RAGTIME DUDES IN A THIN PLACE

Ragtime Dudes in a Thin Place

RICHARD GARTEE

Lake and Emerald Publications

Books by Richard Gartee
Published by Lake & Emerald Publications
—Fiction—
Lancelot's Grail
Lancelot's Disciple
Ragtime Dudes at the World's Fair
Ragtime Dudes in a Thin Place
Ragtime Dudes Meet a Paris Flapper
—Poetry—
Mountain Breathing
Watching Waves
Canyon Falls
—Non-Fiction—
Skating on Skim Ice
Information about the author and a complete list of his currently available titles can be found at
www.gartee.com

Published by Lake & Emerald Publications, LLC
www.lepublications.com

Library of Congress Control Number: 2019902572
ISBN: 978-0-9906768-6-7 (Trade paperback)
ISBN: 978-0-9906768-7-4 (e-book edition)

Typesetting services by BOOKOW.COM

*For Victoria Woodhull and Tennessee Claflin
sisters who advocated free love and equality
between sexes a century before the hippies.*

CHAPTER 1

May 1904, New York City

The woman who would eat her child—or at least his ambitions—was most likely still sleeping and wouldn't be up for hours. But Bryce Holloway's raging hangover drove him from his bed in search of a headache powder.

He found none, so he put on his dressing coat and stumbled into the parlor where he helped himself to a hefty draught of his father's brandy.

It didn't help as much as he'd hoped, so he staggered to the dining room and rang for coffee, which arrived promptly. Jenkins poured it into a delicate china cup that barely held two swallows.

"Leave the carafe," Bryce said.

"Sir?"

"I want the coffee close at hand. I need all I can get. I'll pour."

"Eggs and toast?"

Bryce's stomach recoiled. "Just coffee for now."

"Juice?"

"Perhaps when Mother gets up."

"Sorry?" Jenkins said, in his most carefully controlled voice. "Sir, it's half-past one. Your mother breakfasted at her regular time and has gone to her Saturday afternoon social."

Oh, damn. "I see. No juice, then."

When the carafe was empty, Bryce went to his room, poured water into the basin, splashed his face, and shaved. Jenkins had laid out a summer-weight outfit while he'd had his coffee. Dressed, he left the house, and waved down a passing hansom. "Fifth Avenue Hotel." Domain of Mother's social circle.

At the hotel, he asked the driver to wait. Truth be told, he was skinned, having spent his last six-bits getting home from the train station last night. He'd be solvent Monday when the bank opened. Until then, he'd have to rely on his parents. Again. Father was in Albany this weekend. Just as well, because Mother was the easier touch.

The white marble Fifth Avenue Hotel spanned the full block between Twenty-third and Twenty-fourth streets and was the social, cultural, and political hub of New York City elite. Bryce entered the vaulted dining room which easily seated 2,200. Lucky for him there was only a smattering of the Social Register there at this time of day. He quickly located his mother and her friends lingering over tea and pastries. He snagged a chair from a nearby table and dropped into it next to his mother. "Good afternoon, ladies. All is well, I hope?"

"Oh, Bryce," said the woman seated next to his mother. "Have some tea. Your mother says you've been to the St. Louis World's Fair. Tell us all about it."

The coffee had already done its work, and the topic at hand reignited his primal fires. "It was enormous—fifteen hundred buildings, including twelve colossal palaces that provided a mind-boggling five million square feet of space. And at night the fair dazzled with electric lights."

"Oh, tell us more. We'll have the waiter bring a place setting for you."

"No, I can't stay. I have a hack waiting out front."

"We simply must hear about your trip." She held out a silver tray. "Here, have a petit four."

"Not today, I'm sorry."

"Bryce, don't be difficult," his mother said.

"I'm sorry, but I really do have a cab waiting," Bryce said. "Mother, why don't you have the ladies over for tea? I've stereoscope cards and a Fair guidebook in my trunk. I can give a proper presentation of the fair and perform the latest Scott Joplin tune for them." Bryce grinned at the ladies. "You know, I had a chance to play with Joplin while we were in St. Louis."

"Ragtime," his mother said, as if it were something one found stuck to one's shoe. "A veritable call of the wild which arouses the pulses of city-bred people."

He couldn't have agreed more, hence its appeal. And he intended to introduce ragtime in the western territories.

He leaned close to his mother's face as if to give her a kiss on the cheek, then spoke into her ear. "Let me have ten dollars until Monday."

"That's a great deal of money."

"I need to pay the driver."

Under the table, she placed a coin on his palm and closed his fingers over it. From its size he knew she'd slipped him a half-eagle. But best not to argue money in front of her friends. He kissed her cheek and bid the ladies farewell.

Bryce changed the five-dollar piece at the hotel cashier. Outside, he gave two bits to the waiting driver. The man snapped the reins, and the cab clattered away, leaving Bryce an unobstructed view of Madison Square Garden on the opposite side of the park that fronted the hotel. Its Beaux-art design reminded him of the neo-classical palaces at the Fair where he and his boyhood chums, Mo Silverstein and Julius Hornsby, had gone for opening day.

Forty-five states and territories and forty-three countries had exhibits. Bryce had found himself returning again and again to the New Mexico pavilion, which resembled an old Spanish mission and featured a pueblo of real Indians. Just the stark beauty, the simplicity of their life, held such an appeal compared to the baroque complexity of New York Society. The pueblo Indians never had to worry about who was in, who was out. They didn't feel any pressure about slotting into a career that would please their parents or working to maintain the family fortune. They just . . . lived.

While he practically camped in the New Mexico pavilion, Julius haunted palaces that exhibited the latest inventions like Marconi's wireless telegraph that allowed visitors to send messages between different stations in the fairgrounds. All three of them were dazzled by Edison's Kinetoscope which projected moving pictures, and fascinated by St. Louis inventor Knute Wideen's solar furnace that harnessed the sun's energy with 40,000 mirrors to create 10,000 degrees Fahrenheit temperatures. "Bryce, imagine if we invented something like that," Julius had said.

Mo, a painter, had to be pried from the Palace of Fine Arts. At dusk when the palaces closed, the friends spent their evenings on the mile-long Pike, where they rode the Ferris wheel, ate, drank, and watched belly dancers. Over suppers, Mo rhapsodized about French impressionists, and the skill of capturing the character of light, while Julius ran on about the coming new world of electro-therapeutics, electro-magnetism, and electro-chemistry.

Bryce generally nodded and smiled, his mind still lost in the sheer simplicity of New Mexico. But the bouncy joy of ragtime, and the belly dancers caught his attention, too.

Their last night at the fair, they dined at Faust's Tyrolean Alps restaurant with several artists Mo had befriended. Their dinner companions mentioned that two European-trained artists were touting the light in Taos, New Mexico as ideal for painters and had moved there to start an arts colony. And that was the seed of the idea.

Over fine continental fare and too many bottles of wine, Bryce, Julius, and Mo decided to open a grand emporium in Taos. Their store would bring the latest music and literature of New York culture along with wondrous inventions they'd seen at the fair. Why, the idea seemed as brilliant as the Edison lights around them.

The following day they hit the exhibits one last time, buying what goods they could for their store. Then Julius and Mo entrained for New Mexico. Meanwhile, Bryce returned to New York to make arrangements with sheet music and book publishers. During most of the train ride home, he had been in the bar car, dreaming of how he and his friends would bring the new world to the primitive west. Finally, he would be free from the constraints of his own old world, a world that didn't allow him the freedom to be himself, that didn't accept one of his best friends because Jewishness offended their Protestant heritage. At last, today, he'd start putting that dream into action.

Well, he supposed he could start today. Publishers might work on Saturday, after all, and Scribner's headquarters was only two blocks away. Still, he hadn't eaten yet. With his hangover abated, his appetites were starting to reassert themselves. Now he required food, liquor, and a warm companion. It had been a hell of a long train ride from St. Louis. Emporium purchases could wait until Monday.

The afternoon sun glinted off the golden statue of Diana high atop her minaret, towering over Madison Square Garden. At the moment, her arrow aimed toward Broadway. He took that as a sign. Pick up a Broadway chorus girl, take her to Keens Steakhouse for mutton chops, and afterwards they'd dance the two-step to the latest ragtime.

Mother wouldn't be pleased. But he wasn't looking for a girl like "dear old mom."

CHAPTER 2

New Mexico, same day

"Hey, Dude!"

Mo glanced up at Julius with a grin. "Hey, dude, yourself." It was obvious they weren't locals returning home. Their fashionable New York waistcoats practically screamed "eastern dandy." He resumed counting the crates, trunks, and suitcases the train porter had piled at his feet.

A young boy pushing an empty hand truck scrambled to keep up with Julius's long strides as he strutted down the train platform. Mo tipped the porter a nickel. "Help that boy get these on the hand truck."

"Yes, sir," the porter said.

"Where the hell are we?" Julius said.

"Tres Piedras," the porter said.

"Thanks, I can read the sign. Mo, I thought we were going to Taos."

"Me, too."

"No, sir, Taos is twenty-five miles from here," the porter said. "You need a horse and wagon. You could take the stagecoach, but the stage don't run regular."

All right. Well, he couldn't expect New York levels of transportation. "Where do we see about the stagecoach?" Mo said.

"Other side of the depot."

The hand truck had a bad wheel and once it was fully loaded, it made a thump, thump, thump as the boy pushed it. When they reached the edge of the platform, Mo said, "Julius, wait with our stuff. I'll see what I can find out." He walked around back of the depot where a chalkboard advertising the stagecoach schedule was nailed to the whitewashed station wall. A dusty-looking fellow wearing a cowboy hat and a handlebar mustache was currying a large horse. It was exactly as he'd pictured it in his mind.

"You the man we see about the stagecoach to Taos?" Mo said.

"I am. Name's Dunn."

"Your schedule says, 'Taos: occasional.' What's that mean?"

"Upon occasion when there're any passengers, or if there's mail for there." Dunn ejected a stream of tobacco juice from between his teeth. It hit the dirt and curled like a desiccated garter snake.

"There's two of us," Mo said. "Is that enough of an occasion?"

"That's fine." Dunn wiped a bit of tobacco spit from his mustache with the back of his hand. "I got mail to take there, anyway."

Mo nodded and entered the depot. The interior was devoid of life. Against the wall were two wooden pews that looked like they'd once been in a church, between them a brass spittoon that needed cleaning. Two flat benches, just boards without backs, sat in the middle of the room, and the ticket counter was unattended. This really was the back of beyond, and apparently they still had a way to go.

The train steamed off and a young man wearing a clerk's cap came in.

"You the man I see about tickets?"

"Train's left. Where you going?"

"Taos."

"You'll want the stage, then. Mr. Dunn's leaving pretty soon."

Mo's hands and clothes were covered in coal soot from the train ride. It'd been hot, and the passengers put all the windows down. Sucked the smoke right in. "We got time to get a bath?"

"Not if you want to catch today's stage. No point to it anyhow. Trail's dusty. You'd need another by the time you got there."

Mo brushed the dust off his clothes best as he could, still wishing for a hot bath. "All right, give me two tickets to Taos."

"No tickets—pay Mr. Dunn directly," the clerk said.

When Mo found him again, Dunn had hitched a team of six to the coach and was helping the boy load the crates and luggage into the boot. Julius was already in the coach, sipping on a flask he kept in his coat pocket. Mo got in and closed the door. Dunn climbed up top, gave a whistle and cracked the reins. The coach surged forward and soon Tres Piedras was behind them.

After seven days of the rhythmic motion and steady clack-clack of the train from St. Louis, the stage ride was jarring. Mo was thrown back and forth on his seat until he braced his feet against the seat opposite. "Not like taking a hansom through Central Park."

Julius, wedged into the opposite corner, pulled back the curtain on the coach window and peered out through a cloud of dust at the reddish-tan colored rocks. "Doesn't look much like Central Park, either."

Mo finagled his own flask out of his jacket and lifted it to his lips. The stage hit a rut, and the contents spilled down his shirt front. "Damn."

"Shameful waste," Julius said.

Mo swiped at his shirt several times and then, using both hands, managed to tip the flask over his mouth. "Empty. Give me some of yours."

Julius didn't hesitate to pass his over, but after Mo had a swallow, he held his hand out for the flask's return. He took one more swig himself and then capped it and slipped it back in his pocket. Mo gave him an appreciative nod of thanks.

"Julius, before we get to Taos, I want to talk to you about something."

"What's that?"

"I've decided to change my name."

"What for?"

"People named Silverstein don't get a lot of respect from gentiles in New York. I doubt it's any better in the Wild West. Besides, everyone comes west to get a fresh start."

"You got a point. These cowboys probably assume every Jew is a tailor. So, what you want to be called?"

"Well, you know Mo is short for Mordecai, and that's not any better. Then, I thought of Morgan. If I drop stein off my last name, I'll be Morgan Silver. What do you think? Can you start calling me Morgan?"

"Morgan. I like it, a real cowboy name, like one of the Earp brothers. I'm not Jewish, but maybe I should have a cowboy name too. How 'bout you call me One-eyed Jack?"

"Sure. Only problem is, you've got two eyes."

"Hmmm, Two-eyed Jack doesn't sound right, does it? Which jacks have one eye?"

"Spades and Hearts."

"So, it'd have to be clubs or diamonds . . . Okay, Jack Diamond's my name. I like the sound of that." He stuck out his hand. "Morgan."

Mo grabbed the offered hand and shook it, "Jack."

Jack and Morgan grinned at each other as though they'd accomplished something. And, well, new names were a beginning.

"We better write Bryce and tell him, soon as we get to Taos," Morgan said.

"Right," Jack said. "If we're gonna make these names stick, we can't have him sending telegrams to Julius and Mordecai."

"I'll do it now. The driver said he does the mail run. He could take our letter back with the outgoing mail from Taos." Morgan pulled out the small pad and pencil he kept in his pocket for making quick sketches. He started the letter three times, then put the pad away. "I can't write anything the way this coach is jerking."

"Do it when we get to Taos," Jack said. "There should be time enough while the driver waters the horses. Tell Bryce not to spread it around the city though. No reason for certain Micks back home to know what we're called out here."

"I hadn't thought of that, but you've got a point. Bryce's supposed to take care of that situation before he comes, but if he screws up—"

"As he's wont to do . . . Jesus, it's hot in here. Hold my hat."

Jack tossed his bowler onto the seat next to Morgan and threw the door open.

Morgan braced himself tighter. The ground raced past and clouds of dust from the horses poured in. "Julius! Have you taken leave of your senses?"

"Julius may have, but Jack's betting it's cooler up top with the driver." In a heartbeat Jack was leaning backward out the door, putting his foot in the window opening.

"Jack, you're crazy, you'll kill yourself."

Jack levered his weight onto the coach window and pulled himself up in one swift move.

And then Morgan was alone in the coach with the door flapping. "Well, I'll be."

Jack leaned over the edge and hung upside down grinning like a fool. "Come on. It's cooler up here."

Well, he came west to enjoy a new life. Morgan doffed his hat and put it on the seat next to Jack's. He peered out the door at certain death rushing by, then decided to embrace it. Morgan turned around and leaned out backward. He struggled to lift his leg high enough to slip his boot in the window frame as Jack had done, but he was shorter than Jack, and couldn't reach. He put one foot on the coach seat which got him a little higher, but put him too far from the door—he was practically lying horizontal. That wouldn't work.

A smart New Yorker like him should be able to solve this problem.

He held onto the door frame with one hand and reached overhead with the other. He found the iron railing that ran around the edge of the coach roof and grabbed hold. He took a deep breath, let go the doorway and got his other hand on the railing too. He tried to pull himself up by doing a chin-up, but all he succeeded in doing was losing his foothold.

Great. Now what?

He hung by both arms, flopping against the bouncing coach like a sack of meal. Finally, Jack reached over the side, grabbed his coat collar and pulled him up.

The driver took his eyes off the team and turned around. "You city fellows planning on dying young? Why didn't you just holler? I'd have stopped and you could have climbed up top like regular folks."

Jack laughed at the driver and pulled out his silver flask. He unscrewed the top, drank deep, and handed it to Morgan who took a long pull.

Jack winked at Morgan, "But his way, we wouldn't have a story to tell Bryce."

Morgan grinned. "You know how Bryce would tell it. He'd have pulled himself up with one hand while shooting some Spaniards."

That cracked Jack up. "Yep, and Teddy Roosevelt would have been riding in the coach, egging him on."

"Don't worry," Morgan said. "I'm sure we'll have plenty more adventures before Bryce gets here."

CHAPTER 3

Earlier the same day, Boston, Massachusetts

Rebecca Sullivan appraised the stairway, its deep-worn treads still dappled with remnants of a spring shower. She hoisted her skirts above her shoe tops and dashed up the half-dozen steps. The puddles made a splashing song as she ascended. When she reached the wide porch of the manse, she let go her skirts and smoothed the fabric where she'd gripped it. She lifted the brass door knocker and rapped twice. A wren in the nearby lilac took flight.

Her grandfather's longtime housekeeper opened the door. "Glory, Miss Sullivan, what a delight to my eyes. It's been a great stretch since I've seen ye—being a college lass as you are."

"Good afternoon, Moria. It's nice to see you as well. Is Granddad in?"

"Reverend Fitzpatrick is in his study, rehearsing tomorrow's sermon. Go on in. I'll bring a pot of tea and a wee plate of scones in a fairy's wink."

Rebecca found her grandfather pacing the room, mumbling to himself. She rushed to embrace him, kissed his cheek, and savored the scent of fragrant pipe smoke in his beard.

The old man patted her affectionately. "Have you come to ask me to proofread your senior thesis?"

"Not exactly."

"Surely, you're finished by now. Graduation is next month."

"Oh, it's done. But I'm thinking of scrapping it and writing something different."

He smiled. "Only you, dear Rebecca. While your classmates are wearing out the nibs of their pens putting on finishing touches before the deadline, you want to start afresh."

"My thesis is too ordinary—I'm sure three others have chosen the topic. Then I remembered you telling us the Celtic myth of Thin Places. I'm sure that's never been presented before. So I'd like to delve into it if you can spare the time."

"For you, of course. But when is your thesis due?"

"Not for two weeks. Will you tell me what you know?"

Moria brought in a silver tray, poured the tea, and left. Reverend Fitzpatrick put tobacco in his pipe and tamped it down. "My Seanmháthair, your great-great grandmother, used to say, 'Heaven and earth are only three feet apart —just out of reach from each other. But in the Thin Places that distance is even smaller.'"

He struck a match and puffed until the tobacco was glowing. "In the old country certain wild places were said to manifest ephemeral or mystical qualities beyond what we experience with our mere senses. Where the gap to heaven was thin, one could perceive a sacred space."

Rebecca handed him his teacup and saucer. He took a sip. "She also believed in fairies and such. Although Universalists are open to diverse ideas, I don't think your thesis advisors will accept Celtic myths for academic research. You wouldn't have reference books or footnotes, just an old man's memories of legends told by his Irish Catholic grandmother."

He set his cup on the table and relit his pipe. "So, tell me about the paper you already wrote. Perhaps it's the wiser choice."

"It's on the serendipity of John Murray being blown off course and finding a church waiting for him in a place he would have never gone otherwise. But I'm sure generations of divinity students have written about him founding the Universalist Church in America. The subject seems so shopworn and predictable. I want to surprise them with a topic no one ever addressed."

With a benign smile he shook his head. "It's enough of a challenge for your professors at Tufts to accept a woman. Submit your paper on Murray. That'll tickle their hearts and get you your diploma. After you graduate, you can expound whatever philosophical beliefs you want."

CHAPTER 4

"Taos," Dunn said, as he pulled to a stop in front of a row of adobe build-ings.

Morgan had been observing the architectural styles as they drove into town, some adobe, others apparently wooden throughout. "Well, it's certainly nothing like New York City."

"Not even like New Jersey." Jack leaped from the top of the coach in a single bound. "I wonder if they have beer here."

Morgan and the driver climbed down. "Are you joking?" Dunn said. "There's a saloon about every fifty feet."

"Juli—I mean, Jack, we ought to find a place to stay first. We can drink later. Mr. Dunn, you know of somewhere we can room?"

"Columbian Hotel is right across the plaza. I run a roulette wheel in the bar there. After you get your room, come down and give it a spin."

"We're planning on living here. Do you know where we'd find a boarding house?"

Dunn pointed to a gap between stores a few buildings down "There's a widow woman runs a rooming house on that back street over there. If she's not filled up."

"What about our crates?"

"No problem. I'll hold them for you at the freight office until you get settled."

"That'd be great," Jack said. "Store everything but the suitcases. We'll take those with us."

While their trunks and crates were unloaded and locked up, Morgan wrote a letter to Bryce and gave it to Dunn along with two cents for a stamp. Then, carrying their suitcases, they crossed the road and passed through a narrow, dusty alleyway to an equally dusty back street and located a large, two-story, wood framed house with two pretty young women sitting on a porch swing. They looked to be in their teens, but maybe late teens, judging by their enormous bosoms.

Once he was able to raise his gaze, Morgan found that both girls had brown hair and brown eyes. The older one wore her hair in long, coiled curls that hung over her pretty pink ears. The younger had a mass of soft wavy hair tied back with a blue velvet ribbon.

Jack gave them a rakish smile. "Is this a place where two handsome gentlemen from back east might find a welcome?"

"Gentlemen?" said the older girl. "You look like a couple of coal miners dressed for church."

"It was a long train ride from St. Louis," Jack said.

"St. Louis!" The younger one nearly squealed. Deep dimples appeared when she smiled.

The older sister's manner softened. "As it happens, we do have a vacant room." She stood and stepped to the edge of the porch, making a quarter turn to show them her generous figure in profile. It was an inspiring sight. "My name is Peaches. Pleased to make your acquaintance . . . Cherry, go tell Mother we have callers."

Cherry—really? The girl pushed back on the swing and let its forward motion propel her as she leaped out and dashed for the door. The screen door swung open before she reached it and there stood mama. An older version of her amply endowed daughters, somewhat fuller in most places, but still fine-figured. Her face, however, had narrow eyes and a sternly pinched mouth that put something of a damper on the prevailing mood.

Jack doffed his hat. "Ma'am."

Morgan took off his, too. "We're looking for accommodation, and your place came highly recommended."

"Is that so? What are your names?"

"I'm Morgan Silver and this is Jack Diamond."

"Humph, what kind of names are those? You're not gamblers are you?"

Uh-oh. He'd chosen a new name without considering what people might infer from it. Well, too late now. Morgan smoothed the brim of his bowler. "Not at all, madam. We're New Yorkers, come to Taos to open an emporium. We'd like to stay with you while we grow our store into a going concern."

Her eyes appraised them from haircut to footwear. "All right, come in. I'll show you what I've got. I'm Mrs. Romero."

Jack held the door for her and for the first time, she smiled. Morgan smiled, too. Jack could charm the severity off a nun. Morgan followed Mrs. Romero inside. Peaches and Cherry slipped in after him, giggling at Jack as they passed him. Jack came in last and let the door smack shut.

Mrs. Romero whirled around, "Don't let it slam."

"Yes, ma'am."

She led Morgan upstairs to an immaculately-kept room with an oak dresser and a double bed. On the dresser was a lovely white basin trimmed with pink roses and a matching water pitcher. A clean porcelain chamber pot sat in the corner. He'd stayed at less salubrious places in New York.

"Very nice," Morgan said.

"Five dollars a week—that includes breakfast and supper. You're on your own for lunch."

Jack and the girls crowded in behind them. Morgan glanced at Jack, who gave a quick nod. A shiver of excitement emanated from the girls.

"This will do nicely," Morgan said. "Let's see Jack's."

Mrs. Romero frowned. "This is the only room I've got open."

"It's only got one bed," Jack said. "Mo and I don't sleep together."

"Mo?" Peaches said.

"He means me," Morgan said.

"Can I call you Mo?" Cherry asked.

"Please don't. Call me Morgan." He slipped his hand in his trouser pocket and jingled a stack of silver dollars. "Isn't there anything else, madam?"

She pursed her lips for a pensive moment and then said, "Let me show you the girls' room. It has two beds."

"I couldn't put these young lovelies out of their beds," Jack said.

"I can. They'll move into this room. The girls won't mind sharing a bed. Will you?"

Cherry showed Jack her dimples and Peaches batted her eyelashes. "No, Mama," they said in unison. It seemed they were willing to sacrifice to have two handsome New Yorkers within reach.

Mrs. Romero led them down the hall, while behind her back, Peaches brushed up against Jack and whispered, "It'd be so romantic, knowing you were staying in my room."

"Our room," Cherry said.

The girls' room wasn't any larger, but it had two comfortable-looking single beds.

"Okay with you Jack?" Morgan said.

"Seven dollars," Mrs. Romero said.

Morgan stopped jingling his money. "You had said five."

"Each. There's two of you, eating twice a day. But since you're sharing a room, I'll only charge you seven."

"Aw, Mama," Cherry said.

"Hush."

"Take the deal, Morgan," Jack said. "I'm so sick of sleeping on trains I'd lie down on any bed that wasn't moving."

"Hold on," Mrs. Romero said. "Those are good linens on the girls' beds. You'll not be sleeping in them until you bathe."

"No argument there," Morgan said. "We've been traveling for a week. A bath sounds delightful."

Mrs. Romero gave a sly smile. "Well, the laundry up the road has baths for twenty-five cents apiece, 'course their tubs are likely full of used wash water. For fifty cents I'll have my girls heat you a tub of nice fresh water and you can have your bath right now."

"Madam, it's a deal," Morgan said.

"Morgan can go first," Jack said. "I'm going to investigate one of those establishments we saw on the main road when we arrived."

"Well, don't take too long," Morgan said. "You don't want a cold bath."

"Don't worry, Mr. Diamond," Peaches said. "I'll heat more for you, if it gets cold."

"Why don't you gentlemen wait on the porch while we get arranged?" Mrs. Romero pushed her girls out of their room. "Peaches, set up the bathtub in the kitchen. Cherry, fill the kettles. While the water's heating, move your stuff to the other room."

The men walked out to the porch. "Kind of like some story about the farmer's daughter, isn't it?" Jack said.

He'd been thinking the same thing, until the moment he met Mrs. Romero. "Don't get any ideas, Jack. We need to live in this town, remember?"

* * *

Jack walked downtown, but was back far sooner than Morgan, knowing Jack's fondness for beer, would have expected. Morgan was in their room, dressed in clean clothes, unpacking his suitcase.

"Mo—Morgan, glad you're dressed. We're going to a party."

"A party? Us?"

"It's *for* us. I was having a few beers with this fellow, Deitwiler. He and his wife just moved here from Minnesota to open a dry goods store. Haven't got it open yet, but they're eager to meet other people. I mentioned we'd been to the World's Fair. The boys in the bar got real excited, and quick as a buggy whip Deitwiler decides to throw a welcome party in our honor at his store—seeing how he hasn't got it set up yet and the building is just sitting empty."

Morgan nodded. "I told you Taos was the right place to come."

"You did, and you were right. By the end of tonight, we'll know everybody important in town."

Morgan took a bottle of liquor from his suitcase and refilled his flask. "Sounds like a big party."

"Well, it's not that big a town. They're rolling a barrel of beer over to Deitwiler's right now. Bunch of local musicians are going to play, too. Shame Bryce didn't come with us. He'd be in his element—introduce Taos to a little ragtime."

"I thought you said it's at a dry goods store. There won't be a piano."

"Sure. I'm just saying Bryce wins us a lot of friends. Hopefully when he gets here we can throw him a party someplace with a piano."

Morgan offered Jack the bottle. "Top off your flask?"

"Thanks. Just leave the bottle out. Right now, I got to get my bath and get ready before all the beer's drunk up." Jack started out the door and then turned back. "Maybe we ought to bring Peaches and Cherry?"

"You're not serious?"

"It's a party for us. I guess we can bring whoever we want."

"Didn't you meet Mrs. Romero? Let's not get evicted before we have a chance to unpack. Go take your bath."

CHAPTER 5

Orange flares of sunset behind the mountains surrounding Taos cast purple shadows over the streets behind them as Jack and Morgan walked into the party. The dry goods store was little more than a hollow shell. A dozen kerosene lanterns had been lit around the room, giving the unfurnished store a cheerful contrast to the falling night. A chorus of voices greeted them. Many seemed to already know Jack. Morgan knew none of them, but they called his name as if they were old friends.

A temporary table had been constructed by laying boards over two sawhorses and draping them with a long tablecloth. A pretty, diminutive woman stood behind a cut-glass punch bowl ladling some fruity drink into matching cups. Many of the women had brought dishes of food, and these were arrayed on either side of the punch bowl. In the corner several men stood around a beer barrel they had wrestled into a wooden cradle.

Music of sorts from an odd assemblage of instruments began to fill the room. A trumpet, a violin, and an accordion were by no means the makings of a symphony at Carnegie Hall, but as the instruments struggled to play together, they added a jovial undertone to the overlapping conversations. Many of the men sounded as if this was not their first beer barrel of the evening. The women's voices, an octave higher, trilled like birds after a rainstorm.

Jack hustled Morgan through the room making a beeline toward the keg, but their trajectory crossed paths with a man too tall to be a dwarf, but too short to play for the Brooklyn Dodgers. It was a wonder Jack hadn't stepped on him. "Herr Deitwiler," Jack said.

"Shush, that was my father." A smile appeared from amidst the man's muttonchops. "In America we now say 'mister,' but, please, just simply call me Fred. We don't go for a lot of formality in the west."

"Sorry. I'm Jack. Remember me from the saloon?"

"Of course. I'm the one who invited you to the party."

"I want to introduce you to my business partner, Morgan."

Morgan shook the odd little man's hand. "Fred, then. Pleased to meet you."

Fred led them to the punch table. "Gentlemen, this is my wife."

Morgan and Jack both tipped their hats. "Mrs. Deitwiler."

"Emma, please," she said with an accent similar to her husband's.

"I'm Morgan, this is Jack. Your accent, is it German?" Morgan had a good ear, and he had spent time among the German immigrants down on Pearl Street.

"Minnesota," Fred said. "We don't notice our accent, but everyone here comments on it."

"I'm sorry. When I heard Deitwiler and the accent I put two and two together and got—"

"Five?" Fred said.

Jack laughed. "He got you on that one, Morgan."

"You're not wrong, of course," Fred said. "My parents came on a boat from Hamburg in 1871. But I was born in Minnesota. Grew up there, met and wed Emma."

Morgan smiled at her. "You have a lovely punch bowl set."

Emma fluttered her eyelashes. "Wedding present. I brought it from Minnesota. Fortunately, it didn't get broken in the move. So many of my good things did."

"Newlyweds?"

"Hardly," Fred said. "We've been married seven years."

"How old are your children Mrs. Deitwiler?" Morgan offered as an ice-breaker.

Emma studiously ladled out more fruit punch.

"We haven't started a family yet," Fred said. "It's just Emma and me."

Jack kept eyeing the keg of beer in the corner where men were drawing off frothy glasses of lukewarm ale into Mrs. Deitwiler's best water glasses. She offered him a dainty little cup. "Punch?"

Jack stared at it. Normal size in her delicate hands, it'd be a glass butterfly in his. He was no stranger to these things. Socialites in New York loved to throw parties at which they wore long frilly dresses and required men to sip from tiny crystal-ware thimbles. Morgan elbowed him in the ribs.

"Yes, thank you." Jack accepted the cup, squeezing its little handle between this thumb and forefinger, pinky extended. He swallowed the nectar in a gulp and set the cup on the table. "Delightful."

"More?" Emma said.

"Not just yet," Jack said. "I see some men I would like to introduce to Morgan. He's just arrived from New York and doesn't know anyone."

"I thought you had, too," Emma said.

"Yes, but I've already met a good number of local citizens that he hasn't." Jack turned toward the keg.

"Oh, but wait," she said. "I didn't get to ask what's in fashion back east. Fred's left it to me to choose what we'll stock in our store. I'd like to offer my customers fabrics and patterns for the latest styles. I was hoping you'd tell me what New York City women are wearing this year."

Jack's eyes were fixed on the knot of men clustered around the beer barrel. "Women's fashion isn't really something I pay attention to. Morgan's the artist. He probably notices things like that more than I do."

Emma looked at Morgan expectantly.

"Jack, why don't you go ahead? I'd be happy to talk with Emma."

Jack gave him a subtle nudge. "Morgan, we really do need to meet a lot of people. While they're . . . while the night is still young."

Morgan touched his hat brim. "If you'll excuse us, Mrs. D—I mean, Emma. I promise I'll come back and talk to you about fashion later in the evening."

As the partners left Emma, Jack stuck his finger in a dish one of the wives had contributed and licked it. "Yum."

Morgan smiled. "I'd like to see you try that at one of Mrs. Holloway's soirées."

"That's why I never attend Bryce's mother's soirées."

"Oh? And here I thought it was because you were never invited."

"Come on, Morgan, this is the frontier. The brave new world, free from outdated mores and reaching toward the future. Open yourself to it."

"With the help of beer."

"Of course."

Fred was already at the barrel. He filled three glasses, handed Morgan and Jack each one, and raised his. "To commerce." The men drank. "Emma's nervous, and excited," Fred said. "We don't have much inventory yet, and she's worried we'll look half empty."

"We don't have much either," Morgan said. "We have a third partner, Bryce. He was with us in St. Louis, but went back east to settle old business and buy more goods while we came west and got set up here."

"How'd you pick Taos?"

"This whole idea really came to us at the World's Fair. Our partner kept visiting the New Mexico pavilion because it had real Pueblo Indians."

"We got plenty of them," said a man in a cowboy hat who was leaning against the keg.

"And then, we learned that European-trained artists have moved here."

The man in the cowboy hat refilled his beer. "Oh yeah, them two art fellows. It don't seem like a real job though, does it? Writers, painters—that lot. I mean a fellow herds cattle or even sheep, digs gold or silver, even a carpenter, that's work. But to sit around painting pictures, that ain't work. Is it?"

"I don't know," Morgan said. "Let's say that miner strikes gold or silver. What's he going to do with the money? Build a fine house, get a wife? And then she's going to want to decorate it with nice things."

"Oh, I see what you mean. Once people have a little money, they're gonna buy those fellows' paintings."

"Exactly. But take it one step further," Morgan said. "Everyone has to make a living, because like the animals, we have to have a warm place to sleep and enough to eat. But animals are satisfied once they have their needs met. Man has to feed his soul, his curiosity, that's where culture comes in. Music, literature, art—they move us, make us feel."

The cowboy, took off his hat, straightened the brim, and put it back on.

"Tell him about the World's Fair," Fred said.

"Now that was really something," Jack said. "Opened our eyes to what the new century is bringing. Unless you go, you cannot believe the wonder of it."

Morgan nodded. "Jack, Bryce, and I conceived of a grand emporium to bring the culture and inventions we'd seen at the Fair to a western city. Taos seems poised to become an oasis of sophistication in the wilderness."

"And the gold doesn't hurt, neither," Fred said. "Emma and I heard the area had a number of gold strikes."

"Historically, sudden wealth raises cultural aspirations in the newly rich," Morgan said.

A man wearing a derby joined them. "Well, you may have missed the train, then. The gold boom's pretty much over. Glen-Woody's closed down. There are still a few mines in Red River, but they'll play out before long."

"We were given to understand that those who made out came here afterwards," Morgan said.

"Some have," the man in the derby said. "Not sure how long they'll stay."

Jack smiled. "Maybe we can give them something to stay for."

"You fellows hunt?" the cowboy said.

Jack and Morgan looked at each other and shook their heads.

"I'm a terrific shot," Fred said. "Used to hunt all the time in Minnesota. I can bring down a stag from two hundred yards. I shot our Christmas dinners every year. One year, I even got a bear."

"We got bear here," the cowboy said, "but mostly it's elk or deer. Bighorn sheep, too. I don't suppose you had those in Minnesota."

"None in New York City, either," Jack said.

"Well, we got geese, turkey, pheasants, and ducks if you prefer," the cowboy said.

Jack gave a little smile. "Truth is, I've never fired a gun."

"Do tell," the cowboy said. "First man I've met who hasn't."

Morgan set his glass down. "I'm going to make a few more acquaintances."

"You go ahead," Jack drew another beer. "I'll catch up with you in a bit."

Morgan worked the room, introducing himself and shaking hands. He repeated the same story for each cluster of couples he encountered. Yes, they were from New York. Yes, they had just come from the St. Louis World's Fair. Yes, he had ridden the 264 foot-tall Ferris wheel with carriages the size of Pullman cars. Yes, the view was tremendous. No, he wasn't scared. He noticed that no one mentioned the real futuristic wonders, like Edison's lights or Victor's Gramophone. They really had no idea what the future had on offer.

As Morgan circulated he met the baker, the butcher, two ranchers and several of their wives. But of all the guests, one woman stood out. Not only because she was the odd wheel in a party of five having an animated conversation in the far corner, but because she was by far the most beautiful woman in the room.

She had a voluptuary's body and didn't mind wearing a décolleté dress to show it. She also had a prey's awareness of being watched. But instead of withdrawing like a frightened fawn, she turned to this man and that as they spoke, giving the rest of the room glimpses of her profile from various perspectives. Yet there was none of the anxious flaunting he'd seen with Peaches and Cherry. After watching her for a while, Morgan gravitated to her corner.

"If I may introduce myself, Miss," he said, "my name is Morgan Silver."

"Abigail Wythe," she said. She then introduced the other members of her party: her sister, Penelope, her brother-in-law, Walter, Mr. Hoffsteader, vice-president of the bank, and his wife, Ida. Names he forgot in Abigail's aura.

Abigail had dark wavy hair, high cheekbones, almond-shaped eyes, and an inviting mouth. A large pink tourmaline on a silver chain hung in the perfect valley between her breasts. Morgan's eyes were transfixed—the color perfectly complemented her skin tone, and the shape drew the eye naturally to its setting. He could see instantly how to paint her. And what would it be like to paint her, nude. The faint blush of her—

"Mr. Silver, my eyes are up here," she said.

"I-I-I was just admiring your beautiful . . . tourmaline."

"Lovely, isn't it?" She lifted it from its sacred swale and invited closer inspection. "Not many men recognize the gem by name."

Morgan leaned in as close as he dared and inhaled her floral essence. "Oh, we saw many precious and semi-precious jewels on display at the Fair."

"Fair?"

"The Louisiana Purchase Exposition—most people call it the St. Louis World's Fair. My partners and I have just come from there."

She let the jewel drop back into her cleavage, and he stepped back. She ran her eyes over him and smiled. Morgan was confident he looked quite dapper in his dress coat and ruffled shirt. It was obvious she thought so, too.

"Wythe," Morgan said, "is that English?"

She dropped her voice to a whisper, "My *ex-husband* was English." Then louder, "My ancestry's Welsh. So, you're the men who are going to bring Eastern refinement to Taos?"

"We heard that Ernie Blumenschein and Bert Phillips have already got that movement started. We're just here to add a little excitement."

"With a new store?"

"A world emporium," he said. "We're going to sell the latest in books and music. We'll sell some artwork, too—I'm something of an artist. And wonderful new inventions we saw at the Fair, things you can hardly imagine. We've a third partner, Bryce, back east right now making purchases and getting things shipped to us."

"A bookstore would be very nice," Abigail said.

"Music, too," Morgan said. "Bryce plays piano, knows ragtime—the latest rage. We'll carry sheet music for sorts of tunes people here have never heard before."

"Ah, but literature is the thing," Abigail said. "You can't buy a book out here unless it's *Tales of the Old West* or dime novels about Kit Carson or Wyatt Earp."

"Careful how you speak about Carson," her brother-in-law said.

Abigail laughed. "Kit Carson's the local hero. He resided here when he was alive."

Again, a chance to mix some business with pleasure. "Would it be forward of me to ask your advice on what books the ladies of Taos would like to read?"

She laughed again. He liked her fine white teeth.

"Around here we say, always be forward, the past is behind." She held out her empty punch glass. "But you'll have to earn my favor."

"It'd be my pleasure."

As he took her fragile cup in his hand, she rapped her knuckle on the faint outline of the flask in his coat pocket. "Perhaps you'll touch it up on your way back?"

Morgan grinned and nodded.

Jack and Emma were alone at the punch table when Morgan approached. Jack wasn't drinking any punch, and Emma was the color of a beet. "I've never had a preference for really big men," she was saying. Morgan hadn't heard the first part of their conversation, but since Jack was drunk, it wasn't difficult to guess he was pushing the boundaries of frontier mores.

Emma eyed Morgan uncertainly as he held out Abigail's cup. "I hope I'm not interrupting."

She seemed relieved he spoke without slurring. "Not at all." She grabbed the cup from his hand and quickly refilled it.

"Partner!" Jack said. "Have you met this adorable little creature? Emma, this is my partner, Mo——"

"We've met," Morgan said. "Emma, let me apologize for whatever he's said. It's lovely of you to throw a party for us. And I hope nothing Jack's said will keep us from being friends tomorrow."

Emma blushed again. "Don't be concerned. It wasn't anything I haven't heard before."

"Also, I want apologize for not getting back over here before now. Earlier, I promised we'd discuss New York fashion so you could get your merchandise ordered."

"It's all right," she said. "I see now, a party isn't the right place to talk business."

"Some other time then. I have some illustrated magazines. I'll bring them by for you to look through."

She smiled "I appreciate it."

Jack raised his head and mumbled something about his offer still stands. "Remember, women who think the way to a man's heart is through his stomach are aiming too high."

"I'll take him away now," Morgan said. "But could I have a second glass of punch?"

Emma filled it, and Morgan set both cups on the table, slipped the flask from his pocket and added two fingers of liquor to each. He glanced up to see if Emma had noticed and found her holding out a cup of her own. He gave her a wink and topped hers off. Morgan picked up his and Abigail's cups, and with Jack in tow, returned to Abigail.

Morgan handed Abigail her punch. "Have you met my business partner, Jack Diamond? Jack, this is Mrs. Wythe."

She extended her hand. "Abigail, please."

Jack took her hand and leaned in, his eyeballs nearly falling into her cleavage. Morgan put his hand on Jack's forehead and pushed his head back.

Jack winked at her. "Do you believe in love at first sight, or should I walk up again?"

Morgan shook his head. "Perhaps you can meet him another time."

Jack tipped his hat. "Excuse me. I think I'll go get a beer."

"Good idea," Morgan said. At least it could do no further harm. Jack usually went directly from overly friendly to passed out, without a mean or sloppy phase in between. As Jack left, Morgan glanced around Abigail's group. "I hope you'll excuse Jack's over-indulgence. Normally when he's drinking, Jack's what you might call a barstool scientist—discussing the latest issue of *Popular Science Monthly* after a couple of drinks. Perhaps tonight he's drunk himself out of reach of scientific theories."

"Oh, he didn't do anything so awful." Abigail took a delicate sip of her punch and ran the tip of her tongue over her upper lip. "Perfect."

Penelope sampled her sister's cup. "Mmmmm, Abigail."

"Would you like me to get you one?" Morgan said.

Penelope glanced at the banker, Hoffsteader, and his wife. "I'd better not."

"I don't know how it is back east," Penelope's husband said. "But out west, drinking is as normal as fleas on a dog. There's little else to divert the mind."

Morgan patted his chest. "I hope we can remedy that."

"So you were saying earlier," Hoffsteader said. "Sheet music?"

"Yes, and other things as well. Are there a lot of pianos in town?"

"Every saloon has one, and some of the better families have them in their homes."

"We have one," Mrs. Hoffsteader said.

"Abigail does too," Penelope added.

Morgan nodded. "That's good. I'd also like to get you ladies' opinions about books. What would interest women in Taos?"

"Jane Austen," Penelope said.

A century out of date, from a world that no longer existed. "Have you read Edith Wharton? She's American, but gaining popularity, and I understand she has another novel coming out next year."

"Balzac," Abigail said. "I don't think you can find a book by Balzac west of the Mississippi. He's French, but there are translations."

"Have you heard of Henry James?" Mrs. Hoffsteader said.

"Oh, yes," Morgan said. This sounded promising. "Our partner, Bryce, knows his publisher. I'm sure he can get some of James' books for us."

Mr. Hoffsteader looked at his wife with a smile. "Mr. Silver, I predict great success for your endeavor. With a mere question you've elevated the conversation at this party." He pulled out his pocket watch and looked at it. "Unfortunately, it's time for us to take our leave. Mrs. Romero's house where you're staying is on our street. Would you care to walk with us?"

Morgan hesitated. Butter up the banker or dally in Abigail's company?

Abigail made the decision for him. She extended her hand. "Penelope and Walter and I are leaving as well. It's been a pleasure. If you'd like further recommendations, please feel free to call on me some afternoon."

Morgan made a slight bow. "You can take that to the bank." He stacked their cups together and said to the Hoffsteaders, "I'll be glad to accompany you. Just give me a moment to return these and bid farewell to our hostess."

The women who had brought food had taken their empty dishes and left. The punch was gone, and Emma was stacking her precious crystal cups carefully in the empty bowl. "Thank you, Morgan. I'm going to take these home before anything gets broken." She nodded toward Jack and the other men hovering around the keg. "Who knows how late this will go on?"

"That crystal looks heavy. Would you like me to carry it for you?"

"No, Fred will do it. We'll come back and clean up this mess in the morning."

"You're going to leave your store unlocked?"

She gestured to the empty room. "What's here to steal, but beer? And that's free."

"Well, I can't thank you enough for the wonderful party. I promise, tomorrow I'll bring over some magazines showing what ladies in New York are currently wearing."

She took the dirty cups from him and held his hand a moment too long. "I don't think you know how excited everyone in Taos is by your arrival."

"Considering the turnout tonight, I think I do." He glanced at the Hoffsteaders. "I don't want to keep them waiting." He grazed the back of her hand with a kiss. "Tomorrow, for sure."

CHAPTER 6

Jack could hear the squeak of the ropes holding the porch swing as he approached the boarding house steps. Morgan was swaying gently back and forth, carefully sipping his coffee. Jack caught a whiff of it. Boy, nothing smells as good as a nice cup of coffee in the morning.

Cherry stood near the swing twirling in circles. Her ruffled skirt, flaring out as she spun, brushed Morgan's arm every third or fourth revolution. Jack noticed her glancing at Morgan from under her eyelashes at every turn, and Morgan answering her naive flirtations with a benign smile.

Didn't Morgan say we should leave these girls alone?

Mrs. Romero's silhouette darkened the doorway and barked through the screen. "Cherry! Stop that whirling—people can see your petticoats. We're going to be late for Mass. Where's your sister?"

"Fixing her hair," Cherry said.

Mrs. Romero turned on her heel and stalked off. "Peaches!"

Jack, a little unsteady, climbed the steps. He'd be right as rain after a few hours' sleep.

"Hi, Jack!" Cherry said. "You missed breakfast, almost missed church. You want me to get you something to eat?"

"Just coffee, darling."

Cherry disappeared inside. Jack took a seat on the porch rail opposite Morgan's swing.

Morgan raised his coffee cup. "I take it you had fun."

Cherry appeared with Jack's coffee.

"Tale for another time," Jack said. "Cherry, you're a lifesaver." He took a large gulp and made a huffing sound. "Hot, too."

Her brow furrowed.

He smiled at her. "It's perfect."

Mrs. Romero and Peaches came outside. "Good morning, Mr. Diamond, I see you woke up in time for Mass."

"Mass?"

"It's Sunday morning, or did you forget?"

"I'm . . . not Catholic."

"Too bad, but there's only one church in Taos, so it'll have to do. You *are* Christian?"

"That's how my mama raised me. But you ladies go ahead. Morgan and I aren't quite ready to turn Catholic yet."

Mrs. Romero snapped her eyes forward and marched down the steps. "Well, you're not the only Protestants in town. Come, girls."

Peaches gave the men a quick smile and sashayed for them as she and Cherry dutifully followed their mother toward the street.

"That older one's trouble," Jack said.

"So's the younger. She was doing everything she could to show me her petticoats before you arrived."

"She gave me a pretty good view as I came up the steps." Jack tipped his cup and blew on it before drinking again. "What a welcome party!"

Morgan nodded. "A very friendly town, as well. Friendly enough to keep you entertained all night."

"You haven't heard half of it." He took another sip. "I take it Mrs. Romero doesn't know."

"I told her at breakfast that you were sleeping in. She said she didn't have time to make breakfast twice, she had church this morning."

"I take it she didn't ask if you were Christian."

"Never came up. She must have assumed I was waiting for them to get ready. Good thing you showed up—I'd have never thought to tell her I was a Protestant."

Jack laughed. "I can't imagine what your mother would say to that. You could have said you weren't Catholic, though. That'd be true enough." Jack took another sip of his coffee then drained the cup in a single swallow. "I'm going to see if there's any more of this. I could use it."

Jack went to the kitchen and Morgan followed. A large blue enameled coffee pot sat on the stove. Jack lightly touched the side of it with his hand. "Still hot." He refilled both their cups. "Are my eyes bloodshot? They feel bloodshot."

"About typical after a night on the town."

"I'll sleep it off. You should have lingered last night."

"The party seemed to be breaking up, and I'd struck up an acquaintance with Hoffsteader, the banker. He and his wife live in that big house across the street, so I walked home with them."

"Well, you missed the entertainment. After the men with wives got out of there and the Deitwilers left, Sneed, who owns the brothel, brought a few of his girls down. They sang, danced and entertained us until dawn."

"Brothel? I've never known you to pay for it."

A smile played on Jack's lips as he remembered pale-skinned, freckled, red haired, Fanny. "I'm sure mine would've done me for free, but Sneed was right there—"

"How much?"

"Hey, it's been a long time since St. Louis. A man's got to dip his wick to keep his lamp bright."

"Jack, that's our store money. How much?"

"Don't worry we'll make it back. I got us both jobs."

"What?"

"Hear me out, I wasn't as drunk as I seemed. The Deitwilers want to pay us to help get their shop ready. I told him I was pretty handy with a hammer, and then I bragged on you as an artist. Mrs. Deitwiler wants you to paint a big sign for their store."

"How big?"

"Sixteen feet long, maybe five foot high—some kind of fancy mural."

"That's taller than she is."

"That's taller than he is, too. Emma's a cute little mouse isn't she? You could pick that tight little body up and put it in your pocket." And given the invite, he might just do that.

"Hold on. If we're working for Fred now, that makes her the boss's wife. I don't think the town is ready for that much modernity quite yet."

"I'm just making an observation. Besides, they've been married seven years with no children to show for it. Maybe old Fred's shooting blanks."

"You're incorrigible. You just left a woman an hour ago."

"Like I said, it's been a while since we met those girls at the fair. It wouldn't do you any harm to visit Mr. Sneed, either. He's got a redhead that would really turn your fancy." Jack wouldn't mind sharing. Back home, he and Bryce and Mo often went out with the same chorus girls—as long as the woman didn't object. "I suspect she'd be willing to step out on Sneed for a couple of handsome New Yorkers."

"Thanks, but no. I woke in my lonely little bed thinking of that lovely woman we met at the party, Miss Abigail."

"I thought someone said *Mrs.* Wythe."

"Divorced," Morgan said. "That doesn't matter to me."

"Me neither. A fellow at the party said Abigail was the upper crust of local society. If Taos had a Park Avenue, she'd be on it."

"Money buys a lot of status. Take it from a Jew. Anyway, I believe I'm going for a stroll, and if it happens to take me near her home, well, happy circumstance. I might call on the lady. A friendly Sunday afternoon visit —all very proper."

Jack smiled. "Go for it."

The men continued to talk and drink coffee until footsteps sounded on the front porch and the door opened. "Girls, get out of your Sunday dresses. Cherry, pick me a pan of beans for supper, and bring wood for the stove. Peaches, feed the chickens, gather any eggs, and kill me a rooster."

When Jack heard them march inside, he stood up. "I'm beat," he said quietly. "I'm going to bed and sleep 'til my head's my own again."

In the foyer they encountered Mrs. Romero unpinning her hat. Jack headed upstairs toward their room.

"Mr. Diamond," she said. "Dinner will be at five o'clock. If you don't want to miss two meals today, I expect you to be prompt." It was like he was twelve, hearing his own mother.

Morgan snatched his hat from the hat rack and pushed open the screen door.

"That goes for you too, Mr. Silver."

"Certainly, madam," Morgan said.

Jack paused on the stairway. "Morgan, while you're out, stop by the Deitwiler's and thank them for the party."

"Will do. Good day, Mrs. Romero." Morgan tipped his hat to her and left whistling.

Jack suspected Morgan's happy tune had everything to do with Abigail. Well, good for him. He continued upstairs. From the landing he heard disappointment in Cherry's voice. "Where did Jack and Morgan go?"

"That's none of your affair, and you should say Mr. Diamond and Mr. Silver."

"They told me to call them by their first names."

"And I'm telling you to respect your elders."

"They're not elders—not old—like you are."

Jack let out a laugh, and then quickly covered his mouth.

"They're too old for you. Now, quit sassing and go pick green beans."

Jack entered his room and closed the door. God, he felt sorry for the Romero sisters, wanting so badly to be women, with a mother trying so hard to keep them girls. But her efforts were doomed. Her chicks weren't going to stay in the hen house. That was obvious. He stripped, tossed his clothes in a pile, and fell into bed exhausted.

CHAPTER 7

Since it was still too early in the day to make an afternoon social call, Morgan swung by the freight office where their trunks were stored to make sure all was well and dig out a couple of magazines. Then he explored the business section of Taos, such as it was—peeping in the windows of shops closed on Sunday and trying to get a feel for what was where. The business district consisted of the plaza square plus a handful of businesses on adjacent streets scattered over what would be about three New York City blocks. But Dunn hadn't been joking. About every third building was a saloon, and most were open, even on Sunday, though they didn't have many customers yet.

When he got to Deitwiler's, the doors were propped open and Fred and Emma were sweeping up last night's mess.

"Morning," Morgan said. Fred scowled at him. Had he done something to earn that, or was it really directed at Jack?

He tipped his hat to Emma, who looked friendlier. "Or should I say, good afternoon?"

"Yes, it's past noon," Fred said. "I expected you two earlier. Where's your partner?"

Morgan turned his palms up and shrugged. "Still recovering from last night. That was a wonderful party, by the way. Thank you so much. It really made us feel welcome here."

Emma put her broom down, brushed off her hands and pinched her cheeks until they looked rosy. She moved near Morgan and said softly, "The pleasure was all ours. Everyone in town is talking about your stories of the World's Fair."

"By everyone, she means herself," Fred said. "She's been going on all morning about you fellows."

"Emma, here are a couple of magazines I brought from New York." Morgan laid them on the edge of the table. "I think there may be others a little deeper in my trunk when I finally unpack it."

Emma stepped in front of Morgan, blocking Fred's view and gave Morgan's hand a little squeeze. Maybe this was what was behind Fred's dirty looks.

Maybe some fence mending was in order. Morgan met Fred's eyes. "Well, I'm not really dressed for it, but you've got quite a mess here. Let me help you clean up." He slipped out of Emma's grip and reached for her broom.

"Emma can get that. Jack said you two would help get the shelves and tables built."

Morgan's posture stiffened. That was it. He shook his head. "Jack's your man for the carpentry stuff, I'm the artist. He told me you wanted a sign painted, but I didn't plan on working Sunday. I just saw you were here and thought I'd stop in to say thanks for last night."

Deitwiler frowned. "We do need a sign, but I've got inventory coming next week and I need shelves to put it on. I got a load of lumber out back that we need to get off the wagon right now. Jack didn't say anything about not working Sunday. You'll have to help me. Emma can't."

Damn Jack. Just like him. He puffed out his cheeks, exhaled, and then shook his head. "No, we can't expect your wife to unload lumber. Let me take my coat off."

"I'll take it." Emma accepted Morgan's coat, draped it over her arm, and petted it. "Nice cut, very nice material."

"I bought it just before we left New York for the Fair. It's the latest fashion, by the way."

"Emma knows her patterns and fabrics," Fred said, friendlier now. "She's the reason we chose the dry goods business."

Emma held the back door open while the men emptied the wagon. By the time the lumber was stacked in the shop, Morgan's shirt was wet with sweat and too dirty for a call on Abigail. Before Fred could suggest any further construction work, Morgan selected a board about three feet long and two feet wide—not quite the right proportions for a sixteen by five foot sign, but it'd do. "Jack said Mrs. Deitwiler wanted me to paint something artistic for your store sign."

"Call me Emma, please." She pointed to the board in his hand. "But I want something much bigger. It should cover nearly the whole storefront."

"I understand. But first I'd like to do a smaller version. Make sure we agree on the design. I have some paints in my trunk over at the freight depot. I'll take this board and see if I can capture some local scenery for the background."

Morgan reclaimed his coat from Emma and made his escape before any more work came to Fred's mind. He retrieved a canvas sack containing his paint and brushes from the freight office and walked up into the hills above town, carrying the board under his arm. The afternoon light falling on the pueblo buildings below gave the scene a depth and sharpness that the smoky air of New York never afforded. Even up in the Catskills, he hadn't seen this kind of clarity.

A rocky prominence further up called to him. From there he saw sage-colored mountains highlighted with lavender hues. Quickly getting out his paints, he propped the board on a rock and began to paint, striving to capture the evanescent sight. It was as though the plane separating earth from sky was a little thinner here, flooding the scene with an ethereal light.

He painted in an inspired frenzy—just what he'd dreamed of since hearing about Taos. After he finished, he headed home for supper carrying the wet painting gently with two hands, held away from his good coat.

As he passed Deitwiler's, Emma spied him and called from inside, "Let me see."

He hesitated, started onward, and hesitated again. She was in the doorway by then, all dimples and curls. "Oh Fred, Morgan's got something done already."

Fred appeared behind her.

"It's late. I was just heading home for supper," Morgan said. "And it's still wet. I may want to do some touchup as it dries."

"Just give her a peek," Fred said. "She'll be uneven all night if you don't."

Morgan carried the painting inside and leaned it against the window. "Don't touch it," he said.

Emma's face fell. "Well . . . it's a nice painting."

"The details are a little fuzzy," Fred said. "Do you normally wear eyeglasses?"

Ah. "It's a style called Impressionism. It's supposed to look like that."

"Oh, it's beautiful. Really," Emma said. "Your partner was right. You're an extraordinary talent."

"But . . ."

Emma blushed. "I'd buy this to hang in my parlor in a heartbeat. In fact, I will buy this, as soon as we get the store open and make a little money. But my thought is that women here already know what the scenery looks like. My sign should have pictures that say to them, 'Here is where a beautiful woman will find the makings for beautiful clothes.' An ideal for them to attain to."

Morgan nodded as she spoke. It seemed he and his friends weren't the only ones with a vision for an emporium. Fred rolled his eyes.

Emma's eyes danced. "Before we moved, I had a magazine illustrated by Aubrey Beardsley, but I can't find it now. Do you know his work?"

This woman was full of shocks. "Art nouveau, I know his work very well. In fact, I'm sure we have some books he illustrated in our crates."

It was only after he said this that he remembered that one of the books was *Lysistrata* and that most of the drawings in it would be banned in Boston. Emma looked like she might be game, but he probably wouldn't show the books to Fred.

"Well, I imagine our name written in fancy lettering," Emma said. "Dry Goods written under that, and a beautiful, Beardsley-type woman on each end. Is that something you could do?"

He could picture how that could work. And Beardsley would be fun to mimic. "I can, but not today. It's nearly supper. Tomorrow I'll sketch out something for you on paper and bring it by."

CHAPTER 8

Cherry had her feet on the rail pushing the swing back and forth when Morgan walked up the steps. She swung her feet to the ground and covered her legs with her skirt. "Oh, good, you're back! Jack's up."

"That's good."

"He's in the parlor with Peaches. They wouldn't let me in. Made me stay out here. Come sit with me."

He wasn't even going to inquire. "Perhaps later. I need to clean up first."

"What's in that canvas sack on your shoulder?"

"Paints and brushes."

"Are you going to paint a picture?"

Morgan nodded. "Already did."

"Where is it?"

"Deitwiler's store. It was for them, more or less."

"I'd love to see it. Walk me there after dinner."

Mrs. Romero's voice came from somewhere inside. "Mr. Silver, is that you?"

Morgan opened the screen door and stepped inside. "It is, ma'am."

Mrs. Romero stuck her head out the kitchen doorway at the far end of the hall. "My lord, you're filthy."

"He's made a painting," Cherry said from behind him. "Imagine, a real artist staying in my room."

"Is that so? I hope you're not planning to sit at my table like that."

"No, ma'am. I was just going to wash and put on a clean shirt."

"Be quick about it. Supper's nearly ready. Cherry, is the table set?"

"Yes, Mother."

Mrs. Romero disappeared back into her kitchen. Morgan went to his room, poured water in the basin, washed, and put on a fresh shirt. When he was dressed, he came down to the kitchen. "I hope I didn't hold up supper."

"You did not." She wrapped her hand in her apron and opened the oven door. "Another fifteen minutes or so." She closed the oven and tried to step past him. "Go wait on the porch with the others. I can't cook with people in my kitchen."

"Even your daughters?"

She set a serving platter on the sideboard and wiped it with a towel. "Last year, I left them in charge while I went to help Mrs. Sanchez birth her first child. They destroyed my kitchen and one of my boarders moved out." She edged him toward the door. "Thankfully, they have good schooling, and soon, proper husbands, so they won't need to run a boarding house."

Morgan wondered how they felt about those plans, but he left her to her work and started for the porch. He passed the parlor with its closed door. Sometimes it was best not to know.

Cherry spoke to him through the screen, "Are you coming to sit with me? We'll have a grown-up conversation. You can tell me about your painting."

On the other hand, maybe it was better to know. "Um, I'm going to say hello to Jack and Peaches first."

Cherry stamped her foot. "Not the parlor. Peaches said I'm not welcome."

"I'm not you," Morgan said.

"Oh, I'm not that young. Don't think I don't know stuff."

Morgan gave a light tap on the door and turned the knob, hesitating just long enough to permit Jack to redo whatever had been undone. When he opened the door Peaches sat leaning languidly against the arm of the settee, fanning herself with an ornate fan. Jack sat in a wicker armchair on the other side of the room.

"I see the dead have revived," Morgan said.

Jack grinned. "I feel like a new man, ready for another night."

"Well, I feel just the opposite," Morgan said. "I stopped by Deitwiler's to thank them for the fine party last night—"

"Oh, Jack was telling me all about it," Peaches said.

Morgan glared at Jack. "Did he tell you he was supposed to go to work today?"

"What?" Jack said.

"Yes, I arrived there and Deitwiler thought you and he'd arranged to start building shelves today. He had an entire wagon of lumber to be unloaded. Worked me like a Brooklyn stevedore. I never made it to Abigail's."

"Abigail?" Peaches said. "Who's Abigail?"

Best to let that lie. "By the time Fred and I finished, I was sweaty and my clothes were dirty. Then Emma wanted a sign painted, so I retrieved my paints from the freight office, and went up in the hills. Actually, that was good. In fact, Jack, you have got to see the place. There is something ineffable about the landscape and the light. Anyway, I think I did it justice . . . Turned out not to be the background Emma wanted for her sign, but maybe we can sell the painting in the emporium when we get it open. She said she'd buy it, but I know they won't. All the Deitwilers' money is tied up in their store."

"Peaches!" Mrs. Romero's voice rang through the house. "Where are you?"

Peaches jumped up and scurried out of the room.

"So you never got to call on Miss Abigail?" Jack said.

"I couldn't go to her looking the way I did after doing *your* work."

"Deitwiler is confused. I said we'd start tomorrow—Monday."

"Yesterday's tomorrow was today," Morgan said.

Jack shrugged. "Well, he should have known what I meant. Sorry if I put you on the spot."

"Peaches! Find your sister and tell the men dinner is being served."

"Yes, ma'am," Peaches said.

But the men had already heard and headed into the dining room when Jack ran into Peaches in the doorway. Peaches pressed herself against his chest and Jack didn't take a step backward. Morgan saw it happen and poked him in the ribs. "Move, Jack, there's other people wanting to eat."

Peaches took Jack by the hand and led him to a chair next to hers, then waited pointedly for him to pull her chair out. Cherry chose the seat next to Morgan and looked at him expectantly. He smiled and made an elaborate show of helping seat her. Cherry flicked her tongue out at Peaches, pulling it back in so quickly Jack missed it, but Peaches certainly didn't.

The table had two extra place settings. A rotund man squeezed through the door and took the seat at the foot of the table, right-angle to Cherry. He was accompanied by a wiry man with a mustache thick as brush bristles, who took the empty seat next to Peaches.

The fat man pressed a sausage-like finger into Cherry's dimple. "How's my little Cherry tart? Did you miss me while I was away?"

Cherry squirmed and scooted her chair closer to Morgan. Morgan stared at the fat man wondering, given Mrs. Romero's temperament, that she tolerated him.

Mrs. Romero entered carrying a tureen which she placed at her end of the table. "I'm sorry, you haven't met. These are my other two borders. Please introduce yourselves while I get the meat."

Morgan stood, leaned across Cherry, and extended his hand toward the fat man. "Morgan Silver. This is my business partner, Jack Diamond. Mister?"

"Smith. This is my associate Mr. Jones." He gripped Morgan's hand in his pork chop sized mitt. "Sounds like money. Get it Jones? Morgan Silverdollar. I'm sure you've heard that a thousand times."

Morgan just nodded and smiled. Should have given more thought to choosing his new name.

The men shook hands all around. Mrs. Romero carried in a platter of roast chicken, set it on the table, and went to her seat. Jack and Morgan both stood. Smith and Jones did not. Morgan held Mrs. Romero's chair for her, and when everyone was seated Jack reached for a drumstick.

"Mr. Diamond! I thought you were a Christian man. We say grace in this house. Peaches, I believe it's your turn."

Peaches mumbled the standard Catholic blessing and everyone crossed themselves except Morgan, who was afraid he'd do it wrong. Mrs. Romero didn't notice and commenced to direct traffic as the dishes were passed around the table. "Mr. Smith and Mr. Jones are land agents," she said during a gap in the serving.

"You work for the government?" Jack said.

"No," Smith said. "We're employed by various law firms around the state to assess and procure land deals. Mostly, large spreads, but if you're looking to start a sheep or cattle ranch, we'd be glad to assist you. A lot of easterners coming to New Mexico, these days."

"How'd you know we're easterners?" Morgan said.

Smith passed Jones the potatoes. "Your accent."

"Well, you guessed right," Jack said. "But we're not here to punch cows."

"What are your ambitions?" Jones said.

"Art, music, literature, and the enjoyment of life," Morgan said.

"And the wonders of our modern age," Jack added.

Smith and Jones looked at each other.

Mrs. Romero explained, "Mr. Diamond and Mr. Silver are shopkeepers."

"Oh, more than that," Jack said.

Morgan nodded. "We intend to inspire, as we were inspired by the culture and sciences of the World's Fair."

"You've been to the exposition in St. Louis?" Smith said.

"Just came from there," Jack said. "It boggles the imagination."

"Smith and I talked about going," Jones said. "But there's always too much to do here."

"Oh, make the time," Jack said. "It was worth every day we spent there."

"How long were you there?" Smith said.

"Two weeks."

"An entire fortnight?" Jones said.

"Can't see all of it in anything less," Morgan said. "The fairgrounds cover 1,200 acres. There are a dozen enormous palaces that rival anything in Europe."

Peaches clutched Jack's arm. "Oh, I wish I could go."

"There's still time," Jack said. "It'll be open until December."

"Two weeks away from work," Smith said. "You must be from wealthy families."

"Not really," Jack said. "But we're single and young, and there may never be another exhibition like it. You could buy anything, from the latest books to the newest inventions."

"Don't misunderstand. It wasn't all play," Morgan said. "We spent a good part of our time purchasing items for our store. What we didn't buy there is currently being contracted for by our third partner back in New York."

"Just what kind of store will this be?" Mrs. Romero said.

Jack swept his hand in the air before them, painting his words in an imaginary arc, "A cultural emporium, as Morgan likes to say."

"Isn't that wonderful, Mother?" Peaches said.

"Why did you pick Taos?" Mrs. Romero said.

"The artists," Morgan said. "We met several European-trained artists at the Fair who said a couple of their peers had already moved here. Have you heard of Phillips or Blumenschein?"

Jones nodded to Smith, "You know Phillips, that painter who married Doc Martin's sister."

"Well," Jack said, "Morgan figured with them here, Taos might be thirsty for some of the cultural and artistic things from back east."

"Blumenschein's not here anymore," Jones said. "He went back to New York."

That was disappointing. He'd planned to introduce himself to Ernest Blumenschein one day next week.

"Morgan's an artist, too," Cherry said.

"Cherry! What did I tell you girls about referring to grownups by their first name?"

"Don't scold them," Jack said. "Morgan and I asked them to."

She fixed her eye on him. "You two shouldn't encourage them. It's difficult enough to bring up mannered young ladies in the western territories."

"It's a new century," Jack said. "There are new manners now."

"Well, I was taught to say Mr. Diamond and Mr. Silver. You don't hear me saying, Jack this, and Jack that."

Jack laughed. "I wish you would. When someone calls me mister, I think they're talking to my dad."

"As I was saying," Cherry looked at her mother. "*Morgan* is an artist. He painted a picture this afternoon for the Deitwilers. Didn't you?"

Morgan nodded.

"Mother, can we go see it after dinner?"

"Absolutely not. You girls have the kitchen to clean, dishes to wash, and homework to do. Mr. Jones, would you please pass the green beans?"

Morgan patted Cherry's hand. "Deitwiler's is probably locked up by now. They may not buy it, anyway. If they don't, I'll bring it home and let you see it."

Mrs. Romero blotted her lips with her napkin and laid it back in her lap. "Gentlemen, Saturday is laundry day as that's when I have the girls home to help me. You missed it this week, but if you have enough clothes to last until next week, I'll wash them for the same price as that laundry up the road, and you won't have to carry them there and back. Your clothes will be clean, ironed, and in your room when your get home."

Throughout the meal Peaches had fawned over Jack, passing him this, re-filling his plate with that. It was a bit worrisome. So, when there came a lull in the conversation, Morgan said, "Madam, Jack and I were wondering what age are your daughters, exactly."

"No, I wasn't," Jack said.

Mrs. Romero scowled, but before she could answer, Peaches piped up, "I'm almost eighteen."

Morgan kicked Jack's shin under the table and arched his eyebrows.

"I'm going to be eighteen, too," Cherry added.

"Liar," Peaches said. "She's fifteen."

"I said I was *going* to be eighteen. Someday is not that far off."

Mrs. Romero looked from Morgan to Jack and back to Morgan, narrowing her eyes. "Why do you ask?"

He was ready for the question. "I was helping the Deitwilers ready their store today, and I wondered if perhaps one of your girls was of an age to clerk there."

Mrs. Romero pursed her lips and looked at the ceiling. "Mercantile occupations are fine for a married couple—if they don't have children—or a spinster, or a widow. But my daughters don't need jobs. They'll find nice husbands and have maids and nannies like Mrs. Hoffsteader. I'll see to that."

Jack pushed his chair back. "That was a very satisfying meal. Gentlemen, I propose a stroll downtown, walk off some of Mrs. Romero's exceptional cooking."

"I'm afraid Jones and I will have to beg off," Smith said. "My feet won't take it. I've a touch of the gout."

Morgan stood and helped Mrs. Romero with her chair. Cherry looked at him. "You going with Jack?"

He nodded. Cherry pouted.

"Girls, get this table cleared," Mrs. Romero said.

"Would you care to perambulate the evening air with us, madam?" Morgan said.

"Thank you, but no. I've got to stay here and make sure these two get their work done."

CHAPTER 9

After breakfast Monday morning, the girls went to school, Jack went to work, and Morgan puttered around with a pencil and paper trying to imagine what Emma Deitwiler would like. He started with a series of overlapping ovals on the left and right edges of the sketch, placeholders for female figures he would add later. Between them he wrote *Deitwiler* in an elaborate calligraphy not unlike the typeface that might be used on the title page of a Bible. Below that in smaller, serif lettering he wrote *Dry Goods*. He made a couple of adjustments to the proportions of the two lines, then played with intertwining vines of ivy around the perimeter, the way Beardsley sometimes did, but it seemed overdone.

Too busy. He erased all but a few inches of leaves under the words Dry Goods.

When he had something he thought would satisfy Emma, he went to his room, changed into his best shirt and put on his dress coat. He had a plan. Get his Beardsley illustrations out of storage, drop the sketch for the proposed sign at Deitwiler's, and then call on Abigail. It had to be today before her pleasant memories of their tête-à-tête at the party started to fade.

At the freight office, he rummaged through his trunk for his copy of *Le Morte d'Arthur*, which Beardsley had illustrated, but couldn't find it. He did find several issues of *The International Studio*, a fine arts magazine to which Beardsley frequently contributed. He thumbed through the pages. The magazine had plenty of nude goddesses—not that he intended to paint any nudes on the dry goods sign. That would be a little too much of the modern world. He wouldn't show Emma those pages. But Art Nouveau magazines had illustrations of amply endowed women in fashionable dresses with deeply cut necklines showing plenty of cleavage. The magazines he'd lent Emma Sunday should have given her a pretty good idea of what women on her sign should be wearing. In fact, if she'd sewn any of the patterns she intended to stock in the store, she might even have such a dress. That would be smart, having a sign showing women attired in the very style you're trying to sell.

The wall clock in the freight office chimed. He looked at the time and decided he'd better visit Abigail first and take the Art Nouveau magazines to Emma on the way home. Why risk missing her again?

As Morgan walked to Abigail's, he thought back over his conversation with Jack last night after dinner. Their evening stroll had inevitably taken them to a saloon. Morgan got a table and Jack brought two beers over and set them down.

"You said at dinner, that Deitwiler might not keep the painting you did today," Jack said.

"That's right," Morgan said. "I think every penny they've got is committed to getting their store off the ground." He clinked his glass against Jack's. "Something we should think about, too."

"Cheers." Jack took a sip and wiped froth from his lip. "I had a notion we might sell your art in our emporium. It'd be a little extra inventory that we wouldn't owe some company back east for."

Jack often had good ideas. That's why they'd been partners, even back in New York City. And the artists in St. Louis had been right—the light in Taos was unique and fascinating. If he could keep in touch with his creative muse, his art might help the store prosper.

"I'll tell you what else," Jack said. "Everyone we talk to is interested in knowing what the Fair looked like. Our emporium should sell those packets of stereoscope cards Bryce bought to show his mother."

"That's a great idea. I wonder who makes them."

"Bryce has several sets. The publisher's name must be on them somewhere."

Morgan nodded. "I'll write Bryce, ask him to find the company, and order us some."

"We should sell the stereoscope viewers, too."

"I don't see why not."

He was still thinking about possible inventory when he arrived at Abigail's large Victorian style house, surrounded by flower gardens. She was outside cutting irises. Morgan paused to admire her shapely derrière before announcing himself. "Good afternoon, Mrs. Wythe."

She straightened up and turned. "Good day to you, Mr. Silver."

"Morgan, please."

"And call me Abigail. I thought we got beyond all this formality Saturday night at the party."

"You're right, of course. Though, I didn't know if we were starting over in the harsh light of day."

"I told you Saturday, be forward, the past is behind."

Morgan laughed. "Yes, I recall."

Abigail tucked the garden shears in her apron pocket, gathered the flowers in one hand, and with her other, tucked a loose strand of hair behind her ear. "I must look a mess."

"Anything but." The whole scene was like a painting that took his breath away—a pre-Raphaelite beauty in a Monet garden. If he'd painted such a picture, he'd have titled it *Auburn-Haired Beauty with Flowers*.

"It's so hot. Won't you please come in?"

Morgan held the door for her and she led him into her kitchen. She worked a hand pump on the sink to fill a vase with water, then arranged the flowers. Next, she took two tall glasses from the cabinet, crushed sprigs of fresh mint in the bottom of each and sprinkled a teaspoonful of sugar over the mint. The kitchen had a modern ice box. She opened the door to the ice block and chipped enough to fill both glasses. "Follow me."

Morgan followed her into the parlor where she filled each glass with brown liquor from a cut-glass decanter. She gave each glass a quick stir with a long spoon and said, "Best to let them steep a minute. Excuse me while I freshen up."

Abigail disappeared upstairs. Morgan set his magazines on a low table in front of the divan and browsed around the room. The walls were painted pale green with gold leaf border at the top. Obviously a wealthy person's room. The piano her sister had mentioned was in the corner—a mahogany upright, decorated with Art Nouveau filigree molded on the upper panel. He didn't play, but Bryce did. Around the parlor hung several museum-quality paintings, misty landscapes and scenes of goddesses—clothed of course. Originals or reproductions? He moved closer for a better look and stepped on a toy locomotive. Children? She didn't say anything about children. Of course, he hadn't asked. But why not? What woman her age didn't have children?

Abigail reappeared, face freshly washed and hair retied. She'd changed into a loose blouse and a clean skirt. He was quite certain she wasn't wearing a corset. He couldn't recall if she'd had one on earlier. She gave the beverages another stir and handed him one. He touched his glass to hers, "To a wonderful day."

"To a wonderful new friendship," she said and took a sip.

He followed suit. It was . . . cool and sweet. "What do you call this?"

"Mint Julep. I might be the only one around here who makes them."

"Then I'll know where to come."

She flicked open a small folded fan and waved it. "Please, have a seat. I didn't mean to leave you standing while I changed."

"It was worth the wait. You look lovely."

"I'll bet you say that to all the women."

"Honestly, in the garden earlier, when you were standing there with your armful of flowers, I thought you would make a perfect painting."

"Oh, that's right. You're an artist, aren't you?"

Morgan nodded. "I was admiring these." He pointed to her artwork. "Do you paint?"

"Oh, no. I'm a bit of a collector, though."

"Well, perhaps, sometime you'll let me paint you in your garden."

"It's already too hot, and it's only going to get worse. You have no idea."

"People around here say that, but you know back in ninety-six, New York had a heat wave that killed 1,500 people in ten days. I still remember it. I was fifteen."

"Well, imagine those ten days extended for the entire summer. A person can sit out for a bit in the early mornings, but not long. I'd be all runny with sweat."

Abigail fingered the magazines Morgan had left on the table. "What are these?"

"Examples of Art Nouveau I'm going to show the Deitwilers later."

"May I?"

Morgan tried to manage the situation by skipping pages with nude drawings and showing her only pictures of clothed women. But while he was busy with that, Abigail picked up one of the other issues and began flipping through it.

She held up a drawing of a cluster of nude fairies and goddesses and pointed to one with petite breasts whose nipples were simply circles of dots. "I ask you, is that realistic?"

Morgan nearly dropped the magazine he was holding. She was . . . well, in New York Society, it would be called scandalously forward. Here it was . . . normal?

Ah, brave new world that hath such creatures in it.

Abigail went to the credenza, pulled open a wide drawer, and removed a large portfolio. She untied the ribbon closure, removed three prints of Peter Paul Rubens' paintings, and spread them on the table before him. He recognized them at once: *Three Graces*, *Feast of Venus*, and *The Judgment of Paris*. He had to admit the full breasts and hints of pubic hair that Reuben's fleshy women sported were truer-to-life.

"Did you think I would be offended by art?" she said.

"I didn't expect—"

"What?"

"To find such . . . open-mindedness in New Mexico. And certainly not in a woman."

"Well, you'll notice these aren't framed and hanging on the wall. Being a divorced woman requires considerable circumspection."

"You mentioned an ex-husband the other night at the party, but I didn't want to pry."

"Oh, you merely had to ask your landlady or any of the other women in town. The wags are always happy to gossip."

"We don't have to discuss it if you don't want."

"May as well get it straight from me than from a pack of female coyotes. My husband brought me to Red River during the gold strikes there. It was no place for a lady. There were twelve saloons, seven brothels, and no plans for a church. The gold boom only lasted a few years, but my husband was one of the lucky ones. When the mine output began to fall off, he took what money he'd made—which was plenty—moved us to Taos, and built this house."

She took a long, honest pull from her drink, which he had noticed had a respectable kick. "Claude planned to open a dance hall here—nothing more than a saloon with live entertainment. He bought a plot, put up a big building, and then discovered Taos already had too much competition and not enough customers. Never even opened it. Next thing I know, he wants to go back to Red River to marry one of the whores he fell in love with."

"I'm . . . sorry."

"Oh, don't be, I'm well shut of him. Fortunately, we were Episcopalian, so I could divorce him. The only church in Taos is Catholic—they'd have never allowed me to get rid of that rotten adulterer. Short of him falling down a mine shaft, I suppose."

Morgan patted her hand.

"Don't feel too bad for me. I got all his Taos property and enough money to live well. Socially though, it'd be easier if the bastard was dead. A widow trying to raise her boy in this town is considered very acceptable. A divorcee creates an awkward situation for the women around here. They don't want me in their little social circle, but I'm so wealthy they can't ignore me. What these proud little housewives don't realize is that their husbands own every-thing. I'm the only woman in town who controls her own money."

"Not Mrs. Romero?"

"Oh, I suppose. But she barely scrapes along, raising two girls on her own."

"I saw toys. I was going to ask."

"Just one, he's in school and won't be home for hours." Abigail leaned in so close Morgan could feel her words on his ear. "I have all afternoon to do . . . whatever you like."

Morgan pulled back a little to read her eyes. In them he saw her bluntness, her honesty. He knew exactly what he'd like to do, but he didn't want her to think that was the only reason he was here.

"Have I shocked you?"

Morgan shook his head.

She put her cheek against his and whispered, "Morgan, I told you, 'Be forward.' Is it your intention to take me to bed?" She slid her mouth along his face until she reached his mouth and pressed her lips against his. Soft, warm, plush—his brain raced for adjectives, but all his blood had gone south. When their lips parted, she said, "We have all afternoon, but we don't have all day. You need to leave before school gets out."

Abigail made love like a woman who enjoyed it. Midway through, she rolled on top, raised herself up slightly and swayed her breasts across his chest, rubbing her nipples against his. He noticed her breasts had gravity, and he liked that.

Afterwards, he traced her lips with his finger. "The moment I saw you at the party I said to myself, in a town where the men outnumber the women two to one, if this woman has to sleep alone at night, it's every man's fault."

"A divorced woman has the same needs as a married one, but somehow when you get divorced you're expected to forget all that. But discretion is paramount. I trust you can keep your mouth shut."

"Except when it's on yours."

She hit him with a pillow and then kissed him again. "Seriously, a woman's social standing in this town is rigidly fixed: wives by their husband's occupations, unmarried girls by their father's, finally widows, divorcees, and prostitutes. Gossip determines if a divorced woman is treated like a widow or a strumpet. The banker's avarice is the only thing keeping me in Ida Hoffsteader's circle. A whiff of scandal and I'd be out."

"Believe me, I know what it's like to live betwixt and between in society."

"You have no idea what it's like for a woman marked with the stigma of divorce."

"And if I told you I was born Mordecai Silverstein?"

"Ah."

He nodded. "A Jew in an Irish-Catholic borough of New York. They don't respect you, but they don't want to offend your money."

She sat up, slid her hand up his thigh, and flicked back the sheet. "Do you mind if I look?"

He wrapped his arm around her taut white waist and pulled her back down, burrowing through her waterfall of hair to nuzzle her neck. She wiggled with pleasure, but then said, "No, no, we can't. Cyrus will be home from school soon."

"Cyrus? What kind of sadist saddles their son with the name Cyrus?"

"My ex-husband's name was Claude, and he tried to lay something equally onerous on his boy."

She stood up and handed him his pants. He noticed she wasn't self-conscious about being seen naked. Maybe he could paint her after all.

"Morgan," she said in a soft voice. "I have to be discreet when we meet in public, but don't think it's because you're a Jew."

"That's good to know. And don't think I have any judgments about you. Every man west of the Mississippi is here because he left his old life behind to begin a new one. Why shouldn't a woman who's been married before be entitled to the same fresh start as a cowboy? You're not only beautiful, but the bravest woman I've met."

She beamed. "I do hope you will call again." She cupped his face in her hands and added, "Frequently."

CHAPTER 10

After leaving Abigail's, Morgan stopped at Deitwiler's as he'd promised. Fred and Jack were nailing racks of shelves to the wall. Work paused when he came in. Jack got a dipper of water from a bucket while Morgan showed Fred his preliminary sketch for the sign.

"I like the lettering," Fred said. "But what are all these circles at either end?"

"Placeholders. When I paint the full size sign, they'll be two stylishly dressed women, representing the kind of customers who patronize Deitwiler's."

Fred hesitated. "Okay, do you have any talent for realistic figures or are these going to be all fuzzy like your scenery picture?"

Jack suppressed a snicker, not entirely successfully.

Morgan flipped open an issue of International Studio to a page he'd dog-eared and firmly gripped the surrounding pages so they wouldn't turn. No nudes, goddesses, or fairies for Fred. "Figures like this."

Fred studied the pen and ink illustration of a woman in a floor-length dress with a large bustle. She was bent slightly forward, resting her weight on the handle of a closed umbrella. The neckline was a modified V, but only the rounded tops of her corseted breasts peeked out. Fred rubbed his neck. "She's pretty, but it looks like an outline drawing. I know Emma has her heart set on a colorful painting."

"The magazine is black and white, but I'll use color."

"Morgan's real skilled at portraits," Jack said from across the room.

"I'll need a live model though." If Abigail would pose for the sign, it would give her a socially acceptable excuse for his visits.

"Oh, Emma would be thrilled to do it."

"Emma? You're sure?"

"She's hardly talked about anything but this sign since we met you." Fred shook his finger in Morgan's face. "But no Impressionism, don't paint Emma blurry."

Morgan grinned at Jack. "I won't." He went over to the pile of lumber and began scrutinizing the boards.

"What are you looking for?" Fred said.

"Boards for the sign. These are long, but there aren't any wide enough. If Emma wants the sign to be tall, we'll have to tongue and groove the edges and glue several of these together. Would you have planes that would let us cut—"

"Oh, Emma's already got the sign at our house," Fred said. "Had the old one taken off the building and painted over when we moved here. Been storing it in our carriage house ever since. Why don't you go over there and see if it'll do?"

"Shouldn't I wait until you finish up here?" Morgan said.

"Nah, Jack and I aren't ready to quit yet. Emma's at home, cooking supper. Take your books and your sketch over to my house for her to look at. She'll show you the old sign, too."

Well, this was all too convenient. Almost as if Fred was pushing them to-gether. Not that anything untoward would happen, even assuming Emma was willing. The Deitwiler home was about a fifteen-minute walk from the store. Morgan got there while it was still daylight, but it wouldn't be for much longer. He decided not to get involved in the specifics of the de-sign until he got a look at the medium he was going to paint on. If what she'd salvaged wasn't right, he'd have Jack and Fred make another from new lumber.

Emma led him around back, to a carriage house with double doors that when fully opened, let in plenty of light. It was also far enough from the road that dust wasn't a worry. It would serve as a makeshift studio. The Deitwilers didn't have a horse or buggy so the reclaimed sign had command of the space. Morgan ran his hand over the wood. The surface had been nicely sanded and prepped with two coats of white paint. No issues there. He stepped back and held his thumb up at arm's length, mentally laying out the sign in his mind. It was going to require a lot of paint. He'd have to mix more.

He turned to leave the carriage house and Emma hooked her arm in his. Her intention was unmistakable. He'd thought he was bringing modern ideas to Taos, and in a single day he'd found two forward women with Belle Époque sensibilities.

He stepped away from her. "Shouldn't we close the doors?"

She walked to one door and he to the other. When they brought the two doors together, she put a bar across two braces to hold it and took his arm again. "It's so important we get this right. Gusdorf's general store sells dry goods, too. So, I'm depending on your artwork to entice the ladies."

"I understand. I've brought a couple of Art Nouveau magazines and made a preliminary sketch for your consideration."

Emma gave a little squeal.

Inside the house, she lit kerosene lanterns as he unfurled his drawing on the table. "These placeholders on the right and left will be replaced by two fashionably dressed women facing in toward the name, Deitwiler. I was thinking of something like this." He opened the magazine to the page he'd shown Fred.

"I love the idea of it," Emma said. "But not the dress. A bustle? That's so Victorian." She began thumbing through the pages of nudes. "Oo-la-la."

"Well, there's a lot of that in Art Nouveau," Morgan said. "Obviously, I won't put partially clothed goddesses on your sign. People might think you were running a brothel."

She laughed. "I don't believe they need to advertise. Besides, we want them thinking about making clothes, not taking them off."

"That's true."

"Not black and white though, I want color, like a fine portrait."

"Certainly. Your husband suggested I use you as my model. Would you be willing?"

She flushed. "I'm flattered, but . . ." She fingered the drawing of a well-endowed nymph. "I'm not quite that . . ."

Then she gripped the bottom edge of her corset through the material of her dress and tugged downward. Two peach-shaped moons crested the top of her bodice.

It was Morgan's turn to blush. "You're absolutely lovely. Moreover, it's fashion you want to promote, not some over-endowed Venus."

"You're right. Our sign should exemplify our fabrics and dress patterns. The magazines you brought Sunday were most helpful. I saw a dress in Vogue very similar to one I made last week. Let me show you." Emma disappeared and returned in a moment holding in front of her a lovely creation of pearl blue satin with white crepe ruffles. "Do you think it will do? Shall I try it on for you?"

Abigail all over again? Morgan, irresistibly drawn to this petite little flower, required all his willpower to shake his head no. "Save it for tomorrow. We'll start in the morning."

"The sketch calls for a second model. I don't know any other women my size. I might have to sew another dress. Do you have anyone in mind?"

Of course his mind jumped to Abigail, but no, she'd never do. This situation already held too much sexual tension. "I'll use you for both sides. Tomorrow you'll pose for the left side and when I'm finished, I'll have you face the opposite direction and paint the right."

"Two of me?"

"Twice as enchanting." Okay, maybe he shouldn't have said that. A divorced woman was one thing. A still-married woman was salacious, even for his modern sensibilities

* * *

The first illicit act occurred the next morning. Fred had already left to meet Jack at the store before Morgan arrived. While Morgan got the studio set up and his paints out, Emma went to change. He propped the five-foot tall sign at an angle he could see over and opened both doors as wide as they would go, to let in maximum light. Even with the doors open, they had plenty of privacy. The carriage house was behind the main house and passers-by could not see into it from the street.

Emma entered the makeshift studio and Morgan stopped breathing for a moment. The dress on the hanger last night was no match for the way it fit her tight little body. The pale cerulean color brought out the baby pink tones of her skin in a heavenly vision.

They opted for the pose of the Victorian lady leaning on the umbrella, although the dress Emma had made couldn't be considered Victorian by any means. It had a much lower-cut neckline and no bustle. They didn't have an umbrella so Morgan substituted a yardstick and told her he'd paint the umbrella in later.

Emma stood bending slightly at the waist with both arms extended, hands resting on the yardstick. Unfortunately, the thin strip of wood wouldn't support any weight so she couldn't actually lean on it. Holding the position would be a strain, but Morgan said it gave a nice form to her derriere, and leaning emphasized her breasts, letting them hang forward instead of being diminished by a more upright posture.

Still, they weren't all they could be.

He went over to adjust her pose and suggested that, to enhance her figure a bit more, she should reach inside her corset and lift herself a little. Instead, she clasped his hand in hers and pushed it inside the top of her dress. "Here why don't you just do it the way you want it."

A wisp of air could have knocked him over. Still, there was nothing for it; his hand was in there now. Her skin felt like velvet, her nipples like bonbons. He gently slipped his fingers underneath and lifted.

"I'm sorry, they're rather small," Emma said.

"No, they're perfectly delightful pippins. I'll paint them like ripe apples." He slid his hand over and did the same to the other one. Emma cooed.

He withdrew and hid behind the sign. Picking up his brush and palette, he started to paint.

They worked until noon, each keeping to their respective sides of the room. Occasionally Emma needed to straighten up from the bent position. When she returned to her pose Morgan stayed firmly rooted and left it to her to arrange her own pippins.

At lunch time Emma called a halt and came around to see herself through Morgan's eyes. "Oh, that's good. I've got to take Fred and Jack something to eat, but the streets are so dirty I don't want to get this dress soiled. I'd better change first." She turned her back to Morgan. "Will you undo me?"

Morgan spun her around, took her hands in his, looked deep into her green eyes, and said, "I think we better not."

Emma blushed and looked away. "You're right. I can do it myself. I'll be back in a little while."

"That's fine. I'll work on the umbrella while you're gone."

In New York, Morgan sometimes bedded his models and sometimes he didn't. It really depended on mutual attraction—he would never push an unwilling woman. True, Morgan was attracted to Emma. They'd teased and flirted a little bit before. But when she'd thrust his hand inside her corset, it was . . . completely new territory. He didn't know what to make of it or how far she wanted to take things. She was married and seemed to genuinely like Fred.

But did it matter, really? The prigs might label them libertines, but the three partners shared a common belief that it didn't matter if a woman was married or not. They'd heard women's rights activist Victoria Woodhull speak at Carnegie hall on free love. Civil War outlawed slavery, she'd argued, it shouldn't be any different for women. Nobody owned a woman, not fathers, husbands, or pimps. Morgan, Jack, and Bryce agreed with her. They believed they had the right, if not the duty, to love anybody who wanted to be loved by them. Of course, that philosophy didn't always meet with understanding spouses, even back east.

Nothing further happened the first day, but the second day Emma packed a basket and sent it to work with Fred so she wouldn't have to get changed to go to the store in the middle of the day. Fred, anxious to get the store finished, was amenable to the idea.

Emma let Morgan paint her until midafternoon when she said, "It's hot and this corset is killing me. Let's take a break. Come in the house and I'll make us some lemonade."

Her lemonade was tart and cold. Morgan sipped it and traced the beads of sweat on his glass while Emma disappeared into her bedroom. When she returned, she came up behind his chair, leaned over his head and ran her hands over his chest. "I've never done this with anyone else, but . . ."

Morgan tilted his head back to look into her face and she clapped her mouth on his. He felt the tip of her nose on his chin. Then he felt the velvet of her breast touch his ear. She was wearing nothing.

Their lips parted, and she swung around him and sat on his lap.

"You're sure about this?" Morgan said. "Don't be unfaithful now and regret it tonight."

"No regrets," she said. "I'm not some young virgin who doesn't know what's coming. Fred and I've been married for seven years, and I've had these urges before. But you're the first man I've found truly irresistible."

"Would Fred be okay with this?"

"Absolutely not, and he's a deadly shot. So, my question for you is, do you want me as much as I want you?"

Morgan did, and she did, and it was nice enough for him to forget about Fred's ability with a gun. And it was just as nice when they did it again on the following afternoon. But sweet afternoons with Emma meant no afternoons with Abigail. Morgan worried that Abigail was going to think herself ill-used and he never intended that. He really liked Abigail. Hell, he liked them both, but Emma was married. That meant there only two ways it could end between them, quietly or badly.

CHAPTER 11

New York City

Bryce Holloway walked down West Twenty-Eighth Street, stopping at each of the firms located along music row. Earlier this week he'd visited book publishers, collected their catalogs and purchased titles that were currently the rage in New York literary circles. The books would be shipped directly to the emporium by the publishers. He'd also set up accounts for the emporium to wire future orders once he moved to Taos.

His week had started awkwardly when he'd mistaken the portrait of G. P. Putnam's Sons' founder for Abraham Lincoln. But by the time he reached Scribner's he had his patter down. Dropping his family name and mentioning that his mother's circle included friends of Pussy Jones and Henry James garnered him lines of credit.

Today he was making similar arrangements with music publishers. His partners knew books and art, but they couldn't play a note between them. When it came to music, Bryce was the decision maker. Yes, they'd carried a crate of sheet music west with them, but he'd chosen the songs. They had no idea what popular music to order. He did.

This morning's post contained two letters from New Mexico. The first informed him of his partners' new names. He laughed when he read them —straight out of a dime novel. Too bad he couldn't follow suit, but he'd already used his given name to secure contracts. Besides, he had a copy of the Rough Riders' enlistment roster with his name in it. That was worth more than all the Irishmen in Brooklyn.

Jack and Morgan may not have grown up on Park Avenue like Bryce, but their lifelong friendship had allowed all three of them to move easily between the highest and lowest ranks of society. Of course, the strata Bryce preferred were the ones his parents considered sullied—ragtime musicians, minstrels, and Broadway chorus girls. He didn't mind using his parents' connections to start his business, but he could hardly wait to leave them and live in New Mexico.

The second letter asked him to find the manufacturer of stereoscopes and photo cards of the St. Louis Fair. Not a bad idea, but that would have to wait for another day. Today he concentrated on the music business. At F. A. Mills' firm on West Twenty-Ninth Street, Bryce ordered a whole case of "Meet Me In St. Louis, Louis," and had it shipped to New Mexico. The tune, written as a promotion for the Fair, was experiencing widespread popularity. He'd discovered, quite by accident while waiting in the lobby of a book publisher, that whistling a few bars caused doe-eyed receptionists to bring up the Fair. The ensuing conversations had twice this week led to evening suppers and late night dalliances.

As he collected music catalogs and set up accounts, Bryce imagined becoming a ragtime composer. He hadn't written anything yet, but he could. Contacts he was making today on music row might one day introduce him to the men in their firms who bought and published hot new tunes. Wouldn't that impress a Broadway girl?

CHAPTER 12

Morgan painted the second Emma on the sign, but in a different dress—one she'd sewn just for the painting. Lord knows when she'd found time. Emma and Morgan had an agreement that he'd leave after they made love. Neither of them had any desire for Fred to discover them in flagrante delicto. Although his departure gave Emma time to cook dinner, unfortunately, it was always too late for him to go to Abigail's. He'd had every intention to, and certainly had sweet memories of her moist loins, but she'd insisted he only come on weekday afternoons and Emma had fully occupied his days. And so the week slipped away.

Morgan unfailingly took supper at Mrs. Romero's. Sometimes Jack missed. One night Jack came late, and she grumbled at him. Another time Fred took Jack home after a long day and asked Emma to feed him. Morgan didn't mind. He and Jack had both squired the same woman numerous times back east. Besides, Fred was there.

Leaving Emma's on Thursday, Morgan decided it was his turn to be late for dinner. He had a plan. Despite Abigail's warning not to call after school, he didn't see another way. He'd just make his call brief and formal to let her know she wasn't used and forgotten.

Abigail answered the door with steel in her eyes. "It's rather late to receive gentlemen callers."

"I know it's been a few days, but—"

"Cyrus is right inside."

Morgan could hear small wheels roll on the hardwood floor and a boy's voice calling, "All aboard."

"I couldn't wait. Any longer and you might presume I was one of those men who love them and leave them."

"Shush." Abigail cast a worried glance down the hall.

"I'm sorry, but I've been painting the sign for Deitwiler's store, and it required daylight hours."

"I knew that. Not much happens in this town that isn't quickly known."

Did that mean someone saw him with Emma? No. You couldn't see into the studio from the street. Besides, they'd been careful. Nothing untoward had happened outside the bedroom, except that first morning when she'd put his hand in her bodice. But Morgan was certain no one had witnessed that, or Fred would have shot him by now.

Morgan gazed at Abigail's mouth and remembered the feel of her lips. She fingered a curl of her hair. He made a quick bow. "Mrs. Wythe, I'd like to make it up to you. I wonder if I might call on you Friday evening." He twisted his hands nervously and said under his breath, "Perhaps your sister would mind Cyrus?"

She touched the corner of her mouth with her tongue and smiled. "Why, Mr. Silver, I believe that can be arranged."

Tiny footsteps clacked up the hallway behind her.

"About this same time?" Morgan said.

"I look forward to it."

Morgan descended the porch stairs and walked toward the street. A small voice behind him said, "Who was that?"

"A man with a message," Abigail said. "You're going to stay with your cousins at Aunt Penelope's tomorrow night."

"Oh, fun!" Cyrus said.

Abigail tousled his hair. "Yes, indeed."

* * *

Jack made it home that evening in time for supper. He went straight to their room and washed off the sawdust and sweat. He'd wanted a cold beer after work worse than anything, but he was hungry too, and Mrs. Romero had strict rules. He and Fred had eaten everything Emma had packed in the basket, but that was hours ago. It didn't seem likely Fred would let him impose on Emma for supper two nights in a row, so his only choice was to eat here and go out later.

Morgan still hadn't come home from Deitwiler's when Mrs. Romero called them to supper. That was unlike him, but maybe it was his turn to have supper with Fred and Emma. Not a bad idea, since Fred was proving to be interesting company, with a lot of good ideas on how to build a business. He hoped Morgan was getting along as well with Emma.

Smith and Jones were away again. Peaches said they were gone most nights, and Cherry said she was glad. Since Jack was the only man at supper, the girls put him between them. Mrs. Romero served a nicely sliced ham on her best platter. Bowls of mashed potatoes, red-eye gravy, and pole beans with butter were passed among the four of them. There were hot biscuits, too.

Morgan came in while they were eating, and Mrs. Romero gave him a fierce look, but didn't scold him. She'd torn into Jack the other night for expecting to be fed after everyone else was done, but Morgan? She just passed him the potatoes and ham. Morgan accepted the platter with a smile. Most Jews Jack knew back home wouldn't eat pork, but Mo had never been that way.

After dinner the men went out to the porch. The girls started to follow, but Mrs. Romero derailed their plans and made them start cleaning up. With the girls out of earshot, Morgan said, "Going out?"

"I thought I would. You want to come?"

"No, I've got plans tomorrow night," Morgan said. "I better rest up."

"Oh, *those* kinds of plans. I'm glad you haven't become a monk."

"Speaking of which, Jack, I've noticed you've not been home quite a few nights this week."

"You've missed me? How sweet."

"No. Just when I wake up at night to use the chamber pot, your bed's empty."

"I've done pretty well at getting in before Mrs. Romero starts breakfast. I don't think she's caught on."

"Don't be ridiculous. She's been running a rooming house for more than a few years. I imagine she doesn't want to say anything that will give her girls ideas."

"Those girls already have ideas."

Morgan raised his eyebrows. "I trust you're leaving that alone."

"Oh, sure. No need tempt fate. I've been doubly occupied."

"How do you stay out all night and still work the next day?"

"Well, my motto is, work hard, drink hard, stay hard, and sleep only when none of those are available."

Morgan laughed. "I know, but I hope you're careful what you're spending. Once we're done with Deitwiler's, we've still got to get the emporium going. Bryce is likely to start shipping goods any day now."

"I'm watching the purse," Jack said. "You remember Sneed's little redhead I told you about? The one you said you didn't want."

"Yes."

"She's taken a fancy to me and treats me when Sneed's not looking. Not costing me a thing."

"That won't last forever. Sneed will find out she's not earning."

"Oh, she earns, just not from me. We meet after Sneed goes to sleep, when the girls take their baths. I wash her back."

"What are you doing until then, drinking?"

"You keep worrying about money."

"One of needs to, and Bryce never has."

He had a point, but Jack had been doing his part more than Morgan knew. "I haven't been drinking as much; only a beer or two, until it gets dark, then I give a young schoolmarm lessons in practical biology."

"Wait, wait, wait. I thought the school was run by nuns."

"They train secular teachers, too. Believe me she's not a nun."

"Is she one of Peaches' and Cherry's teachers?"

"We're being very discreet," Jack said. "Now, I've told you mine, you tell me yours."

Morgan bit his lip. "Discreet, that's a good word. Secret is even better. You can't tell a soul."

Jack leaned toward him, all the better to emphasize their privacy. "Come on Mo, we've known each other since we were kids. I talk about nobody's business but my own. Spill."

"You remember Abigail from the party?"

"Do I ever. Word is she's queen bee of this town."

Morgan nodded. "I almost screwed up though. I saw her last Monday and then didn't get back all week."

"Why not?"

"That's the other . . . well, Emma."

And here Jack had been worried about Morgan living like a monk. "Emma, too? You rascal." Jack slapped his knee.

"Don't let on to Fred. Emma says he's a dead shot."

"He says so, too. But why would I say anything to Fred?" Jack shook his head. "Emma . . . And she told me she didn't like big men."

"I'll tell you, Jack, I don't know what's with the women in this town."

"I understand what you mean," Jack said. "Obviously, the men here aren't meeting their duty. I guess it's up to us."

CHAPTER 13

Emma had carefully limited her indiscretions to hours she knew Fred was heavily engaged at work. At breakfast, she and Fred discussed what he and Jack were doing that day or what time he was picking up the freight from Santa Fe. She packed him a basket every morning, so he'd have no reason to come home for lunch. There was always risk though. The house was within walking distance of the store and he could have popped home at any time for something he forgot or to ask her opinion on where certain things should go. What made her sure he wouldn't was his drive to get the store open and customers coming. "To stop the bleeding purse," he said.

Morgan was . . . delicious. The only time in seven years she'd been unfaithful to Fred. There was one fearful incident where wet paint from Morgan's hand got smeared on her naked body in a place where, if Fred saw it, she'd be hard pressed to explain how it got there. She'd rubbed herself raw trying to get it off. Luckily for her, Fred had been too tired to be amorous of late.

Emma was willing to try any new position Morgan suggested, and he had some creative suggestions. The only thing she resisted was when he advised her to continue making love with Fred to allay his suspicions. "We haven't been intimate very often since starting the store," she said. "Wouldn't a sudden interest on my part seem curious?"

Morgan chuckled. "I assure you, men in general are so happy to get love they never question it."

"If you say so."

"Trust me."

She would give it a try.

Work on the store had progressed well, and it was nearly ready. Emma anticipated Fred would work late that night, pushing to finish. She made him a cold plate, bathed, and slipped between fresh sheets. She undid her hair and fanned it out on the pillows, trying her best to look like Miss As–will-be-done-by, and turned the bedroom lamp down low.

Emma heard Fred come in, pull his shoes off and drop them by the back-door. She called from the bedroom, "You're so late, Fred, I wasn't sure when you'd be home for supper, so I left you a cold lamb sandwich in the ice box."

Fred removed the plate from the ice box. "That was sweet of you." He took a large bite and said, with his mouth full, "We got all the stock put up today. That's why I was so late. We can open tomorrow or the next day, if Morgan ever finishes our sign."

"Not tomorrow," she said. "I might want to rearrange things."

"You haven't been there this week to help. I wasn't sure where you wanted everything, but I unpacked it all so I could see what we actually had." Fred swallowed the last bit, put his dish in the sink, and came to the bedroom doorway. "Problem is, everything we've got doesn't half fill the space. It makes the place look vacant—more like a store going out of business than one starting. We might have to string a rope across the room and hang fabrics on it to hide the empty side."

"Fred, put out the lamp and come to bed."

Fred went back to the kitchen, blew out the lantern, and returned to their room. Dropping his clothes by the bed, he climbed in. "You're right. We'll give it another day. I'm so exhausted I might sleep in tomorrow and open the next day."

Her breath caught in her throat. "What? And pay Jack for waiting while you sleep at home? No, tomorrow morning I'll make you a hearty breakfast and you'll be good as new."

"You're right. I'm not thinking straight. I just need a good night's sleep. Besides, if we hold off opening tomorrow, it'll give Morgan an extra day to finish his darn sign. I haven't even gotten home one night this week when it was light enough to see it. Is it everything you hoped?"

"Oh it's more than I hoped," Emma scooted against him.

He laid his arm over her and patted her backside. "Why, Emma, you're naked."

"It's been a long time, and you've worked so hard . . ."

He rolled over and kissed her briefly on the mouth. "It's a sweet idea, but I'm so tired, I honestly don't think I can."

Emma tugged the draw string loose on his underwear and slipped her hand inside. "Are you sure? Let's check."

Fred chuckled. "I can't remember the last time you acted like this."

"As I said, it's been a long while. You've been working so hard I thought you needed to be reminded why it's all worth it."

Fred took her in his arms and pressed her to him. "I never forget."

She wrapped her legs around him. "Prove it."

Afterward, her hair lay across his chest like damp corn silk. She stoked the hairy line above his navel with her finger. "I have an idea, Fred."

"Mmmm?"

"If the building is half empty, why don't we ask Jack and Morgan if they want to rent half our space?"

He sat up at that. "What? No."

"Why not? It'd be better than having to hide our empty shelves behind a curtain. They're just starting out, we're just starting out."

"But we're not in the same business."

"Exactly. We wouldn't be competing with each other. Maybe their emporium would bring us extra customers, too." The rigidity in his body told her he wasn't convinced. She squirmed seductively against him. "It would only be until they get their own place."

He kissed the top of her head. "I don't think it's a good idea."

"Fred . . ."

"Yes, Emma."

"Suppose Morgan would trade what we owe him for the sign for their first month's rent. We'd be able to hold on to more of our working capital."

That was the ticket. She felt his body relax.

"Why would he agree to that?"

"Because they need to get their store open, too, and we've got space for them."

Fred turned on his side. "Okay. We can ask."

"Morgan needs one more session with me to finish the sign. I'll bring it up then."

"Fine, Emma. Good night . . . Oh, Emma?"

"Yes, Fred?"

"Thank you for tonight."

She kissed the back of his neck and snuggled against him. She'd enjoyed it as well. Though someday, she'd have to suggest some of Morgan's positions.

* * *

Morgan arrived at the studio Friday morning and propped the doors open. The squeak of the hinges brought Emma to the back door. She was wearing a housedress and apron. Perhaps she was still cleaning up from breakfast.

"You're not changed. Do you need me to fasten your dress?"

Emma held her finger across her lips making the universal sign for silence. In the kitchen behind her, someone whistled a merry tune. "Fred's getting a late start this morning. Poor man is tuckered out. Have you eaten? I can make you some eggs."

"Mrs. Romero fed Jack and me a large breakfast, but thank you for offering."

"Jack! Oh, Fred you better get going. Morgan says Jack's waiting at the store."

"He's got a key," Fred said. "He knows what's left to do this morning." Fred carried his cup to the backdoor. "Good morning, Morgan. Come in and have some coffee."

Morgan glanced at Emma. She shrugged and nodded her head.

Fred started down the back steps. "No, wait, I'll come there. I want to see our sign. Emma, bring Morgan's coffee out here, will you, sweetie?"

Fred crossed the yard almost dancing a jig. He looked happier than Morgan had seen him since they'd met. The image of an overgrown leprechaun jumped into Morgan's mind—a German leprechaun.

"It's not quite finished," Morgan said as they entered the studio.

"That's what Emma said, but I don't understand. You painted a whole picture of the Taos hills in a single afternoon. Why's it taking so many days to paint Emma?"

"Different technique, more time consuming. Beside, your wife isn't a sage bush."

Fred studied the images of Emma. "No, she's not, is she?" He paused and appraised the sign. "My God, she looks so beautiful."

"She's a beautiful subject."

Emma arrived and handed Morgan his coffee. Fred put his arm around her. "You were right, dear. It's perfect. I don't see what's left to be done."

"One more session to wrap things up," Emma said.

Fred looked to Morgan for confirmation. Morgan nodded his head. "Some final shading and outlining. I'll get Jack to help me hang it tomorrow."

"About that," Fred said. "Emma and I were wondering if you and Jack would like to rent the unused portion of our store to get your emporium started. I'd be willing to trade you first month's rent for the work you did on our sign."

"Just temporary, to get you started," Emma said.

And like that, over coffee in the morning, the emporium moved from a dream to reality. "I'll need to confer with Jack. But my work is worth far more than a single month's rent."

Fred admired the lovely portraits of his wife. "You're right. I was being too cheap. Would you agree to three months' rent?"

"That sounds fair, but I still have to ask Jack." It was a capital idea, the two stores drawing in customers for one another. But how long could he and Emma work in close proximity without Fred noticing their every expression?

"I'm headed for the store right now," Fred said. "You won't mind if I mention it to him?"

"Go ahead," Morgan said. "But we may not be ready yet. We only brought a few crates of inventory with us. Our partner back east is supposed to be buying and shipping more."

"I know what you mean. When we got everything spread out yesterday, I discovered we had the same problem. You can only have a certain number of half-filled shelves before it looks like you don't have anything."

"Oh, yes, Jack and I should wire Bryce before giving you a definite answer."

"That's understandable. Listen, I better get to the store. Jack's waiting. Emma, is our lunch made?"

"It's all packed. Let me get the basket."

Fred shook Morgan's hand. "You've done a heck of a job. Jack has too. I think sharing a space will make it easier for both our stores. Can you finish doing Emma this morning?"

Morgan choked on his coffee.

"If we're going to open tomorrow, I need her to come in this afternoon and arrange everything the way she wants."

"I will, dear." Emma handed Fred his lunch, kissed his cheek and sent him on his way.

As soon as he was well down the road, she led Morgan into the house. She took off her apron and pushed him into the bedroom, unbuttoning her dress as they went. "I want you. I want you, right now!"

Emma had her way with him, and afterward lay on her side, hips pressed into the curve of his waist, knees embracing his thigh. "I didn't know what I'd feel, having just been with Fred a few hours ago. I wasn't sure I even could. It seemed so lascivious, being with two different men . . . but I find it rather licentious. What was it like for you? Could you tell? I mean I washed this morning, but did you mind?"

Morgan kissed her nose. "I knew the moment I heard Fred whistling. And no, I didn't mind. Making love with you is a precious gift. I'm happy to share."

Emma kissed him hard. When their lips parted he said, "We'll have to be careful how we act around each other if we share our stores."

A tear leaked from her eye and wet his cheek. "I feel as if we've just made love for the last time. This was a chance that happens once in life. And only because I knew Fred's commitment to his store, he'd never quit and come home early."

"He practically threw us together."

"This has been a magical week, but we'll never have an excuse to spend time together like this again. Very soon, I have to go arrange ribbons and buttons."

"You can leave for the store as soon as you're dressed. I didn't tell Fred, but I can finish without you."

Emma stuck her lip out. "That's it? I tell you we can no longer be lovers and you're done with me?"

"Emma, sweet Emma, I don't need you to model anymore because I have every inch of your firm, lithe body in my mind."

That made her smile. She rolled over and pulled him on top of her. "Once more, for our memories."

CHAPTER 14

Morgan finished the sign after Emma left. While it dried, he went to Deitwiler's store to discuss Fred's proposition with Jack. When he arrived, Jack wasn't there. Emma and Fred were fussing with the table displays. Emma looked up and gave Morgan a shy smile.

Fred said, "Jack helped me move a couple of tables, but as soon as the work ran out he left—didn't even stay to eat Emma's lunch. I supposed he'd gone to my house to discuss my proposition with you."

Morgan knew Jack knew about Emma, and Jack wouldn't risk embarrassing her by popping into the studio. Also, Jack hadn't come home 'til dawn, so he might be taking a nap. But probably not. It was past noon, and it was hot. Most likely Jack was celebrating his afternoon off with a cold beer. Morgan said goodbye to the Deitwilers and started checking saloons along the plaza.

Sounds of merriment and a flurry of movement in a side alley drew his attention as Cherry, Peaches and two older boys dashed behind the livery. Peaches stepped back into the alley, caught his eye, and made a zipping gesture across her lips.

Morgan nodded. He was beginning to see where they got their ideas from. She smiled and disappeared.

Jack was in the bar two doors down, with a pretty redhead on his knee. She wore a thin white dress, pulled low on her freckled shoulders, and didn't appear to be wearing anything underneath. Her breasts wiggled as she squirmed on Jack's lap. Jack was holding up a hand mirror. "Now, if you look at the reflection of the bar mirror behind us, you see this mirror, reflecting that mirror, reflecting this mirror—it continues an infinite number of times."

She pulled on one of her red curls and let it spring back. "You're so smart, Jack."

Morgan came up behind them, laughing. "Infinitely smart."

"Morgan!" Jack said. "This is Fanny. She has cute little freckles on her nose and everywhere, even down here . . ." He tugged lightly on her bodice.

She grabbed his hand and giggled.

Morgan took her free hand and kissed it gently, wondering how Sneed hadn't found out yet, if Jack was being this open with her. "I believe Jack has mentioned you. Pleased to make your acquaintance."

"Your friend is so gentlemanly," Fanny said.

"All us New Yorkers are." Jack pushed her off his lap and let his fingers linger a moment on her butt. "Get Morgan a beer, will you? And bring a couple more for you and me."

"Early in the day," Morgan said.

"Just got paid."

"Fred said he told you about his offer. What do you think?"

"I say, yes. Hell, yes. This is what we came here for. Let's get started."

"You know it's just temporary?"

"Fred said he traded you three months' rent. Damn nice of you to give up your pay."

"Three months ought to be about right. If both businesses are successful, we should need our own building about the time they need more space."

"Any concerns about . . . entanglements with the little lady?"

"She and I discussed it—won't be an issue."

"It's never that easy," Jack said.

"What's not?" Fanny set three glasses of beer on the table.

"Starting a new business," Morgan said quickly.

"Jack was telling me," she said.

"Should we ask Bryce?" Morgan said.

"I don't see any reason to spend money on Western Union. We're the ones who've seen the place. He'll just be glad we're open. Besides it's only temporary, we might not even be there by the time he arrives."

"God, I hope it doesn't take him another three months to clean up that situation back east and get out here."

"If we're the only votes, then it's a done deal. Go get Fred and we'll buy him a drink to seal it."

"Let's not. No reason to give him the impression we're the kind of guys who drink all day."

"Not *all* day—it's after twelve." Jack pulled out his watch. "Hell, it's after three."

"Tomorrow will be soon enough. I need you to help me carry his sign over and hang it in the morning. We can tell him then."

Jack drained his glass and slammed it on the table. "All right, I want to dance with my Fanny. Where's that piano player? Damn, I wish Bryce was here. Fanny, our partner Bryce is the best ragtime piano man you ever heard. When he gets here, I'm going to dance you right off your feet."

Fanny ran her hands through Jack's hair, which he had let grow long since coming to Taos. "You want another beer?"

"Sure, and one for Morgan, too."

She took their glasses and started for the bar.

"Fanny," Morgan said. She stopped and looked back. "See if the bartender has a blank piece of paper."

She nodded.

"What for?" Jack said.

"To make a list. We need lumber to make shelves and tables of our own. Help me figure out how much to buy."

"We'll need a sign, too."

"I'll paint one, that won't be a problem."

"You have to help with the carpentry this time. It can't be like Deitwiler's where I do all the manual labor while you get laid."

"Listen, I did my part. We got a store rent free, didn't we?"

Fanny returned with three beers, including one for herself, and Morgan wondered if Jack was being charged a premium for Sneed on his drinks. He decided to ignore that. She gave Morgan a piece of brown butcher's paper, and he pulled a drawing pencil out of his jacket pocket. He took his jacket off and hung it on the back of his chair. It was too hot to dress as they did in New York.

Morgan recalled an ancient seafarer's map he'd once seen that showed the Atlantic trade routes from Europe. Emulating the layout he'd used for Deitwiler's, he planned to frame the store name with an object on either end. In this case he chose a stylized Europe on the right and America on the left. He'd paint the space in the middle sea blue as background for the lettering. On the European side he sketched the Big Ben clock tower over Britain and the Eiffel Tower over France. Everyone would recognize Italy from the boot-shaped peninsula, so it didn't need a building.

On the American side he drew an exaggerated New York City skyline with pushed perspective so New York's dominance was magnified. He didn't need another city did he? New York was the business capitol, even if it wasn't the actual capitol, and he and his partners were, after all, New Yorkers. Over the Atlantic Ocean, he lettered, *New Yorker's Emporium*. He turned the paper around for Jack and Fanny to see.

"Weren't we going to just call it The Emporium," Jack said.

"Everyone around here calls us the New Yorkers. I figured they're going to refer to our store that way, so we might as well go along with it."

"Kind of smacks of eastern elitism—Bryce might resent that."

"And if Bryce were here, he might have a say," Morgan said.

"Don't get me wrong. I like the overall concept. The whole Europe to America map gives it a nice World Fair quality. After all, an emporium is a world marketplace, isn't it?"

"Jack, you're a genius." Morgan fished a gum eraser out of his pocket and spun the drawing around toward him. He erased *Yorker's* and replaced it with "World." He showed Jack. "New World Emporium, what do you think?"

"I like it. What do you think Fanny?"

"It sounds like something new."

Jack raised his mug. "New ideas for a new century."

CHAPTER 15

Saturday morning Jack and Morgan walked to Deitwiler's house and got the sign out of the studio. The paint was still a little wet, but they were careful as they carried it to the store. Fred was standing out front, proud as a new papa. He'd been expecting them and had a ladder ready. Hanging the sign was easy because there were already brackets where the old one had hung.

Emma was inside fussing around the tables. Morgan waved at her—they were friends after all—but he stayed out front with the men to discuss where to position the New World Emporium sign. "It'll be smaller than yours, of course," Morgan said.

"I suggest we center it just below yours," Jack said.

Fred looked up. "Seems about right. Are you going to use that board of mine you painted the fuzzy picture on for your sign?"

"No, Morgan's got a new idea. We'll sell that painting in the store. We don't have much inventory yet."

"Speaking of which, we better get to the telegraph office and wire Bryce," Morgan said. "We need him to send more inventory."

A crowd gathered, admiring the sign. "Are you open yet?" said a woman in a flowered hat.

"You bettcha." Fred opened the door for her and several others to enter. "Jack, do me a favor, and put that ladder out back."

Morgan followed the women inside, tipped his hat to Emma, and went to pace off the space Fred had allotted for the Emporium. He wrote down the measurements and then met Jack at the telegraph office where they sent Bryce a terse, economical message—Western Union charged by the word. Their next stop was the sawmill, which was a fair walk from town. Since they didn't have a wagon, they had to pay extra to have the lumber delivered, but at least they got a ride back.

By the time they returned, clusters of curious women filled the store. Emma hopped from group to group like a little elf. Fred was overwhelmed and hid behind the cash register, a smile on his face. When he saw Jack come in the backdoor, he said, "Emma, I've got to step out for a minute." She nodded and returned to showing her customer some cast silver buttons.

Fred surveyed the wagonload of lumber. "Jack, I hope you understand you'll have to do your carpentry out in the alley. I can't have sawdust and hammering going on while the store's open. Build what you can out here and I'll help you bring it in after we close. You can use my tools, they're in the storeroom."

"Seems reasonable," Jack said.

The wagon driver pushed up the brim of his hat and wiped his brow with his forearm. "You fellows going to help me unload this or are you going to stand there yammering?"

Fred ducked back in the store, and Morgan and Jack helped the driver unload and stack the wood. When the wagon left, Jack found the sawhorses he'd used to cut Fred's shelves and set them up. He got Fred's tools while Morgan looked over the boards and selected one for their sign. "This wood's grainy, but I can use the effect to portray waves in the Atlantic and contours on land. Cut me two pieces about four feet long. We'll butt them together to make a taller sign."

Jack scratched his head. "You want to start the sign first? It seems like we've got a lot of other stuff to make before we need that."

"I want the wood to cure in the midday sun for a few days. If it's going to warp, I want to know it before I put a lot of work into it."

* * *

Jack and Morgan built tables and unassembled shelving units during the daytime. At night, Fred helped carry them in and assemble them by lantern light. This schedule didn't allow Morgan time to see Abigail, nor Jack his school teacher. But Jack was still seeing Fanny in the wee hours—the man never seemed to require sleep. Peaches stopped by to bother them, but got distracted by all of Emma's pretty things and left them alone.

Nothing arrived from Bryce except a telegram saying he'd shipped several more crates. It didn't say what was in them. Morgan helped Jack move the goods they had stored at the freight depot over to their new emporium and then left to paint their sign while Jack unpacked.

When the New World sign was finished, they hung it, still wet, centered below Deitwiler's. By Wednesday, Deitwiler's had been open several days and the crowds had slacked off. The ladies had perused their fabrics, purchased their patterns, and were home, busy sewing. There'd be a whole new parade of fashion in Taos the first chance the women had for a social event. But hanging the new sign signaled the emporium was finally here. It brought a second surge of curious customers, this time including men.

They weren't entirely ready. They didn't have a cash register yet, just a tin money box, and Bryce's shipments still hadn't arrived. Jack had spread things out as best he could to keep it from looking empty, but Morgan would have to paint more artwork to hold them over until the freight arrived.

Smith and Jones were back in town, and Jones came by to look the store over. "I thought this was supposed to be some big emporium, but it's really just a bookstore isn't it?"

"No, we have piano music, too." Jack pointed to a rack behind him. "A lot of things we saw at the Fair are coming, but the freight delivery isn't very regular here."

"True enough," Jones said. "Your best bet is to have it shipped to Santa Fe and pick it up yourself from there in a wagon. Dunn owns the bridge on the road from Tres Piedras and charges a hefty toll."

"We don't have a wagon."

"You can hire one, but if it becomes a regular thing, you may be better off buying a team."

Unfortunately, none of the three New Yorkers knew how to drive a team. There wasn't any need for it in the city—that's what teamsters were for. Even carriage rides could be had by merely hailing a hansom. Fred's shipments were coming through Santa Fe. Maybe he'd go in with them on buying a rig.

Later in the day, Fred left to see the banker and Jack was gone to wherever Jack went, leaving Morgan and Emma alone in the store. They acted with friendly propriety, she staying on her side and he on his. Then, Abigail came in. It was the first time Abigail had visited. She knew Emma from the party but hadn't socialized with her since.

Abigail reintroduced herself and Emma said she remembered her. Emma unfurled bolts of fabric and Abigail fingered them while eyeing Morgan. Something palpable arose among the three of them—an electric current carrying information as surely as a telegraph line. Morgan busied himself dusting books, uncertain how this was going to play out.

Emma trailed Abigail as she ambled over to Morgan's side of the store. "Mr. Silver."

Morgan saluted from his brow as if tipping a hat. "Mrs. Wythe."

"Call me Abigail, please."

"Then please call me Morgan."

"I don't see any Balzac."

"Ah. I'm sure his books are on their way."

"You two know each other?" Emma said.

"We met at your party, dear." Abigail turned her back on Emma to give Morgan her full attention.

Emma crossed her arms and drummed her fingers on her biceps.

Not going well. He needed a distraction. Morgan grabbed the nearest two books from the table, glancing at the titles. "Emma, do you read Jane Austen?"

"When I was in school."

Abigail turned, "Which one?"

"*Pride and Prejudice*, of course."

"No, I meant which school."

Emma's tight smile bared her teeth ever so slightly, like a raccoon protecting its food. "Up in Minnesota." She stepped over to Morgan and straightened the lapel on his coat. "Abigail, you know the women here much better than I. Tell me, do they make their husbands' clothes? Should I start carrying patterns and material for men's clothing as well?"

Abigail wandered over to peruse the book table. "You're married, Emma. Do you make Fred's clothes?"

"Why yes, I do."

"There's your answer, dear. Although I expect you'll find men have less interest in the latest New York fashion than we ladies. We're your market." Abigail put her hand on Morgan's arm and spun him toward the book display. "Morgan, don't you think if Emma enjoyed *Pride and Prejudice*, she should read *Sense and Sensibility* as well?"

Morgan's mouth was dry. Being the center of a cat fight between Taos' most prominent woman and the town's newest merchant was not an auspicious way to start a business. "Well . . . well, that book did come out first."

Abigail handed the book to Emma. "Why don't you take this and read it? I'll buy it for you."

Emma's cheeks looked as if they were on fire. "That's not necessary."

Abigail made a throaty laugh. "Please, it's a gift. One woman to another." She walked over to the rack of sheet music. "Do you play, Emma?"

"Since I was five. But I don't have a piano anymore. Fred said it was too expensive to move it."

Abigail said, "Hmmmm," but the sound was somewhere between a purr and the growl of a feral cat.

The front door opened and Fred and Jack came in together. Morgan exhaled loudly and motioned Jack over. Fred came, too. "Jack, do you remember Abigail? You met briefly at the party."

Jack doffed his hat. "I'm afraid I didn't make a terribly good impression. Pleased to meet you again."

"Fred, you know Mrs. Wythe," Emma said.

"That's a lovely dress you're wearing," Fred said. "Did you make it?"

"I did. And Emma has been showing me some of your beautiful fabrics. Don't worry. I won't leave today without purchasing several. Just now though, we were discussing music." She touched Morgan's arm. "Weren't we?"

Emma sniffed, her nostrils widening.

"Emma tells us she's been playing since she was a child," Abigail said.

Fred beamed. "Back home Emma was a real virtuosa."

"My sister, Penelope, is the talent in our family," Abigail said. "She has a wonderful singing voice. Perhaps we should have a musical social at my house Sunday afternoon. Shall we say two o'clock? Morgan, you and Jack come, too."

"That sounds wonderful," Fred said. "Wait until you hear Emma play."

"I look forward to it. Now, if you and Emma would measure off about five yards of that calico with the blue periwinkles and five of that emerald satin, I'll be right over as soon as Morgan and I select some music for Sunday."

Emma's eyes never left them as Fred guided her to the measuring table. "Emma, let me help you. Show me which fabrics Mrs. Wythe wants."

At that moment, he had a deep appreciation for Fred.

* * *

Before Abigail's Sunday social, Jack had been asked by Morgan to help create a little misdirection. They'd convince Emma that Abigail had come to the store looking for Jack. Conversely, Abigail should be made to believe Emma's attraction was actually for Jack and she'd feigned interest in Morgan merely to deceive Fred. Jack didn't mind being thought the subject of two women's attention, and it would be better for the emporium to turn down tensions a bit. He recognized the ploy came straight from *Much Ado About Nothing*, but if it worked for Shakespeare, it might work for Morgan.

The machinations were unnecessary, for in the company of family and community Abigail acted no more attentive to Morgan than to any other guest. Likewise, Emma offered nothing beyond polite conversation and hung on Fred's arm whenever she wasn't playing the piano.

Abigail's guests were served cucumber sandwiches, petit fours, and sherry. Sherry wasn't really Jack's beverage of choice, but it was all that was on offer, so he drank it. Jack preferred beer because he drank in quantity. Over the years, he'd discovered a pint of beer every half hour would let him drink all night and keep him in that happy, inebriated state without crossing over to falling down drunk. Whiskey and wine were too strong. A pint of either would push him over the edge and shorten his night.

Emma sight-read the unfamiliar new tunes and played every bit as well as Fred had bragged. Penelope sat next to her on the piano bench, reading the lyrics and singing with perfection. Penelope's husband, Walter, couldn't come, but she'd brought her children, who were playing outside with Abigail's son, Cyrus. Neighbors and women of Abigail's social circle also attended. After each song they applauded Emma and Penelope enthusiastically.

The two women performed until nearly four o'clock, when they called for a rest and offered the instrument to someone else. But since no one wanted to risk comparison, that was the end of the music. Jack, who had been guzzling sherry like beer, was well past his limit, but he couldn't see why that should slow him down. He gathered three fresh glasses and brought them over to Emma and Penelope.

"Here, Penelope." He offered her a glass. "Something for your throat. Here Emma, one for you, too. What nimble fingers on such tiny hands."

The women accepted the drinks with a smile and a nod.

"Wonderful, wonderful," Jack said. "You've been prisoners in this parlor all afternoon, though. Shall we go out on the porch?"

"I believe Fred and I will pass," Emma said. "I've hardly had a chance to say a word to any of the ladies here." She pressed Fred into a group of Abigail's friends, where she received flowery complements on her playing.

"I'll go," Penelope said. "I need to check on the children, anyway."

As Penelope led the way through the crowd, Jack's eyes strayed down her sleeveless gown, to her slightly swaying hips. She didn't wear a bustle, so the action he saw was purely natural. And the lack of petticoats in the heat allowed his imagination free play.

On the porch she counted the number of children running amok and, with all accounted for, turned her back on them. "I see you've opened your store in Deitwiler's. How is that faring?"

"Well, it's just a start. You can't fit all of modern culture into the space Fred allotted us. When our other partner gets here we'll move to someplace bigger, with bright windows—we'll be displaying some artwork and will need plenty of natural light. Besides, the light here is so . . ." He realized he was wandering from his theme. "Anyway, we're planning on walls full of bookshelves, a reading area, with tasteful chairs where people can meet and talk ideas, many more racks of sheet music, stereoscopes and picture cards of the St. Louis Fair, maybe even electric lights—"

"Pardon me, what?"

"Surely, you've heard of Edison's invention? It's going to do away with gas lamps and kerosene lanterns. At the St. Louis World's Fair electric lights lit the whole place up at night, bright as daylight. And speaking of which, may I remark on how lovely the afternoon light makes your shoulders look?"

She smiled at him, much as she had smiled at her children earlier. "I'm married, Jack."

"I have a philosophy about that."

Penelope took a sip of sherry. "I'm sure you do."

"I'm telling you, this is a new century. The Victorian era is over and their moralistic ideas should be, too. The French have the right idea."

"I got the impression marital fidelity has been around long before the Victorians."

"Well, a woman should have the right to follow her heart. A man expects his wife to share him with his mistress. Why shouldn't she be entitled to the same consideration?"

Still smiling, she pressed a finger pensively to her lips. "I take it you're not married."

Lovely lips, a lot like her sister's. "No, but if I was, I'd encourage a little adultery."

"Good luck finding a wife with that philosophy."

"Who says I'm looking?" He brushed her bare shoulder with his fingertips. "Are you… looking?"

Penelope didn't pull away, but she said, "Is that the way it is with women back east?"

"Not as many as you might think."

"It's not that I mind the attention, Jack. But I'm not the kind that cheats."

"Ever?"

"Never."

CHAPTER 16

June 15, 1904, Tufts College, Medford, Massachusetts

"Rebecca Anne Sullivan, School of Theology," President Capen said.

Reverend Fitzpatrick beamed from the front row as his granddaughter strode across the stage and received her sheepskin. Imagine, his granddaughter following in his footsteps into the ministry. His only regret was that his stubborn daughter and her backward husband refused to attend. Silly, really. How many families in Boston could brag they had a daughter with a college degree? To stand her up was unacceptable, no matter what her father's priest said.

Were they going to put her through the same pains he had to endure? He could still remember the family discord when he'd left the Catholic Church to become a Universalist minister. His own daughter succumbed to pressure from her in-laws and left his church to return to Catholicism when she married the Sullivan boy. It was some years before Rebecca's mother felt comfortable inviting him into her home. And when his granddaughter followed him away from the superstitions of holy relics and an infallible pope, the battles had begun anew.

His other grandchildren had followed their parents' wishes, marrying Catholics and adhering to ancestral beliefs. But Rebecca wouldn't settle for some outdated religion. She was smart, strong willed, and wanted an education. Moreover, she had an altruist's heart and a theist's mind. She wanted to follow in her grandfather's footsteps and he'd been happy to help her. Against her parent's wishes, he had secured her admission to Tufts, and now, if she didn't find a position once she was ordained, he was going to make her associate pastor at his church, even if that caused yet another rift in their family.

He caught Rebecca's eye as she returned to her seat and gave her a broad smile. She smiled back, a justifiable pride swelling between them.

* * *

Same day, New York City

Bryce bounded down the stairs of music publisher Remick & Company, where he had tried to sell three of his songs. Jerome Remick hadn't exactly sprung from his office to offer him a contract, but the men Bryce played his tunes for did say they would get back to him. It was not likely he'd hear from anyone before Monday.

He started out the door when he spied two Irish pugilists loitering across West Twenty-Eighth Street. He immediately reversed direction and returned to the girl at the reception desk. "Is there a backdoor?"

She pointed down the hall. "Last door on the right is shipping and receiving. It connects to an alley on Sixth Avenue, used by printers and teamsters."

"That'll do." Bryce sprinted through the door, out to the loading dock, and looked up and down the alley. The coast was clear. He hoofed it back to the hotel where he'd been living since a disagreement with his parents. On the way, he stopped at a corner drugstore and bought a roll of adhesive tape.

He took out his suitcase, trunk, and a tin box containing ten and twenty-dollar gold pieces. He laid two strips of tape, adhesive side up, and arranged a row of double eagles on one. These, he secured in place with the second piece of tape. He took off his trousers and wrapped the strips of coins around his waist.

When he was dressed again, he divided his ten-dollar gold pieces between his pants pockets. He hastily tossed a few days' change of clothes in his suitcase and emptied the remainder of the armoire into his trunk.

Bryce threw open the window and leaned out to see if there was anyone sketchy. The street seemed filled with ordinary passersby, so he went to the lobby and ask the porter to bring down his trunk and hail him a carriage. It wasn't that far from the hotel to the train terminal, but he had no other way to get his luggage there. While the porter was gone, Bryce settled his bill, and designated the New England Conservatory as his forwarding address. Anyone trying to follow his trail would wind up in Boston.

Outside the hotel, a newsboy waved the afternoon edition. "Steamship sinks in East River, thousand dead!"

Bryce wasn't going east.

At the terminal, he bought a ticket to Camden, New Jersey. He breathed a sigh of relief when the train pulled out with not an Irishman in sight.

In Camden, he stored his trunks in the station, grabbed a quick sandwich and beer at the lunch counter, then took a cab to the Victor Talking Machine Company where he met with the sales department. He returned to the train station with four crates and an arrangement to receive shipments of more inventory as needed. Next he purchased a ticket for St. Louis. Only after reaching St. Louis would he buy a ticket for his actual destination.

And who knew? He might linger a few days in St. Louis to look up Scott Joplin.

CHAPTER 17

A month had gone by since Morgan and Jack opened the emporium. Shipments of books and sheet music started arriving from Bryce, and the shelves filled up. They made enough sales to pay for the goods and a small profit. They'd received the requested stereoscopes and the photo cards of the World's Fair sold out immediately. But most people already owned a stereoscope so the unsold devices were just getting dusty and taking up space. Abigail suggested they order more World Fair photo cards and present a lecture on their experiences there. Morgan thought that was a good idea and ordered double the original quantity.

With the store rent covered by Morgan's deal with Fred, profits from their sales seemed like free money. Their only personal expenses were what they paid Mrs. Romero for rent, laundry, and whatever other incidental charges she dreamed up. Morgan and Jack had big dreams, but their store wasn't much of an emporium, yet. Aside from the stereoscope cards of the Fair, they didn't seem to have anything representing the coming new world. Worse, they'd failed to reinvest any of the profits to expand, so their business was holding even only because Bryce kept shipping more goods.

They fell into a routine. Morgan would awaken first, breakfast at Mrs. Romero's, and then open the store. Jack, who typically stayed out until dawn, slept through breakfast, but Mrs. Romero agreed to save him a cold biscuit and make him fresh coffee for a nickel extra a day. He'd rise midday, drink his coffee, and then take Morgan's place at the store. Jack closed up when Fred did, at suppertime. By then, Jack was voraciously hungry so he'd meet Morgan for dinner at Mrs. Romero's. Afterwards, the two men would take their evening constitutional, invariably ending up at a bar, where they'd spend some of the day's profits. Jack was not alone in this. Morgan drank his fair share. And why not? They'd done a day's work. Nothing wrong with having a drink.

During Jack's shift, Morgan sometimes painted landscapes. These were offered for sale in the emporium, but Abigail was the only one who bought them. Still, it kept them in beer money. The problem was, on afternoons when he wasn't painting, Abigail demanded her conjugal visits. It made Morgan nervous—like their relationship gave her the right to presume he owed her something. He told himself his worry was irrational. Abigail kept up a front of social propriety for the town wives. She never made him escort her to social functions, never acted like his paramour in public. Whenever they both attended the same dinner or party, they came and left separately. Abigail definitely knew how to avoid gossip. And now that school was out, she had her sister watch Cyrus during their afternoons together. Emma might have been suspicious—that first day in the store. But that was a month ago, and Emma had her own secret to keep.

Abigail's clandestine secret collapsed one afternoon with a knock on the door while she and Morgan lay *in flagrant.*

"Pretend no one is home," she whispered.

That was her first instinct. But as the pounding grew more insistent, she realized it must be important. "Something could have happened to Cyrus," she said.

It would take too long to get into the full rig of women's clothing. Time she might not have. She grabbed the thickest, least transparent, dress she owned and pulled it on. Shutting Morgan in the bedroom, she descended the stairway far enough to see a man's silhouette through the frosted pane of the front door.

Abigail rushed the rest of the way downstairs, pausing only to check her appearance in the foyer mirror and tuck her hair up a bit more—she could always claim she'd been taking a nap.

She threw open the door. "Jack?"

Jack touched his hat brim. "Abigail."

Think quickly. "What is it? Is Morgan all right?"

"I don't know, is he?"

"Whatever do you mean?"

"I need to talk to him, right now."

Oh, dear. "I, uh, I . . ."

"Abigail, don't worry, your secret's safe with me. Just get him, please. It's important."

Abigail bit her lip, hesitating only a minute. Then, she spun on her heel, stalked to the bedroom, and threw open the door. "Jack's here," she said with daggers in her eyes.

"Jack?"

"He knows. Get dressed."

Morgan dressed in seconds and hurried out, closing the door behind him he descended the stairs two steps at a time.

"Jack? What the hell?"

"Telegram just came from Bryce." Jack held the flimsy Western Union form out for Morgan to read: "Am in Kansas • Arriving the 30th • Bryce •"

"Succinct," Morgan said. "Wait . . . When did he send that? Today's the first."

"Exactly. That's why I asked Emma to watch our store while I came to get you."

"Go back to the store in case he's there now. I'll be along directly."

Jack nodded and left. Morgan returned to Abigail's room and knocked softly. "He's gone."

She let him in. "But how did he know? I thought we agreed not to tell anyone."

"Jack won't tell anybody. I trust him with everything."

"But how can I trust you? Men brag. It's in their nature."

"I wasn't boasting to Jack about you. If it hadn't been urgent, he would've never let you know that he knew. Besides, are you pretending you never told Penelope?"

Abigail wouldn't meet his eyes, so he'd made a lucky guess. "Okay, but just Penelope. It's a thing between sisters."

"And Jack and Bryce are like my brothers."

"So what was the emergency?"

"Bryce could arrive any second. According to his telegram he was supposed to get here last night. Although I don't know for the life of me, why he didn't wire us when he left New York, or at least from St. Louis. I've got to go." Morgan kissed her, lingering long enough to show her he was sorry for Jack's interruption. "Say, why don't you come along and meet him? He's an event in himself."

"I can't. I have to pick up Cyrus."

"I'm sure we'll throw Bryce an impromptu party tonight. You should come."

"Well, I do want to meet this Bryce I've heard so much about. Let me ask Penelope if Cyrus can spend the night. I'll meet you at the store."

* * *

The stagecoach was late. A small group had gathered for a welcome party that hadn't happened yet. In addition to Morgan, Jack, Fred, and Emma, Penelope had fed the kids and left them with Walter so she could accompany Abigail. Penelope's neighbor lady came, too. Also men they didn't know very well had showed up, figuring that any party meant free drinks. They crowded the store waiting for Bryce.

Jack kept opening the door and looking down the road. Morgan kept apologizing for the delay although he had no reason to—the whole town knew the stage was irregular at best. Finally, Fred said he was going to lock up and go home even if nobody else was. Jack went over to the saloon to see if they could move the party there.

Fred locked up and he and Emma were just leaving when the stagecoach pulled up. No one got out. A half-dozen party goers peered in the coach window and began to snigger. Jack pushed through them and opened the door. Inside, a slovenly figure lay passed out on the seat.

Great. Jack shook his leg. "Bryce? Is that you? Get up. You're here."

Bryce struggled to get himself upright and stumbled out, missing the step and falling face first in the street. Jack helped him up, but it was apparent he was filthy, stinking, drunk. Most of the women took a step back and held hankies over their noses. This was their big city partner who was bringing them the future? What an advertisement for the emporium.

"Julius!" Bryce said with a grin.

"I'm sorry," Morgan said. "We'll have to postpone the party. It seems one of us has had enough party for the day. Jack, you hold him on one side and I'll get the other. We'll take him home and let him sleep it off."

Jack and Morgan half-dragged Bryce toward Mrs. Romero's. Jack called over his shoulder. "Sorry to disappoint everyone. Tomorrow's Saturday night. We'll have Bryce's party then. Please come."

"Jack, are you staying out tonight?" Morgan said.

"Don't know. Why?"

"I thought we might put him in your bed."

"He'll stink it up."

"Well, where could he get a bath at this hour? The laundry up the street is closed, and we don't want our landlady to meet him in this condition."

At the boarding house, as Jack and Morgan carried Bryce up the porch stairs, Bryce's feet began to bounce against the steps, thump, thump.

"Shit," Jack said, in a hoarse whisper. "Mrs. Romero will hear."

"Flip him on his back and take his upper body. I'll get his feet and we'll tote him up to our room like a rolled carpet."

Morgan flopped Bryce over, and Jack caught him by the shoulders. Bryce emitted a slobbering sigh and started to mumble.

Jack clamped his hand over Bryce's mouth. "Shush, don't disturb the landlady."

Morgan propped the screen door open and grabbed Bryce's feet. They made it in the house and started toward their second story room when a stair creaked. They stopped and listened. The dining room conversation continued unaware. They resumed their trek, taking the steps carefully. Eventually, they reached their room and tossed Bryce on Jack's bed like a sack of grain.

"You know," Jack said. "This evening started with the promise of cold beer, which I didn't get."

"Yet."

"Yet," Jack said. "I believe it's time to fulfill that promise. I'll see you in the morning."

Morgan shook his head. "Go ahead. I'm going to see if there is any dinner left."

When Jack returned at dawn, Bryce was still sprawled on his bed, dead to the world. "Where am I going to sleep?" he said.

"Here, take my bed. I was about to get up, anyway."

"Listen, Morgan, I expect, after last night's fiasco, Fred won't want us to hold Bryce's welcome party in the store."

"Well, he'd have a good point. Too great a risk of someone spilling a drink on our goods or his."

"So I talked to the owner of the saloon and he's going to let us hold the party there tonight. Tell Fred, Emma, and anyone else you think should come."

"Um, I'm a little worried what a party there will cost us," Morgan said.

"Bryce brought money with him, he must have. We'll spring for the party and he can put his money into the store. Besides, a party like this is advertising."

"Jack, I think the whole town knows we're here by now."

"Well, public relations, then."

Jack fell into bed and slept until noon. When he woke up Bryce was still snoring. Jack washed, dressed and went into the kitchen. Being Saturday, the girls were helping their mother with laundry.

As Cherry made his coffee, Jack said, "How'd you like to make a shiny new dime?"

Cherry hesitated. "That's a lot of money. What do I have to do for it?"

"There's a man in my bed—"

Her eyes grew wide. "There is?"

"Yes. His name is Bryce, and when he wakes up, he won't know where he is. You keep watch for him and tell him Morgan and I have gone to work. Also, he's going to need you to fix him a bath. Can you do that for me?"

"Mama charges a quarter for a bath."

"She'll get her quarter. What I want you to do is change my sheets while he's taking his bath. When you're done, tell him I said to pay you ten cents. He will."

"How do you know he will?"

"He's our partner. He's just come from New York and he's got money."

"His name is Bryce and I get a dime, just for changing his sheets?"

"Yes. Thank you so much, Cherry. I've got to go to the store now."

At the store, Jack and Morgan put together a list of whom to invite to the party that evening. They agreed the list should include not only their friends, but also members of the Taos community likely to become future customers.

Morgan spent the afternoon inviting people and then returned to the store to update Jack on the expected guests. They closed up, checked at the saloon to make sure everything was set, and then walked home for supper.

CHAPTER 18

The girls' laughter could be heard half a block away. As Morgan and Jack approached the house, Bryce was sitting on the porch rail with his back to the street. He had his feet on the swing between Peaches and Cherry, pushing them back and forth while he simulated playing an imaginary piano. "After the war, while I was in New Orleans waiting to be mustered out, I used to sit in on piano at a little club down in Storyville. Then last week, I stopped over in St. Louis, and had a chance to play Maple Leaf Rag in a duet with Scott Joplin. Are you ladies familiar with ragtime?"

The girls' curls jiggled as they shook their heads.

"So . . . I take it you've never danced the Rag Time Two Step?"

They shook their heads again, all wide-eyed and innocent.

"I'll play it for you sometime."

"Oh, Mama," Peaches said. "I wish we had a piano."

Mrs. Romero, sitting in a white rocking chair, put her hand over her heart and sighed. "I wish we did, too. I'd love to hear Mr. Holloway perform Beethoven. I'm sure you also play classical music. Don't you?"

"Twelve years of lessons," Bryce said. "Nothing would pleasure me more than to delight you, madam."

Dear God, Bryce had won over Mrs. Romero!

"Sounds like balderdash," Jack said as they came up the steps.

Bryce jumped to his feet, sending the girls' swing careening. "Mo! Jules!"

Mrs. Romero stood up. "Mr. Diamond, Mr. Silver, you failed to tell me we had another guest. We need to talk after dinner before you take your usual evening perambulation."

"I apologize," Morgan said. "Things were hectic last night. Let me introduce our third partner, Bryce Holloway."

"We've met. He introduced himself and kept us entertained until you arrived. Mr. Holloway, if you'll excuse me, I'll check on supper. Girls, come in and set the table."

The women disappeared into the house and the men exchanged bear hugs. Bryce was wearing one of Morgan's shirts and a pair of his pants—and a beaded leather vest. On his head was a Mexican cowboy hat with little bells dangling from the brim.

"Try to remember, our names are Jack and Morgan now," Jack said. "And what the hell are you wearing?"

"Got the vest at a Harvey House in Kansas and the hat from a boy selling them at the depot," Bryce said. "You like it?"

"No," Morgan said. "And are those my pants and shirt?"

"Had to. I've no idea where my luggage went, and Jack's clothes are too big for me."

"Your bags are probably in the freight office. We'll get them tomorrow."

"Tomorrow's Sunday," Bryce said.

"Doesn't matter, the office is always open," Morgan said. "Now jettison the tourist getup. We've got important people coming to meet you tonight."

"Here?"

"No, uptown, after dinner," Jack said. "The party we planned for you last night and had to postpone, for reasons you were probably too drunk to remember."

"Have you read this?" Bryce showed them a dog-eared copy of *Tales of the Trail: Short Stories of Western Life*, by Henry Inman. "Bought it off a news butcher on the train. Great stuff. We're in the real west now, aren't we boys?"

"We've sold everyone on the idea we're cultured, sophisticated New Yorkers, not some budding desperado."

Bryce clutched his book. "Well, Billy the Kid was from New York City. Did you know that? And Kit Carson used to live right here in Taos."

"And both of them died decades ago. This is a different century," Jack said. "New Mexico will probably be a state in less than ten years. People are already talking about it."

"I see you've charmed the landlady and her daughters," Morgan said.

"A couple of real cuties."

"Don't even think about it, Bryce. They're both too young, and their mother is far too old-fashioned."

"You know what I say, old enough to—"

"Bryce!" Morgan said. "I'm serious. Leave them be. Don't start something where we live."

"I didn't start anything," Bryce said. "They did. Made me a nice bath and then kept hovering around the kitchen until their mother caught them."

"We know," Jack said. "We've been living around them for six weeks. They'll push up against you and give you an engraved invitation to trouble. But trouble has a mountain lion for a mama."

"Problems we don't need," Morgan said. "People are starting to accept us here. It isn't like New York, where you can bed a girl down in Bed-Stuy, then never run into her again. People know each other here, and they talk to one another. Don't do anything to jeopardize us. Trust me, you'll find plenty of women in this town wanting your attention."

"Okay, okay. But why did the young one say Jack told her I'd pay them?"

"For stinking up my sheets. I told Cherry to change my bed and said you'd give her ten cents for it."

"Didn't know. I gave a dime to each of them. Peaches didn't say different."

Morgan laughed. "Maybe she's more like her mother than we thought."

"What's that mean?" Bryce said.

"Mrs. Romero charges for everything. I have to pay a nickel a day extra for coffee 'cause I sleep through breakfast."

"I wasn't aware you'd been paying that," Morgan said.

Jack shrugged. "After dinner, she'll tell us we owe her for your bath today. Did she wash your clothes? Today was laundry day."

"I don't know. If so, I haven't got them back. That's why I had to wear Morgan's."

"She'll charge you if she did."

"Who charges?" said Peaches from the door.

"Apparently, you do, you rascal," Jack said.

Peaches batted her eyelashes. "Whatever do you mean?"

"Did you get Bryce to give you ten cents today?"

Peaches moved over and leaned against Bryce. "No. He just gave each of us a dime. Never said why. We hid them anyway. Never told Mama."

Jack took her by the arm and steered her away from Bryce, toward the door. "Did you come to call us for supper?"

"Oh, yeah, that. Dinner's ready." She put her hand over Jack's. "I've heard there's going to be a big party tonight to welcome Bryce."

"Where'd you hear that?"

"From Mr. Hoffsteader's daughter. Will you take me?"

"What would your mother say?"

"Oh, Jack, you know what Mama would say. That's why I'm asking you."

"Well, I'm with your Mama on this," Jack said. "We don't want to be tossed out onto the street."

"It's Bryce's party," Peaches said. "When I asked him about it, he said I could come."

"Bryce is not your mother," Jack said. "Let's get to the dining room before she comes looking for us."

An extra chair had been added to the dining room table beside Peaches, and she connived to be seated with Jack on her left and Bryce on her right. Although Bryce ate with impeccable manners, he hadn't had a thing since yesterday. He allowed Peaches to refill his plate several times. He complimented Mrs. Romero on every dish and repeated it each time Peaches gave him another helping. Peaches gave equal attention to Jack, but, between caring for one man or the other, consequently didn't eat much herself.

"Did you know Bryce can wiggle his ears like a bunny?" Cherry said.

"Yes," Morgan said.

"I don't mean with his fingers. He can make them move all by themselves."

"We know," Jack said. When they were twelve Bryce discovered how to control some muscle other people couldn't access. He'd been using this questionable talent to wile women ever since. Something subtly unspoken, just a movement that caught their eyes, nearly always prompting a conversation that led into bed.

Dessert was served. Bryce tasted a fork full of pie and declared, "Madam, there isn't a restaurant in New York that has a better pastry chef."

Mrs. Romero's chest swelled and her chin lifted. "Surely, that's flattery, Mr. Holloway."

"It doesn't make it any less true," Bryce said.

Uncharacteristically, Peaches began clearing the dishes and cleaning up without being told. She didn't even nag Cherry to help her.

"Gentlemen," Mrs. Romero said, "shall we adjourn to the parlor? Cherry, get to the kitchen work."

Peaches washed dishes and Cherry dried. Peaches finished first, paused to listen briefly outside the parlor door, and then slipped up to her room to change. Bryce was politicking for Teddy Roosevelt's re-election in November, even though her mother couldn't vote.

Peaches expected Mother would let Bryce stay. She'd seen right away how much her mother liked him. Peaches could do that now—tell when a girl liked the same boy she did. It was like she'd acquired a new sense.

Jack tapped his foot nervously. "It's getting late, we better go. Are you sure you wouldn't like to come with us, Mrs. Romero?"

"Thank you, no. I've got church in the morning."

The men started to rise when Mrs. Romero said, "It's been an interesting conversation, but we haven't discussed an arrangement for Mr. Holloway. I still don't have an empty room."

Morgan glanced at Jack. "I guess he could share ours. We might fit a third bed in there if we put the wardrobe out in the hall."

"I don't have a third bed," she said.

"Well, Bryce, it looks as if you'll have to sleep on the floor," Jack said.

"Oh, poor Mr. Holloway," she said. "I have extra pillows we could take apart. I'll buy some ticking and have the girls sew you a feather mattress."

"How thoughtful," Bryce said.

"Now about the rent—"

"Rent?" Morgan said. "He doesn't have a room or a bed."

"Yes, but he certainly demonstrated that he has an appetite. That makes an extra set of feet under my table at breakfast and dinner."

"Jack doesn't eat breakfast. He tells me you've been charging him extra for coffee when he gets up," Morgan said.

"Because it's more work for me. Breakfast is served when it's served. I'm not running a restaurant here."

"Let it go, Morgan," Jack said. "I don't mind."

Mrs. Romero pursed her lips. "Shall we say ten dollars for all three of you?"

"Fine," Morgan said.

"And Mr. Holloway, baths are twenty-five cents, and laundry is extra."

Jack put his hand on the parlor door. "Give her a quarter, Bryce. It's time to go."

Bryce fed a coin into Mrs. Romero's palm and held her hand. "It's a real pleasure to have made you acquaintance. You are truly a wonderful cook and I thank you for making a place for me in your lovely home."

Jack was already out the front door.

Morgan and Bryce caught up to him.

Peaches slipped out the backdoor and trailed a safe distance behind.

CHAPTER 19

Peaches read the sign on the door the men had entered: "Closed for Private Party." She hesitated. She'd never been in a place like this in her life. Nice girls didn't even walk downtown in the evenings for fear of what they might see. Yellow lantern light spilled out etched-glass windows, painting her invitation on the boardwalk. The laughter of men and women and a tinkling piano tickled her ears. She touched the door handle, and it vibrated from the thunderous feet of dancers.

She dropped her hand and peeked through the glass. Mother would die.

She saw Bryce at the piano. It was his music she was hearing, that raggedy stuff. She reached out again and pushed the door open, ever so slowly. When it was open just wide enough to squeeze through, she slipped in. People were drinking and laughing loudly. Peaches realized how many of them knew her mother and eased around the periphery of the party toward an old upright piano.

Finally, Peaches rested her chin on the piano lid and felt the notes resonate through her bones—a strange rhythm that sounded unsteady and almost mistaken. But it made a kind of sense, and made her feet want to start tapping. This must be the new wild music that the priest was warning them about.

When the piano player's eyes traveled up her figure and reached her face, she batted her eyelashes. "Hello, Bryce, I made it." Bryce gave her a smile that turned her body into warm butter on a hot day. While his left hand continued to play the bass notes, bouncing around erratically, with jumps and slides of more than an octave, he took his right hand briefly off the keys and patted the piano bench invitingly. He resumed the melody notes and slid over. Peaches didn't have to be asked twice. She sat down and scooted against him. "Teach me."

The room was a cacophony of ragtime music and merry voices. Morgan and Abigail were drinking with Jack and Penelope. Behind them a dozen couples were doing a lively dance that was definitely not a quadrille.

No one took attendance, but if they had, Jack's schoolteacher would have been marked absent. Fanny hadn't been invited, either, and Penelope was blatantly flirting with Jack.

Abigail grasped her sister by the waist and rotated her away from Jack. "Here, let me retie your bow."

While Abigail undid and redid the ribbon on the back of Penelope's dress she whispered in her hair, "What are you doing?"

"Reminding myself what it's like."

"You can't do that with a rake like Jack. He'll get the wrong idea."

"Don't be ridiculous. Jack knows I would never betray Walter. But it's fun pretending."

"Be careful, sis, I wouldn't trust Jack as far as I could throw a freight train."

While the two sisters were huddled, Morgan scanned the room and was pleased with the turnout. The ratio of potential customers versus party freeloaders weighed heavily in their favor. When his eyes fell on Bryce, he elbowed Jack.

"What?" Jack said.

"The woman next to Bryce."

"My God, is that?"

"Yes, Peaches."

"How'd she get in here?"

"That's not the question. The question is how do we get her out of here?"

"Think of something," Jack said. "If she gets caught, we'll get the blame."

Morgan spotted the Deitwilers and quickly formulated a plan. Abigail and Penelope had finished their tête-à-tête and rejoined the men. Morgan gave Jack a wink and said, "Ladies, Jack is going to give a toast for Bryce. Why don't you accompany him to the bar for refills while I get Bryce?" He left the sisters in Jack's care and headed for the Deitwilers.

"Emma, Fred, are you enjoying the party?"

"Your partner can really play," Fred said.

"He can." Morgan looked into Emma's eyes. "Fred, I wonder if I can impose on your wife for a moment."

Emma linked elbows with Fred.

"You see the girl sitting on the piano bench with Bryce?" Morgan said. "That's our landlady's underage daughter."

Emma gave him a hard look. "That's one of the Romero girls."

He held up his hands as if she had him at gunpoint. "We had nothing to do with it, honest. She snuck in on her own. No one's recognized her yet, but half the people in this room go to her mother's church."

"Why come to us?" Fred said.

"Three reasons: you're not Catholic, I hope we're friends, and Emma's a woman. Peaches needs to go home, right now, but I can't do it. If she were seen leaving alone with a man, people who haven't noticed her suddenly would." He smiled at Emma. "Won't you help extricate this young woman from a situation she shouldn't have gotten herself into?"

Emma nodded and looked at Fred. "We should."

"Please come back after you get her home," Morgan said.

"We'll see," Fred said. "How do you want to do this?"

"I know this tune. Bryce is near the end. When he finishes, I'll take Bryce up front where Jack's going to give a toast. When that happens, everyone will be looking at us, and you can spirit her out the door."

Morgan and the Deitwilers made their way to the piano. "Hello, Peaches."

She looked up, all dimples and delight. "Hi, Morgan. Surprise!"

"Have you met Mr. and Mrs. Deitwiler? Emma, Fred, this is Peaches Romero."

"We've met," Peaches said. "Mama brought my sister and me to your store several times. I just love your fabrics. I wish I could buy them all."

Bryce finished the song with a flourish, running his hand the length of the keyboard. Morgan inserted his arm between Bryce and Peaches and turned Bryce toward the front of the room. "That's enough for now. Jack wants us to join him for a toast." Bryce stood up and Morgan steered him toward the bar, away from Peaches. "Let's get you a refill first."

Fred offered Peaches his arm and Emma took her other hand. "We're going to walk you home, dear."

Peaches didn't even raise an argument. "Are you going to tell Mama?"

Emma shook her head. "It's not our place to say."

Peaches squeezed Emma's hand and accepted Fred's arm.

Jack was standing near the bar. Morgan planted Bryce next to him. "Everything's arranged. Toast time."

Jack threw his arm across Bryce's shoulder. "If I can have your attention, I want to make a toast. If you don't have a drink, get one."

The guests turned toward Jack as a unified body.

"By now, you've all had a chance to meet Bryce, but I want to tell you a few things about him you may not know. Bryce not only plays damn fine ragtime, but he's a genuine war hero. That's right. Bryce served in Cuba with our President, Teddy Roosevelt."

A cheer went up and Bryce made a quick bow.

Jack raised his glass. "So let's drink to Teddy's boy, Bryce, and to the President's re-election in November."

After the toast, a surge of people surrounded them. In the corner, someone picked up an accordion and the music resumed. It wasn't ragtime, but those who wanted to dance began to polka.

The banker, Hoffsteader, said to Bryce, "Funny, you don't look old enough to have been in the Spanish-American War."

"Well, I wasn't quite. But I was tall for my age, and the recruiter didn't ask too many questions."

Abigail and Penelope joined them, mixing in with those clustered around Bryce. Morgan made his way over to the sisters. All eyes were focused on Bryce anyway as he recounted some war story Morgan had heard a dozen times. Morgan understood Abigail's desire to avoid calumny, and so he acted the casual acquaintance in public. But in private she still seemed to be driving for a more committed relationship than he had in mind. Any shift toward marital thinking was an unwelcome deviation from the unabashed free spirit he'd admired in her.

Bryce's flamboyant, enthusiastic stories enthralled his audience, especially the women. Abigail was no exception. Morgan could almost see her thoughts and desires mesh like the gears in her hall clock. If she was considering changing partners, it would provide a graceful exit for him, and they'd likely remain friends. Bryce wouldn't object or even know. Bryce was a practicing, new century voluptuary. Put in a compromising situation, he'd gladly be compromised.

Not only would Morgan not stand in their way, he'd push things along.

CHAPTER 20

Sunday morning, the emporium partners slept in. Only Smith and Jones were present at breakfast. Mrs. Romero hurried Peaches and Cherry to get ready for church. As usual, Smith and Jones declined to go with her, saying they had to be in Albuquerque by Monday and were leaving right after they ate.

Walking to Mass with her mother and sister, Peaches said, "Mama, why can't we get a piano?"

"Because they're very expensive. If you're thinking I should provide one for our gentlemen boarders, it's out of the question."

"Well, it would be for us, too."

"You girls don't know how to play."

"Bryce said he'd teach me Jellyroll."

"Don't use that word. Although I find Mr. Holloway charming and amusing, these New Yorkers' influence have led to a breakdown in decorum in you girls. Calling adults by their first names, now vulgar language—"

"What's wrong with Jellyroll?"

"It's not nice."

"Why not?"

Mrs. Romero stopped walking and hastily looked around. Satisfied they were alone, she said, "It's Negro slang for a woman's . . . private parts."

"Really?" Cherry said.

"It is not," Peaches said.

Mrs. Romero narrowed her eyes. "I don't want either of you to use that term again? Understand me?"

"Bryce said it was his piano teacher's name."

"I'm certain even a Creole mother would never name her son that."

"But—"

"You heard what I said, and I'll have no more of it."

Peaches fell a step behind and stuck out her tongue. Cherry saw her and laughed.

* * *

Monday, with their hangovers finally abated, the three partners ate breakfast and went to the store early. Bryce stood in front of the building and studied the sign. "New World?"

"Well, you weren't here to vote," Jack said. "We thought it was a good name."

Bryce shook his head. "It makes me think of Pilgrims trading beads with the Indians."

"You're ignoring the map," Morgan said. "The message is, we offer wonders from Europe and New York."

"Deitwiler's sign is much bigger. Ours is like a footnote."

"Well, it *is* their store," Morgan said. "They're just letting us share their space."

Jack unlocked the door. "But the rent's free."

The three men entered and Bryce's face fell. "I thought we were opening a grand emporium. All we've got here is a little cubby in the corner of a dry goods store."

Jack slapped Bryce on the back. "Like I said, the rent's free."

"It was only meant to get us started," Morgan said. "Now you're here, we can afford a bigger space of our own."

"I would hope so. Have you got someplace in mind, or do we have to build?"

"Abigail owns a building up the street," Morgan said. "We haven't been inside, but according to her, it's huge. We hadn't bothered with it yet, because we barely had enough inventory to fill this space, and not enough capital to buy more."

"But we have plenty of copies of 'Meet Me in St. Louis,'" Jack said.

"Still? It's very popular in New York."

Morgan laughed. "Popular here, too. But you sent us more copies than there are pianos in Taos. We started giving them away for free with any purchase."

"Well, how was I to know? Anyhow, let's get this emporium growing. You said you knew where the stage driver stored my stuff?"

"Freight office is in the back of Western Union," Morgan said.

"Have you brought goods with you?" Jack said.

"Yes," Bryce said. "Something extraordinary. Remember, one of the big hits of the World's Fair was the new Gramophone that used platters instead of cylinders?"

"You've got one?" Morgan said.

"I've brought three. They're in my crates. And I brought musical recordings to sell, too. That's where the money's going to be. Sell a customer one Gramophone, and he'll keep buying more records. There's a company back east that's bought the Gramophone patents and invented a way to stamp recordings on shellac discs. Before I left, I set us up with The Victor Talking Machine Company. They're going to ship us as many players and discs as we can sell."

"I remember their exhibit at the Fair—always had a crowd around it," Jack said. "We'll be rich, boys."

"Let's go find this freight office," Bryce said.

* * *

Emma arrived with Fred at the regular opening time and had to push their way through the mob of curiosity seekers. The crowd was gathered around a device sitting on a pedestal made of packing crates, putting out a waltz by a tinny orchestra. Bryce, standing next to it, nodded to Emma as he turned a crank. Once inside, they were accosted by a different tune from a second device Jack was guarding. Morgan was unpacking and arranging paper-sleeved ten-inch disks on a table. A dozen customers were congregated on the emporium side of the store, so Emma pulled Fred over there to study the apparatus Jack was operating.

Music was coming from a large silver-colored cone, whose narrow end snaked out to a needle following grooves in a black platter that revolved like a Lazy Susan. She had heard that Edison had been selling a phonograph device that used hollow wax tubes, but this was a revolution, even she could see that. The disks would store on a shelf like books rather than in a pile like cylinders or piano rolls. And as the song continued, she realized the platters held much more music.

When the song ended, Jack lifted the needle and replaced the disk with another. He gave the crank a half-dozen turns and set the needle on the outer edge of the platter. A lively fiddle tune poured out of the machine. "Makes you want to dance, doesn't it?"

"It's a little early for that." Fred bent over and watched the tip of the needle ride the groove, spiraling toward the center of the record.

Jack grabbed Emma and began to whirl her around the room, bumping into customers as they went. By the time the song ended she found herself laughing.

Jack gave a quick bow, "Thank you, ma'am." She brushed the wrinkles from her skirt, and Jack went over to show Fred how to restart the song. "Just give this handle a few turns and gently lower the needle on the outer edge of the disk."

Fred did, and the fiddle ripped out of the machine straight into Fred's ear. He jumped up and said, "Have you got a symphony or something less jarring?"

Jack laughed. "Ask Morgan what he's unpacked."

The influx of people coming to see the new marvel pleased Emma, but as the morning wore on Fred complained about the constant loud music and warned it would drive lady customers away. Her husband and the New Yorkers wrangled over the issue. Emma asked Morgan to play gentler selections, and he did. That pacified Fred. But whenever Bryce or Jack ran the Gramophone, they choose lively tunes that Fred said made the store sound like a dance hall.

In the afternoon, Abigail and Penelope brought Cyrus and his cousins to the emporium to see the new marvel that had everyone talking. While their mothers were engaged in conversation with the men who owned the store, the boys put their noses right up to the whirling disk and, when no one was looking, touched it with their fingers. The singer's voice would drop several octaves and the words would drag out. Whichever boy had done it would let go and the music would resume the normal tempo.

"Quit touching that," Penelope said.

Cyrus ran over to his mom. "Can we buy one? Please, please."

"Sorry, I'm afraid they're all sold," Jack said.

Abigail pointed to the Gramophone the boys were fooling with. "What about that one?"

"Already spoken for by Ida Hoffsteader," Morgan said. "She's gone to get money from her husband."

Bryce smirked. "As my Nana used to say, 'she who hesitates is lost.'"

Abigail raised her eyebrows. "Nana?"

Jack stuck his finger in Bryce's ribs and wiggled it. "His nanny."

Here was a glimpse into a different world. "You had a nanny?"

Bryce smiled nostalgically. "She was coal-black, fat as a stuffed turkey, but sweet as chocolate toffee. While Mother ran her precious charities, it was my Nana who raised me."

"Oh, poor little rich Bryce," Jack said.

Abigail saw that kids in the store were making Fred nervous. He kept trying to corral them to the emporium side of the room.

"Maybe I should get a nanny," Abigail said.

Bryce's face lost all humor. "Don't. Unless you want Cyrus to love someone better than you."

Fred approached, dragging two of Penelope's children by their arms. "It's closing time," he said, handing them over to their mother.

"I agree," Jack said. "We sold all three Gramophones the first day. We should celebrate."

"Shouldn't we wait for Ida to come back?" Morgan said.

"Nah, she'd never be able to carry it, anyway. We'll deliver it to her home later."

"Sound's like a plan." Bryce sided up to Abigail. "I hope you're joining us."

Abigail bit her lip and studied Bryce's handsome face. Possibilities opened in her mind.

"Let me take you out for a drink," Bryce said. "I'll even stop at Western Union and order another Gramophone, just for you."

Abigail leaned toward him. "I'd love to, but I have a child here."

Penelope whispered, "If you want, I can take Cyrus with me."

"Penelope! I can't be seen in a saloon with three men, unaccompanied."

Jack threw his arm across Fred's shoulder. "Bring your wife, come help us celebrate our best day so far. It'll be our treat."

"Oh, Fred, let's go," Emma said.

"Yes, Emma," Abigail said. "Please come."

Fred just shook his head.

"Fred Deitwiler," Emma said. "We've hardly had a bit of fun since the store opened."

"That's not true. We were just at Bryce's welcome party Saturday night."

"That was cut short." Emma jerked her thumb toward Morgan.

"I do owe you both another drink," Morgan said.

"Well, I guess we could celebrate that all the noisy Gramophones are gone."

"Are we going to the same bar we were at Saturday?" Bryce said.

"No," Abigail said. "Let's go to Salazar's. Being seen there isn't quite so harmful to a lady's reputation. They have table cloths and serve wine in nice stemware glasses."

Fred ushered everyone out and locked the store.

Salazar's was an intimate little place Morgan had never been to. A beautifully carved mahogany bar dominated a very tiny room full of round tables covered with red tablecloths. The windows had red velvet curtains and passersby could not see in. The ladies' drinks were served in fancy glasses and the men's beer steins were clean. Certainly a step up from most of the saloons he and Jack had frequented. It was nice to see that Taos had some upscale pretensions—that could only help their cause.

A piano sat unused in the corner.

"What time does the piano player start?" Jack said.

"Don't have one. He quit and moved to Albuquerque," the barkeep said.

Jack jerked his thumb toward Bryce. "Do you mind if my friend tickles the ivories?"

"Not as long as the other customers don't object."

"Bryce, give us some free advertising," Jack said.

"Only if Abigail comes with me."

"Oh, I don't play in public," she said.

"That's okay. Just help me hold down the bench."

Sharing the piano stool, Abigail and Bryce shifted into brazen flirting while Bryce let some Joplin roll. Perhaps she was still trying to misdirect Emma's suspicions of their affair.

Bryce finished "Maple Leaf Rag" with a flourish, running his fingers back and forth across the keys. Abigail oozed compliments.

"I'm a little rusty," he said.

"Don't be modest. I heard you play Saturday night. Remember?"

"No, seriously. I need more practice."

Abigail twisted a curl of hair around her finger. "I have a piano in my parlor. You're welcome to use it. It'd have to be in the afternoons though, so it wouldn't disturb my son."

Morgan had a pretty good inkling what afternoon piano practice at Abigail's implied, but it would nicely extricate him from the relationship.

After more songs and several drinks Jack suggested they all sing, "My Girl's a New Yorker." But the locals didn't know it.

"Come on, Morgan. You, and Bryce, and I will teach it to them."

Morgan joined Jack and Bryce at the piano, and they began to sing:

> My girl's a corker, she's a New Yorker
>
> I buy her everything to keep her in style
>
> She's got a pair of legs, just like two whiskey kegs
>
> Hey boys, that's where my money goes-oes-oes

During the second verse Jack ran back to their table and pulled Fred and Emma over to the piano.

"Third verse," Bryce said.

When we go walkin', she does the talkin'
And when my arm's round her, how time does fly
She does the teasin', I do the sqeezin'
Hey boys . . .

The New Yorkers forgot some of the words and filled in with:

dah-da, dah-da-dah,
dah-da, dah-da-dah,
And when the lights go out, she wears silk underwear,
I wear my latest pair. She's where my money goes.

At that line, Fred stopped singing and led Emma to the door.

"Hey! Where are you going?" Jack said.

"Home," Fred snapped.

Jack waved them off and turned back to Bryce. "Can't anyone remember the rest? Something like, 'She's got a pair of hips, just like two battle ships.'"

The song broke up in laughter, and Bryce stopped playing. "Who needs another beer?" Jack said.

The door opened, and Walter came in. "Abigail, Penelope thought perhaps you needed an escort home."

"Aw, don't go," Bryce said.

Abigail looked around the all-male room. "I'm afraid Penelope knows best. Jack, thank you for the drinks, and Bryce, do come over and play some afternoon." Abigail offered Morgan her hand. "I hope you don't have any objection."

"You knew I wouldn't," Morgan said.

Abigail took Walter's arm and left. Bryce struck up the song again:

"My girl's a corker, she's a New Yorker . . ."

CHAPTER 21

Bryce managed to not only charm Mrs. Romero. He won over the people of Taos. In addition to being musically talented, he was funny. His conversations were peppered with clever puns and humorous expressions, most of which he'd borrowed from someone else, but the locals wouldn't know that. About underage girls he'd quip, "Fifteen will get you twenty," and his definition of a lifespan was, "From sperm to worm."

Bryce also had a repertoire of fabulous adventure tales and well-rehearsed exaggerations that he trotted out whenever presented with a new acquaintance. His war stories about being in Cuba with Teddy Roosevelt's Rough Riders enthralled men in the saloons and his jovial patter about New York upper curst seduced many women, Abigail among them. Morgan and Jack had heard it all before, of course, but he still made them laugh. Bryce was definitely a bullshitter, but a charming one.

The thing Jack had forgotten was how much trouble Bryce could be, almost as if there was a tax levied on anyone closely involved with him by some omnipotent overseer. *You want to be entertained by the snake charmer? Then you have to put the snakes back in the basket after the show is over.* On one such day, Jack and Morgan were in the store unpacking the latest shipment of books when gunfire broke out.

Kit Carson and Billy the Kid were distant memories. Taos was a quiet town now. The Indians performed peaceful ceremonial dances in front of McCarthy's on special occasions, and gunshots were never heard. Yet, against all common sense, the sound of shooting caused people to run out of their homes and shops toward the source of commotion. Jack was no exception.

With Morgan on his heels, they burst out of the emporium and ran with the crowd to behind the livery stable.

Oh, damn.

Bryce, wearing a low-slung holster like a gunslinger, was holding a Colt in his hand, taking shots at a target tied to a stack of hay bales. Bad shots—there were far fewer holes in the target than they had heard shots.

The owner of the livery ran up to Jack. "Stop him. He's spooking the horses."

Jack marched over to Bryce with Morgan at his side. "What the hell?"

Bryce paused to reload, pretending not to be aware of the crowd that had gathered. A heckler shouted, "You aim first, then pull the trigger. You're doing it the other way around."

Bryce was wearing the Mexican cowboy hat he'd bought on the train, but he'd pinned one side of the brim up. It looked to Jack like he'd just walked off the stage of a cheap vaudeville production. Bryce snapped the cylinder shut, and fired six more shots, missing the target again, but making little puffs of hay fly out of the bales. Jack and Morgan covered their ears.

Someone in the crowd said loudly, "I thought he was a Rough Rider. Roosevelt claimed they could shoot."

"Pistol takes some getting used to," Bryce said. "Only officers were issued side arms. All we infantrymen got were rifles." He pointed to his hat. "We fastened the right brim of our hat out of the way, so the ejected cartridges didn't hit it. That's how you know a real rifleman."

He emptied the spent shells from the revolver and reloaded again. This time he hit the paper target three times, nowhere near the center. The townspeople laughed.

"Well, you get what you pay for," Bryce said to the crowd. "Bought this gun on the cheap, and it has a bad sight."

"Then put it away before someone tries to take it away from you," Jack said.

"We're not gunslingers, we're artists," Morgan added. "Take off that holster and let's get back to the store."

Bryce tipped his hat to the crowd. "To be continued . . . another time, another day." He picked up the box of ammunition and left with Morgan and Jack. "Not a very good show," he said when they were out of earshot of the crowd.

"Well," Jack said, "you got us some attention . . . just not the kind we want."

Despite Jack and Morgan practically begging him not to, Bryce continued wearing his .45 around town like some desperado, except in the boarding house where Mrs. Romero wouldn't allow it. Fred and Emma were frightened he would draw challengers to their store and demanded Morgan and Jack do something about it. Peaches, however, thought it only added to Bryce's mystique as a war hero.

One night at dinner, Jones said, "Bryce, I'm sure you're aware more than half of the Rough Riders were from New Mexico—most from a little town near Santa Fe named Las Vegas. Smith and I go right by there. You ought to come with us sometime, see all your war buddies."

Bryce choked on his food and coughed it into his plate.

"Goodness, Mr. Holloway, are you all right?" Mrs. Romero said. Peaches patted his back and wiped the corner of his mouth with her napkin.

Bryce took a swallow of water. "Fine. Fine. Something went down wrong that's all."

Bryce's gunslinger period ended when he got drunk one night. Morgan and Jack hid his gun and wouldn't give it back. The next time Smith and Jones went to Albuquerque, Morgan gave it to Jones to sell. But Bryce, determined to live out the fantasies of pulp Westerns he'd read on the train, decided to latch onto the Indian tribes. Embracing their peyote religion, he left with a one-toothed medicine man.

It didn't go well. Bryce went missing for three days.

* * *

An angry fist pounded the bedroom door. "Mr. Silver, Mr. Diamond, get decent and come out here."

Jack, who had just gone to bed, groaned, got up, pulled his pants on. He woke Morgan from a deep sleep, tossed him his robe, and opened the door. "What is it Mrs. Romero?"

"Come with me." She charged downstairs.

Morgan rubbed his eyes. "What time is it?"

"Must be near sunrise," Jack said. "I just got home a few minutes ago."

"Gentlemen, I'm waiting," she shouted from the foot of the stairs.

Jack and Morgan followed her into the parlor where Bryce lay shirtless on her good settee. A split second after the sight came the smell. Jack held his nose. "Whew, he smells like he's dead."

"He might be for all I know." Bryce had one leg dangling off the couch and she kicked it. "I came down to start breakfast and smelled some awful odor. I followed the stench to the parlor and found him like this."

Bryce lifted his leg back up on the settee.

"Look, he moved. At least he's among the living," Morgan said.

"Well, get him out of here. He's ruined the upholstery. I'll never get the stink out."

Jack shook him hard. "Come on, buddy. Get up." But Bryce didn't wake. Jack jostled him again, to no avail.

"Mr. Diamond, pick up his feet. Mr. Silver, get his shoulders, and carry him to the porch. I want him out of my house, now!"

The men carried Bryce out and tried to lay him on the swing.

"Not the swing," she said. "Put him on the floor."

Morgan set him down slowly in the spot she indicated. Jack let Bryce's feet drop with a clunk and wiped the dirt from Bryce's boot off his hands.

"Mr. Holloway may be witty and amusing, but I find his recent behavior unacceptable. He is no longer welcome here."

"What do you mean?" Jack said, though he'd already guessed.

"You and Mr. Silver have been good tenants, I'll grant you that. You can continue to stay if you want, but your associate has got to go. He's irreparably damaged the only good piece of furniture I had in the parlor. It's going to have to be reupholstered, and someone has to pay for that."

Peaches came outside in her dressing gown to see what all the yelling was about. "Oh, poor Bryce, what's happened to him?"

"Never you mind, young lady. And get back in the house. You shouldn't be on the front porch undressed like that."

Since even dropping him on the porch had failed to rouse Bryce, Jack and Morgan just left him. They ate breakfast and went to the store to unpack a new shipment of Gramophones. The record players had been arriving steadily and selling well ever since Ida Hoffsteader and Abigail Wythe had purchased theirs. Now, every woman in their social circle just had to have one, too. Even small New Mexico towns had society leaders, and followers determined to keep up with them. On their evening walks to the saloon, Jack had taken satisfaction in hearing the music drifting out of open windows. It was just what they'd envisioned—bringing culture and technology to the frontier.

While the men pried open crates, Bryce's stench still haunted Jack's memory. "You get on well with Mrs. Romero. What will it take to make her relent on this situation with Bryce?"

"I don't think she will."

"Even if we pay for her settee?"

Morgan laughed sarcastically. "She's already said we have to do that, anyway. No, I think her mind's set against Bryce. Us too, if he doesn't get off her porch."

Jack went silent, making himself incredibly busy prying lids off crates. Finally, he said too quickly, "You know Bryce has been seeing Abigail?"

Morgan smiled. "I know, but thanks for telling me. I don't mind."

"Maybe she'll let him stay there. She has a big house, plenty of rooms."

"She won't."

"Why not?"

"The scandal. Abigail has to keep up appearances."

"Where else can he stay?" Jack said. "With his new Indian friends?"

"Hardly. And I'm not sure they want him. The store's been doing really well. It's probably time to get a place of our own."

"Will we have enough after we pay Mrs. Romero for the damage?"

"We'll have to see what *that* costs, but we're a bit above breaking even. I think it's time we start looking."

* * *

Bryce slept on the porch like a dog while the summer winds off Wheeler Peak aired him some. When her mother went into town, Peaches came out, knelt down, and stroked his face until his eyes opened. "Wake up, Bryce. I'm going to make you a bath."

She set up the tub in the kitchen and started heating water when her mother came in. "What are you doing?"

"I'm fixing Bryce a bath."

"You are not. He is not to come back inside this house. Take that water off the stove and put the tub back where you found it."

"He needs a bath, Mother."

"I agree, but he can get one at the laundry down the street."

"Oh, Mother."

"No. My mind's made up. He's not to set one foot inside this house."

"He needs clean clothes from his room."

"Well, fetch them for him. Then get him off my porch before the whole neighborhood sees . . . And smells him."

* * *

Bryce accepted the stack of clothing from Peaches and made his way to the laundry where he had his bath and left his smelly clothes to be washed. Next, he went to the barber shop, got a shave, and came out smelling of Bay Rum.

Well, the peyote ceremony had been a wonderful experience, but it had left him homeless, and a bit embarrassed, especially in front of Peaches. But what he had seen . . . The dime novels never mentioned that.

Instead of going to the store, or back home, he went to Abigail's. He needed to share what had happened with someone, and he didn't think Jack and Morgan would be prone to listen. But school was still out for summer and she wouldn't let him beyond the porch. He poured out his tale of woe and did his best to wheedle a place in one of her rooms, but she held firm.

Bryce took supper at Salazar's and then wandered the town until late when he let himself into the store and locked the door behind him.

He selected a couple of bolts of Emma's fabrics for a blanket and pillow —making sure to choose dark colors that wouldn't show dirt. He curled up behind the counter. Not that he expected he'd be able to sleep after being passed out for most of the previous twenty-four hours. But within ten minutes, he was out like a light.

CHAPTER 22

The next morning Morgan was running late, trying to figure a way around Mrs. Romero. And wondering where Bryce had stayed last night. He hoped it was one of the cheaper hotels, especially since they needed their funds to rent their own place.

As Morgan opened the door to the emporium, the bell above it jangled, interrupting a heated quarrel. One glance inside, and he realized he had another Bryce-lit fire to put out.

Fred turned. "Morgan, your three months are up. Find someplace else for your store—today, if possible."

"Fred, we can't move in a day. You're not serious."

"Deadly. I've given you guys the keys to my place and look what he's done to it."

Morgan took in the bolts of expensive, dark wool, arranged into a bedroll behind the counter. He knew what Emma charged for that cloth. And he had to admit that Fred, like Mrs. Romero, had a point.

But he should at least put up a fight. "Our Gramophones brought you a lot of customers."

"And how many have been driven out?"

Bryce put his oar in. "You wouldn't recognize a good thing if it bit you in the ass."

"Bryce, stop baiting Fred," Morgan said, with some iron in his voice. "He and I will talk this out. You go get Jack."

"I'm not allowed there," Bryce said.

Fred sneered. "I'm not surprised."

"Just go," Morgan said. "Ask one of the girls to wake Jack. And Bryce—"

"Yeah?"

"Don't get into it with Mrs. Romero."

"What do I look like, an idiot?"

Morgan refrained from commenting.

Bryce left. Morgan talked and talked to Fred, and then talked some more, but the stubborn German would not be persuaded. When Bryce returned with Jack, Morgan was standing outside. "Jack, watch the store while Bryce and I go to Abigail's. Fred is throwing us out."

"What?" Jack said.

"I'll explain it when we get back. For now, don't rile Fred any further. He might start tossing records out on the road."

Abigail was outside supervising Cyrus weeding the garden when she saw Bryce and Morgan walk up her carriageway. Abigail chewed the inside of her cheek. She and Morgan had never formally broken it off. She'd just sort of rolled off one man and onto the other. Now they were both here at the same time.

But surely, Morgan must know about her and Bryce. Morgan had stopped calling on her right after Bryce started. Which, now that she thought of it, seemed a bit suspicious. Had she traded men, or had she been traded like one of Cyrus's baseball cards?

Morgan tipped his hat and elbowed Bryce who then did the same. Bryce gave her a boyish grin and added a wink. Abigail swallowed the lump in her throat and looked from man to man. She motioned toward Cyrus with her eyes. He was on his hands and knees with his back to them as yet unaware of the visitors. She trusted Morgan would be cautious about what was said, but would Bryce? He'd showed up yesterday with the absurd suggestion that she allow him to live here. At least Morgan had some grasp of how tenuous her hold on Taos society really was.

Well, she'd decided to live life on her terms. It was too late now to thread the needle and quietly take up cross-stitch.

Finally, she spoke. "This . . . is unexpected."

Cyrus jerked his head around, jumped up, and ran over to her.

"Hello, Cyrus," Morgan said.

Abigail put an arm around Cyrus. "Do you remember Morgan and Bryce? They own the store where we bought the Gramophone."

"I sure do. Did you bring any new records? I've listened to all of ours a hundred times."

"No, they're back at the store," Bryce said. "You'll have to come in sometime and peruse them."

Abigail cleared her throat, glancing from Morgan's eyes to Bryce's and back to Morgan.

"Don't look so worried," Morgan said. "Bryce and I haven't come to put you on the spot. We merely want to ask you to show us that commercial building you said you owned."

"Now?"

"If it wouldn't be too inconvenient," Morgan said.

"The sooner, the better," Bryce added.

Morgan nodded. "It *is* a matter of some urgency."

Cyrus tugged on her skirt. "Can I come, too?"

Abigail ruffled his hair. "I can't very well leave you alone, can I? Go wash your hands while I get the key."

Cyrus dashed to the watering can, plunged his hands in, and ran back wiping them on his knickers.

Bryce laughed. "Clean enough to eat with, I guess."

Cyrus grinned sheepishly. Abigail returned with the key and the four of them set out with Cyrus happily skipping down the street ahead of them.

The business property Abigail had received in her divorce was a white clapboard building shaped like an inverted T; the center was two stories tall, with one story extensions on either side. Abigail unlocked the front door. Cyrus pushed it open and charged in ahead of everyone, then stopped and backtracked to his mother.

It was dark, darker than she remembered. The second story had windows around the balcony, but they were covered with brown paper and what little light spilled through the front door was swallowed within a few feet.

Abigail lifted the globe off a lantern on the nearest table and Bryce struck a match. Morgan walked to another table and lit a second lantern. At the far end of the room was a stage. Staircases on the right and left of the entrance led to a U-shaped balcony overhead.

Cyrus raced upstairs.

"Cyrus, be careful," Abigail said. "I don't know what's up there."

He stomped back down the steps. "There's just a bunch of chairs."

Bryce extended both arms, embracing the large room, "Now, this is a fitting site for an emporium."

Abigail shook her head. "You really aren't very good businessmen are you?"

"What do you mean?"

"It's too much space for what little you've got. In fact, one reason it's still vacant is that no one in town has anything that will fill it. Except maybe a dance hall, which was my ex-husband's original intention. Bring the lanterns. I'll show you what you need."

Under the left stairway was an unfinished bar. Behind it was a door to the left wing of the building. Through it they entered a storeroom nearly the size of Deitwiler's store. "My ex-husband planned to make beer here, so he made the storeroom extra-large." She pointed to the opposite wall. "That's the outside wall. Put a couple of windows in it for light, a nice door on the front side, and you'll have a cute little shop. You could even put a partial wall across the back to section off some storage space."

A distant voice called, "Mama, where are you?"

"In here, Cyrus."

"It's dark. I can't find you."

Abigail hastened back to the main room carrying a lantern. "I'm right here."

"I can't find my way."

Morgan and Bryce rushed to Abigail's side. Morgan lit a third lantern and said, "Cyrus, can you see us better now?"

"No-o-o."

"Stay where you are and keep talking," Abigail said. "We'll find you."

"Mommy."

Abigail pointed across the room. "He's in that wing over there. The door must have closed behind him."

She opened a door near the stage and they entered a hallway that connected to several dressing rooms. They threw open doors until they found him. Cyrus wrapped his arms around his mother's leg.

"What is this place?" Bryce said.

"Dressing rooms and guest accommodations for out-of-town entertainers. Part of the whole dance hall design."

"Interesting," Morgan said. "You know Bryce is in need of a place."

"He told me," Abigail said. "But as I explained, I can't possibly—"

"I understand your situation," Morgan said. "But if we rented your store, no one would say anything against him living here."

Abigail shrugged. "Well, the place has been sitting empty—might as well make use of it."

Bryce grinned. "And who could object to a landlady coming by to check on her property?"

Abigail put her hands over Cyrus's ears. "Bryce, some discretion, please."

Bryce put his hand to his mouth. "Oops."

Morgan stepped between them and stuck out his hand. "Let's make a deal. We'll take the storeroom and dressing rooms. Is twenty dollars a week agreeable?"

Abigail shook Morgan's hand and gave him the key. "Better than what I'm getting for it now."

CHAPTER 23

Morgan managed to convince Fred to let them keep their space in the dry goods store while the new place was readied. Fred's only condition was that Bryce give back his key and not sleep there. Morgan assured him that Bryce now had a cozy little room at their new location.

Jack's initial reaction when he learned Bryce was the cause of their eviction was, "We should have let him keep his gun. Someone would have shot him by now." He had a point.

Morgan didn't have time to paint that week. He worked the emporium full-time while Jack and Bryce remodeled the storeroom in Abigail's building. The windows and sashes were an unexpected expense—they had to pay a man to build them as Jack's carpentry skills didn't extend to that level and Bryce had none at all. Bryce's main contribution was to hold boards while Jack sawed or nailed. However, he kept Jack laughing as they worked. Bryce was a terrific mimic and would imitate Fred's voice, "I'm a dead shot . . . a dead shot."

With more money going out than coming in at the moment, Morgan suggested he and Jack also move out of Mrs. Romero's. "You'll have your own room next to the store and you won't have to sneak in before dawn."

"Yeah, but who'll cook for us? You?" Jack said.

"Hey, I make a mean fried eggs sandwich. We'll buy a kerosene stove and take turns."

"Or eat at Salazar's," Jack said.

"Not if the idea is to save money. We've spent a lot getting this place ready."

"You guys need to relax," Bryce said. "This town loves us, and they love what we're giving them. We'll do fine."

The agreement with Fred was they'd move out on a Sunday when Deitwiler's was closed. Morgan said they couldn't afford to hire a wagon, so the three men carried the tables, shelves, and inventory themselves. It took all day, and by dusk they were exhausted. Last to go was the New World Emporium sign. After it was down, Jack wanted to quit for the night and put it up the next morning, but Morgan said, "No. We need to borrow Fred's ladder to hang it, and I want to return it tonight before he knows different."

"Isn't that a little paranoid?" Jack said.

"I agree with Morgan," Bryce said. "Let's just be done with Fred."

* * *

Monday morning, Abigail came to the store with Cyrus and a basket of muffins. Jack and Morgan were arranging sheet music, books, and records, which had been haphazardly stacked on the tables and shelves during the move. Cyrus went to look through the records.

"Where's Bryce?" Abigail said.

"Sleeping," Morgan said.

"You know I don't mind if you use some of the furniture from the dance hall. It's just sitting there collecting dust. Jack, would you get us four chairs?"

Abigail set her basket on a table while Jack went to get the chairs. When he came back, Bryce was with him, carrying two of the chairs.

"Hi, darling," Bryce said.

Abigail made a slight shake of her head. She was beginning to understand what Morgan had meant when he said Bryce was 'unbridled.' She would have used the word 'childish,' herself.

Morgan cleared space on the table. Jack arranged the chairs and held one for Abigail. Bryce flipped back a hand towel covering the basket and snatched a muffin. "Yum."

Morgan went to a kerosene stove in back and returned with a shiny-new enameled coffee pot and three cups. As he poured he said, "I hope you don't take cream? I'm sorry, we don't have any."

"This is fine," she said. "Aren't you having any?"

"We only have three cups. I'll just share Jack's."

"Morgan doesn't have anything I don't have," Jack said.

"Does that include women?" Bryce said.

Abigail kicked him in the shin.

"Ow."

Morgan and Jack laughed.

Abigail handed out napkins and passed around the basket of muffins. Soon the men's mouths were full, and she was rewarded with murmurs of appreciation. Good time to bring up the reason for her visit. "Last week I said you weren't very good businessmen."

"You did?" Jack said.

Morgan and Bryce nodded. Bryce took another muffin.

"I hope you weren't offended."

"Not at all," Bryce said. "We were never born to be shopkeepers. What we came to do is bring excitement into people's lives. The world's at the edge of a whole new century, and we represent it."

Abigail smiled. "That's a lofty ideal, but—"

Cyrus interrupted by climbing onto her lap. He broke off a corner of her muffin and ate it.

"Sorry, we don't have any milk for you, Cyrus," Jack said.

"That's okay." Cyrus slid off his mother's lap and continued exploring.

Abigail took a sip of her coffee. "Before I was interrupted, I was about to make a suggestion."

"We're open to new ideas," Morgan said.

"Most wives work long hours—cleaning, cooking, and doing laundry. But that's not true of everyone. Ladies of Ida Hoffsteader's ilk employ cooks and housekeepers."

Bryce nodded. "Like my dear old mother."

"These ladies are my friends, and I know for a fact they have time on their hands and nothing to fill it with. School starts this week and Taos just doesn't have enough social events to keep them occupied."

Bryce grinned. "There are only three of us, we can't occupy them all."

Abigail slapped his face, though not hard. He was apparently a slow learner.

Morgan touched her sleeve. "Ignore him—we do. Go on."

"I suggest you start a ladies' book club with afternoon tea."

Bryce wrinkled his nose. "Book club?"

Jack picked up his coffee cup and extended his pinky finger. "Afternoon teas?"

"Consider it," Abigail said. "Give women a reason to make your store a regular place to congregate. Their husbands have money, and they'll probably buy something every time they come."

Morgan nodded enthusiastically. "Don't you see, boys? Bringing Taos the modern world is more than just handing them books, music, and new-fangled gadgets. Stimulating conversation about literature, sophisticated European thinking—our emporium becomes a hothouse for ideas. Abigail, that's brilliant!"

Abigail laughed. "I wouldn't let my expectations go quite that far."

Bryce shook his head. "I left New York to get away from my mother's afternoon socials with dainty cakes. The conversation usually ran to how hard it was to find good servants."

"Cakes?" Jack said. "I don't think we'll be able to manage anything like that."

"You won't have to," Abigail said. "The women will provide petit fours, and probably even compete to see whose pastry is the best, even if their cooks do the actual baking. All you need to bring to the table is a good pot of tea."

Bryce banged his coffee mug on the table. "And serve it in these?"

"Oh, Bryce, don't be obstinate. I have a nice tea set you boys can use."

Morgan was all smiles. "Bryce, Jack, quit fighting it. Can't you see Abigail's given us a terrific way to draw our female customers from Deitwiler's to our new location?"

Abigail took charge. Someone had to. "Bryce, you and Jack carry one of the round tables over from the dance hall, and a few more chairs. Morgan, you're going to need a tablecloth, napkins, tea set, forks, and small plates. I can loan you all that. I think the book club should meet twice a week. Let's start with Balzac's *Le Vicaire des Ardennes*—the English translation of course. Do you have six copies?"

"If not, I'm sure we can get them. Don't you think that book's a little . . . risqué for Taos?"

"It'll set their eyeballs on fire. But under their petticoat propriety they're craving a little titillation. Once the whispers about Balzac start, it'll double the attendance."

While Jack and Bryce fetched the furniture, Morgan took her hand. "We never really discussed what happened—"

She put her finger across his lips and cocked her head toward Cyrus. "There's nothing to discuss. I'm happy, you're happy, and we are friends. Good friends. That's the best possible ending."

As Bryce and Jack wrangled a table through the doorway, Morgan and Abigail separated to let them pass. Cyrus took the opportunity to scoot into the dance hall.

"Cyrus, come back here. We're leaving. One of you can stop by the house this afternoon to pick up my china and table linens."

"Bryce will," Morgan said.

She nodded. "That'll be fine." Abigail glanced at the doorway to make sure Cyrus was still in the other room. "I shouldn't have to remind you, I'm putting you in with my social circle. An errant remark or unwise quip from any of you could be my undoing."

Morgan pantomimed locking his lips with a key. Jack nodded. Bryce turned his palms up and made puppy dog eyes.

Abigail struck Bryce's forehead lightly with her palm. "Cyrus, Mother's leaving." She opened the front door and Cyrus came running.

When they'd gone, Jack said, "Imagine our emporium entirely filled with idle women—"

"Temptation on tap every Tuesday and Thursday," Bryce said.

"Tread carefully," Morgan said. "I think Abigail sees the book club as a way for her to gain a hold over the other ladies by secretly sharing salacious literature. But if anything changes their fantasy life into genuine scandal, the whole thing blows up—for her, and for us."

Bryce smirked. "If we're bringing them the latest ideas of our times, why not free love?"

"Let's start with Balzac," Jack said.

CHAPTER 24

The Ladies Afternoon Tea and Book Club, as it came to be called, began regular meetings the following week. The New Yorkers were perfect gentlemen and gracious hosts. As Abigail promised, the ladies brought cakes.

Morgan began the first meeting with a somewhat pompous talk about the enlightening nature of literature and the aspirations of the book club. He proceeded to give a short biography of Honoré de Balzac and describe his influence on noted writers such as Charles Dickens and even contemporary novelists such as Henry James, whom Morgan promised they would read later in the year. He warned them that although the first selection they would be reading, *Vicar of the Bulge*, might make some of them blush, its redemption was that Balzac's novels were considered the beginning of European realism. And, Morgan hinted, could even be considered a literary precursor of La Belle Époque, the vibrant creative movement current in Europe.

"Henry James recently returned to New York to lecture on Balzac," Bryce added. "I attended. Fascinating man."

The ladies purchased the books and several of them bought other items as well. The women complimented Jack on the tea and he them on their cakes. Over tea, Bryce entertained them with tales of his adventures in Cuba with Roosevelt.

"How remarkable that you knew our president," Ida Hoffsteader said.

Bryce backpedalled. "Oh, I didn't know him personally—he had a lot of men under his command."

By the next meeting, those ladies who were quick readers had already reached the good parts. Morgan noticed they seemed reticent to discuss the salient points in front of the men and he discretely led Jack and Bryce into the kitchen to allow the women to whisper. But their whispers soon became full-voiced, and in subsequent meetings, after the majority of their members finished the book, the women were bursting with the urge to talk about the Marquee in love with a young priest, and the naughty morals of the French. What a liberating thing it was to gossip about fictional characters who, unlike real people, wouldn't be able to turn on them.

As owners and hosts of the book club, the men were not only accepted into the circle, but their opinions of books were solicited. Especially after the group read Henry James' *Washington Square*, which was set in an area of New York City the partners could describe first-hand.

Abigail remained the default leader of the group, posing opening questions to stimulate lively debate, organizing whose turn it was to bring the tea cakes, and, with Morgan's help, suggesting upcoming titles. But as was destined to happen, after formal discussion of the book at hand, conversations naturally turned to local intrigues, issues of speculation, and unsubstantiated rumor.

The women clasped to their hearts the idea of twice weekly teas with their friends and damned be the husband who complained about money spent on books. Their numbers swelled and so did the profits—the partners actually started ending the day with more in the cashbox than when they began. Other opportunities came out of the book club as well. One week Ida Hoffsteader, after admiring Morgan's artwork which hung throughout the store, said, "Do you accept portrait commissions? It's readily apparent the woman on Deitwiler's sign is Emma, herself. I understand that's your work, isn't it?"

"Sure is." Jack slapped him on the back. "Don't be shy, Morgan."

"Excellent. I've been looking for someone who could do an oil painting of my husband and me for our parlor."

Morgan accepted the commission—it was another source of revenue. Once the Hoffsteaders' portrait was finished, the other women envied it, and

Morgan soon had a steady waiting list. This added substantially to the likelihood the store would thrive even though it meant the other partners had to cover Morgan's hours.

The teas also offered the opportunity for the women to air grievances. One recurring subject was the lack of an alternative to the Catholic Church. There were Presbyterians in the next town south, but they were a dour lot and not worth the carriage ride. Many of the ladies had been raised in other Protestant denominations. Although some families held small prayer groups in their homes, it really wasn't a substitute for a proper church. Over the years, it had been suggested that a building committee be organized, but nothing had come of it.

One member of the book club, Faye Wentworth, said she had a sister back east who knew of a group that sends ministers to western communities. She would write her about finding them a Protestant minister. Mrs. Wentworth felt sure that as soon as they found a pastor willing to come to Taos, the community would rise to the occasion and build him a church.

* * *

Rebecca Sullivan was raking the maple leaves in her grandfather's front lawn into huge piles. Several neighbors up and down the street already had their piles lit, and the sweet, smoky smell she forever associated with autumn drifted on the crisp morning air. She wasn't yet "officially" his associate pastor, but since her ordination, she'd been assisting him with church duties and he'd even let her conduct several Sunday services. The thrill of being in the pulpit, opening herself to Divine inspiration and sharing it with an eager congregation, was everything she'd gone into the ministry for.

Moria, her grandfather's longtime housekeeper came out onto the porch. "Miss Sullivan—I'm sorry—Reverend Sullivan . . . I can't get used to calling you that."

Rebecca smiled. She was barely used to it herself. "That's all right, Moria. What is it you need?"

"Reverend Fitzpatrick would like to see you in his study."

"I'll come at once." Rebecca leaned the rake against the porch banister, pulled off her gardening gloves, lifted her skirt above her ankles and vigorously shook it to dislodge any clinging leaves before following Moria inside and hanging her coat on a hook.

The study fireplace held a couple of crackling logs. Rebecca warmed her hands and then turned to warm her backside. It wasn't that cold outside yet, but the fire felt good. Granddad was sitting at his desk filling his pipe. He struck a match and puffed until the tobacco gave off a cheery glow and a fragrant scent.

"Moria said you asked to see me," she said. "Am I leading another service?"

"Many." His eyes twinkled. "I received a letter from one of your former professors at Tufts asking if I could replace my new associate pastor."

Rebecca bristled. "Replace? I've done nothing wrong."

"You certainly haven't. He's recommended you to a group seeking a full-time minister for a new church." He smiled. "Unless I object, of course."

Rebecca rushed behind the desk and threw her arms around him. "Oh! My own church!" This was so sudden. She'd fully expected to serve as an associate for several years before she'd earn a position somewhere as head pastor. Unless—

She pushed away. "Granddad, you'll tell him you don't object, won't you? I mean, unless you think I'm not ready, and if so, I'll understand. I haven't done that many services."

He put his arms around her and pulled her tight. She could feel the pipe smoke wafting past her eyes.

"No, dear, I'll not hold you back." He let go. "There are a couple of factors to consider though."

"Factors?"

Reverend Fitzpatrick took a long draw on his pipe. "First, the position is at a church in New Mexico. You'll have to leave friends, family, and everything remotely familiar."

Rebecca patted his hand. "Isn't that what our founder John Murray did?"

Reverend Fitzpatrick chuckled. "Yes, but you may encounter more resistance in your new land than he did."

"Murray found a church prepared for his arrival and waiting for his message. How will this be any different? As for family, Father, Mother, and the rest of the Sullivan clan haven't had much to do with me since I started serving at your church."

The old man closed his eyes. "So foolish. Someday, I hope, they will realize what a jewel you are." His eyes popped open. "Well, there's plenty of time. From the professor's letter, I take it you won't be going there until after Christmas. Maybe the holiday spirit will bring your family around. Good will to fellow men and all that."

Where her father was concerned, she wouldn't count on it, but she was used to being cut off. "What was the other thing? You said there were several."

"Oh, that. He hasn't told them he's sending a woman."

She laughed. "They'll figure it out pretty quick. There aren't any men named Rebecca."

"He's only been using your initials: R. A. Sullivan."

Rebecca felt her face grow hot. "That's deceptive. And unnecessary. The Universalists have been ordaining women since 1863, and the Congregationalists a decade before that. There's no reason for him to hide it."

"Calm down my little suffragette. We don't know his reasoning. Perhaps he's waiting to be sure they actually want a Universalist. His letter indicated he's dealing with multiple intermediaries."

Rebecca cooled off and nodded. She hadn't realized the arrangements were so complicated. Surely, he'd tell them everything as negotiations progressed. "Well, if I'm not leaving until the New Year, I'll be able to help you with Christmas. I was thinking we could have the children perform a Christmas pageant. I can start rehearsals right after Thanksgiving."

Her grandfather smiled. "That sounds wonderful. You go right ahead and plan it."

"I will. But right now I'm going to burn the leaves I raked before a wind comes along and scatters them."

Rebecca kissed his cheek and left smiling. Today was a date she would never forget—the day she got offered a church of her own.

CHAPTER 25

Bryce was setting the table for tea when Peaches entered the store, followed by Cherry and Mrs. Romero. Bryce hadn't seen any of them since his first experiments with peyote, but they looked every bit as charming as he remembered. At least the girls did—dressed up like it was Sunday—Peaches in a pink organdy dress with ruffles and her sister in a lavender and green gingham plaid. Mrs. Romero wore a new hat and her old pinched expression. Peaches greeted Bryce enthusiastically and then asked where Jack was.

"He's in the back with Morgan, making tea."

The girls rushed off, leaving Bryce with Mrs. Romero, who stood sternly watching him fold napkins and arrange cups and saucers. He ignored her withering looks. He'd had plenty of practice at that with his mother.

Finally, she said, "I wouldn't have guessed you had the grace to lay a proper table."

"Madam. I come from the upper layers of New York society."

"Is that so?"

Bryce continued to work his way around the table. "This for the Ladies' Tea and Book Club."

"I assumed. The girls have been badgering me to let them come. They didn't have school today and insisted they were old enough to join a ladies' literary society."

Peaches and Cherry could be heard in the back of the store telling Morgan and Jack how dull the house was now that they'd moved away and offering unsolicited advice on straining loose-leaf tea.

Mrs. Romero sniffed. "Your partners paid to reupholster my settee—very honorable of them."

Bryce nodded and laid the forks.

"I'm sorry I had to put you out. But you understand, slovenly furnishings attract only the roughest boarders. I must keep measure of the kind of men my girls are around."

Bryce stopped what he was doing and walked over to her. He took her hand and kissed it lightly. "Dear madam, paying for the damage wasn't enough. Let me offer my heartfelt apology."

She blushed but didn't jerk her hand away. "We are taught to forgive. And I hope it's evident from my presence here, that indeed I have."

Bryce pantomimed tipping an imaginary hat. "All three Romero women, in full force."

"Frankly, I was surprised when the girls suggested it. I didn't think they were that eager for reading. But they convinced me joining with women of social standing would better prepare them for proper society and make them more marriageable. Lord knows living in a house full of male boarders isn't doing it. I just hope this isn't some exclusive Anglo coterie."

Bryce, whose mother and sisters belonged to cliques exactly like that, said, "I assure you, it's not."

"Of course, I wouldn't let them join without seeing for myself what kinds of books are being read."

Fortunately, last week Morgan had suggested an American author, Edith Wharton, for their next selection. Bryce picked up a copy of *Sanctuary*, Wharton's most recent novel, and handed it to Mrs. Romero. "This is what they're reading this week. It's the story of a widow dedicated to instilling morality in her child as he grows up."

"You have no idea what a trial that can be." Mrs. Romero leafed through the book, reading a few passages, and found the price penciled inside the back cover. She frowned. "Seems like fit reading, but I can only afford one copy. The girls will have to share."

While Mrs. Romero dug around in her purse for coins, the other ladies started arriving. Each one gave her a polite nod and Bryce a warm smile. Bryce began helping the ladies with their chairs. Mrs. Romero paid for the book and said, "Are there assigned seats?"

Bryce pulled out a chair next to Abigail. "Here, take mine."

Abigail's eyes snapped to his, which was kind of fun to see.

"Mrs. Romero and her daughters will be joining us this afternoon," Bryce said.

The other women studiously adjusted the placement of their teaspoons and cups.

"Oh, I won't be staying," Mrs. Romero said. "I don't have the luxury of time to sip tea. I've only come to introduce my girls. Peaches, Cherry, come out here."

Cherry appeared, carrying a steaming pot of tea on a tray. Morgan accompanied her. Jack and Peaches followed. Cherry put the teapot on the table, and Morgan took the tray away. Mrs. Romero called the girls to her, and when they came near, she held the book she had purchased in front of her face and whispered to Cherry, "You're not here to be servants." She handed Cherry the book and asked Morgan to make formal introductions, though several of the women already knew the girls. Morgan did, and when he finished, Cherry sat in the chair Bryce was holding, so Morgan offered Peaches his seat and said, "Jack, would you bring in a couple more chairs for Bryce and me?"

Mrs. Romero turned to Ida. "I feel confident leaving my daughters in such esteemed company, but Mrs. Hoffsteader, would you mind if the girls walked home with you afterward?"

Ida blinked twice and nodded curtly.

* * *

The following morning, the Ladies Book Club convened an emergency conclave at the emporium, without the Romero girls. Morgan was minding the store, but had nothing set up for an impromptu meeting.

"That's all right," Abigail said. "We don't need anything formal, just brew some tea."

The women took their seats and Ida Hoffsteader began. "The Romeros have lived across the street from me for years. In fact, my daughter Henrietta and Peaches are the same age. I've always considered Mrs. Romero to be very upright, so I'm surprised she'd expose her daughters to . . . some of the books we've been reading. Of course the Spanish may have different moral standards for their daughters."

Several of the women gave knowing nods of agreement, even though Morgan full-well knew Mrs. Romero was not of Spanish descent.

It was time for Morgan to get involved. "I should think you would want to encourage young ladies to read."

"Yes, but not *with* us," said the short gray-haired women sitting next to Abigail—wife of someone who had made money in mining, as he recalled. "They should be reading Jane Austen at their age, not Balzac."

"I think you'll find Wharton is more or less the American Jane Austen," Morgan said.

"That may be true for this week's book," the gray-haired woman said, "but we don't want our reading selections limited to only what is fit for young girls."

"Or our topics of discussion," Faye Wentworth added.

Morgan scratched his head. "Well, here's our dilemma. We have no basis to ask them to leave. We've never restricted participation in the book club by age or ancestry."

"Oh!" Ida said. "It has nothing to do with them not being pure Anglos—"

"Certainly, no one implied that," another woman said. "This is our time to socialize away from our children. We don't want to spend it having to pussyfoot around someone else's."

Morgan nodded to her. "A valid concern. Yet, you must agree pursuit of literature is a desirable use of after school hours for young ladies of a certain age."

"I have only a son," Abigail said, "so perhaps it's not my place to suggest this. But what if we created a young ladies book society? We could select what books they read, but they would meet separate from us, on a different day."

Morgan looked at Ida. "Mrs. Hoffsteader, would you send your daughter to a book club for young ladies?"

"I have no objection to Henrietta socializing with the Romero girls. She and Peaches are at school together."

Several of the women volunteered their daughters, and Ida suggested names of other girls the same age. It was decided by consensus of the meeting to form the Young Ladies Book Society, which would meet on Wednesdays and Fridays and whose reading selections would be guided by the Ladies Afternoon Tea and Book Club. Ida agreed to inform Mrs. Romero about the change.

And it seemed the Emporium would start selling more Jane Austen.

With the fate of the girls settled, Faye Wentworth cleared her throat. "Some exciting news." She laid a wrinkled Western Union envelope on the table and smoothed out the creases. Throughout the meeting she had squeezed it in her hand, straightened it out, and then clutched it again. Now she opened the envelope and removed the telegram. "My sister in Boston has wired that her husband spoke with a professor at the divinity school who knows of a Protestant minister he thinks will come west and pastor our church."

"When?" Abigail said.

"I imagine as soon as we have a church ready for him to preach in."

"This is all so sudden," Ida said. "We haven't even started building."

"If we delay too long, he may take another post," Faye said.

"Well, we can't conjure a building out of thin air," said another woman. "It's not like there are empty churches sitting around."

Abigail leaned toward Morgan and whispered, "Is Bryce decent?"

Morgan chuckled. "Not even when he's clothed. But I don't think he's here."

Abigail stood and tapped her teacup with her spoon. "May I offer a solution? Follow me ladies."

She led them through the doorway that connected the emporium to the dance hall. They squinted in the dim ocher light filtering through the paper-covered windows on the second floor. "Morgan, be a dear, run upstairs and uncover a few windows."

Morgan went up to the balcony and began tearing paper off the windows, anticipating what she was about to suggest. Hot autumn light streamed down in yellow shafts. He threw open several sashes and an updraft of warm air rushed out. Abigail unlocked the front doors and propped them open.

"This will never do," Faye said. "It's a saloon."

"Actually, it was supposed to be an entertainment palace," Abigail said. "But it never opened. So, it is not now, nor has it ever been a saloon."

"But it has a bar," one of the women pointed out.

"That can be dismantled, and the tables removed," Abigail said. "The stage can serve as a dais, a lectern is easy enough to build, and we already have dozens of chairs. What do you think?"

Ida looked up at the U-shaped balcony. "The first floor is a little dark—we'd have to hang chandeliers. But whoever designed the place gave good thought to venting out summer heat."

Ida's remark seemed like tacit approval, so the other women began nodding their heads.

"Is the Reverend married?" Ida said. "If so, he'll expect us to provide him a manse." Her question inaugurated a round of furrowed brows and puzzled looks.

Abigail suggested Faye telegraph her sister for information as to how they might contact the Reverend. "Once we establish direct communications with him, all else will be revealed. Meanwhile, I'll hire someone to dismantle the bar and store the tables."

At the close of the meeting, it was agreed there was no reason to arouse ire in the Catholic community with any public discussion of a Protestant church or minister prior to the good Reverend's arrival.

Later that afternoon, Ida Hoffsteader called on Mrs. Romero to inform her that she had inspired them to organize a Young Ladies Book Society for the edification of young women, and that Henrietta would be attending with Peaches and Cherry. The members of Ida's group would make book selections appropriate for them.

"But I've already paid for *Sanctuary*," Mrs. Romero said.

"Wharton's perfectly fine. The girls club can start with her book."

Mrs. Romero gave a sigh of relief.

"But generally the two book clubs will not be reading the same books, as ours tends toward the more . . . mature themes in literature."

Mrs. Romero raised her eyebrows. "It never occurred to me you would be reading anything inappropriate."

"A married woman may read what her daughters may not imbibe. Wouldn't you agree?"

"I don't know. I was married twenty-two years and I've yet to allow an indecent book in my house."

Ida sniffed. "Indecent is your term. I assure you the books we select for our daughters' book club will be suitable to instilling proper values in their tender minds."

Mrs. Romero sniffed back. "I would expect nothing less."

Mrs. Romero considered canceling her girls' participation upon learning they would be separated from the older women's group. After all, exposure to women of propriety was the whole reason she'd consented. Nonetheless, the price of the book was already spent, so her girls would be permitted to continue at least until the club finished *Sanctuary*. "But you better read every last page of it," she warned.

"I'm trying, Mama," Cherry said. "Peaches is hogging it and not giving me a turn."

"We didn't have many books when I was a girl. Our family used to gather in the parlor and read aloud. Should we try that?"

"Oh, no. That would feel like school." Peaches raked her fingers through her hair. She found a piece of straw which she quickly balled up in her fist. "I'll do better at sharing with Cherry."

"Best you do, then. I've half a mind to take you two out of the club all together."

"Don't, Mama," Cherry said. "Peaches and I will work it out between us."

The inaugural meeting of the Young Ladies Book Society started with four members as Henrietta had brought a friend. Peaches and Cherry had initially been upset about being put out of the women's group, but it quickly dawned on them they would have the undivided attention of three handsome men twice a week.

None of the girls really cared for the taste of tea, but they insisted on it because that's what society women served. Enough milk and a lot of sugar made it palatable. Henrietta brought a brown paper bag of cookies her family's housekeeper made. She gave them to Morgan, who arranged them on a plate and set it in the middle of the table for all to share. Bryce took the first cookie and declared the Hoffsteader housekeeper a culinary wizard.

Cherry vowed to have her mother bake something for next time.

CHAPTER 26

With four meetings a week being held at the emporium, the store was selling more books than anything else. They could have sold a Gramophone or two, but the October shipment never arrived and it was already November.

Jack had just started his shift when Faye Wentworth burst through the door in a fluster.

"Calm yourself, madam." Jack offered her a chair. "The meeting doesn't start for another hour."

She perched on the edge of the seat and clutched her chest.

"Do you need some water?"

She patted her face with an embroidered hankie. "It's so distressing."

"What is?"

"I met Abigail on her way to get the doctor. It's her turn to lead the book discussion today, but she can't. She told me to have you do it."

"Tell me what's happened?"

"The most terrible thing—Abigail's brother-in-law, Walter, was repairing the roof when he fell off. Now, he's just lying there, like he's dead."

"Is he dead or isn't he?"

"I don't think so, not yet. Otherwise Abigail wouldn't need to find Doc."

"That's . . . terrible." Abigail must be frantic. "Come on, we should go there."

Mrs. Wentworth bit her fingers. "I don't know what we could do, and the other ladies will be arriving shortly. We should wait right here."

"You wait if you want. I'm going to go see what I can do."

"What about our meeting?"

"Is that really what's important here?"

She stood up. "What about the store? You can't close up when you know the others are coming."

Jack jerked the front door open. "You watch the store. I'm going to Walter's."

"But, but, I've never worked in a store. I don't have any idea what to do."

"Just make tea. Everything you need is in the back. I'm sure Bryce and Morgan will be back any moment. Tell them what's happened and where I've gone."

Jack closed the door and left Faye standing there with her mouth open.

* * *

Walter lay prone in the front yard like a corpse laid out by an undertaker. Penelope knelt over him, her shoulders quaking. Three wailing children clung to her.

Jack walked over and tapped her on the shoulder. She looked up with obvious surprise. He leaned past and looked into Walter's slack face. Walter's eyes were open and fixed. Some said dead men's eyes stayed open. It was hard for Jack to tell if Walter was staring at the sky or dead gone.

Suddenly Walter's eyes flicked to Penelope and back to Jack. "Mmmumph rhvaie."

"Oh, thank God!" Penelope said.

"I . . . can't . . . move," Walter said.

"Don't try," Jack said. "Abigail's bringing the doctor. They should be here any minute."

A trail of spittle leaked out one corner of Walter's mouth. He tried to catch it with his tongue. Penelope dabbed it with the hem of her skirt.

Walter fixed his eyes on Jack. "I know you."

"Yes, it's Jack," Penelope said. "Jack's here."

"Here? Where am I?"

"Home, dear, you're home."

A tear ran from the corner of Walter's eye. "I can't remember your name."

Her voice caught. She swallowed. "Penelope . . . I'm your wife."

"Wife. Good." Walter closed his eyes and rested.

Penelope broke down crying. The children picked up on her distress and increased the volume of their wailing. She turned and clasped them to her.

Jack gently patted her on the back. He wasn't sure what else to do.

Abigail came rushing into the yard with the doctor and stopped. She took in the scene: prostrate brother-in-law, wailing family. And there was Jack rubbing her sister's back. She grabbed Jack by the ear and dragged him away like an errant schoolboy. "Have a little decency. I know you made a play for my sister at the Sunday social, but her husband's body isn't even cold."

Jack pried her fingers from his earlobe. "I'm not making a play, and he's not dead."

"What?"

"Walter spoke to us. He's alive."

Abigail rushed to the doctor's side. Walter had his eyes open again.

"He's got a pulse," Doc said. "Walter, can you wiggle your fingers?"

Walter's hand moved.

"Good, good. Mrs. Wythe, please unlace and remove his shoes. I want to see if he can move his toes."

"Shouldn't we carry him inside?" Abigail said.

"Doc, I doubt the women can lift him," Jack said. "But I can heft his shoulders if you—"

"No!" Doc said. "If his back's broken, that might kill him."

"You can't just leave him out in the yard 'til he mends," Penelope said.

Doc looked at Jack. "We need something to carry him on—maybe a wide board."

Jack jumped up. "I'll find something." He ran to the barn and returned in a moment with a twelve-inch-wide plank.

"That'll do," Doc said. "Ladies, help me. Gently roll him just enough for Jack to slide the board under him."

As soon as they moved him, Walter groaned and Penelope shrieked. Abigail gritted her teeth and kept Walter's shoulder raised while Jack got the board in place. They slowly eased Walter's body back down.

"Damn hard bed," Walter said.

Everyone laughed with relief.

Jack and Doc carried Walter into the bedroom.

"Set him down on the bed," Doc said, "but leave the board under him until I figure out what's busted."

While Doc finished his examination, the women and children hovered around. A few minutes later, Abigail heard hammering.

Abigail came out to see what the racket was and found Jack on the roof, nailing the remaining shingles. "Jack! What are you doing up there?"

"I can't foresee Walter getting back up here anytime soon, and I couldn't leave him with a hole in his roof."

"You surprise me, Jack."

"I'll take that as a compliment. Tell Walter I'm sorry for the noise. I'll finish quick as I can."

Abigail nodded. "Jack, thanks for thinking of that. And . . . I'm sorry for what I said earlier."

"You were upset. Don't think of it again."

She nodded. "And you be careful up there. One broken man is enough."

Abigail went back in the house. The doctor was repacking his bag. "I don't think Walter's back is broken, but he may have a spine injury. He shouldn't get up for some time."

"I can't anyway," Walter said.

At least he was talking again. "Is there anything more that can be done?" Abigail said. "A specialist, perhaps?"

"I've heard of a doctor at the medical college in Denver who specializes in spinal injuries," Doc said, "but the only way to get Walter to the train station would be to lay him in the back of a buckboard and I fear the jarring would do him more harm than the doctor could do him good. I think your best option is to keep him here and see if a few weeks' rest mends him. I'll leave you a bottle of laudanum to ease his pain, and I'll come by again tomorrow."

* * *

The following Thursday, Abigail returned to the book group. There was little else she could do for her sister. Penelope was overrun with helpful neighbors and hadn't had to cook since the accident. Abigail offered to pay to bring the Denver specialist down by train, but then Walter started moving and was now able to roll over on his own—which Doc said showed the back wasn't broken after all. Walter still couldn't sit up. Whenever he tried, waves of dizziness and nausea struck him. Walter also belched for days. Doc said it was gases in his body released by the fall. Walter's boys thought his burping hilarious, but he still had gaps in his memory and couldn't always remember their names.

It was apparent to Abigail that it would be a long time before Walter would be able to work, and it was too much for Penelope to keep the place up on her own. If she couldn't spend her money on a specialist, Abigail said, she would pay for a hired hand to do whatever chores the boys couldn't until Walter recovered, no matter how long that was.

That's when Penelope told her there was no need; Jack had been doing all the work that needed to be done.

"You're joking," Abigail said.

"Not at all. Jack comes before dawn, milks the cow, wakes the boys up, and makes them do their chores. By the time he leaves, everything I need a man for is finished. The kids and I can do the rest."

"Well, call me suspicious, but we both know the man's a lothario. With Walter crippled up, he may be banking against some future reciprocity."

"I don't think so," Penelope said. "I admit, he was very forward when we first met, but since Walter's accident, he's shown his better side. He consults Walter every day about what work Walter wants done and they've become good friends."

"And he expects nothing in return?"

"Breakfast. I make him breakfast."

"Ah-ha."

"Abigail, it's just breakfast."

"If you say so."

CHAPTER 27

Jack continued spending his mornings helping Walter and Penelope. He'd always been a night owl and seldom took the morning shift, anyway. Since most evenings the three friends went out after dinner, business conferences tended to occur spontaneously over drinks in any convenient bar. Tonight they were toasting the good results of the book clubs—one reason they were able to eat out more—and drinking to Walter's speedy recovery.

"Walter can sit up now," Jack said. "He still gets dizzy when he tries to stand, but Doc says he's going to be all right. Hopefully, he'll be up and around by Christmas. His kids would sure like it."

Bryce raised his glass. "To Walter. And to Saint Jack."

Jack slapped him affectionately on the back of his head.

"Speaking of saints," Morgan said. "Bryce, did Abigail tell you the Ladies Tea group is fostering a Protestant rebellion?"

"No. What are you talking about?"

"Yeah," Jack said. "Abigail told Penelope, they're starting a church in the unused dance hall next to us."

Bryce said in a sonorous voice, "Communion is now served—by the pint or by the quart. Congregants may now step over to the bar."

Morgan shook his head. "They're serious. They've already hired a minister from Boston, a man named Sullivan."

Bryce blanched. "You know, Big Tim Sullivan's the Tammany leader in the Bowery."

"What of it?" Jack said.

"Boston and New York aren't that far apart. What if this Sullivan is related to Big Tim and tells our Irish friends where to find us?"

"Nah," Jack said. "The minister is Irish-Protestant. The Catholic-Irish won't even speak to him."

"Probably right," Bryce said. "You heard about the Irishman who got engaged to a whore? Brought her home to meet his mother who said, 'Tell me about yourself.' The lass replied, 'I'm a prostitute.' The old lady clutched her chest. 'Lord, you gave me a fright. For a moment, I thought you said Protestant.'"

"Careful there," Jack said. "My grandmother's Irish, that's my people you're talking about."

Bryce held his hand like a gun. "Yeah? Then it's your people who were after our asses."

"Why worry?" Morgan said. "You took care of that situation. Right, Bryce?"

Bryce hesitated a bit too long before replying. "Well, I'm not saying we have to worry, but there is no reason to invite old grievances to Taos, is there?"

"Order another round," Jack said. "Then I'll tell you something we *do* have to worry about."

Bryce frowned. "What's that?"

"Beer first." Jack signaled the barman.

When they had fresh beers, Jack said, "You won't believe this. Deitwiler is selling Gramophones."

"How do you know?" Morgan said.

"My schoolmarm told me. She's clerking there after school, helping Emma with the Christmas sales."

"We should have hired her," Bryce said. "A school teacher would be a perfect salesperson for a bookstore. She could have run the book clubs, too."

Morgan and Jack emphatically shook their heads.

"We can't afford an employee right now," Morgan said. "There's barely enough work for the three of us."

"Besides," Jack said. "It'd be mighty inconvenient to have one of my lady friends involved in my work life."

"What a kick in the ass," Bryce said. "He threw us out because he said the Gramophones were too noisy, and now he's hawking them."

"Bryce," Morgan said, "you know he didn't evict us over Gramophones."

"Okay, okay. But he complained about them plenty, didn't he?"

"Yes, he did," Morgan said. "And we don't even have one in stock. In fact, we haven't received a shipment in two months and we're about sold out of records, too."

"Bryce," Jack said, "you better telegraph the company tomorrow and find out where our order is."

"I'll do it first thing."

But Jack was beginning to have his doubts.

Those doubts were confirmed the next morning, when the stagecoach mail arrived with an official-looking letter from The Victor Talking Machine Company, informing them that the company had granted exclusive rights to sell Gramophones in Taos to a more established firm and would therefore no longer be able to accept orders from other merchants.

Bryce and Jack were in the store, sitting at a table, staring at the letter, when Morgan burst through the door as angry as they'd ever seen him.

"I guess you heard," Jack said.

"Heard? I've seen it with my own eyes. What an offense to art, and an affront to me personally."

"To all of us really," Bryce said.

"I take it you've seen it then?"

Jack shook his head. They were having two different conversations. "Whatever you're upset about, I don't think you know half of it."

"Some amateur has butchered the beautiful sign I made for Deitwiler's. Painted out the ivy and wrote '& Gramophones' in penmanship that would embarrass a fifth grader."

Jack handed him the letter. "If you're outraged by a sign, wait until you read this."

Morgan scanned the page. "Fred, you little fox."

Jack cleared his throat. "You don't think Fred's doing this to us because he found out about Emma?"

Morgan shook his head. "Definitely not. If that were it, he'd simply shoot me."

"What's this got to do with Emma?" Bryce said.

"Before you came, Morgan had a little fling with Emma."

Bryce grinned. "Forbidden fruit certainly makes a sticky jam."

Morgan slammed his hand on the table. "This is no time for wit. No one knows about Emma except me, her, Jack, and now you." Morgan gripped Bryce's arm hard. "And you're to keep it between us, got it? I was serious about the shooting."

Bryce jerked his arm away. "I'll bet you're sorry I lost my gun."

"Not in the least," Jack said.

"I think it's pretty rich, you two blaming me all this time for Fred kicking us out, when it actually might be Morgan's fault."

Morgan threw down the letter and stomped the length of the room and back in smoldering silence.

Jack wasn't in the mood to let Bryce off. "No, getting us evicted was all your doing. But it doesn't matter anymore. We're in our own place now."

"I'll tell you how we get even," Bryce said. "Let's get an exclusive deal with Singer to sell sewing machines. His customers will come running to our store."

"Hell, no," Jack said. "We're not going to be the kind of cutthroat businessmen who pull underhanded stunts. That's not who we are or what we came here to do."

"So you'd rather get screwed over and not do anything back to him?"

"Yes. Right, Morgan?"

After two laps around the store, Morgan calmed down enough to say, "Fred's part in this doesn't count. It's just smart business." He picked up the letter and waved it. "This is what matters."

Jack nodded. Morgan was absolutely right. "So, let's think of something we can do about it."

Morgan's eyes scanned the letter again. "I bet it's because we used Deitwiler's address for all our previous shipments. Someone in New Jersey is confused about who they made the original deal with. Bryce should go there and remind them."

"Oh, it's a long and expensive train ride back east," Bryce said. "Let's just send them a letter."

Bryce told Abigail about it, jokingly calling it the Gramophone war. She said she had an idea and sent him to fetch Jack and Morgan. When the New Yorkers arrived at her house, a wagon was backed up to her front porch, with a team of four hitched up and waiting.

"I'm moving my piano to the emporium," she said. "Help the driver load it on the wagon. It'll take all four of you. It's heavy."

"That's very generous of you," Morgan said. "But why are you doing this?"

"Bryce told me you can't sell Gramophones anymore, but you still sell sheet music, don't you? I figure you can stimulate music sales the way you did Gramophone records, by having Bryce give performances of the newest tunes. I suggest you have him play at the afternoon book clubs. All those ladies own pianos and their husbands have money."

"Damn nice of you," Jack said.

"Well, I feel more kindly disposed toward you since I saw the way you've been helping Walter and Penelope."

Heavy planks were laid between the porch and the wagon. The combined efforts of the four men got the piano loaded while Abigail tried to keep Cyrus from underfoot.

"Tie it securely," she said. "I don't want it damaged."

"Yes, ma'am," Jack said.

"Don't ma'am me," Abigail said. "And take those boards along. You'll need them to unload it."

Jack had to admit, Abigail was one hell of a good woman, generous to a fault.

CHAPTER 28

Abigail's scheme to sell more sheet music worked. Bryce, who enjoyed entertaining even when it didn't pay, played for the Ladies Afternoon Tea group and sales increased. He also performed for the Young Ladies Book Society and attendance escalated. Unfortunately, the girls didn't have money. Bryce was playing purely to beguile them.

At the Ladies Tea meetings, Bryce played Christmas carols and a selection of classical pieces. Both styles sold well. The young ladies preferred ragtime. After a few meetings, he switched the older ladies' group from Chopin to Scott Joplin as well. Bryce's mother would have said Joplin was a more corrupting influence on good women than even Balzac, and Mrs. Romero might have agreed, had she been familiar with the works of either man. The ladies of Taos society didn't seem to mind ragtime. Bryce also gave weekend performances to draw in male customers and women who were not in either book club.

The society ladies were currently reading *A Tillyloss Scandal*, which turned out to be a compilation of short stories and not all that scandalous. For the Young Ladies Society they had selected a safe choice, *Pride and Prejudice*. Since Mrs. Romero already owned a copy, she allowed Peaches and Cherry to continue with the group. Neither girl told her that time spent discussing the Bennet's story had dwindled as time spent listening to Bryce's ragtime increased. Instead they told her how well acquainted they were becoming with the daughters of the social elite. It seemed to be what she wanted to hear.

Bryce latched onto Jack's latest *Popular Science Monthly* as soon as it arrived. The November issue featured the science congress at the St. Louis World's

Fair and included ten pages of photos that Bryce used to impress people. By the time Jack got his magazine, its pages were as frayed as a street dog's fur.

On the plus side, Bryce's efforts with the magazine had brought a brief resurgence in sales of the emporium's overstock of World's Fair stereo cards. And his demanding performance schedule had another good effect. Before Abigail gave them her piano, he'd been shirking work to spend time with his peyote friends. Jack, who had been stuck covering shifts for both partners, was relieved to have Bryce showing up for work regularly for a change.

Jack felt his other partner's absence was justified. They needed the extra money Morgan was earning painting portraits. However, Taos was about out of families who could afford oil portraits and then Morgan would take his shifts back. Once that happened and Walter recovered, Jack could resume the carefree life he'd lived last summer.

Unfortunately, Morgan had yet to find another subject that sold well to the locals. He even painted a few of Bryce's Indian friends, but customers weren't buying pictures of gnarled old men or pretty Indian maidens any more that they did the familiar Taos landscapes. Why own portraits of people you could see on every street? Morgan mentioned sending them to a few galleries back east where there seemed to be a fascination with all things western. Jack told him he should. What harm could it do?

One night, over drinks at Salazar's, Morgan said to his partners, "We're making pennies on sheet music, when we could be making nickels on records and dollars on Gramophones. One of us needs to go back east and see if we can straighten out the situation with The Victor Company. Just writing a letter didn't work. This probably needs to be done in person."

Jack said, "That person should be you, Bryce. You set us up originally. You must know someone at the company."

Bryce turned ashen and rubbed the back of his neck with his hand. "Oh, why waste money on train tickets? They didn't even respond to our letter. There isn't any hope as long as Deitwiler has an exclusive."

"It won't hurt to try," Morgan said. "Gramophones and records were a big piece of our business."

Bryce put his finger in his shirt collar and stretched it like it had suddenly shrunk. "Look, I don't know anyone special there. I just walked in, talked to the sales department, and left. That was six months ago, they wouldn't know me from Adam. Besides, I can't go back now. We're selling more sheet music than ever. Who'd play piano if I went east?"

"Can't argue with that," Jack said.

"No, I guess we can't afford to send Bryce," Morgan said.

* * *

Monday afternoon, Bryce was off with some Indian doing God knew what and Jack and Morgan were alone in the store when the stagecoach pulled in and unloaded a couple of crates from Victor for Deitwiler's.

Morgan jumped up. "To hell with Bryce, I'm investing my own money in a train ticket. I'm going to show my paintings to some New York galleries. On the way, I'll stop in New Jersey and get us back our record deal."

Jack nodded. "I don't mind. I've gotten used to working your shifts while you paint portraits, anyway."

Morgan packed a suitcase and wrapped three of his paintings in brown paper. "I'll carry these with me on the train. I'm afraid they'd be damaged in the baggage car. When Bryce gets here, tell him I'll be back in about a month."

"Will do," Jack said. "Have a good trip, and write when you know something."

* * *

It wasn't until the day after Morgan left that Bryce came back, looking a little worse for wear, and learned he was gone. "Shit, shit," Bryce said, nervously pacing around the store.

"Stop, before you wear a hole in the floor," Jack said.

Bryce's eyes darted around the room. "I've got to send a telegram."

"Right now? The Ladies' Tea starts in a half-hour. You'll have to do it after."

"No, no, I've got to warn Morgan not to go into the city."

Jack had had niggling doubts. Now it was clear something was up. "Why, Bryce?"

Bryce hemmed and hawed and finally said, "I never took care of that difficulty we had with the Irish. I just skipped town and hopped the train here."

"I thought you said—"

"No, I just let you guys think that. The day I left New York, I saw two or three of them waiting outside. They might have been looking for us."

So . . . they could never go back to New York? "I feel like I've been kicked by a mule."

"Understandable. I'm sorry. Very sorry. But we've got to reach Morgan."

Jack shook his head. "I wouldn't even know where to send a wire."

"Where is he now?"

"Someplace between here and New Jersey."

Bryce paced some more. "He should be all right in Camden. Just as long as he doesn't cross the river into New York."

"Oh, he's going there for sure. He's taking his paintings to some galleries."

"Shit, shit, shit. Why didn't he stay here?"

"Well, Bryce, why didn't you take care of the matter before you came west, like you said you did?"

Bryce hung his head. "Because I'm a screw-up." He gave a heavy sigh. "Well, he might be able to sneak into Manhattan, but he better not cross the East River into Brooklyn or Queens."

CHAPTER 29

January 1905

Morgan had been gone three weeks when Monday's stagecoach brought the mail and a single passenger. As soon as Jack saw the stage pull up, he left Bryce to man the store while he went to see the postmaster. He'd done this every time the stage came for the last two weeks. Today the long-awaited letter finally arrived. He tore it open and read it as he walked back to the store.

"Is that from Morgan?" Bryce said.

Jack nodded.

"At least we know he's not dead," Bryce said. "Did he say he had trouble with anyone?"

Jack shook his head and kept reading. "Had to buy new clothes. Said living in New Mexico, we've forgotten how people in the city dress."

"Better him than me," Bryce said.

"He says the city was all decorated up for Christmas." Jack looked up wistfully. "I never liked winters there, but Christmases were pretty. Festive, much nicer than here."

"I thought Christmas would be warmer here. It was so hot last summer I expected winter to be balmy. But it snowed here most of December, and look, it's snowing again today . . . What's he say about the Gramophones?"

"He wasn't able to persuade Victor to rescind the Deitwiler's exclusivity, but the company's going to ship us records." Jack finished and handed him the letter. "Here, read for yourself."

Bryce took the letter from him and began reading. "Good, he bought a Gramophone for the store."

"Yeah, and he says under no circumstances is it for sale. He had to pay retail for it. Says it's for our customers to hear records before they buy them."

"I just read that part. He says he's shipped it here with four cases of records. Was there any freight on the stagecoach?"

"No, just that passenger's luggage. Did you get to the part about taking the train to Washington, D.C.?"

"Just getting there . . . Going to meet with executives at Columbia Records, a new company that's licensed Victor's patents to manufacture records. Says they plan to release a large catalog of recorded music."

"See Bryce, we should have sent you. You could have called on Teddy Roosevelt—gotten the President to intervene with those people at Gramophone."

"Oh, he doesn't know me."

"Yeah, but I've read he welcomes all former Rough Riders to stop by."

Bryce imitated the President's oft-photographed pose. "Holloway? Holloway? I thought we left you at the port in Tampa."

They both laughed.

Their laughter was interrupted by a tentative rap on their door, like a bird pecking on bark.

"No need to knock," Bryce said. "We're open for business. Come on in."

The stage coach's only passenger stood in the doorway, holding her suitcase in one hand and a leather valise in the other. The tall, plump woman wore a gray suit with a long skirt, a starched white blouse with a lace collar, and a matching gray hat over her dark hair. She had green eyes. Unlike her timid knock, her resonant voice filled the store. "I wonder if you gentlemen could help me. I was given the address next door for the ladies' committee forming the new church, but the place is locked and there doesn't seem to be anyone inside. Are either of you acquainted with the women on the committee?"

Jack smiled. "Are we ever."

"If you're looking to join the committee, most of them attend the Afternoon Tea Book Club we hold here," Bryce said. "But today's not a meeting day."

"They've been working next door to get the place ready for the new minister," Jack said. "But if the door's locked then they're obviously gone."

"I see. I'm rather lost here. Would you help me locate someone on the committee?"

"I'm sorry, we've been rude," Bryce said. "Please, put down your things and have a seat. I'll go get Abigail for you. Jack, why don't you put on some tea?"

"That would be so kind of you." She placed her suitcase against the wall and accepted the proffered chair.

Bryce took his hat and coat from the rack and started for the door. "Are you expected? May I know your name, so I can tell Abigail?"

"Rebecca Anne Sullivan. . . . Reverend Sullivan, from Boston."

CHAPTER 30

Abigail answered the knock on her door to find Bryce with January snow falling on his head. He didn't seem to notice. She glanced toward Cyrus playing in the other room. Bryce wasn't supposed to call at this hour. She scowled at him. He knew the rules.

He tipped his hat and snow fell at her feet. "Sorry about that mess." He looked up. "Reverend Sullivan arrived on today's stage. She's waiting for you at the emporium."

It took a moment. Abigail wasn't sure she'd heard correctly. "She?"

"Tits and all." Bryce quipped.

Abigail gave him a stern look. "Language, please. Cyrus has ears."

He peeked inside. "Sorry. Conservatively dressed, stocky, nearly as tall as I am, but a woman, I'm sure of it."

Abigail chewed her lip.

"You didn't know?"

"No. Correspondence concerning the Reverend only used his initials, R. A. Sullivan."

"Her initials."

"Apparently. Well, go back to the emporium and make her comfortable. I'll drop Cyrus off at Penelope's and gather the rest of the committee. We'll meet at your store shortly."

* * *

Word spread from member to member of the ladies' society like tumble-weeds on a windy day. By the time the full committee converged on the emporium, Reverend Sullivan and Bryce were engaged in a nostalgic discussion about New York City. She fondly described the time Granddad had taken her to a Universalist state convention there. Meanwhile, Jack was in the back making more tea for the impromptu meeting Bryce had warned him was on its way.

The ladies stamped snow off their high-top shoes and shook it from their capes. Faye Wentworth brought a pound cake. "I made this for my husband's dessert, but he'll have to do without." She handed it to Bryce, who set it in the center of the table.

Jack carried in a steaming teapot as Bryce raced to set the table. Jack spied the cake and returned to the kitchen for a knife.

Rebecca checked her hair, tied in a tight chignon at the back of her neck, and rose to meet them. Her grandfather had advised her that being open and frank was the best way to impress her new congregation.

The committeewomen introduced themselves and then studied their shoes, apparently as surprised by her gender as Bryce and Jack had been. Obviously, her professor had maintained his ruse to the very end, leaving her to deal with the consequences. She'd have preferred fewer intermediaries and a direct correspondence with the committee. She could have cleared everything up with the stroke of a pen.

The tick of the wall clock echoed awkwardly.

Finally, Bryce pulled out a chair. "Reverend, will you have more tea? As you see, Mrs. Wentworth has brought cake."

"Thank you." Rebecca settled herself as graciously as she could.

The committee ladies took their places at the table and consumed more quiet time pouring tea, passing sugar and cream, and serving cake, without meaningful conversation. Between sips of tea, the ladies gave each other furtive glances.

It was time to take Granddad's advice and be forthcoming. "I sense my arrival has caused consternation among you."

"Consternation might be too strong a word," Abigail said. "Perhaps surprise would be more accurate."

"That I'm a woman?"

"We had no idea that a minister could be of our own sex," Faye said.

"Why not?" Rebecca said. "I assure you, my degree and ordination are legitimate." Rebecca removed a sheath of papers from her valise and began laying them out on the table. "Here is my Divinity Degree, here is my Certificate of Ordination, here is the letter from your committee offering me the position." She sat back. "And here I am."

The women stared at the documents on the table as if they were evidence in court. Faye fingered the letter bearing her signature.

"Well, you are here, indeed," said Ida Hoffsteader. "Now, we must find someplace for you to stay. The Columbian is too rough a place for a single woman."

"We can't board her at Romero's," Faye said. "They're Catholic."

"Another person's religion doesn't matter to a Universalist," Rebecca said.

"No, but it will to Mrs. Romero," Abigail said. "You see, the Catholics have the predominant church in town."

"Until now," Bryce interjected.

Abigail nodded. "Until now. You're here to provide Protestants an alternative, and the Catholics aren't going to be happy about it."

"Too bad you didn't arrive in time for Christmas service," said the women next to Abigail, whose name escaped Rebecca. The other ladies nodded.

Yes, and too bad they hadn't seen the Christmas pageant she'd organized.

Ida cleared her throat. "It seems, until we can find other accommodations, Reverend Sullivan will have to stay with one of us."

The committee members uniformly turned to Abigail.

"Why are you all looking at me?"

"Well, you have a rather large house," Faye said.

"So do the Hoffsteaders."

"Yes," Ida said with a smile. "But you don't need your husband's permission."

"But I have Cyrus. The Reverend may find it difficult to prepare her sermons amidst the ruckus of an energetic young boy."

"I grew up in a large family," Rebecca said. "Children are no problem."

Abigail nodded. "Well, then. Jack, would you take the Reverend's things to my home?"

"Oh, I can carry my bags, thank you," Rebecca said. "I travel quite light."

"These gentlemen wouldn't think of allowing that," Faye said.

"It'd be my pleasure," Jack said.

Rebecca looked at Abigail, who was clearly still a bit on edge about the prospect. "You're sure it won't be an imposition?"

Abigail held up her hand. "Of course not, this is our fault. We should have had a place ready for you. It will only be temporary until we can make arrangements."

The meeting broke up with cordial farewells. Abigail and Rebecca walked in silence. The snow had stopped falling and wasn't deep. Jack trailed behind, carrying Rebecca's suitcase and valise, which weighed almost nothing. She could have carried them herself.

Abigail's home was indeed fairly substantial, even by Boston standards. Jack set Rebecca's luggage in the foyer, tipped his hat and left.

Rebecca had been leery of what sort of reception she might receive and was even prepared to be turned around and sent back on the next stage. But in talking with Bryce, she learned that the modern world had developed a toehold out here in Taos. And that might include room for a woman pastor.

Now, all she had to do was convince the town she was a good idea.

CHAPTER 31

Finishing touches to the church were hurriedly made in preparation for Reverend Sullivan's first service. The coffin maker had been pressed into service to construct a pulpit. The result wasn't fancy, but at least it didn't look like a casket. The wealthy emptied their conservatories and decorated the dais with enough flowers that an undertaker would have felt right at home. Although the church looked ready for a funeral, the abundance of blossoms in wintry January delighted the senses.

The crate of hymnals arrived in time for the first service and the ladies' committee placed them on chairs they'd arranged in neat, orderly rows. There hadn't been time to install a stove, so there was no heat. The congregation was encouraged to fetch lap robes from their carriages. As the room filled, the collective assemblage created some accumulation of body heat, but the cold drove families to scoot their chairs together in clumps, ruining the symmetry of the once tidy rows.

Rebecca stepped up onto the dais and the room quieted. She wasn't wearing a robe or any vestments, just her best navy-blue wool suit, which consisted of a floor-length skirt and a nicely tailored matching jacket. She didn't wear makeup, for her cheeks were naturally pink and her lips had that rosy color of young women. She also refused to wear a corset which she considered an instrument of torture designed to please the male ideal of beauty. She wore her hair up in a tight bun but elected not to wear a hat.

Rebecca had a strong singing voice, and, after a brief invocation, led them in several hymns a cappella. The congregation quickly discovered that her style of service didn't require all the standing and kneeling of the Catholics so there was less heat loss, and everyone could stay snuggled in their blankets.

As the collection plate was passed, she announced that the day's offering would be directed toward purchase of a wood-burning stove. Contributions were generous.

When it was time for the sermon, Rebecca gripped the pulpit in both hands and gave it a shake, both to test its stability and her own. The coffin maker had done good work. Her pulpit was solid and did not rock or tilt.

Rebecca looked out at her audience, cleared her throat and began. "Let me introduce myself. I am Rebecca Sullivan, a Universalist minister, a graduate of Tufts College Divinity School, and ordained by the Massachusetts Universalist Convention."

Her breath in the cold air hung like fog. But her voice was not weak or her manner timid. Her words reached even those furthest to the rear that had come merely to see the curiosity, a woman preacher. "When I was called to serve here, I assumed you knew what upon my arrival, I learned you did not. However, I am not discouraged and I hope you will not be disappointed. Our situation reminds me of the story of the first Universalist to come to America."

There was a creaking of chairs in the front row, but she still held most of the eyes in the room. It may just be over the novelty of her being there, but she would use it.

"During our country's colonial period, Thomas Potter, a colonist living near the New Jersey coastline, had a vision that if he built a chapel, a minister would come and preach there. So Potter built his church and waited . . . and waited.

"In 1770, John Murray, a Universalist minister from England, set sail for the colonies. His ship, blown off-course, was becalmed off the coast of . . . yes, New Jersey. Reverend Murray went ashore to obtain provisions for the men on his sloop, and who was the first person he met? If you guessed Thomas Potter, you are correct. Potter showed him the church he'd built, and Murray did indeed preach there—the first Universalist sermon in America.

"Now, I cannot speak to the prescient abilities of the ladies' committee who organized this church, and I do not pretend to compare myself to our great founder John Murray. But I do ask you to consider that God works in mysterious ways, and great things can start from happy coincidences."

There were knowing nods of agreement from several of the committee-women.

Good. She was bringing them along.

"From speaking with Mrs. Wythe, Mrs. Wentworth and Mrs. Hoffsteader, I understand this congregation is drawn from many different denominations. I want to assure you that back east there are Baptist Universalists, Quaker Universalists, as well as Universalists from Congregational, Lutheran, and various German sects. Even our American founder, John Murray was a Methodist. So I hope you will take comfort that we are a church that welcomes all faiths."

Two of Penelope's children began to prod one another. She separated them by changing places and putting herself between them. Rebecca waited for the commotion to settle.

"Reverend Murray's style was not to preach Universalist doctrine, but to cite scripture that supports the precept of universal salvation. For example, Romans 5:18 refutes the idea that all men are condemned by Adam's sin. Saint Paul says that if by the offence of one man—Adam—judgment came upon all men, then by the act of one man—Christ—the free gift of salvation came upon all men."

Her audience straightened up in their seats.

Ah. They had not been prepared with an understanding of what Universalism meant.

"God is not a wrathful deity, but a loving deity. As God is unlimited, God's love is also without bounds. The true message of the gospel is ultimate salvation of all."

From that point, Rebecca wrapped up her sermon quickly and discharged her congregation. Perhaps some were disappointed with her brevity, but she didn't want to overwhelm them with too much change too quickly.

* * *

As the service let out, Jack was standing outside, leaning against the emporium door. He had the morning shift, but it was Sunday, and there hadn't been any customers. Maybe if they saw he was open, someone would wander over after church and buy something. He stomped his feet to ward off the cold. At least it wasn't snowing.

The Deitwilers came out of church and started to walk by. Jack tipped his hat to Emma, and they stopped. Fred shook his hand.

"How was it?" Jack said.

Emma cocked her head. "You didn't go?"

"Me? No. Morgan is . . . out of town. And I had to work the store. Besides, religion isn't really my strong suit."

"Being from Minnesota, I hoped for something a bit more Lutheran," Fred said.

"Everyone back home who's not Catholic is Lutheran," Emma said.

"I guess we've got to take what we get, though." Fred pressed his hand into the small of Emma's back. "Let's go home, dear."

* * *

Rebecca considered her challenge no different from that faced by stalwart predecessors, James Relly and John Murray. But they had decades of experience before breaking ground. This was her first church. To intrigue people to return a second time, Rebecca let it be known her upcoming sermon was titled Eternal Damnation.

Protestants who had been raised with the drama and spectacle of fire and brimstone preaching came with high expectations. The crowd filled even the balcony. The new stove had arrived from Albuquerque and been installed that week. Rebecca lit the wood hours before the service, and the church felt toasty warm.

After several hymns were sung and the offering collected, Rebecca took to the pulpit. "Without resorting to creed or dogma, I shall attempt this week to present the essence of Universalism."

Rebecca opened her Bible. "Let us begin on that day in ancient Athens, when Saint Paul spoke on Mars Hill. I am reading from Acts, Chapter 17:

God that made the world and all things therein, seeing that he is Lord of heaven and earth, dwelleth not in temples made with hands; Neither is worshipped with men's hands, as though he needed anything, seeing he giveth to all life, and breath, and all things."

Rebecca looked up from her reading and added, "God does not need to be reconciled to humanity. Rather human beings need to be reconciled to God." She paused to let that sink in.

"Let us continue with verse 27:

That they should seek the Lord, if haply they might feel after him, and find him, though he be not far from every one of us: For in him we live, and move, and have our being . . . For we are also his offspring."

Rebecca closed her Bible and gazed at the expectant faces. She gave a small smile and let the moment linger.

"Today, I promised to elucidate Universalist views on eternal punishment. Our view is quite simple. It doesn't exist."

A sharp, collective inhalation sprung from her audience.

"Yes, you heard me correctly." She stepped away from the pulpit to engage them more directly. "Universalists believe that God is a loving God. Reward for our merits and punishment for our transgressions may be meted out in our lifetime. But unlike papist doctrines, we do not believe we can be eternally condemned after we die."

The ladies in the front row looked at each other and furrowed their brows.

"As we read today in scripture, God has made all according to his plan. We are his offspring and in him we have our being. At death we are reconciled to him. Anything less than universal salvation is unthinkable since it would imply failure of the Divine plan."

A man in the audience could not restrain himself. "What about the unrepentant sinner?"

Rebecca scanned the audience, but couldn't identify the speaker so she answered the congregation at large. "God is all powerful. It is not possible for any human to frustrate God's love or God's design."

Rebecca smiled at a woman in the second row with a large family of children. "Hosea Ballou, a great Universalist minister, used the following parable: 'Your child has fallen into the mire, and its body and garments are defiled. You cleanse it and array it in new robes.' Reverend Ballou's query was this: 'Do you love your child because you washed it? Or did you wash your child because you loved it?'"

Women in the church smiled at that. She was getting somewhere.

"The whole idea of damnation makes no sense. Reverend Ballou studied all the Old Testament accounts of God's retribution for wrong acts and found it was always imposed immediately. Not once did God say punishment would be deferred until after death. Any sins we commit are finite, limited. Eternal damnation is infinite, unending. Does it make sense for God to punish us eternally for sins committed over a few years? Or to wash us of our errors as any mother would."

She had gone about as far as she dared for now. "I leave you to consider this week, why, if in Old Testament scripture there is not one instance of God condemning his children to eternal hell after death, would you accept any doctrine that says you are to fear him instead of love him? As Jesus Himself said, perfect love casts out all fear. And God is love. He gave life and breath to all, then why would he do anything less than give all salvation?"

CHAPTER 32

Rebecca's sermon certainly gave the people of Taos something to talk about. Not just Protestants who were in attendance, but the whole town. As rumors circulated, Rebecca's words were exaggerated, and soon it was being said that she did not believe in punishing sinners. Or in sin at all. By the time her message was spread, it had become, 'Anything you wanted to do is fine with God.'

While Rebecca worked on her sermon for next week, the Ladies Tea group busied themselves discussing the new minister's opinions and busy formulating a way to quell the town's reaction. Jack and Bryce hadn't attended the service and certainly didn't want to get mixed up in some religious melodrama—people on both sides were customers. Since the ladies weren't discussing books or interested in hearing Bryce play piano, the men decided to make themselves scarce.

"We'll be in the back if any customers come in," Jack said.

They stayed there until the meeting wrapped up. They heard the ladies leaving, but then Ida scurried into the back room, looking like she'd just found a snake in her handbag. "Some rough-looking characters have come in. They don't look the type who read books."

Jack peeked around the doorframe. Oh, shit.

"Bryce, escort Mrs. Hoffsteader, will you, please?"

"Certainly." Bryce offered Ida his arm and walked her past Sneed and his men. He opened the door for her. "Would you like me to accompany you the rest of the way home?"

"No, I'll be all right, thank you. I just didn't like the cut of those fellows."

When he heard Bryce close the door, Jack stepped out of the back room. "Mr. Sneed."

Bryce made to move toward Jack, but Sneed's two henchmen stopped him.

Sneed strode toward Jack. "You owe me."

"For what?"

"Fanny."

Jack's mind raced back to Christmas. The schoolmarm's job in Emma's store had made her less available, so he'd been seeing Fanny more frequently. By the time school resumed, he and the teacher had just fallen by the wayside. Besides, Fanny had fewer designs on settling him down.

"Look," he said, "Fanny and I had an arrangement between ourselves. It doesn't—"

Sneed pulled a Bowie knife from his belt and held it against Jack's throat. Oh, shit.

Sneed's face was no more than an inch from his own. "There's a price a man has to pay for putting himself between the legs of one of my girls."

Bryce lunged. "Let him be!" But Sneed's men held him back.

"Don't interfere," one of them said.

Bryce clenched his teeth. "You don't know who you're messing with. I was a Rough Rider back in ninety-eight."

"You don't look so rough."

"I don't have to be. Half of Roosevelt's company lives in a little town south of here. You so much as nick Jack's neck and I'll have a hundred of them up here in a heartbeat."

Remarkably, Sneed bought Bryce's bullshit. He lowered the knife and stepped back. "Hold on, we're not trying to start a war. But you got to pay your debts."

"What debt?" Bryce said.

"My little redhead," Sneed said.

"You mean Jack's girlfriend?"

"I mean my whore."

"You don't own Fanny," Jack said. "Slavery's over. The thirteenth amendment ended that. It's unconstitutional to own a person."

"You a damned lawyer? Fine, she's my employee and those who take a taste of her pay for the pleasure, same as you pay a bartender for a drink. Difference is, you can run a tab in a saloon. I don't extend credit."

"What Fanny does after work is her business."

"Yeah? Just because she thinks she's in love doesn't mean I'm not due." Sneed waved the knife at him. "Start digging in your pockets. How much money you got?"

Jack pulled his pockets inside out. A few silver dollars fell on the floor.

"That's not going to cover it."

"Well, that's all I've got."

Sneed looked around. "This is your place, right? Where's the cash box?"

"Over there," one of the henchmen said.

"Bring it here."

Sneed opened it and spilled the contents on the table.

"Hey!" Jack said. "That doesn't belong to me. I've got partners."

"And I got expensive whores." Sneed counted the money. "I don't know exactly how many nights you and Fanny were together, but I'll take this and say we're even."

Bryce bristled. "Jack already told you that's not his money. It belongs to all of us."

"Then you just bought his debt. Better he owes you than me. Let's go, boys." Sneed started for the door, stopped midway, and turned back to Jack. "I'm calling us square, but between the two of us, I think you and Fanny were together more times than I know. So you got a bargain today, but that's finished. No more free ones. You got to pay to play like everyone else, love be damned."

Sneed and his men left.

Jack dropped into a chair. People in Taos might be saying the new Reverend didn't believe in hell, but Jack felt as if he'd just been through it.

He looked around at the shelving. Still had a fair amount of stock, even though they had bills to pay with the funds Sneed just walked out with. They might get by.

"We'll make the money back," Jack said. "No reason to bother Morgan about this."

"You know," Bryce said, "if you'd let me keep my gun, this incident would have had a different ending."

"Yeah." Jack actually laughed. "I'd have my gullet slit, and you'd have a bullet hole in the toe of your shoe."

* * *

Sunday, Rebecca's sermon addressed the question of hell directly. "Christians who support the doctrine of hell may find it useful for enforcing social order," she said. "But social convenience doesn't always make for good theology."

Her congregation waited.

"There are those who say lack of fear of future retribution might weaken the moral order, but from what I have seen here on the frontier, the prospect of hell isn't having much effect on morals."

The congregation laughed. Always a good sign.

"Abraham Lincoln argued that biblical punishment was parental—intended for the good of the offender, and the punishment ceased once justice was satisfied. If there has been any distortion of the Universalist ideals I explained last week, then heed Lincoln. Simply stated, Universalists believe God is a loving God, who will never condemn anyone eternally. Each being is created in God's divinity, and He reunites us with the whole as soon as feasible after we die."

Rebecca heard someone in the back whisper loudly, "Smacks of predestination."

"Whoever said that is referring to the Calvinist doctrine of election to grace, which holds that before the dawn of time God chose those who would be saved. Anyone not so elected is powerless to obtain salvation. I will not quarrel with a Calvinist or Presbyterian whether prior to creation God chose whom to save, except to say that all are elected and therefore destined to be saved."

Several Presbyterians in the audience looked to heaven—or at the chandelier —it was hard for Rebecca to know which.

"Does that mean Universalism denies free will?" Rebecca said. "A Calvinist certainly does, asking, if mankind had free will and we removed the threat of punishment in the hereafter, what would make men moral?"

Her audience waited expectantly.

"First, God has fit us with a subtle system to guide us. Reward and retribution for our acts need not be violent and eternal. In every interaction man has the free will to choose to be part of God's plan, or to resist it.

"Choose to participate, even facilitate, God's plan and you experience a sense of wellbeing even during times of difficulty. It can be sensed as surely as a sweet scent on a spring breeze. Use free will to act in opposition to God's plan and a sense of restlessness comes like a biting chill in a winter gale, even in times of prosperity."

Several among the congregation coughed.

"Second, it's not that we are too good to be damned, but that God is too loving to make a place such as Hell and eternally damn us to it."

From various quarters of the room came the sound of chair legs scraping the floor. Rebecca decided to cut her sermon short. She closed the service with a hymn and said a benediction.

CHAPTER 33

Abigail put a spoonful of marmalade on her toast, passed the dish to Rebecca, and spread the preserves with her knife. She eyed Cyrus's plate. "Eat your eggs, so you can get to school on time."

Cyrus stabbed the yolk with his fork and scooped up a bite. It dribbled on the table. Abigail wiped the table with a corner of her napkin. "Do you need me to cut that up for you?"

"No, Mama. I can do it." He picked up his table knife and noisily slashed his fried egg into tiny squares. These he shoveled into his mouth until his cheeks bulged. He looked at Rebecca. "Reverend?"

"Don't talk with your mouth full," Abigail said.

Cyrus grabbed his glass of milk, chugged a quarter of it, and swallowed. "Are you a real minister?"

"Cyrus! Of course, she's a real minister."

"My schoolteacher says no. Only men can be ministers."

Abigail fumed. "Your teacher and I need to have a talk."

"If you talk back, she makes you stay after school."

Rebecca smiled. "Cyrus, women have been ordained ministers for the last fifty years. Your teacher just didn't get word of it yet."

Abigail laughed.

Cyrus cocked his head. "What's so funny?"

"People in this town. Finish your milk and get your coat on. It's time for you to leave."

Cyrus stood and Abigail wiped his face with her napkin. She pulled his stockings up for the fourth time this morning and tucked them under his knickers. Abigail walked him to the foyer, helped him button his coat, kissed him goodbye, and sent him out the door.

Abigail returned to the dining room and began to stack the dirty dishes. "Are you finished?"

"Yes, I am, thank you. But if you're not in a hurry, I'd like for us to share another cup of coffee and a little conversation."

With a nod, Abigail carried the dishes into the kitchen and returned with the coffee pot. She refilled their cups and set the pot on a trivet. "I apologize for Cyrus."

"Oh, please don't. What I would like to learn is how you've succeeded in this male-dominated culture."

"Are you surprised to encounter resistance? Isn't it still a man's world back east as well?"

Rebecca studied her fingernails. "Yes, that's true everywhere. But in Boston I had the support of my granddad, and some of my professors. They knew of other women ministers, and, well, college was different from real life."

Abigail sipped her coffee and waited.

"It wasn't an isolated struggle. Tufts had a number of women students. Here I'm fighting on my own."

"No, you're not. Don't forget, it was the ladies of Taos who stood up against the status quo, started a church, and brought you from Boston."

Rebecca chuckled. "Quite by accident, though, you'll admit."

"Yes, we had no idea we were getting a woman. Still, they accepted it, jumped to the task, organized a church, and made their husbands come."

"What about the rest, like Cyrus's teacher?"

"You can't win over everybody. I seriously doubt if she's ever heard you preach, and I don't recall seeing her in church."

"Exactly. Maligned by women who never met me. And the men are no better. You seem to be well respected. How did you do it?"

Abigail shook her head. "Our circumstances are different. I have wealth, and important men are afraid I'll take it elsewhere. That makes their wives fall in line. But you already have a position that commands deference. You're a minister, for Heaven's sake. Every Christian has been raised to show reverence toward a man of the cloth, even those of a different denomination."

"Well, *a man of the cloth*. That's the problem isn't it?"

"Yes, being a woman is a struggle, a female clergy, probably doubly so. What I'm saying is, your job title alone grants you a status in society that only Father Ignacio shares. Hold your head up high, and demand equal treatment. You have a college degree. Most likely you're the only person in this town that does. You earned the right to be respected. The only thing you can do wrong is let them ignore it."

Rebecca shook her head. "I didn't come to New Mexico seeking accolades. I came to bring modern theology to the west."

Abigail smiled. "That sounds like Jack and Morgan's dream of bringing modern ideas to Taos."

"I know. We've had several interesting talks. It's fitting my first church is adjacent to the emporium. I believe our visions are interconnected in more ways than sharing the same building. The Universalists' dream of bringing realization through enlightened preaching and freedom from the strictures of tradition, is every bit as exciting as the technological new world that Jack and Morgan saw at the World's Fair. I want people to see that God is loving, not wrathful and vengeful, and that ordinary mortals can experience the Kingdom of—"

Abigail held up her hand. "Whoa, you're not on the pulpit."

"Sorry."

"Paradoxically, I'm afraid Mrs. Romero and the Catholics see the same interconnection between the church and the emporium as you do, but not in a good way. I worry if either of you will survive."

"Oh, we don't want anything like that to happen. Is there anything I can do?"

Make your sermons a little less unorthodox, Abigail thought.

She refilled Rebecca's cup. "Why don't you get to know some of your congregation socially, outside of church? Show them what a bright, intelligent person you are off the dais."

"You think so?"

"Rebecca, I like you. Living together, dining together, I've come to know you in a way the other ladies haven't. Give them a chance to see you as I do. You're well read. We have a book club. Maybe you should attend."

As soon as she said it, she remembered the scene of Madame Bovary in the carriage. Too racy for a minister, even an eastern liberal, and the ladies would feel awkward.

"No, here's a better idea. Why don't you host a tea here in my home? I'll help. Perhaps some of the ladies will reciprocate and invite you to dinner at theirs. That way you'll get to know their husbands and children, as well."

Rebecca laid her hand on Abigail's. "Thank you so much for everything you've done, and this talk has been so helpful."

CHAPTER 34

The first week in February, the Ladies Afternoon Tea Book Club was reading *The Awakening*, by Kate Chopin. Faye Wentworth said, "It's hard to believe this was written by a woman."

"It certainly couldn't have been written by a man," Abigail said.

The other members were unwilling to discuss its frank portrayal of female marital infidelity in mixed company, so Abigail kept sending Jack and Bryce on little errands to get things from the kitchen until finally Jack resolved to just stay in the back and experiment with his electric generator. Bryce joined him.

Inspired by Morgan's letter mentioning the dazzling Christmas lights in New York, Jack had ordered several hand-cranked electric generators from a scientific supply company along with incandescent bulbs and wiring. These he predicted would sell well. They hadn't. Oh, they were a novelty that drew in customers, but no one was going to stand around their house cranking a generator all night when it was easier to touch a match to a lantern. Now, the store had another bit of inventory gathering dust. Jack put it to use though, trying different electro-magnetic experiments he read about in *Popular Science*. At least he could enjoy the benefits of modernity.

In contrast to the scandalous book the women were reading, the ladies had selected *Sense and Sensibility* for the girls. At the Young Ladies meeting the following day, Henrietta and Peaches were arguing in favor of Marianne Dashwood and handsome John Willoughby, when Cherry noticed the stagecoach had pulled into the plaza. Morgan stepped out.

"He's back!"

"Who?" Peaches said.

"Morgan. I just saw him through the window, getting off the coach."

Bryce rushed out the door. Jack followed, yelling, "Mind the store, girls."

"Aw, we want to come," Cherry said.

"It's too muddy. You'll ruin your dresses," Jack said over his shoulder. "Don't worry, Morgan will be here in a minute."

"Then why are you guys going?"

"He's brought new merchandise and needs our help to carry the boxes."

Morgan had indeed brought a new Gramophone and four crates of records. It took two trips, but when all five wooden boxes had been carried into the store and Morgan had been effusively welcomed back by the girls, Jack got a pry bar and set about opening the crates. The girls gave up their book discussion and enthusiastically unpacked records while Bryce set up the Gramophone. Soon the emporium filled with music.

Morgan, exhausted from the journey, left the festivities and went to the back to get a drink. He found a bottle of whiskey, poured a good measure into a teacup, and returned to watch.

Rebecca came through the side door that connected to the church, bumping into him just as he was taking a sip. Whiskey dribbled down his chin and onto his vest.

"Oh, goodness. I'm sorry," she said. "I heard music and wanted to see where it was coming from." She had her hair down today in two braids that made her look young, closer to her actual age of twenty-three.

Morgan wiped the whiskey from his chin. "My fault, I'm sure. It's just that no one except us ever uses that door. You must be a new member of Abigail's committee." Morgan dried his whiskey-dampened hand on his pants and offered it. "I'm Morgan. I don't believe I've had the pleasure . . ."

"Rebecca." She shook his hand and sniffed his teacup. "Smells like good stuff. Is there any more?"

Morgan's smiled. "Would you like some?"

"Please."

"It's in the back. Let me get you a cup."

Rebecca followed him into the kitchen. He handed her a cup and saucer and poured two fingers. "More?"

"No. That's enough, thank you."

"Our emporium hosts afternoon teas, although this isn't the usual beverage."

Rebecca took a small sip. "Irish?"

"Unfortunately not. Something local . . ." He examined the bottle. "Made in Albuquerque, I think. I just returned from New York. I could have brought a case of Irish whiskey home with me, but it never crossed my mind."

"This isn't that bad. Albuquerque apparently knows what it's doing."

"Let's not kid ourselves. It's nothing like you get back east . . . Your accent, you're from somewhere in New England?"

"Boston. So, you didn't bring whiskey. Anything besides the music?"

"Cadmium red, burnt umber, chromium yellow, ultramarine."

"What?"

"Oil paints. The main difficulty with the West is everything here has to come from somewhere else, so I'm perpetually waiting for materials."

"Oh, you're the artist. Are those yours?" Rebecca gestured at the land-scapes hanging around the store and walked over to admire one. "They're beautiful."

"Thank you, but people in Taos aren't buying them. They claim they get the same view for free by looking out their window."

"I'll buy one—once I get paid."

He looked at her hand. "I notice you're not married. What brings you here—no, let me guess. You appear well educated. Are you a new schoolteacher?"

She shook her head. "Close. I'm the new minister."

"Minister?" He glanced at the cup and saucer in her hand and back to her face.

Her eyes danced. "There are Universalist teetotalers, I'm sure. I'm not one of them."

"Apparently not."

"We share a wall."

"I'm sorry?"

"My church is the room next door."

Morgan nodded. "There was talk of that before I left."

"Come, see for yourself." Rebecca opened the connecting door to the former dance hall. Henrietta glanced at them as they passed by, but the other girls were fully caught up playing records with Bryce.

Jack gave Rebecca a small wave. "Afternoon, Reverend. Bringing a lost sheep home?"

"I'll try."

Morgan entered and stood agape at the transformation of the room. Gone were the bar and tables. The chairs had been arranged in neat rows. On the stage was a table draped with a floor-length white tablecloth, on it a candelabra. Not a menorah, but throw in an ark for the Torah and it could be his parents' synagogue. A wooden podium occupied the front corner of the stage. A stovepipe from a wood stove on the right side of the room snaked up past the balcony and out the roof.

He gave a low whistle. "Did Abigail do all this?"

"Not alone. But it was done by women. It's my understanding that their committee was the impetus to organize the church."

Morgan looked up. The butcher paper had been removed from the upstairs windows and the glass cleaned. Light now streamed in. Chandeliers were suspended from pulleys in the ceiling which allowed them to be lowered to light the lamps. In New York, Morgan thought, they would have been electric.

Rebecca was flushed. The whiskey had done its work. She leaned toward Morgan and said, "My first church."

"Mine, too."

"What do you mean?"

"I've never been in one before."

Rebecca's eyes widened. "Really? You are a lost sheep."

Morgan smiled. She was near his height, her green eyes level with his.

"Well, I'm here every Sunday."

"I'm here every day," Morgan said.

She laughed and handed him her cup and saucer. "You're the first person in this town to offer me a drink. I thank you for that, but I've got to go work on my sermon."

"It was lovely meeting you."

"Likewise," she said.

Morgan walked back into the store and looked at the clock. "Girls, your mothers are going to wonder why you're not home."

"Aw," Cherry said. "We haven't even had a chance to hear about your trip."

"Yes, tell us everything about New York," Peaches said.

"Next meeting. You best go home before Mama comes looking."

"You other girls, too," Jack added.

The Young Ladies Society members left, and Morgan strolled around the room looking over the inventory. He came to a display of silver jewelry. "What's this?"

"Indian stuff," Jack said. "From Bryce's friends."

He picked up a piece. The hammer marks showed, and the design was plainer than the baroque excesses current in New York. But it did have the virtue of simplicity. Still . . . He set it back down. "It'll never sell."

"Oh, give it a chance," Bryce said.

Morgan pointed at a painting he'd done of an old medicine man. "No, I know what'll happen. The locals don't buy things they can find here. They come to our emporium seeking the exotic and sophisticated. You could sell Indian jewelry in New York, maybe—there it'd be exotic. Here it's ordinary."

"Speaking of New York," Bryce said. "Everything go all right?"

"Swell. Several galleries are interested in Western art, and I got us lots of records."

Jack laughed. "Swell?"

"Popular expression in New York, right now." Morgan picked up a silver bracelet with mismatched turquoise stones, examined it, and set it back down. "I guess it doesn't cost us anything to let them show their pieces here. I assume if it sells we'll get a commission. Right?"

Bryce stroked his mustache. "You didn't run into any angry Irishmen back east?"

"Why would I? They don't care about us anymore."

"They don't?"

"Not any thanks to you. You let us believe your father made a deal with the bishop and you'd paid the diocese to forget us."

Bryce shrugged. "He may have. I haven't spoken with him since I left."

"So what happened?" Jack said.

"I heard that while fighting back against her family, she blurted out the truth about sleeping with us. Her uncle, the bishop, confined her to a convent. She slipped the noose, ran off with a young fisherman from Brooklyn, and got well and properly pregnant. The bishop performed the nuptials and said we were never to be spoken of again."

"None of that means my father wouldn't have talked to the bishop," Bryce said. "Anyway, did you notice we've got electric lights?"

A length of wire connected a row of unlit bulbs strung above the bookcase on the far wall.

"Did Taos get electrified?" Morgan said.

"Just us." Jack walked over to a table next to the bookcase and began to crank the generator. The bulbs threw off a blaze of white light.

Morgan's eyes glistened. "Just like the World's Fair. I'll bet that draws in customers."

Jack nodded, grinning. "No one's ever seen anything like it."

"One step closer to our dream emporium."

Bryce tugged on Morgan's sleeve. "Listen, before we close up, help me push the piano into the church."

Jack stopped cranking. The lights dimmed to yellow and went out. "Why would we do that?"

"Now we've got records and a Gramophone, we don't need it. I'm sure the Reverend will love having a piano to accompany the hymns."

"What are you going to play sheet music on?" Morgan said.

"Oh, I'm done with that."

Sheet music was one of their steadier sellers. "Tell me this is one of your jokes."

"Look, Morgan, you've been gone six weeks. My fingers are bleeding." Bryce extended his hands, palms up.

Morgan looked at them. "They seem fine to me."

"Playing piano puts the burden for selling music on me. With the Gramophone, any of us can do it and I don't have to be here. Now, push."

Morgan looked to Jack who merely shrugged. "Okay, Morgan, let's get this thing out of here."

Bryce propped the connecting door open and then got in front of the piano and pulled. "By the way, Morgan, you haven't told us how you got the Victor Company to sell you records."

Morgan got on the opposite side and shoved. "Oh, that. I kind of saw an opportunity and took it."

"Do tell," Jack said, helping Morgan push.

"It turns out Deitwiler's exclusive is only on the players, which I realized doesn't hurt us."

They had the piano inside the church by then. Bryce stopped. "Let's not go any further until the ladies tell us where they want it."

"Why doesn't Fred's deal matter?" Jack said.

"We've always known we'd only sell a finite number of machines. Once you own a Gramophone, you don't need another. The real money is in the music. You buy one player, but you keep buying more disks. The record market is unlimited."

Bryce grinned. "And Fred doesn't know shit about music."

"No, he doesn't," Morgan said. "And he doesn't know about Columbia Records, either."

CHAPTER 35

From Boston to New York, the oft-quoted adage was that March comes in like a lion and leaves like a lamb. But in Taos, early March seemed like a polar bear that just wouldn't go home. Rebecca and the New Yorkers were allied in their expectation that somehow New Mexico should have been warmer. While they waited for winter to break, Morgan hoped for a word from an agent or gallery about his paintings. Bryce had forsaken piano in favor of playing records, but once more disappeared, leaving Morgan and Jack to take up his shifts. They'd sold the four crates of records Morgan brought, and additional shipments continued to arrive. The store was finally doing well again, and the church was happy to have Abigail's piano.

After a prolonged absence, Bryce reappeared on a Sunday morning. The refrain of "Nearer My God to Thee," accompanied by some unlucky piano student, pierced the adjoining wall. Bryce winced as the pianist lost the left hand and played a bar or two of discordant notes, then paused, and got himself righted.

He walked into the kitchen and poured himself a cup of coffee. The coffee pot was still pretty full, so he found an enameled saucepan with a lid and put it on the kerosene stove. He ladled it three-quarters full of water, lit the burner, and added a dozen dried, disk-shaped cactus buttons retrieved from his pocket. When the water boiled, he put the lid on and turned the flame down to simmer.

Jack came in from the outhouse. "Making breakfast?"

"You might say."

"Smells like a dead rat."

"Where's Morgan?"

"Out front, clearing ice from in front of the door."

"You expecting customers?"

"Nah. Seldom get many on Sunday. But the ice won't go away by itself. Where you been?"

"Indian medicine ceremony. I brought us a little present."

Morgan came in huffing warm breath on his fingers. He held his hands over the steaming kettle and rubbed them together. "Damn near frostbitten."

"You think it's cold here, you ought to feel it up in the mountains," Bryce said.

"That where you been?"

"Yeah."

"What's in the pot?"

"Peyote."

"Huh?"

"Cactus buttons the natives use in their Big Moon ceremony. You can chew them or make them into a tea. They taste bad, so the tea is a little easier to swallow."

"What the hell for?" Jack said.

Bryce hesitated. One of the problems with what he'd been finding is that it extended some ways beyond language. "How can I . . . The world we think we know is not all there is. You drink this and you're going to see something you've never seen before."

"Is it safe?" Morgan said.

"Indians have used it for five thousand years, and they're still here. They've got an elaborate ceremony with a water drum, peyote rattles, and a magic stick. They read the Bible, too—they've folded some Christianity into their indigenous ritual. But I'm convinced the cactus buttons are what causes the effect, so I brought a few home to share with my partners."

Bryce lifted the lid and sniffed the pungent broth. Satisfied, he emptied their coffee cups and poured in the tea.

When his cup had cooled sufficiently to drink, Bryce took a swallow. "Drink."

Jack took a sip and spat it out. "You weren't kidding. And that's the easy stuff to swallow?"

"You only have to choke down one cupful. Trust me, the experience is worth it."

"Where's the sugar?"

"It won't help."

Jack ignored Bryce's advice and added several spoons of sugar. He tasted it again and made a face. "You're right. Sugar didn't hide it. How about salt?"

Bryce put his hand out to stop him. "Keep up and you're really not going to be able to drink it. Just chug it all in one go, like a glass of cheap whiskey, and be done with it."

Jack nodded, drained his cup, and gagged.

"Morgan, you too," Bryce said.

Morgan clanked his cup against Bryce's. "Bottoms up."

The singing next door stopped. Rebecca was probably giving her sermon, but they couldn't be sure. The sound of one person's voice didn't carry through the walls unless the connecting door was open.

Jack clutched his stomach. "Bryce, you bastard, you poisoned me! I'm going to puke."

"Probably all that sugar you put in it," Morgan said.

"A brief period of nausea is normal at first," Bryce said. "It'll pass."

After the queasiness dissipated, Jack and Morgan waited for something to happen. Nothing did, or so they thought. Bryce knew and was waiting for it.

Presently, Morgan wandered over to a stack of paintings he'd been waiting to ship east and flipped through the canvases. "I never realized how accurately I've been able to capture the light in these scenes. Look how sunlight emits from the image."

Bryce came over to see. The painting was amazing, a revelation. It was of a waterfall, and it captured the motion, the majesty of the water, the stuff of life, pouring itself out onto the desert. And the colors . . . "Look at the hues. You've managed to achieve colors that don't exist in a paint tube. Jack, have you seen these?"

Jack joined them and looked over Morgan's shoulder. "Very nice . . . That one is making me thirsty."

"Don't drink anything except water, Jack. Trust me. I've taken this several times."

Jack walked to the kitchen and ladled water into a glass. He held it up to the light, studied it, and then slowly poured it back into the bucket. He refilled his glass and then watched as he emptied it again.

The colors in the landscape paintings became too intense to bear, forcing Morgan and Bryce to leave them. They took seats at the table.

Morgan picked up a teacup and studied it. "What if physical objects are only tokens of a reality behind reality?"

Bryce nodded. "The medicine men say that true knowledge about natural things prepares the mind for insights of its own." He wagged his finger. "But they are not the source."

Morgan set the cup down. "It's that way in art. However perfect, art can never be the thing it portrays. The effort of the artist is naught because what he sees belongs to a higher order that can never be fully captured on canvas."

"Yes. You get it."

"At the place on the mountain where I painted those landscapes, the separation between worlds seems thinner."

The men were silent. Bryce was indifferent to the loud tick of the wall clock. The sound of falling water could be heard coming from the kitchen.

After an undetermined period, Bryce said, "Do you think church is out?"

"I don't know. Why?"

"I might go next door and play the piano."

"Been a while since you wanted to play."

"Has it?"

"Yes. A while since you wanted to participate in the store, too. Why is that?"

The question wasn't an accusation. Morgan truly wanted to know, and Bryce felt he deserved an answer. "In the ordinary world we are . . . selfs. In the spirit world you become Not-Self, perceiving Not-Self things."

"Why don't you open the door and see?"

"What?"

"If church is out."

"Nah, I don't want to bother them . . . Have you ever been?"

"Where?"

"To one of Rebecca's services?"

"No."

"Because you're Jewish?"

"No, just haven't. Should we go sometime?"

Bryce belched; it tasted like peyote. "Why?"

"She's like us, young and from back east. Maybe she needs support against all the backlash she's getting here."

"She's nice enough, but after this—" His gesture took in the waterfall, the amazing teacup, the clock. "Well, who needs church? How come you're not religious?"

"None of us are."

"True, but it seemed when we were growing up your parents were really drilling that stuff into you. More than ours did."

Morgan nodded. "Hebrew class, bar mitzvah, and everything, but you know what bothered me most? The first word."

Bryce waited.

Morgan drew Hebrew letters on the table with his finger. "Everyone translates the first word of Genesis as, 'In the beginning.' But actually it says, 'In *a* beginning.' After I learned that, I lost all interest in dogma, my own or anyone else's. It seemed to me God's own words were implying this has all happened before and may someday happen again."

"Transience," Bryce said. "Eternal, yet perishing and becoming."

"Exactly." Morgan looked around. "Where's Jack?"

"Getting a drink of water."

"Sounds good to me. Aren't you thirsty yet?"

They walked into the kitchen and found Jack refilling the water glass.

"I'll take that," Morgan said.

"Fill one for me, too," Bryce said.

Jack gave them both water and filled a third glass for himself. "I think I'm really sozzled."

"Yeah, that's what happens," Bryce said.

They heard the door open, so they walked back into the store. A man in a russet cape came in and took off his derby. He was completely, perfectly bald. "Do you have any books on transcendentalism?" The man's teeth whistled as he spoke.

The partners looked at one another and laughed—a perfect comic strip character, come to life and walking into their store.

Jack recovered first and walked along the bookshelves, running his thumbnail across the spines. It made an oddly musical thrrrr noise.

"Tran-scen-dent-al," Bryce said. "Has a melodic sound. Doesn't it?"

"Certainly does," Morgan said.

The man wiped his bald spot with his hand. "Well, do you have any books or not?"

"Books, we got books of every color." Jack turned to his partners. "You know, we should sort these books by color. Put all the red covers together, then the blue covers, and the green covers."

Bryce studied the bookshelves. The letters on the spine seemed to dance and swirl. Each book had its own pattern. "I see what you mean," Bryce said. Wait, he'd just mimicked the whistle in the man's speech.

"Are you fellows making fun of me?" the bald man said.

Apparently he had.

"Not at all," Morgan said. "We can sell you letter shapes on sheaves of paper bound between hard covers, but reading isn't experiencing the transcendentalist's vision, merely his description of it."

"Very poetic," Bryce said.

"Poet? Yes, that's it. Jack, give the man Whitman's *Leaves of Grass*."

With some help from Bryce, Jack located the book and gave it to the man.

"How much do I owe you?"

"Owe us?" Morgan said.

"For the book. What's the price?"

"Who can put a price on enlightenment?"

The man shook his head, put on his hat and cloak, and said, "Very odd business you're running here." He picked up the copy of Whitman, looked for a price, and found it written in pencil inside the front cover. He put a coin on the counter and waited. The New Yorkers stared at it. Finally, the man said, "Keep the change, it's only a penny." He opened the door.

"Wait," Bryce said, following him outside. "Is church out?"

"I believe it is." He tucked the book under his cloak and strode off.

"Hey, it's snowing," Bryce said.

Jack and Morgan came out. Bryce tilted his face to the sky and watched the snow swirl. "It's a ballet. The snowflakes are ballerinas."

"They say no two snowflakes are alike," Jack said.

"How do they know?" Morgan said.

"I'm not sure." Jack paused. "*That* was strange."

Bryce continued to stare up at the sky. "The dance of the snowflakes?"

"No, the bald man with the derby."

Bryce shivered. "If the church is empty, I'm going to play piano."

Jack and Morgan followed Bryce into the store.

"Lock the door," Jack said. "I don't think we can deal with any more customers today."

"I agree." Morgan put the key in the lock and turned it.

Bryce went into the church and sat at the piano. Shafts of sunlight from the balcony windows pierced the room diagonally, giving it a cathedral-like atmosphere. A composition by Beethoven that Bryce hadn't performed in years came to his mind, and he suddenly hungered to play it. Every note was arrayed before him, in a dance as intricate as the snowflakes.

He began to play.

When he reached the fourth movement, the storm, the bass clef notes reminded him of Joplin's left-hand stride rhythm. He quadrupled the tempo and began playing Beethoven with manic ragtime variations.

Rebecca appeared from nowhere. "I was enjoying the earlier movements."

Bryce stopped. "Where did you come from? I thought everyone was gone."

"I was up in the balcony, watching the snow through the windows, waiting for inspiration, when I heard *The Pastoral*. You are a phenomenal musician. I've only ever heard it performed by a full orchestra. I had no idea it could be played by a solo pianist."

"Franz Liszt transcribed it for piano."

"Not that last part."

Bryce laughed. "No, that was inspired by Scott Joplin."

"Beethoven probably rolled in his grave."

"Good thing he was deaf," Bryce said. He stepped on the sustain pedal, struck middle C, and listened until the note existed no longer. He waited an equal length of time and struck C sharp, again letting it hang in the air, seemingly forever. Next he played a sustained B flat and listened. "The problem with music is, it's so dependent on the interval between notes. Yet men long to be delivered from the world of time."

"You're in an odd state of mind today."

Bryce played the B and C simultaneously and a jarring sound echoed through the room. "Dissonance. Two notes as close as can be on a keyboard, yet seeming to violate natural law."

"Certainly unappealing," Rebecca said.

Bryce played C and C sharp together, which created the same effect. He did it again and again, obsessing on the atonal sound it produced.

Rebecca put her hands over her ears. "I believe I'm going to look for inspiration elsewhere," she said, and left.

Bryce began to compose a song played only on the black keys. It had a strangely foreign character that reminded him of the oriental pavilions at the World's Fair. He'd been working on it for some time when Morgan and Jack came in. "Listen, doesn't this remind you of the China or Japan pavilion?"

"More like Siam," Morgan said.

The sound of someone knocking on the emporium front door came from the other room.

"Did you hear that?" Morgan said.

"What?" Jack said.

"Someone wants into the store."

Jack patted Bryce's shoulder. "Keep playing Bryce. They'll go away."

But they didn't. The knocking escalated to pounding.

"May as well see who it is," Morgan said.

"Aw, let's not," Jack said.

Bryce slid off the piano stool and accompanied his partners back to their store. Morgan unlocked the door and Abigail shoved it open. Cyrus burst in, tracking snow on the floor.

"Why are you locked up in the middle of the afternoon?" Abigail said.

Jack locked the door behind her. "We couldn't deal with any more customers today."

"What?"

"We were next door, listening to Bryce play piano," Morgan said. "It's an astonishing experience."

Abigail brushed snowflakes off her shoulder. "'Astonishing' was not one of the words Rebecca used when she described it. She said Bryce drove her out."

"I waited until everyone left," Bryce said. "I thought she was gone."

"That shouldn't have happened. It *is* her church after all."

Morgan was gazing off abstractedly. "You know what the most absurd sentence is? I don't want that to have happened. By definition, it already did."

Abigail tilted her head. "Morgan, what a peculiar thing to say."

"Not any less true, though."

Cyrus tugged on Bryce's pant leg and held up a toy locomotive. "Hey, Bryce, you want to see my new train? The wheels work."

Bryce took it from him and studied its elaborate detail. Tiny metal rods connected to the wheels slid pistons in and out as the wheels turned. It was fascinating and called into question the whole concept of "size" and "scale." In a way, so did Morgan's paintings.

"Um . . . you can play with it, if you want," Cyrus said.

Bryce realized he'd been monopolizing the wonder. He handed it back and patted Cyrus's head. "I've been playing piano. I wrote a song. Do you want to hear it?"

"Is it a train song?"

"No. Morgan says it sounds Siamese."

"What's that?"

"Come on and I'll show you."

"I can't today. I've got to go home and play with my train set. We just came to get some records. Do you have anything new?"

"A whole box full. Let's look." Bryce and Cyrus went over to the record section and began pulling out discs.

Abigail patted her hair where the melted snow had made it damp. "I'll be glad when spring comes. I miss the color green."

"Green?" Jack said. "There's more green in Central Park than I saw in New Mexico all last year."

"That can't be true. Isn't New York all buildings?"

Jack nodded. "Don't get me wrong, I love it here. But it's greener back east. You should visit the Catskills sometime."

"The mountains here are beautiful," Morgan said. "And better light."

Cyrus and Bryce joined them, carrying armloads of records. "We're ready to go, Mama."

"Cyrus, you can't buy all those records. I said you could have *two*."

"Oh, you don't have to buy them," Bryce said. "We're going to take them to your house to tickle our ears while we play trains."

"You are, are you? Listen, Bryce, I know what you have on your mind, but we can't. Penelope and Walter are in Santa Fe. Besides, tomorrow is a school day, so Cyrus will be with us tonight."

"You're misreading my intentions." He could hardly blame her for not recognizing the draw of innocence that had just overcome him. "Cyrus has reminded me what it's like to be a child. We really *are* going to your house to play with his trains."

"Please, Mommy," Cyrus said. "I've no one to play with this afternoon."

Abigail rubbed her forehead. "All right. But Bryce, I'm not going to be charmed into changing my mind. You know Rebecca is living with us, so when Cyrus goes to bed, I'm absolutely kicking you out."

"That will be fine, I promise."

Bryce set the records down, put on his coat, and picked them back up. Abigail and Cyrus said goodbye and took Bryce with them. As Jack and Morgan watched them go, the waterfall in Morgan's painting began to overflow the frame. When the water met the floor it froze into a pond where snowflakes wearing tiny figure skates glided and whirled around the ice.

CHAPTER 36

Abigail unlocked her front door. Bryce and Cyrus pushed past her and rushed into the parlor. Bryce cranked the Gramophone and put a record on while Cyrus fetched the rest of his train set. Bryce joined him on the floor and the two literally began to play. And Bryce seemed to be genuinely involved and enjoying himself. Whenever a song ended, one or the other would change the record and wind the crank. They'd brought a lot of records.

Abigail left for a while and returned with a mug of hot cocoa for Cyrus and hot toddies for the adults. When she handed Bryce his, he shook his head. "I'll have what he's having, if you don't mind."

"That's a first." She went to the kitchen and came back with another cup of chocolate.

After an hour, Abigail grew bored watching them. "You really did come to play with Cyrus. I thought you were just . . . Anyway, I'm amazed. I've never seen a grown man get down on the floor and play with children. Not even Walter."

"Well, then, they do not know what they were missing."

"We're having fun." Cyrus pushed his train around the track. "Whoo, whoo."

"I see you are. I'm going to start supper."

Bryce looked up. "What? Oh, okay, bye. Cyrus, you should see Grand Central Terminal—dozens of tracks with trains coming and going all the time."

Abigail went into the kitchen and fired up the kerosene stove to sear some pork chops. She kept an ear cocked toward the music and laughter coming from the living room.

She moved a pot of potatoes she'd prepared earlier onto one burner, set a frying pan on another, and spooned in some lard and watched it sizzle. The New Yorkers had certainly spiced up her life since they arrived, and not just in bed. They brought a different outlook on life, one that was a pleasant contrast to the practical sheep farmers, cattlemen and shopkeepers who represented the male sex here. There was an innocence and optimism to them—even before Bryce began playing in earnest with her son.

She became aware that the needle of the Gramophone had gotten stuck on one of the songs, and the same phrase had been repeating for some time. Cyrus and Bryce were laughing pretty hard.

She turned off the flame under the frying pan and stepped back into the dining room just as Rebecca came downstairs.

Rebecca walked over and looked at the Gramophone. "Do you like it stuck in the groove? Don't you like records that go smooth?"

Cyrus giggled. Bryce gave her a dopey smile. "It's like a chant."

Rebecca lifted the needle off the record. "Chants are soothing. This is . . . disconcerting."

The silence was abrupt, broken a moment later by Abigail. "I'm sorry, Reverend. Were the boys disturbing you? I'll have supper ready shortly."

"Oh, did I forget to tell you? I'm dining at the Wentworth's tonight. I was just leaving."

Well, they'd need one less pork chop.

"Dress warm," Bryce said. "The snowflakes are still dancing."

"The what? Oh, is it still snowing?"

"It was when we came home," Abigail said. "Do you want to borrow the carriage? The mare's not hitched up, but I'm sure Bryce would do it for you."

"No, I can't," Bryce said.

"Thank you, but I was going to walk, anyway." Rebecca bundled up and departed.

Abigail frowned. "Bryce, you were rather rude to the reverend. You should have hitched up the buggy for her."

Bryce stared at the floor. "No, I really couldn't. I don't know how."

"You're joking." Hitching a single, compliant horse into harness was something Walter's kids could do.

"Honest, I don't. I grew up on Park Avenue. The only thing my family taught me how to do was ask the doorman to call for a hansom."

"You rode with the Rough Riders. Surely they taught you to handle horses."

"Nah, I was a foot soldier. We marched up San Juan Hill stepping in Roosevelt's horseshit."

"Bryce! Language."

"Sorry, Cyrus."

"All right, *children*, pick up your trains and get washed up for supper."

"Not yet, Mommy."

"School tomorrow, Cyrus. Wash, supper, bed."

They ate together, and afterwards, Abigail tucked Cyrus into bed. When she came back downstairs Bryce was waiting on the couch in the parlor.

"I meant what I said at the store, Bryce. You can't stay. We can't even fool around. No telling when Rebecca will be back."

"I understand, and I won't try anything. Just sit. We'll talk."

Abigail sat next to him and smoothed her skirt.

"The Indians aren't savages, like people think, you know," Bryce said. "They have an ancient and powerful medicine, unknown to the white man, that opens doors of consciousness more effectively than any other substance."

This was not the conversation she was expecting from Bryce. Normally he struck her as charming and shallow. Fun, but all surface with no depth. "What are you talking about?"

"Becoming aware of awareness. You have to try it."

"Try what?"

"Peyote. It gives you visions—knowledge of what lies beneath ordinary reality."

"Give me an example."

"I'm just coming down from it right now. I'll try to describe what I see."

"Wait. You're under the influence of that stuff now?"

Bryce nodded. "Morgan, Jack, and I took some this morning. There isn't any left, but I'll get more so you can try it."

"I don't know if I want to. But at least now I understand why you three were acting so strangely."

"Strange and wonderful. Simply hearing about an extraordinary vision is not having it; you only have the description of it, not the experience. Once we were lovers—"

"More than once. But we're done with that."

Bryce's smile faded. "I know. But what I'm saying is that during the act the man becomes a steed spurred by a mad charioteer, driven into your depths, to fuse our ecstasies."

"That's very poetic."

Bryce shook his head. "But we are doomed to separate experiences, for we are each, within our own mind, perceiving individual bodily sensations."

Abigail stroked his cheek. She had the impression he wasn't going to make much sense. But it was at least more interesting nonsense than when men drank whiskey. "That doesn't mean they weren't nice."

"No, but it means we live isolated realities . . . In fact, nothing we say is real. Language is an invention of man, and nothing he says is true . . . Nothing I've ever said is true."

Bryce was silent a long time. The house creaked, but Bryce didn't speak. Finally, he wept. "Abigail, I am a terrible person."

She brushed tears from his cheeks, like she would Cyrus. "No, you're not."

"I am. I'm a compulsive liar."

She sat back. "What?"

"I lied about everything. I never took care of our problems with the Irish back east; I just let Jack and Morgan think I did. I was never in the Rough Riders, never been to Cuba, never even shot a gun before I came to Taos. I didn't play piano in New Orleans or meet Scott Joplin, I just liked the music."

"But Bryce, you described your military experience in detail—where you trained, where the Rough Riders shipped out from and landed, where the battles were, how the riflemen wore their hats."

"When I grew up, Roosevelt was the police commissioner of New York City. Papers were full of stories about Teddy back them. When the war started, and he said he was forming a company to go fight the Spanish, I tried to join up. But I never got beyond signing the roster. Hell, I couldn't even ride a horse. I already told you that. After the war, Roosevelt wrote a series of articles in Scribner Magazine. That's where I got my information."

"Why, Bryce?"

"I wanted to do things my family wouldn't let me do. When I couldn't, I just made up stories that I'd done those things, and when I told others, people loved my tales. I loved entertaining. The lies got more convoluted. Then, we left all that behind and came west, where my life could be whatever I wanted it to be."

"But you didn't leave it behind," she said. "You brought it into Jack and Morgan's life. They've built a business and relationships in this town all based on your lies. You can't imagine how proud they are of you. How they bragged to everyone about you before you came."

Bryce started to sob. "I know. But what do I do?"

Abigail lifted his chin until he looked her in the eye. "Start by telling your partners."

Bryce nodded. She let go of his chin and he fell sideways, laying his head in her lap. She stroked his hair and his cries grew softer.

The front door opened. Rebecca came past the parlor and stopped. "Oh, sorry, I saw the light."

Abigail lifted Bryce's head from her lap and pushed him upright. "Sit up, Bryce. Time to go home."

Bryce stood and moved slowly toward the coat rack. He put his coat and hat on, as if both were made of lead, and reached for the door handle.

Abigail turned the knob and opened the door for him. "Tell them, Bryce. Tell them tonight."

"Good night, Bryce," Rebecca said.

"Good night, Reverend. Good night, Abigail, and thank you for listening."

She closed the door behind him, and Rebecca went to her room.

Abigail returned to the parlor and began putting Cyrus's train set into the toy box. Even though her affair with Bryce was finished, she couldn't keep the Reverend as a houseguest much longer. His poetic speech about steeds reminded her she'd eventually need to find another charioteer. And she couldn't do that with a preacher living upstairs.

CHAPTER 37

The following Tuesday, Abigail arrived early for the book club meeting and discovered Bryce setting the table. "Bryce, I'm surprised to see you."

"That's what the blind carpenter said—when he picked up his hammer and saw."

"Did you tell Jack and Morgan what you told me Sunday night?"

"That I lie like a rug and they should beat me like a carpet? Yeah. They didn't though."

Abigail shook her head. "Is Jack here?"

"In the back, making tea."

Abigail went to the kitchen and found Jack staring into a kettle of water on the stove. "You know what they say about a watched pot?"

Jack looked up. "Oh, hi. I'm testing that theory. In the interest of science."

"I thought you were making tea for the book club meeting."

"That too. I can do multiple things at once."

"Can you stand with your arms out?" Abigail opened her purse and removed a cloth measuring tape, a notepad, and a pencil. She closed in on Jack and wrapped the tape around his waist. "Come on, raise your arms." She moved the tape higher and measured his chest.

"What are you doing?"

"Taking your measurements." She wet the tip of the pencil with her tongue and wrote figures on her notepad.

"What for?"

Abigail moved behind Jack and measured the length of his arm, from the center of his shoulder to his cuff. "I'm surprised you still have Bryce around. He's such a . . . bullshitter, I believe, is the only word for it."

"Morgan and I aren't ones to hold a grudge. We've all stretched the truth sometimes. Mark Twain made up funny stories about life on the Mississippi and the old west. Not true, but entertaining. What's the difference?"

"The difference is, Twain doesn't tell everyone the stories are true and involve other people in his lies."

Abigail wrapped the tape around Jack's neck and pulled it.

"That's too tight. Why are you doing this, anyway?"

"I'm ordering you a new suit. The Hoffsteaders hold a spring soirée every May. It's a dress-up affair for which I need an escort. Thank you for volunteering."

"I'm flattered, but I'm not a 'spring formal' kind of guy. What about Bryce? He was bred for Park Avenue galas."

"Was he? Or is that something else he made up?"

"No, that part is true. I've seen it."

Abigail shook her head. "What if he disappears at the last minute or shows up on peyote blathering about the underlying unity of the cosmos? No, I can't chance it. You've proven you're reliable."

"Why not Morgan, then?"

"You're taller, and in the right suit you'll look downright handsome." Abigail kneeled in front of him. "Now, don't get any ideas. I'm just measuring your inseam."

When she had her measurement, Abigail stood and brushed the wrinkles from her skirt. By then the unwatched water had come to a furious boil. Jack turned off the burner and filled the teapot.

She heard the other ladies arriving and went to join them. This week the group was reading *Sister Carrie* by Theodore Dreiser.

"This book is quite scandalous—vulgar, immoral, risqué," Ida Hoffsteader said. "I liked it."

Faye Wentworth shook her head. "I pity poor Carrie. How many men was she mistress to?"

"But she becomes a celebrated actress," Ida said. "Theatrical types have had dubious morals for . . . well, forever."

Abigail bit her lip and let the other ladies carry the conversation——her own life was a little too close to Carrie's. When they had thoroughly worked over the questionable character of Carrie Meeber, Chicago, and big city moral standards in general, the meeting broke up. As the ladies were leaving, Peaches came in.

"You've come a day early," Morgan said. "Your meeting's tomorrow."

"I was looking for Bryce."

Abigail raised her eyebrows.

"It's something for class . . . a report."

"A school report?" Abigail said. "You sure you want Bryce's help?"

Peaches nodded.

"He's in the back," Morgan said.

"What's your report on?" Abigail said.

"Uh . . . Um . . . Mozart." Peaches disappeared into the kitchen and returned with Bryce, leading him through the connecting door to the church. She smiled at Abigail and Morgan. "I'm just going to close this so we won't bother anybody."

Considering it was Bryce, Peaches would be better off leaving it open. But even he wouldn't try anything in a church, would he?

Abigail was the last to leave. As she said goodbye, Morgan saw the stage-coach pull up, so he grabbed his coat and walked over to see if they had any mail. They did—bills from both Victor and Columbia. He came back to the store and slit them open.

The overdue amounts staggered him. He'd never told Jack and Bryce the records they'd been selling had been obtained on credit. Now, it was time to pay.

He opened their strong box and counted the cash on hand—twice. It was nowhere near enough. They'd been paying Abigail rent and contributing the usual amounts to the saloons, but business had been good. There should be more money in the box. Perhaps Jack and Bryce had tucked some of the profits in the bank while he was away.

In any case, they'd have to moderate their expenditures, at least until their debts were cleared. He put the bills in the bottom of the strong box and locked it.

CHAPTER 38

Spring rains that began, appropriately enough, on April Fool's day showed no signs of stopping. The roads turned to soupy mud. The Ladies Afternoon Tea Book Club had become preoccupied with church problems. In the months since Reverend Sullivan's arrival, the Catholics had closed ranks against her ideology. The local padre, Father Ignacio began featuring her in his homilies—women could not be priests, so she was a heretic and a fraud. Discontent between the Catholics and Protestants arose, and the ladies formed various subcommittees to figure out what to do about it.

The combination of poor roads and religious strife was having a detrimental effect on the emporium's business. Catholics were told not to go anywhere near the Protestant church, so having the store next door cost them half the town as customers. Book sales to the Afternoon Tea group fell off as the ladies committed less time to reading and more to religious politics. The Young Ladies Society still met regularly after school on Wednesdays and Fridays, but the girls spent their meetings playing records with Bryce and dancing with each other. This meant their mothers weren't buying them books. Unfortunately, the girls' delight in music didn't help sales, since they had no money of their own to buy tunes they fancied.

The New World Emporium had been envisioned as a source of culture, a glimpse into the future. Now it was becoming a place with entertaining meetings, but too few sales to show for it.

Still, Bryce tried to be optimistic. "Jack, Morgan, before you arrived, there were only two things in this town you could do with your evenings—get drunk or get laid. On a good night you might do both. We created a third alternative—you could have fun because we're good-time music kind of guys."

Jack snorted. "We wanted to herald the twentieth century, and instead we're running a tea shop and social circle."

"Now, Jack, Bryce has a point. New ideas take a while to settle in, and we've not even been here a year. We'll drag this town into the modern era yet."

"Not by reigniting a religious conflict that's been going on for 400 years," Jack said.

With that, Jack and Morgan said farewell and left him to set up for the Young Ladies Society.

Bryce's partners no longer attended the Young Ladies' group because he got all the attention. Also, letting him run the meetings gave Morgan time to paint and Jack to do . . . other things. Things Bryce suspected had to do with Abigail. Not that he would have objected even if it had been his place. The partners had a long history of keeping company with the same woman —not at the same time of course. But it was dead certain Jack knew he'd have several hours every Wednesday and Friday when Bryce couldn't leave the store.

At the Friday afternoon meeting, the Gramophone was cranked, a half-dozen girls were dancing with each other, and Peaches with Bryce. Then the shop door opened and in the doorway stood Mrs. Romero, fierce as a New Mexican jaguar. "What in the world is going on here?"

Scott Joplin continued to play in the background.

Mrs. Romero yanked Peaches away from Bryce. "Mr. Holloway!" She spied her second daughter near the Gramophone. "Cherry, turn that devil music off."

Cherry picked up the needle, and the abrupt silence caused the remaining girls to flock together, leaving Peaches, Bryce, and Cherry stranded before Mrs. Romero's wrath.

"Father Ignacio warned the parish that there were evil doings at the church next door, so I came to see what kind of influence the Protestants were having on the girls' book club. And what do I find? No book club at all. Just a disreputable man leading girls into hooliganism."

"We were just dancing, Mama," Peaches said.

"That wasn't proper dance music. I wasted good money on books for this club to help you become cultured ladies of society and I find you playing records instead."

"But, Mama," Cherry said, "we have been reading—Jane Austen, Edith Wharton, Charlotte Brontë."

"When? Last fall? This spring? What have you read lately? Or have you just been coming here for this, this . . . ragtime?"

"Now, hold on," Bryce said.

"I will not hold on." Mrs. Romero whirled on the rest of the girls, who huddled like guinea hens facing a bobcat. "I don't know what your mothers think you're doing here after school, but when I tell them what I found, I'm sure it will shock even a Protestant."

"Why is music any less cultural than literature?" Bryce said.

"Brahms, Chopin, certainly, but that wasn't what I heard, Mr. Holloway. I was under the impression Morgan was overseeing this book club. I have no confidence in your influence on young minds. Peaches, Cherry, you're through with this Young Ladies Society business."

"No!" Peaches edged toward Bryce. "I'm not quitting."

"Don't be impudent. You'll do as I say."

"I'm eighteen now, and I can do what I want."

"You may have had a birthday, but you're still in school and living under my roof, so you will respect your mother." She grabbed Peaches and Cherry by their arms. "You girls are coming with me."

In the wake of the Romeros' departure the other girls made a hasty exit. The Young Ladies Book Society may have just disintegrated, but this was only Friday. Bryce would wait to see if anyone showed up next Wednesday. No need to worry Jack and Morgan until he knew for sure.

* * *

Saturday, Rebecca came in. "Good morning, Morgan."

Morgan set his cup in the saucer. "Good day, Rebecca. There's a fresh pot, if you'd like a cup."

"No thanks, I had coffee at Abigail's."

"How can I help you?"

"I was wondering if you had any books on Celtic beliefs or lore."

"I don't think so. Tell me what you're looking for, maybe it's in another book."

"The ancient pagan Celts, and later, Irish Christians, had a saying that heaven and earth are only three feet apart—just out of reach—but there are places where that distance is even shorter. They call them thin places, and I wanted to research them."

Morgan took a sip of his coffee. "What's a thin place?"

"I don't know exactly. It was a legend from the old country Granddad Fitzpatrick used to tell us. Ancient people, especially in Ireland, Britain, and Wales, believed certain places had ephemeral or mystical qualities that made spiritual experiences more likely."

"I've never heard of it, but there are places near Taos that . . . well, I might almost believe it of them."

"Granddad said thin places aren't perceived with our five senses. Experiencing them goes beyond—" Rebecca's throat tightened. Her grandfather could speak about thin places without getting choked up, but just thinking about them was making her emotional. "They say in thin places, one catches a glimpse of the divine, the transcendent, the infinite."

"Surely, such places aren't limited to Ireland. There must be thin places in America, too."

"I don't see why not. The Irish might be particularly blessed in other ways, but God is omnipresent, after all."

"There's a place I found in the mountains that inspires me to paint—where I almost see into a world beyond this one."

"What do you mean?"

"I'm not religious, but it's a place where you sense . . . Dare I say it? The divine. I don't mean Moses on Mount Sinai, burning bush and all, but *something* about the place makes your thoughts fall away, until only a luminous quality remains."

Rebecca's eyes widened. "That sounds like just what I'm looking for. Can you describe that something?"

"It's difficult to put in words. There is a mysterious hum, and the quality of light affects you, like the presence of an inscrutable power."

Morgan's words made her spine shiver. "I need to go there."

"It'd be too far to hike in a dress. Perhaps we can borrow Abigail's carriage one day."

"I wouldn't want to impose, she's too generous as it is. But if this is really a thin place . . . Granddad said thin places not only transcend the senses but also transcend the boundaries of time and space. While you're there, time seems to stand still, and there is a sense of the infinite."

"That's interesting—sounds a bit like Bryce. Do you think this transcendence is strictly an effect of location, or might an extraordinary event produce temporary thinness in an otherwise ordinary setting?"

"I suppose, but I don't know much. That's why I was looking for a book."

"I'm sure we don't have anything in the store. I could order something, but I'd need a title or author."

"I'll wire my granddad and ask."

"He may be able to send you a book from Boston quicker than if I order it."

Rebecca raised her eyebrows. "Yes, but then you'd lose the sale."

"That doesn't matter, as long as you get what you need."

"You're not a very good businessman, are you?"

"You're not the first woman to tell me that. Anyway, if your grandfather sends you the information about thin places, let me know. I'd be interested to learn more."

"I might give a sermon on it. You should come."

Morgan toyed with his cup and saucer. "Church? I'm not sure about that."

"Well, at least consider it. In any case, I definitely want to visit your thin place."

CHAPTER 39

April showers continued into the following week and business remained slow. The mail brought final due notices from the Columbia and Victor companies. Morgan put them in the strongbox with the others. He'd checked with the bank, and the emporium did not have an account there.

Wednesday, none of the girls showed up for the Young Ladies Book Society. Morgan and Jack returned at closing time. "All the girls gone?" Morgan said.

Bryce looked away. "You might say that." He took the tea no one had come to drink outside and poured it on the ground.

Morgan recognized Bryce's evasive tone of voice, but he didn't have time to deal with that now. When Bryce came back in, Morgan locked the door and put the strongbox on the table. "Have a seat, friends."

Bryce eyed the strongbox. "We having a meeting?"

Morgan nodded. "We are."

"If we're closed for the day, I need a drink," Jack said.

"No, stay," Morgan said. "We'll go out later."

Jack walked away. "No need to go out. I've got a bottle in back." He returned with the whiskey and three glasses. "To get things rolling, it always helps to grease the axles." He poured three drinks, drank his in a single gulp, and refilled it.

Morgan took a smaller sip. "Make it last, Jack. Money's going to be tight."

Bryce chewed his lip. "Tighter than a tick."

Morgan looked up. "What do you know?"

"We've lost the girls' book club."

"How?" Jack said.

"Mrs. Romero paid a surprise visit last Friday and caught Peaches and me —"

Morgan jumped up. "We told you to leave the Romero girls alone."

"Dancing, we were just dancing. But Mrs. Romero was in high dudgeon. Well, higher than usual. Said she was going to pull her girls out and tell the other mothers. Which I assume she did."

Jack's face turned an unhealthy shade of purple. He undid his belt buckle, whipped his belt off, wrapped it around his hand, and strode toward Bryce.

Morgan moved to intervene—bloodshed wouldn't help, satisfying as it might be—but Jack brushed past both of them, stormed out the door, and thrashed the hitching rail with his belt. He continued to lash it, cursing all the while, until he'd poured out the last of his anger. He came back in, and when he spoke, his voice had an unnatural calm. "Bryce, when were you going to tell us?"

"Jesus, Jack, no reason to overreact. I didn't know if she'd really do it. I thought I'd wait until today and see if anyone came. No reason to yell 'Fire' if there isn't any smoke."

"How were we ever going to pay the money back with you chasing away business?" Jack said.

Pay the money back? Morgan looked at Jack. "You two already know?"

"We've been aware for a while now."

"Well . . . let's look at the situation."

Morgan opened the strongbox, stacked the money on the table, and retrieved some papers from the bottom of the box. "We're in deep trouble.

I've counted the money three times and there isn't nearly enough. At first, I assumed you'd put some in the bank while I was gone, but I talked to Mr. Hoffsteader. Apparently that didn't happen."

Jack tipped over a stack of gold eagles and counted them. "There's enough here to pay rent and buy more inventory. The problem is, who are we going to sell to? Being next to the church has tarred us. Father Ignacio is driving the Catholics away. And now, Bryce has lost us the Young Ladies Society. That might cost us their mothers' business, too."

Morgan shook his head and restacked the money. "I don't see how you figure we can buy more. There isn't enough here to pay what we owe."

"Owe?" Jack said. "Sneed said we were square."

"Sneed?" Morgan said. "What would he know about it? I'm talking about Victor and Columbia. We're so overdue, they're cutting us off. No more shipments until we're paid up. Cash up front, after that." He pointed to the papers on the table.

"What are you talking about?" Bryce said.

Oh, Shit. "I thought you knew. You both said you knew money had to be paid."

Jack picked up the notice, skimmed it, and gave a low whistle. "Wow! This is serious money."

Morgan handed him the other bill. "That's only half of it. Here's what we owe Columbia Records."

Jack accepted it and passed the first one to Bryce.

"How would we know this?" Bryce said. "You never said you were buying the records on credit."

"I've been putting the bills in the strongbox regularly. From what you two said, I thought you'd seen them."

"Nah. I never look at that stuff in the bottom," Jack said. "We just take out what we need for beer each evening and lock it back up."

Terrific. "Well, we've all been guilty of that. Drinking our profits and never worrying about what we spent."

Bryce laughed. "What did you think, Morgan? Bury the bills under the gold and they'd get paid by the money fairy?"

"Honestly, I thought we'd built up a surplus. I don't know what happened to it."

Bryce winked at Jack. "Easy to come, hard to go."

"Shut up, Bryce," Jack said. "Morgan, what I don't understand is how you got them to extend us credit."

"Well, Columbia was just starting up and eager for any business they could get. At Victor, I made the salesman feel guilty about the way they treated us with the Deitwiler deal. But Jack, you knew I didn't take any store money with me. How else would I come back with a Gramophone and four cases of records?"

Jack shrugged. "Sold the paintings you took with you?"

"I told you I left those with an agent who I'm still waiting to hear from." Morgan paced around the room. He picked up a silver and turquoise neck-lace. "Bryce, would your Indians mind if we shipped their consignment pieces back east? These might sell better in New York."

"Ship them anywhere you want."

"Won't the Indians assume we sold them and want their money?"

"They've already got their money."

"What are you talking about?"

"I paid them when they delivered the jewelry."

Jack jumped in. "Without asking us?"

"Ask you when? Morgan was out of town and you were off with red-haired Fanny. You leave me to run the store, and I'm going to make some decisions on my own. Besides, they needed the money more than we did. These people are so poor they have to pick up loose tobacco out of the dirt to fill their pipes. We should feel honored that we could help them."

Morgan threw down the necklace. "How much did you give them? I thought a lot of money was missing—"

"All right, maybe I was a bit generous with my payments."

"Because you're enamored with them."

"They may be poor as titmice, but they're rich in spirit-world knowledge."

"Bryce, how much?"

"Hey! I'm not the one who lost all our money."

"What are you talking about?"

Bryce looked at Jack. Jack glared back.

"Sneed," Bryce said.

Morgan shook his head like he had a mosquito in his ear. "Sneed?"

"While you were back east, Sneed and two of his boys came in and strong-armed us. Said Jack owed him for Fanny and emptied the money box."

"And you let him get away with it?"

Bryce stretched his hands apart. "He held a knife this long to Jack's throat."

"That's robbery," Morgan said.

"Sneed didn't see it that way, and I'm not sure a New Mexico jury would, either. Jack owed him for Fanny's services. Sneed took the money and said Jack was paid up." Bryce smirked. "As you'd say in Yiddish, it's the shtup'n we get for the shtup'n Jack got."

"I didn't owe him shit," Jack said. "Fanny was in love. Besides, we made the money back. Only, we didn't know we were selling records we didn't really own."

Morgan looked from one man to the other. "I can't believe the two of you never told me where our money went."

"Listen, I never made any deal with Indians," Jack said.

"No, but you bought lights and generators and stereoscopes that never sold."

"You were party to the stereoscope decision."

"Let's just all get off our high horses," Bryce said. "I never explained the jewelry, Jack said nothing about Sneed, and Morgan didn't tell us he put us in debt. Face it. Nobody told everybody everything. Some partnership we are."

Jack poured them fresh drinks and lifted his glass for a toast. "Partners, still. We'll figure something out."

CHAPTER 40

The partners had agreed to meet the next morning for coffee before the store opened. Morgan arrived late, suit freshly pressed, shoes shined, and smelling of lilac water.

Jack sniffed the air. "Is there a funeral I didn't hear about?"

"Besides ours, you mean?" Bryce said.

"No. I got an idea. I don't know why we didn't think of it sooner—the bank."

Bryce drew an imaginary gun from its imaginary holster. "Stick-up?"

Morgan shook his head. "Last fall, I painted the Hoffsteaders' family portrait. He and I became pretty good friends. I'm going to the bank this morning and ask him for a loan, enough to pay off our suppliers and buy more records and books. We can keep this place afloat."

"Genius," Jack said.

Morgan checked his pocket watch. "I'm going there now. I want to be the first person in his office when the bank opens. One of you take my shift this morning."

Mr. Hoffsteader shook Morgan's hand, welcomed him into his office, and invited him to sit. "How's business?"

"Great! So good in fact that I've come to ask for a loan."

"A loan?"

"Yes. We need some short-term cash to restock our inventory and expand into other lines."

Hoffsteader furrowed his brow. "A loan? You don't even have an account here."

"Well, we've been meaning to open one since we got here. Maybe we can do that right now."

"You definitely should. How much would you like to deposit?"

"Oh, let's put in the full amount of the loan and then we'll draw it out as needed to pay our suppliers."

Hoffsteader smiled. "It doesn't work like that. You open an account by depositing some cash. The loan is a separate matter. But yes, if the bank approves your loan, we can credit it to your account. How much were you going to deposit?"

Morgan tried to remember how much was in the cash box, and estimate what they could spare. It looked like they'd have to spend money to get money. "How much do folks usually deposit?"

Hoffsteader scratched his head. "Have you never had a bank account before?"

Morgan gave the slightest shake of his head. "Like I said, we intended to."

"As you should. A prosperous business can't keep its profits secure in the store. Some scoundrel might rob you."

Was Hoffsteader hinting he knew about and Jack's dustup with Sneed? How could he? Morgan smoothed his mustache. "We'll definitely open an account. Now, will we be able start drawing on the loan today? There are some record companies back east wanting to be paid, and we need to place another order."

"Well, first I need to review your books. I assume you brought them with you."

"Um . . . books?" They had shelves of them.

Hoffsteader slid a pencil behind his ear, looked at Morgan, and tapped his fingernails on the desk. "Your ledger?"

"We . . . don't have one."

"You what?"

"We just file invoices and such in a box. Do you want me to get them?"

The banker let out an exasperated sigh. "Yes, please."

Morgan rushed to the store, grabbed the pile of invoices, pulled out the overdue notices, and left those behind. When Morgan returned to the bank, Hoffsteader had a blank, lined ledger page on his desk. He accepted the stack of papers and began copying figures into one of the columns, writing in tiny, neat numerals. When he reached the last bill, he handed them back. "Now, the receipts."

"Receipts? Oh, we don't give receipts. Never had a customer ask for one."

"Okay . . . How do you keep track of sales?"

"By the amount of money in the cashbox."

Hoffsteader's jaw dropped. "This whole time? How do you know what inventory has sold and what to reorder?"

"We eyeball it. The store isn't that big."

"That isn't proper business practice." Hoffsteader labeled the columns and turned the ledger sheet so Morgan could read it. "You need to keep records. This is called double-entry bookkeeping. It's been around for five hundred years. Write your income—sales—in one column and your expenses in the other. Do this every day. I'm surprised you didn't know this."

"This is our first venture."

Hoffsteader held up the ledger page by its corner. "Well, the bank can't base a loan on this tidbit of information."

Morgan tugged his lower lip. "I thought we were friends."

"Look, I like you Morgan, and you're an excellent painter. But this is business. I can't make a loan without knowing how big the risk is, and you and your partners haven't kept proper records."

Morgan hung his head. He knew Hoffsteader was waiting for him to leave, but he didn't have anywhere else to turn. "Isn't there a way?"

"It's not my money, Morgan. It belongs to the bank and the trustees require collateral."

Morgan waited.

Hoffsteader sighed. "This is going to involve some work." He handed Morgan several blank ledger pages. "Take inventory. Write the name of every item in your store in the first column. Then count them and write the quantity in the second. Next, put the retail price in the third, and then look at your invoices and find out what it cost you. The difference will be the net value of your assets. When you're done, bring it back, and I'll see how much we can loan you."

The three partners worked through the night. Morgan took the sheets back to Hoffsteader in the morning. The banker studied them and compared them to the list of debts he'd prepared the previous day. Morgan could tell he wasn't pleased.

"You don't have any collateral at all. Most of what you list as inventory hasn't been paid for. You don't own it. The store's debts far exceed its assets."

"I know. That's why we need the loan."

"But as I explained yesterday—"

"No, listen, please, you never got to St. Louis before the Fair closed. If you had, you would better understand the emporium's potential. This isn't just the beginning of a new century; this is the beginning of a whole new world. In fact, that's why we named our store the New World Emporium. There are all kinds of wonderful things being invented every day. We just need to stay afloat long enough to realize our vision. Taos is going to be a better place because of us."

"That's an admirable ideal, and I admire you for investing in it. But the bank needs tangible security."

"What about the silver jewelry? That's paid in full. Surely, it counts as a tangible asset."

Hoffsteader looked at the inventory sheet. "It does. But its total value isn't close to what you owe your creditors. If you don't pay them, they can take everything and you won't be able to repay the bank."

Morgan shook his head. "I really don't understand. We've brought art, music, literature, and new ideas here and there's more to come. Somehow Taos ought to lend us some help."

Hoffsteader tapped the ledger with his pencil. "There is one way."

"What!"

"Find someone to cosign the note. You've painted portraits for all the wealthy families and made a lot of friends. See if one of them will act as your guarantor."

"Then the bank will give us the loan?"

Hoffsteader nodded. "As long as the man owns property and isn't too deep in debt himself."

"What about you?"

Hoffsteader coughed. "Not me. I couldn't possibly. I have a family. Try one of the older ranchers or another businessman."

* * *

Thursday, before the ladies book club met, Morgan told his partners the banker's decision, and that no loan would be forthcoming. They'd have to work their way out of debt themselves. He didn't tell them he'd approached Abigail about cosigning and she'd refused.

"If you default, I'm on the hook for everything. I love you guys, but I can't risk Cyrus's future."

Jack shrugged. "Arthur Manby is building a nineteen-room house. His contractor's looking for carpenters who can do finish work. The two of you can handle the store between you. I'm going to take a job over there to help pay off what we owe."

Morgan nodded. "We can manage without you. Bryce, why don't we return the jewelry, and get our money back from the Indians?"

"I thought you said it would sell back east?"

"I said it *might*. Even if it does sell, shipping it there and waiting for payment will take a while. We need money now. Let's just give it back."

"The Indians don't have any money. They barely make it a day on a dime. What we paid them is long spent." Bryce went to the kitchen and got the coffee pot. He refilled their cups and returned it to the stove. When he came back, he said, "Poor as they are, there is something magnificent hidden in their ancient knowledge. I am really drawn to finding it. I was lying in bed last night ruminating about it, and I've decided I don't want to do this anymore."

"Do what?" Jack said.

"The emporium, the ladies' teas—"

"That's crap," Jack said. "You got us into this mess as much as anyone here, and now you want to bail out? Get a job, show up for your shifts, help pay our bills. Grow up."

Bryce shook his head. "Look around you. Can either of you honestly say this is the grand emporium you envisioned when we were standing in the Palace of Fine Arts pavilion at the World's Fair?"

"No, it's not," Morgan said. "But we've lived off it nearly a year, and that's pretty good considering how undercapitalized we were."

"True, but I've lost interest in commerce. What I really want to do is go on a vision quest."

Jack snorted. "I've read lots of books about knights' quests, but I've never heard mention of that kind."

"I've decided to become a shaman. The medicine men say I have to have a vision first, so I'm going to go seek one."

"Sounds like an excuse for you to stick us with the work while you go take peyote with your friends."

Bryce grinned. "I'm sure peyote will be involved. But seriously, I'm just weighing you down. Why don't you buy me out? Then you'll only have two mouths to feed, and you'll each get a bigger split."

"We couldn't buy you out even if we wanted to," Morgan added. "We're strapped, remember?"

"Besides," Jack said, "Hoffsteader says the emporium owes more than it has. Your share is in the negative."

"Oh hell, shamans don't need money. They're exploring worlds where money doesn't matter. You and Jack can keep the money. Just let me walk away."

"No, that wouldn't be fair to you, Bryce." Morgan spied the jewelry—the only fully owned asset they had at the moment. "We can't buy you out with cash, but why don't you take the silver. If you can't sell it, you can always melt it down. It's worth something."

"That's a generous offer, but I can't carry it where I'm going, and I wouldn't want the Indians to see me with it and think I'm dishonest. Keep it here, try to sell it for me, and pay me when you do."

Morgan nodded.

"Oh, great," Jack said. "Another debt we owe—this one to you."

"Jack," Bryce said, "now you and Morgan own the store fifty-fifty."

Jack grumbled. "All right." He gave Bryce an affectionate Dutch rub with his knuckles. "Hey, buddy, we never wanted to cut you out."

"I know that. This is all my idea."

"Well, at least stay and help Morgan with the ladies' tea, today. I've got to see a man about a job."

"Sure. Hey, fellows, stake me to a few dollars traveling money, will you?"

Jack felt his pockets. "Sorry, I'm tapped out."

Morgan opened the strongbox, took out a ten-dollar gold-piece, and handed it to Bryce.

"Oh, that's too much," Bryce said.

"Better take it," Morgan said. "Money's not a sure thing around here."

CHAPTER 41

As soon as Jack applied to work on the Manby house, the contractor snapped him up and wanted him to start immediately, leaving it to Bryce and Morgan to host the Thursday afternoon tea.

The women said nothing about the dissolution of the Young Ladies Book Society, though several of their daughters had been members. They were too busy discussing books Mrs. Romero would never approve and the distressing rumors Father Ignacio kept spreading about their church.

After the ladies' meeting broke up, Bryce and Abigail went off in a corner of the store to talk. Morgan took the teapot and dishes to the kitchen. As he returned, Bryce embraced Abigail and left.

Abigail wiped her eyes. Morgan said, "I thought it was over between you and Bryce a while ago."

"It was . . . is. But I worry for him. He's been acting pretty crazy, making a lot of mistakes—giving up the store, going off to live with the natives. Aren't you worried about him taking peyote all the time?"

"Not really. Jack and I tried peyote once. It's interesting, awakens your awareness."

"Yes, but you didn't run away to go live like a pack of dogs."

"Well, you've got to understand. Bryce was never particularly well-rooted even when we lived in New York. Besides, he wants to be the first white peyote shaman. I guess there are worse things to do with your life."

Abigail shook her head. "Pueblo Indians will never tell a white man their secret religion." She patted her hair, making sure it was in place. "Let's see if Jack wants to go for a drink after work. Penelope has Cyrus. I can be late picking him up."

"Jack? I'll bet he does." Morgan locked up the store. "You're not worried about being seen drinking with two men?"

"It's suppertime. Salazar's serves food. We'll go there and no one will think anything of it."

The inside of Arthur Manby's place was a mess—stacks of boards, unfinished doorways, and bare lath walls awaiting plaster. No wonder the contractor was glad to have a skilled hand. Morgan waved to Jack. "Ready for a drink?"

Jack turned to a heavyset man with a ruddy complexion. "Boss, we about done for the day?"

"Sure, come back in the morning. You're pretty good."

Jack wiped the sawdust off himself with his kerchief and grinned at Abigail. "Hear that? I'm pretty good."

"Working for Arthur Manby, you better count your fingers at the end of the day," she said. "He has a reputation for taking advantage of people."

"Nah, I'm not working for Manby directly. He's the builder's worry."

The three of them walked to Salazar's. Morgan ordered beers for him and Jack and a red wine for Abigail.

"Bryce get off?" Jack said.

Morgan nodded. "Headed out right after the meeting."

Abigail shook her head. "Jack, why didn't you talk Bryce out of it?"

"Couldn't. Like Walter says, 'Never wrestle a pig. You both get dirty and the pig likes it.'"

Abigail laughed. "Well, if Bryce keeps on living like there's no tomorrow, one day he'll be right."

The drinks came. They clinked glasses and took a few sips.

"Tastes mighty good," Jack said. "Anyone say anything about—"

"No," Morgan said. "They were all up-in-arms over what the Catholics are saying about Rebecca and her church."

Jack looked at Abigail, but she didn't add anything. She seemed to be looking out the window, but couldn't be. Salazar's windows were covered with velvet curtains.

"That's the trouble with committees," Jack said. "Everyone takes a pee in the bathwater and then complains how it tastes."

"Sounds like something Bryce would say," Morgan said.

"Well, somebody's got to pick up the slack. Speaking of which, with Bryce gone, you're going to have to do everything. I didn't plan on Bryce leaving when I offered to take the carpentry job."

"I can handle it. We need the money."

Abigail drummed her fingers on the table.

Jack finished his beer. "Abigail, you want another glass of wine?"

"What? Oh, no, I haven't finished this one."

"I'll get you one anyway, so you'll have it when you're ready. Barkeep, another round."

Abigail waited until they had their drinks. She poured the remainder of her wine in the new one and pushed the empty glass aside. "Lot of changes today."

The men nodded. Jack drank half his beer and set the glass down.

Abigail ran her tongue over her lips and then pressed them together. She took a deep breath. "Only two months of school left, you know." She took a sip of wine. "I need to find the good Reverend a place to stay, so I can have my house back." She swiveled her glass with her fingers. "With Bryce gone, I was thinking you could maybe move back to Mrs. Romero's. She liked you. He was the only reason you got kicked out."

"We didn't get kicked out," Jack said. "We left when he did to save money."

"Okay. Well, I'll reduce your rent by whatever you have to pay Romero. That way your cost won't be any different. Those dressing rooms you're using would make a cute little apartment for Rebecca—right next to her church."

"Be real convenient for her," Jack said. "And for you, too."

Abigail smiled and took another sip of wine. "A woman has needs."

Jack laughed.

Morgan's eyes darted to Jack. "Um . . . I don't know if either of us can go back to Romero's."

"Be mighty nice," Jack said. "Home-cooked meals after work and a bath whenever I can come up with a quarter. Be heaven for me."

"You're forgetting last Friday," Morgan said

"Oh, that."

"Friday?" Abigail said.

"You tell her. I've got to use the privy," Jack left.

"Mrs. Romero caught Peaches and Bryce in the store. Dancing, he says. Anyway, she went off like a powder keg, blew up the whole Young Ladies book club. You hadn't heard? I thought sure it'd be all over town by now."

"If word was going around, I missed it. Father Ignacio spread so many derogatory things about Rebecca and the church this week, dancing at a book club might not have led the gossip parade."

"Well, she's shut down the Young Ladies Book Society, and I have no idea if she'll welcome Jack and me back or lump us together with the evil, dreaded Bryce."

"Tell her Bryce has quit the store and left town. Better yet, tell her you threw him out. That should reassure her."

"Maybe."

Abigail narrowed her eyes. "You know, last week I thought something was up when Peaches and Bryce went off to do her homework."

"Oh, I'm sure nothing like you're suggesting happened," Morgan said. "Bryce has better sense than that, even if Peaches doesn't."

"Don't be naïve. Women are not fooled, we read the subtext."

"But Bryce wouldn't—"

"It might not be up to Bryce. When a gal decides she's gonna, she's gonna. Take it from one who knows."

"Well, I hope you're mistaken about Peaches."

"Why? The girl's of age. Virginity? A bunch of hooey. Jack says Victoria Woodhull had it right thirty years ago. And I agree." She tucked a wisp of hair back into place. "Free love means a woman has the right to love whom she wants, when she wants."

"You're always so careful in public. Aren't you afraid of being overheard?"

Abigail looked around. "Who's to hear?"

Morgan shrugged. "What time are you picking up Cyrus?"

"Goodness, I forgot!" She stood up as Jack returned. Abigail put four bits on the table. "My treat. I'm buying." She took Jack's hand. "Talk to Mrs. Romero tomorrow about letting you and Morgan room there. Hopefully, she's amenable, and I can get my privacy back."

The men finished their beers and returned to the store. Jack started toward his room, but Morgan said, "Wait. Help me rearrange those boxes in back."

Morgan stacked boxes of unsold stereoscopes against the wall and attempted to do the same with the crates containing the generators. "Umph, these things are heavy. Give me a hand."

"What are you doing?"

"Making a living space for myself."

"I thought we were moving back to Mrs. Romero's."

"If she'll allow it. That's not a given."

"Oh, she will."

"Still, you're earning money and can pay her. I'm not going give her money from the store while we're trying to get out of debt."

"Now, you're making me feel guilty."

"Look, Jack, construction is hard work and you should move there if she'll let you. But that doesn't mean I have to."

"Come on, Morgan. One for all. I'll pay for us both."

Hoffsteader's comments about how they'd run their business gnawed at the back of his mind. "Thanks, Jack, but it doesn't make sense to spend more than we have to right now. You go. I'll stay."

Jack shook his head.

Morgan patted him on the shoulder. "Just until we get this place back to where we dreamed it would be."

Morgan started to disassemble some electrical contraption Jack had built.

"Wait! That's my experiment."

"Sorry, Jack, but this is where I'm going to put my cot."

"Well, just let me show it to you first." Jack closed a knife switch and cranked the generator. A metal sphere leapt about an inch in the air and began spinning in a clockwise direction. Jack kept cranking and moved the switch to the opposite side. The ball instantly reversed direction.

"What is it?"

"Electromagnetism. I remembered it from a back issue of a science maga-zine. I thought, no one's buying these generators anyway, I may as well use them for my experiments."

Morgan shook his head in wonder. "Amazing. Why don't you put it out in the store? I'm sure customers would come in just to see the novelty of it."

"All right. Where should I put it?"

"Just move some of that jewelry out of the way and set it up there."

"Thanks, Morgan. I will. We'll show Hoffsteader and his bunch that there's always something new at our emporium."

CHAPTER 42

In 1905 Easter came late, April twenty-third to be precise. Not having had a minister for Christmas services, the Protestants of Taos awaited Easter with anticipation. It would be the first major Christian holiday they could celebrate in their own church. Certainly, in previous years they'd met in someone's parlor for prayer services—they weren't pagans after all. But this year they expected full and glorious rituals and were a little upset when Reverend Sullivan didn't serve communion on Maundy Thursday.

The ladies had sewn Easter dresses for their daughters, fashioned new hats for themselves, pressed their husband's suits, and made their sons wear clean knickers. The church was so packed, chairs had to be borrowed from the emporium next door. Morgan and Jack carried them over, and Rebecca persuaded them to stay for the service.

The scene was lovely—a field of flowery hats, lilies from Ida Hoffsteader's conservatory decorated the dais. Spring light streamed from the balcony windows giving the room a fairy air. And Reverend Sullivan had traded her dark clothes for a cream-colored suit.

The music was nice, too. Familiar hymns predominated the service. Jack sang along, but Morgan seemed to be pretending to mouth the words.

After a rousing hymn that practically drowned out the piano, Rebecca stepped to the pulpit and cleared her throat. "Although my ancestors are Irish, I've never been to Ireland. Our family immigrated to America sixty years ago, two generations before I was born. Of course, growing up in Boston, my relatives and neighbors told many Celtic legends. Recently, the beautiful mountains surrounding Taos reminded me of one of them."

The door to the street creaked open and someone, late for service, slipped in and pressed herself against the wall.

"In Ireland, Scotland, Wales, and some parts of Britain, people say the earthly plane and heaven are only separated by a short distance." She held her hands apart. "Almost close enough to touch. And they hold that, in certain wild and beautiful places, the gap between heaven and earth is even thinner."

Rebecca saw a man in the second row scratch his head, quizzically.

"These are locations where the veil between heaven and earth, between our mundane lives and the spiritual realities that underlie them, becomes so thin that one can see or move into sacred spaces. Ancient peoples, even before the Celts, called these 'thin places.' The Apache proverb 'Wisdom sits in places,' suggests the natives here hold a similar belief."

Mrs. Wentworth pursed her lips. Rebecca had no doubt she was wondering what Apache had to do with Easter.

"Celtic Christians continue to believe that in certain locations God's presence is easier to see—where the line between holy and earthly seems to touch."

Rebecca glanced at Morgan. "I was discussing this with a . . . friend who suggested Taos might have thin places, too. For he'd found vistas in the mountains that seemed ephemeral, where one may experience transcendence. Then, he posed a question that set me to wondering. Are thin places merely locations in the landscape where the Creator left ajar a door in the fabric of creation that we might peek through? Or could they also be sites briefly opened by a miraculous event?"

Ida whispered to Mr. Hoffsteader, "This is a very strange Easter sermon."

"First, we must ask, are there any Biblical records of thin places? Well, the Garden of Eden jumps to mind, a place where the man and woman saw God and they conversed with ease. The line separating the heavenly realm must have been unimaginably thin. Unfortunately, after they were cast out, no one could find Eden again."

A wooden chair creaked as a heavyset man shifted his weight.

"Next, we turn to Exodus, where Moses finds a place in the mountains extraordinarily thin, for Moses saw and heard God, and felt holy terror for days. A place where God gave the commandments we still follow, and instructed the people to celebrate Passover, which Jesus partook of on the night he was taken. And this brings us to Easter."

There were sighs of relief from several quarters of the church.

"The distance between heaven and earth had to be very slender on the mount where Jesus was seen talking with Moses and Elijah. Yet there are those who can be in a thin place and not know it. His disciples just wanted the thin place to go away. Then they could not stay awake in the Garden of Gethsemane as he prayed. The guards who came into the garden to arrest Jesus did not perceive it as a thin place. Next, we have that first Easter morning when the women visit his tomb and encounter heavenly beings—multiple times. Did the angels *appear* as we have been told? Or had Mary Magdalene simply stepped into a place of thinness?"

Cyrus began to fidget. Abigail laid her hand on his leg and he stopped.

"We go to thin places because they transform us—or more accurately, they have a transformative quality that we may be lucky enough to experience. For the women, the tomb was a thin place, but that doesn't mean their experience was pleasant. It was exhilarating, yet frightening. Their spirits were awake and God was near, but they ran away. Thin places may disorient and confuse us, changing the way we see the world. And, yes, that can be scary."

Rebecca noticed she'd made some of her congregation uncomfortable. They weren't going to like her any better for that. But they would probably be better for it.

She forged ahead. "Do thin places exist? As I am of Irish descent, I hope someday to visit my ancestral land to find out. Yet, my Taos friend is sure his thin place lies only a few miles from here, making me suspect that, like beauty, thin places are often in the eye of the beholder." Rebecca gave Morgan a smile.

"However, Universalists believe God is everywhere. Then why would one place be thin and another not? Maybe the whole *world* is thin, but sometimes we're too thick to recognize it. Perhaps the purpose of thin places is to help us realize that the divine who transcends time and space cannot be limited to a specific locale, and that anyplace can become thin."

She glanced at Morgan, who merely shrugged.

"The idea of thin places is that this world and the heavenly world are separated by a thin barrier. As Universalists, we believe it is not God who is kept separate from us, but we who keep separate from him. If we can but thin out our own barriers, the things inside of us keeping us from God, then wherever we go becomes thin. And of those of us who do so, it may be said, the man or woman who sees God, sees God everywhere."

After the benediction, the Wentworths and Deitwilers were walking out together. Faye laid her hand on Emma's arm. "Did you hear her? 'As Universalists, we believe,' she says. I was raised Lutheran."

"Me, too," Emma said.

"That wasn't much of an Easter sermon," Mr. Wentworth said.

"No. It wasn't," Fred agreed. "She never even mentioned the resurrection."

CHAPTER 43

"Knock, knock," Rebecca said, entering through the connecting door from the church, the Friday after Easter.

"Oh, hello, come on in." Morgan was studying a stack of oil paintings.

"I hope I'm not bothering you. I thought since I live next door now, we should become better friends." On the table was a long, wide, shallow box, holding an expensive man's suit. Rebecca touched the lapel. "You're selling clothes now?"

"No, the suit's Jack's. I planned to use the box to ship my paintings, but I'm afraid it's not sturdy enough to protect them. I expect I'll have to make crates." Morgan put the lid on the box and removed it from the table. "Have a seat. You want coffee?"

Rebecca laughed. "You're always offering me coffee. How much coffee do you New Yorkers drink a day?"

"Usually not enough. Something stronger?"

"Goodness no, it's still morning."

"I can make a pot of tea, if you like."

"Tea would be nice, if it wouldn't be too much trouble."

"No trouble. We have twice as much tea as we need now that the Young Ladies Society is defunct."

Morgan went to the kitchen, put a kettle of water on the stove, and placed the teapot, cup, saucer, cream, and sugar on a tray. When the water boiled, he poured it in the teapot and carried the tray out to Rebecca.

"Aren't you having any?"

Morgan raised his mug. "I've still got coffee."

"Oh, you didn't have to do all this for me."

"No bother, we're neighbors now."

"I feel kind of bad, like I put you out of your home."

"Don't give it a thought. Jack's happy to be back at Romero's. She's a good cook. Has a hot meal waiting for him every night."

She smiled. "I noticed you and Jack came to Easter service."

Morgan nodded.

"How'd you like it?"

"Interesting. I gather your grandfather sent the book you wanted."

"No, he didn't have a book on it, but he wrote me a long letter relating stories his parents told about thin places in Ireland."

"Your sermon gave the impression this was a well-documented Celtic philosophy."

"Well . . . the idea of thin places is ancient, pre-dating the Celts by centuries, but it wasn't the Easter my congregation expected. Overall, they're not too pleased with me."

"I liked the way you worked Moses into your sermon. You know I'm Jewish?"

"No, I didn't. I mean, the day we met, you said you'd never been to church, but I'd just arrived, and had no idea if that was a common affliction in the West."

Morgan laughed. "Affliction?"

Rebecca blushed and busied herself pouring tea, adding cream and sugar. When she felt her natural coloring return, she said, "Anyway, I'm glad you came. Our discussion was what sparked that sermon."

"You're trying to flatter me. You already knew about thin places—you asked me for a book about them."

"Yes, but you were the one who brought up Moses on Mount Sinai, which inspired me to think about thin places elsewhere in the Bible. My original intent in asking for a book was to plan a trip so I could see for myself."

"To Ireland? A trip like that would take months. Could you leave the church for that long?"

"I may not have a choice in the matter. There are many people in Taos who would like to see me gone."

"You're not serious."

"Oh, yes. Ever since my sermon on hell, people have been raising questions about Lucifer, and implying I'm friendly with him."

"How absurd."

Rebecca sipped her tea. "These questions are from those who would like to tar me with a brush and put words into my mouth intended to ambush me. Father Ignacio has convinced people I'm a Satanist."

"Sounds like the priest is jealous."

"No, I understand this enmity goes back decades, to when Presbyterian evangelists tried to root out the Catholics' penitent brotherhood. They've resisted any Protestant incursion since."

"Well, I don't have a dog in the fight either way, but I find it strange that people who profess a belief in One God are so obsessed with Satan."

"Universalists say that even if such a being as Lucifer existed, he'd have to be reconciled back to God in the end." She smiled. "Don't tell Father Ignacio I said that."

"Why would your congregation care what he says? Aren't they all good Protestants?"

"A lot of them are also businessmen. They have to do business with his parishioners. I suppose they don't want to offend any customers."

"Shouldn't the Protestants who brought you here be more supportive?"

"They're not as broad-minded as I naively expected."

Morgan furrowed his brow. "We're finding that, too. Is there any way I can help you keep your job?"

"Maybe the ladies' book club could read James George Frazer's *The Golden Bough*, next. It would broaden their view of religion."

"I've heard of it, but I've never read it."

"We read it when I was in divinity school. Frazer was an anthropologist who visited many foreign lands and wrote about strange peoples with even stranger customs—places where magic was conspicuously present and religion conspicuously absent."

"Reminds me of the Philippine village at the World's Fair—a forty-seven acre reservation set up by our government for anthropologists to study Filipinos."

"Frazer's thesis is that civilized races today all passed through similar phases in some period of their history. That religion is an evolutionary result, not unlike Darwin's theory of species."

Morgan raised his eyebrows. "And you think that's somehow going to help?"

"The women I've met in Taos may be reticent to let their husbands know, but they are extremely perspicacious. An intelligent reader of *The Golden Bough* is going to arrive at the logical extrapolation that Universalism is the evolution of Christianity beyond legend, dogma, and ritual."

"If I tell the ladies that, I'm sure they won't want to read it."

"You can tell them Frazer has been influencing other writers since 1890. The latest edition consists of three volumes. You'll sell thrice as many books."

"So is Frazer a Universalist?"

"Hardly, but his book will make what I'm preaching seem mild in comparison."

"Anything in it about thin places?"

"Surprisingly, not. But do remember, I still want you to show me your special place sometime."

"I don't know when. Jack's working on the Manby house and Bryce is off trying to become a shaman through peyote, so I've got to be in the store full-time. I don't even get out to paint anymore. In fact, I may need to set up my easel and paint in here—if the turpentine doesn't smell the place up too bad."

"Well, it sounds like I better let you get to work. Thank you for the tea and the conversation."

"Come by every day, if you want. It's pretty lonely with my partners gone and the girl's club broke up. Thank God for the Tuesday and Thursday Ladies' Teas; I'd go mad without them."

"Recommend *The Golden Bough*."

"I will, but why don't you attend? You can tell them about it yourself."

"Abigail suggested I join the ladies' book club, and perhaps I shall. But I think it would be better if they were unaware that this particular book was my suggestion."

CHAPTER 44

The Ladies Afternoon Tea and Book Club purchased all three volumes of Frazer's *The Golden Bough*, but found it dense and much too serious. Although Frazer related some gruesome practices, it lacked innuendo, titillation, or even the merely suggestive that the members looked for in a book club selection. Rebecca came to one meeting but quickly picked up on the members' sentiments regarding the book and backed away from the discussion. Her attendance made things awkward for some within the book club were working to replace her with a more traditional minister.

Rebecca didn't come back a second time, and the ladies abandoned *The Golden Bough* in favor of *Jude the Obscure*. Although Thomas Hardy's book was published a decade earlier, the ladies had never read it. The story gave them a perverse, tantalizing seductress to rail against, frank sexuality, and an indictment against marriage. It was exactly the curative they were seeking to relieve their minds of all the religious troubles they'd brought on Taos by hiring the quirky, ungainly woman minister.

When Morgan asked Abigail if it was true the ladies were searching for another minister, she said, "Reverend Sullivan's not the right fit. People are looking for someone who will tell them they're going to hell, then give them communion and tell them they're saved. If the Universalist message is that they're saved from the beginning, they figure, why bother going to church?"

Rebecca visited Morgan more often and one day admitted that recommending *The Golden Bough* had been a mistake. "It only fed their ideas that everything that isn't Presbyterian or Lutheran is sacrilegious. Rather than insist they keep me on, I'll ask Granddad Fitzpatrick to take me to Ireland. He's retired now, and we could search out some thin places together."

"And give up your church?"

Tears started to pool in her green eyes. "I came west with such high expectations. I was going to bring them the good news that would bring light into their lives. As it turns out I'm no John Murray. And they don't have a lot of interest in light."

"I'm a painter. I love light."

"Thank you for that." She dabbed her eyes with a hankie. "Excuse me. I need to prepare next week's sermon." She crossed to the connecting door.

If her dismissal came to pass, he'd be sorry to see her go. Morgan and Rebecca had become more than neighbors. Friends. But not lovers, something he wouldn't have thought possible before. As far as he could determine, she'd never had a man, and he had no intention of being her first.

Besides, she was a minister in a town that already half-believed she was a heretic and libertine. True, Henry Ward Beecher, the most famous preacher in America, had been accused of extramarital affairs and managed to keep his church. But that didn't mean a woman minister could. What had Hamlet said to Ophelia? "Be thou as chaste as ice, as pure as snow, thou shalt not escape calumny." If Rebecca wanted to find a position in another church, she'd best stay a virgin until she found a husband. And Morgan didn't intend to wed before he was at least thirty.

Morgan wandered around the store, dusted, and straightened the merchandise, and drank his thirteenth cup of coffee. He had begun tracking their income and expenses more carefully, and the emporium was not doing that well. Although sales of the three-volume Frazer set, followed in short order by the Hardy book, made them a little extra profit in May, the most popular Gramophone records had sold out and what inventory remained wasn't moving. Jack's steady income was working to pay off the record companies, but any new discs they ordered had to be paid for with cash they didn't have.

Morgan didn't mind sleeping on a cot in the storeroom. It was the least he could do. His partner was working full-time; he could sacrifice a little comfort. They'd be out of debt by the time Jack's job was finished. Jack would take shifts in the store again, and Morgan could get back to his artwork. An agent in New York representing some interested galleries had suggested he build up his portfolio. How to do that and run the store full-time, he hadn't figured out. Of course, given how slow business was, he might as well just lock up and go paint scenery.

The door opened and Cherry came in. She was wearing a pale-green gingham dress with puffy sleeves, accented by a wide pink sash around her waist and a matching pink ribbon in her hair. "Hello, Morgan," she said with a flutter of her eyelashes.

"Hi, Cherry. What a nice surprise. Is your mother allowing you girls to attend the book club again? Should we restart it?"

"She doesn't know I'm here. You won't tell on me, will you?"

Morgan smiled. "You were certain I wouldn't, or you wouldn't have come. Anyway, I'm glad for the company. Since you girls quit, it's pretty lonely here. Jack's working, and I'm by myself all day."

"We didn't quit. Mama made such a stink over Peaches dancing that none of us were allowed here anymore. I hope she dies."

"Don't say that."

"Why not? I hate her." Cherry wandered over and flipped through the records, made a face at the remaining selections, and walked along the book shelves, running her fingers over the spines in the philosophy section. "Do you believe what's written in all these books? Is this what Reverend Sullivan preaches?"

"The wonderful thing about books is that authors with completely different ideas sit right next to each other. You never see a book push another one off the shelf because it doesn't like what the other one says."

Cherry laughed. "You're hilarious. Books can't move."

"No, but they move us, don't they? Even though your mama stopped the book club, don't let that stop you girls from reading. Books can expand your thinking, explain ideas the adults around you aren't even aware of."

A mischievous smile crinkled the corners of Cherry's eyes. "Our parents would be very surprised to find out what we know." She ran her hand across the door that connected to the church. "I went to a service there once."

"Despite what Father Ignacio says?"

"Because of what he says. I wanted to see what everyone was talking about."

"What did you think?"

"It was interesting, seeing a woman in charge and people listening to her. Doing whatever she said—stand, or bow their heads and pray."

Interesting. Morgan had never thought of it like that. "How did you feel about what she had to say?"

"About places in nature that make you feel special?" Cherry shook her head. "I don't think I've been to any yet. Maybe when I'm old as she is."

Morgan laughed. "Rebecca Sullivan's younger than I am."

"Well, Easter week, Father told us her church were pagans because they didn't celebrate Holy Communion, which is the most important rite in God's church. They were going to hell, and if we attended their church, we'd go with them."

"You don't believe you're going to hell, do you?"

"Not for listening to the Reverend." She meandered into the back and saw Morgan's cot. "Are you living here?"

Morgan looked away.

"I wondered why you didn't move to our house when Jack did. I miss you. At first, I guessed you went to live at Mrs. Wythe's when the Reverend moved out, because Peaches said you used to be sweethearts. But then Jack and Mrs. Wythe went to Hoffsteader's ball, like they were a couple, so I knew Peaches was wrong. Jack looked so handsome in his new suit."

"I'm sure he did."

"So, why didn't you move back to our house when Jack did? Then I'd see you every day and wouldn't have to sneak around Mama to come to your store."

Morgan swallowed the lump in his throat. This was embarrassing to say out loud to anyone. "Well, Cherry, finances are tight right now, and we can't afford it."

"Jack's there."

"Jack is doing heavy work every day. He needs a place where he can have a meal ready for him when he gets home. I can make do with this little cot and fried egg sandwiches until we're back in the money."

"If it's cause of money, let me talk to Mama."

"No, don't do that. Your mother needs rent from all her boarders to take care of you girls."

"Well, I sure miss you living with us. I had the biggest crush on you when I was a kid. About broke my heart when you and Jack moved away after Mama threw Bryce out."

Morgan laughed. "You mean, last fall when you were a kid? You may not understand why, but you and Peaches are both too young for men like us."

"I'm not a kid. I'll tell you something, but you got to promise not to tell Mama."

Morgan patted her head.

Cherry pushed his hand away. "Promise. Say it."

He had no idea what he was opening himself up for, but it was probably better that he knew rather than not. "I promise."

Cherry's eyes darted around the room, as if to make sure there wasn't anyone else in the store to overhear. "Mama thinks Peaches and I are virgins. We're not."

Morgan coughed. "You've heard that word at church a lot, I'm sure, but I'm not sure you understand what that actually entails."

"It means a girl's been with a man and he's put his . . . his private part inside her. But remember, you promised not to tell. If Mama ever found out we weren't her perfect little virgin daughters, she'd throw us over to Mr. Sneed.

I don't want to go to work for Mr. Sneed. But I don't want to marry some sheepherder, either."

Okay, he had opened himself to this. What the hell was he supposed to say to that? Morgan mumbled something incomprehensible.

Cherry didn't listen anyway. "Doesn't seem likely any man will ever take me away from Taos."

For the first time, Morgan wondered where this was going. This was starting to look less and less like a friendly visit.

Cherry flounced, her skirt swirled. "Remember Reverend Sullivan talking about thin places? Well, I heard she's going away, and I was wondering if maybe I could go with her and see some of those places."

Morgan laughed. "What makes you think your mother would let you leave town with a Protestant minister?"

She chewed the corner of her bottom lip. "But if I had to go, would Reverend Sullivan take me?"

"I honestly couldn't say, you'd have to ask her. But if you want her to say yes, tell her about your mother's threat to sell you to a brothel. That might sway her."

"Then she'd know I wasn't a virgin."

"It's all right. A minister can't tell anyone what you say to her in confidence, same as a priest."

Cherry shook her head.

"Reverend Sullivan will feel obligated to protect you if she knows you're at risk of being sold into prostitution."

"I've never even told Father Ignacio that in confession."

"Maybe if you had, he'd keep you safe."

"No-o-o, none of the girls tell him about that. He might tell our mothers."

An even worse thought intruded. "Cherry, you're not pregnant, are you? That's often why girls your age have to go away."

"No, definitely not. I'm being careful. Peaches told me to make the boys promise to pull out. Of course, boys don't always do what they promise. Sometimes they just do what they like."

The door opened, and Cyrus and Abigail entered. Thank God. The conversation was far afield of anything he ever imagined.

"Is Bryce here?" Cyrus said.

Morgan squatted down to Cyrus's eye-level. "You know that Bryce quit the store and left town, right?"

"I told him that," Abigail said. "But he didn't believe me and wanted to come see for himself."

"Your mother was right. Bryce has gone away, possibly for good."

Cyrus's face fell. "He was fun."

"Yes, he was," Morgan said.

"Cherry? Fancy meeting you here." Abigail shot him a glance. "Alone."

"Good afternoon, Mrs. Wythe."

Abigail gave her a tight smile. "Cherry, I bet Cyrus would like to hear a record. Would you crank the Gramophone for him?"

"I can do it," Cyrus said.

"No. This player doesn't belong to us. Let Cherry do it."

Cyrus took Cherry's hand and pulled her over to the records. "I'll show you which songs to play."

Abigail pushed Morgan toward the kitchen. When they were out of earshot, and the music was playing, she whispered, "What's she doing here? Her mother darn near put you out of business last time she caught the girls here."

"That was Bryce's doing. Her mother's not mad at Jack and me. In fact, Jack's living there again."

"Aren't you as well?"

Morgan glanced at Cherry and Cyrus. "We have something more important to talk about."

"Cherry?"

"And Peaches, thank you. Cherry and I just had an unimaginably uncomfortable conversation in which she informed me that she and her sister are having relations with boys."

"I'm not surprised."

"Well, I am, and I'm worried as hell the girls are going to get themselves pregnant. Right now, they're depending on getting the boy to pull out, and I can't imagine that working very well. I don't know what women do, but you never asked me to do that, and you haven't had another kid since Cyrus was born. You obviously do something."

Abigail sighed. "What do you want from me?"

"How about if I take Cyrus for a walk, while you give Cherry some advice?"

"That's something her mother should do."

"Mrs. Romero?"

"Right, I wasn't thinking."

"Cherry says if their mother finds out they're having sex she'll send them to Sneed. I believe her."

"You're not serious?"

"Knowing how zealously righteous Mrs. Romero is, do you doubt it?"

"Yes. Wouldn't she just make them marry the boy, like so many other mothers do?"

"Boys—apparently plural. If Mrs. Romero learned that, she'd call her daughters harlots, disown them, and send them straight down the street to Sneed."

Abigail shook her head. "Women are their own worst enemies. How is our sex ever going to get anywhere like this?"

"So, talk to her. Tell her how . . . how to be the liberated woman you are."

"What are you two talking about?" Cherry said from across the room.

Abigail walked over to them. "Cyrus, is Cherry helping you?"

Cyrus, clapping his tiny hands to the beat, nodded.

"Cherry, come here a moment," Morgan said. When she was near, he said, "Will you and Abigail watch the store a minute while I take Cyrus for a walk?"

"Why?"

"I want to give you and Abigail—Mrs. Wythe, a chance to talk."

Cherry stuck out her lip. "About what?"

"Female matters."

"Morgan, you promised—"

"I promised not to tell your mother. Abigail's not like her. She's going to help you."

"First you say tell Reverend Sullivan, now Mrs. Wythe. You keep trying to get me to tell other women my secrets. One thing I know from Mama is, I can't trust women."

"All women are not like your mother. You don't have to tell Abigail anything, just listen, and take her advice."

"Why can't you just tell me what to do?"

"Because there are some things women don't tell men. You can trust Abigail. All right?"

Morgan walked over to Cyrus, and Cherry followed. "Cyrus, it's kind of hot. Why don't we go down to the ice house and see if they'll give us some chunks to cool off with?"

"Can I, Mama?"

Abigail pulled a clean hanky from her purse. "Here, wrap the ice in this, so you won't get your fingers frosted."

Morgan took Cyrus by the hand and made a hasty exit.

Abigail and Cherry eyed each other for a moment. Abigail still hadn't decided whether or not to be mad, if so, should she be mad at Cherry or Morgan?

"Sit with me," Abigail said, taking a seat at the table.

Cherry picked at her fingernails, not meeting Abigail's eyes.

She was a child, and she needed womanly help she wasn't going to get from her actual mother. Abigail opened her purse and removed a small tablet of notepaper and a pencil. "Sit. I'm going to make you a list."

Cherry pulled out a chair and sat sideways to her. When Abigail finished writing, she tore off the sheet of paper, and put the pencil and tablet back in her bag. Next, she took out a brocade change-purse with a gold clasp, opened it, and removed five pennies. She laid them on the table in front of Cherry.

"Morgan told me—" Abigail said.

"But I never—"

"Cherry, I'm not judging you. Do what I say, and you'll be in command of your own womanhood. You can have all the men you want, but you can't leave *anything* up to them."

Cherry blinked rapidly, then looked down at the paper.

"First, go to the apothecary and buy a penny's worth of sulfate of iron. I wrote the name down for you." Abigail pointed to the list. "Next, buy a small sponge at the general store."

"Mama already has lots of bath sponges."

"No. Buy a new one, one that's never been used. It doesn't have to be big. Last stop, Deitwiler's. Tell Emma you want a yard of silk thread—pure silk, not cotton."

Cherry nodded.

"Don't tell Emma, or anyone else, why you're buying these things."

"I don't know myself."

"You will in a minute. When you get home, find Peaches and go someplace private. Break off two walnut-size pieces of the sponge, and with a needle, thread fourteen inches of the silk half-way through each sponge. Tie a couple of good knots in the silk, so it won't come out. When you're done, there should be about six inches of thread hanging off the sponge."

Cherry scooted her chair closer to Abigail.

"Find a small jar with a lid you can close tight. Doesn't your mother make jam?"

"Blackberry all summer, mint jelly in the spring, and apple butter in the fall."

"Good. A Ball jar will work fine. Wash it clean in hot water, then put in about a cup of water and add just enough sulfate of iron to make it look like weak tea."

Cherry looked at the list. "This doesn't say any of that. It's just a shopping list."

"Don't worry, you won't forget. And teach this to Peaches, too. That'll help you remember it."

"She won't listen. She says 'cause she's eighteen, she knows better than me."

Abigail took Cherry's hand in hers. "Listen, Peaches doesn't know what I'm telling you and she needs to, as much as you do." Abigail glanced at the door. "We'd better finish before Cyrus and Morgan get back." She took a deep breath and looked to heaven for inspiration. "Cherry, if I use the word 'intercourse,' do you understand what I mean?"

"Sex with boys."

"That's right. From now on, every time, before you have intercourse, you soak your little sponge in the iron sulfate solution."

"You mean the jar of tea?"

"Yes. Then part your legs and push the sponge way up inside you."

"In the place where the man puts . . . himself?"

"Yes, but leave the string dangling out."

"I could never do that with a boy watching."

"Oh, you don't have to do this in his presence, you do it ahead of time. But always put in your sponge if there's even a chance you and a boy are going to have intercourse. Afterwards, pull on the silk thread and the sponge will come out. You can wash it and use it again."

"Does Mama know about this?"

"I don't know. I doubt it—the Catholic Church definitely would not approve. But keep your jar and sponge hidden. You wouldn't want her to find it, in case she does."

The door banged open. Morgan and Cyrus came in, melting ice dropping a trail of water on the floor. "You want a lick, Mommy?"

Abigail pressed the coins and the list into Cherry's hand. "You understand what to do. Teach Peaches, and if either of you have any questions, you come find me. All right?"

Well, Jack had told her he and his partners wanted to bring enlightenment to New Mexico. Maybe this was how it happened—one person at a time.

CHAPTER 45

The pleasant May weather allowed Morgan to leave the windows open all day. He'd started painting in the store, and the fresh air kept the place from smelling too much like turpentine and linseed oil. Not that there were any customers to be offended by the odor.

Morgan's agent had sent an encouraging letter promising something would happen soon and told him to keep expanding his portfolio. The letter suggested he add colorful locals to some of his paintings—squaws, senoritas, perhaps a buffalo hunter. His agent obviously had an outdated idea of New Mexico. People here dressed like New Yorkers did—ten years ago.

Then again, his New York customers might not know that. He smiled. He was about to go from bringing modern New York to old-fashioned New Mexico to bringing old New Mexico to modern New York.

He touched up a landscape painting on the easel and considered whether to add a figure in the distance, or immediate foreground. Perhaps, a face in the lower left quadrant gazing at the vista would invite viewers into the painting more effectively, and would help balance the composition. This might work.

What he would love to do was close the store early and go up in the hills to paint May wildflowers. They wouldn't bloom forever.

"Hi, Morgan."

He turned with a start. "Peaches, I didn't hear you come in."

"You were busy."

Morgan swished his brush in a jar of turpentine and dried the bristles. He wiped his hands with a rag. Not another Romero girl. He had enough troubles without the wrath of Mama—no reason to stir her up. If it was more female matters, he wished the Romero girls would just go to Abigail.

Perhaps he was reading too much into it. Maybe Peaches needed a book for a school report.

"Is Bryce around?"

So, not a book for school. "Bryce? No, he left weeks ago."

"Not for New York, I hope."

Morgan laughed. "No, he's off with the Indians."

"Oh, good."

"Good?"

"I'm glad he hasn't gone east yet. Bryce promised to take me with him, and I won't be out of school for a few more weeks."

"Well, he definitely didn't go to New York. And it's a good thing he didn't take you wherever he's gone."

"So, do you know when he's coming back? When he's leaving for New York?"

"No telling if Bryce is ever coming back, but I'm pretty sure he's not going east again."

Peaches clenched her fists and stamped her foot. "But Bryce promised to take me when he went. Men always promise they'll take me with them when they leave, but then they don't. What I want to know is, how do you make men keep their promises?"

"Some men keep their word and some don't. Frankly, you're better off that Bryce didn't take you with him. He may be in a place he'll never come back from."

"You're from New York. Can you answer something for me?"

"Depends on what it is."

"Do people in the city know more about sex than people out here in the territories?"

Morgan was speechless. The question was so direct, so open that it was almost innocent. Finally, he said, "Is that why you're looking for Bryce? He's too old for you—"

"That's not true. How old are you guys, twenty-three, twenty-four? I'm eighteen. That's not much difference." Her fingertips brushed her lips and slid down her throat to her cleavage. "There's something about Bryce that's irresistible. He's like a stick of candy from the general store. You see it and you just want it."

"I've seen him have that effect on women, and I can't explain it for the life of me. But we told him to leave you girls alone."

"Bryce? Oh, you think he listened? I had him for my eighteenth birthday —as many times as he could. He has such . . . intensity. When he starts loving you, the passion is just overwhelming. I haven't seen him much since —he kind of went loco. But I need a man who will get me out of this little anthill."

God. Conversations with these girls were completely out of hand. Cherry the other day, now Peaches. Was it a strange phase of the moon, or something in the water? "Well, don't think of sex as your way out."

"No? What if I was a model? Bryce showed me your Studio magazines with all the goddesses and naked ladies." Peaches ran her hands up her body and hefted her bosom. "I've got a better figure than any of those pictures."

He saw where she was going, but he daren't react to it. He picked up a brush that didn't need cleaning and cleaned it again.

"I'd pose for you."

"Oh, that's not a good idea."

"Why? I don't care if a man sees me naked. In fact, I kind of like it. I go skinny-dipping in the Rio Pueblo with boys all the time. I like the way my body looks, and I like the way men look at it."

Peaches probably expected him to be shocked. He wasn't. He'd always suspected as much, confirmed earlier this week by her sister's revelation of their sexuality. But he was still aware of just what a powder keg he'd be sitting on. Father Ignacio was already accusing Rebecca and the partners of bringing corruption to Taos. Being caught with the daughter of a prominent catholic *in flagrante*—well, that would be the end of it. "Cherry says your mother will sell you to Sneed if she finds out."

"She can't. I'm eighteen. And I wouldn't mind being naked in a painting hanging on a wall. As soon as I can find a way to New York, I'm going to become a model for a famous artist."

"Fine. If you want to pose in the buff, go to New York City, but you can't do it here. You said yourself, this is a small town. You're not considering the social complications it would create for you. You know how the town treats Sneed's girls? Well, that's how they'd treat you."

She stomped her foot again. "I don't understand. I thought you wanted to bring New York values to Taos. I've heard the things your Ladies' Book Club talks about."

He was about to answer her, but he realized she was right. One of the values they believed in was free love—that a woman had the right over her own body and to sleep with whom she liked, when she liked. And Peaches was of age.

But to see her throwing herself first at Jack, then Bryce, and probably any boy interested in getting between her legs, it just seemed . . . wrong. No, that was hypocritical—he admired that same free-spirit in Abigail. But she knew how to manage it.

"I really wish you'd have this conversation with Mrs. Wythe."

"I don't want to talk to Mrs. Wythe. I want you to paint me—even with my clothes on."

"Your mother won't allow it, and I don't want to get Jack and myself on her bad side."

"Would you do it, though? If she said I could?"

Morgan rubbed his face. His agent had asked him to add people to some of his paintings. Peaches had an exotic beauty. "I suppose . . . If she came here and told me herself that you had her permission."

Peaches clapped her hands. "Oh, goody."

"But why do you want to get your face on a canvas so bad?"

"I've heard galleries in New York are going to show your paintings. If I go there and other artists recognize me in your pictures, I can get work."

"That isn't how they find models." He thought of all those Pre-Raphaelite redheads. "Artists, good artists, have a certain look they want. You can either provide or you can't."

Peaches showed him her profile and tugged a curl of her hair. "You know I have the looks."

"Well, I haven't got any shows yet. Besides, your mother will never consent."

"Let me handle her."

Morgan looked out the window. What was he getting himself into? How did this eighteen-year-old girl lead everyone to do what she wanted?

Emma Deitwiler walked by and Morgan noticed a distinctive bump protruding from her abdomen. Just when his life couldn't fit another complication.

He raced to the door while Peaches continued to blather on about her fantasy. He stuck his head out and looked in both directions, but Emma had disappeared.

"Morgan! Are you listening? Where are you going?"

He leaned back in and closed the door. "Nowhere, I guess." Morgan slammed his fist against the door jamb. Fred would kill him if he found out who the real father was.

Peaches was still talking. "So, what I was saying . . ."

Where were Bryce and his gun, now he might actually be needed? It didn't matter; Bryce was a terrible shot, and a fake soldier to boot.

". . . And then, when I get to New York . . . well, of course, I'm not going to tell Mama that part."

"Of course," Morgan said. Of course. Why would Emma *ever* tell Fred?

Peaches pushed him out of the way so she could the open door. "Bye."

"Yeah, okay, bye."

It was only after she was gone that he realized he'd just agreed to something without having any clear idea what. That was all he needed.

In less than an hour, Peaches was back, with her mother in tow. To his surprise, Mrs. Romero seemed relatively calm.

"Good afternoon, Mr. Silver. Peaches tells me you're willing to paint her portrait. The whole town's seen the fine pictures you made of Emma Deitwiler, and I've seen the nice portrait you did of the Hoffsteaders. But I don't have their kind of money, so I don't understand what this is all about."

"I told you, Mother, we don't have to pay him."

"Why would he do it for free? The man's got to make a living."

Peaches exhaled loudly. "I've already explained it twice. He's not painting a picture for our parlor. It's going to a gallery in New York, where they sell oil paintings."

"Is it true, Mr. Silver? It won't cost me anything?"

What had Peaches gotten him into? Still, her comeliness would make a pleasing addition to his work. And his intentions were actually innocent. Likely more innocent than hers.

"It's true, Mrs. Romero. I'd like to add figures to some of my landscapes and Peaches offered to model for me."

She narrowed her eyes. "Where would you two be doing this?"

"Right here in the store." He pointed at the canvas on his easel.

"What about Mr. Holloway?"

"He's gone. Doesn't work here anymore. Surely, Jack told you."

"Just checking." She bowed her head, pressed her fingertips to her forehead, and was silent a while. "Father Ignacio won't like you being so close to the devil's church."

"Mother, it's no different than when we used to come to the book club."

"Yes, and we saw how that turned out."

Morgan walked over and gazed at the landscape painting on the easel. In his mind's-eye he could see where he would position a young senorita. "Do you have a Mexican style dress?"

Mrs. Romero puffed herself up. "My daughters aren't Mexican."

"No, of course they're not. I was only thinking of a pose—the costume of a senorita from days gone by."

"I could borrow the dress Margarita Lopez wore for her Quinceañera," Peaches said.

Mrs. Romero flapped her hand dismissively at Peaches and turned her attention to Morgan. "All right, she can be in your picture. But you have to work here. You can't take her anywhere else. I always know where my daughters are."

Not strictly true, but he wasn't going to mention it. "I assure you, madam, I have no intention of doing otherwise."

"I trust you, Mr. Silver. I was merely clarifying my conditions."

Her terms suited Morgan. He positively didn't want to be up in the mountains alone with Peaches. That would be certain trouble, despite his intentions.

CHAPTER 46

Margarita Lopez was as full figured as Peaches, but only stood about four feet nine. The upper part of the dress fit Peaches fine, but the skirt, floor length on Margarita, barely covered Peaches' calves. Mrs. Romero wouldn't allow her to wear it out in public, so she'd brought it with her and changed in the back room. Morgan was only painting her from the waist up, so no one would ever know. The dress had a scoop neck and Peaches kept pulling it down to bare her shoulders and show more cleavage. And Morgan kept telling her to pull it back up. Mama wouldn't like that.

Morgan asked Peaches to take the ribbon from her hair, allowing it to cascade over her shoulders in soft brown waves. He was adding her profile over an existing vista he'd painted of the hills above Taos. When completed, it would appear he'd painted her plein-air, but he'd not violated Mrs. Romero's rule. Peaches had beautiful features and was easy to paint. As he worked away, he imagined the next painting—a young frontier wife cooking supper. Peaches had that fresh-faced glow of a new bride. She could wear one of her mother's dresses and he would pose her in the store kitchen next to the stove.

"Morgan, tell me about New York City," Peaches said, without breaking her pose. When she got down to it, she did exhibit some professionalism.

"What do you want to know?"

"Anything. What's it like living there?"

"Hmmmm." Morgan thought for a minute. "Everything moves much faster."

"What do you mean?"

"There are elevated trains, the BMT and IRT, which take you to other boroughs, and a line that runs the whole length of Manhattan. You can get on it anytime of day and be uptown or downtown in minutes, for just a nickel. When I was back there at Christmastime, they'd finally opened the subway, a train that runs underground, below the city streets. That wasn't finished when we came west."

Peaches shuddered. "An underground train?"

"No different than going through an endlessly long tunnel."

"But I've never ridden a train, let alone through a tunnel."

"Sorry, I forgot you hadn't."

"What else is there?"

"Let's see . . . There are lots more buildings, taller and closer together, not like out here. The streets are paved, so mud isn't such a problem. Oh, and gas lights. The streets are brightly lit at night by overhead lights, so you can always see where you're going."

Peaches sighed. "Imagine a place where you don't have to be home before dark."

"At the St. Louis World's Fair the lights were electric instead of gas. Almost as bright as daylight, with no flicker. People in New York say soon they're going to replace the gas lights with electric."

"Like those?" She pointed toward a string of bulbs Jack had hanging above a bookcase. "But do they have people crank the generators all night?"

"Oh, no, the electricity comes from a hydroelectric dam, way, way up north in New York State. So far, only a few neighborhoods have been electrified. But the city already has telephone wires everywhere."

"What are telephones?"

"Wonderful time savers. Like a telegraph, but with voice, right in your business and even some homes. You just pick up an earpiece and a woman answers. You tell her who you want to talk to and she connects your telephone to theirs. The person can be on the other side of town or even in another city, and the two of you can carry on a conversation as easily as you and I are right now."

"That's amazing, but I doubt this backward place will ever get telephones."

"Oh, I think eventually they'll be everywhere."

"Well, I'm not waiting for eventually. Tell me more about the city."

"Everything is there, goods of every kind are for sale somewhere in the city." Morgan stopped painting and his voice became distant. "Museums, art galleries, and theaters abound. There is a whole block of nothing but music publishers, and there are concerts every week."

Peaches eyes glistened. "Aren't you sorry you left all that to move here?"

He shook off the memories. "No. I love it here."

"I can't imagine why anyone would choose this place over New York City."

"You don't realize how beautiful it is here."

She sighed. "I can hardly wait to get out."

"You've said that before. I suspect, wherever you're raised seems too ordinary, and a distant place has an exotic appeal. For me, that's Taos. Perhaps for you, it's New York."

"You won't ever go back?"

"Oh, I will, sometime this summer. My agent has nearly completed negotiations for two showings of my work. I'll go back for the openings, but I won't stay. This is my home now." He realized it was true, even as he said it. Even if they failed to keep the emporium afloat, he wanted to live near the thin places he'd found.

"Take me with you when you go," she said. "You can introduce me to artists who will hire me to model for them."

"Your mother will never allow that. Besides, it takes money, and I haven't even enough for one person, let alone two."

Peaches crossed her arms. "Can we take a break?"

"Don't get mad, Peaches."

"I'm not. I need to use the privy."

"Oh, I'm sorry. I should have given you a rest sooner. Go ahead."

While Peaches went to the outhouse, Morgan stretched his back. They'd been at work for a couple of hours. It amazed him how long she held a pose. Perhaps she could be a model.

A movement outside the window caught his eye. Emma! Morgan hadn't run into Emma for months, now twice in two days. He studied her figure, but the meaning of her protruding round belly was unmistakable. He pondered how to phrase a question he didn't want the answer to.

Could he ask someone else? Not Mrs. Romero, or Cherry, or Peaches. They wouldn't know. Certainly not Rebecca. Definitely not Abigail. Too many suspicions between her and Emma from long ago. Not Jack—if he knew, he'd have already said. But maybe, if he asked, Jack might wheedle information out of Abigail. They were a couple now and seemed to be getting serious.

Or he could stop being a coward. Emma was right here. He rushed into the street and contrived to brush against her by "accident."

"Excuse me . . . Oh, Emma, what a nice surprise. I haven't run into you and Fred since . . . since, before Christmas. I went back east for a while. Had you heard?"

Emma fanned herself in the midday heat.

"How thoughtless of me, you need to get out of the sun. Shall we go somewhere shady?"

"No, thanks, I'm on my way home."

Morgan felt himself flush. "Oh, your . . . um . . . er . . . condition."

"You can say it, Morgan. I'm going to have a baby."

"Does Fred know?"

Emma chuckled. "I think he noticed."

"Seven years of nothing, then . . . He must suspect."

Emma turned red, but then she laughed out loud. "Morgan, don't you know anything? A woman's pregnancy lasts nine months. It's been almost a year since we—since I posed for you. I'm only six months along. Good God, if you're this bad at arithmetic, how can you run a business?"

Morgan was so relieved he didn't have time to feel stupid. "Not ours."

Emma patted her stomach. "This baby's absolutely Fred's."

"But seven years, no children. Now suddenly?"

"Morgan, you were the only dalliance I ever had, and I don't regret it for a moment." She rubbed her belly. "It was as if there was a log jam that kept Fred and me from getting a family started. You fixed that—broke it loose and everything started working. I can never tell anyone how grateful I am to you, but I am."

Morgan wasn't sure if he was relieved or disappointed.

Emma glanced in both directions and then put her hand on his. "And Morgan, thank you for your discretion. You're the only man I ever knew who didn't brag to everyone he'd had a girl. That's real, old-fashioned chivalry." She gave his hand a little squeeze. "I've got to go."

Morgan watched Emma walk away and continued to stare after her until she turned a corner. He went back in the store and found Peaches studying his painting.

"Was that Mrs. Deitwiler?"

"Yes."

"Your picture makes me look pretty."

"You are pretty."

"Thank you for saying so. My father would have hated it though."

"Why?"

"I look too much like a senorita."

"That was the whole idea."

"Sure. But did you ever wonder why two girls named Romero weren't called Maria and Lucia?"

"I never gave it any mind. Why don't you get back in pose and we'll see if we can finish this up today."

"Oh, I don't want it to be over."

"It's not the end. I've already thought of another painting you can model for."

"Oh, I'm so glad." Peaches naturally fell back into her earlier pose.

Morgan squeezed a little dab of black paint on his palette and feathered it with the bristles of his brush.

Peaches reached up, scratched the tip of her nose with her fingernail, and then put her hand back down. "Our father—he's dead now—he said before the war there was a general distrust of people of Spanish descent. So he gave us names that didn't sound Spanish or Catholic."

Morgan laughed. "Well, Peaches and Cherry are about as far from Spanish and Catholic as he could get."

"Mother wasn't Spanish anyhow, so she let him. But their priest nearly had a fit. I don't mean Father Ignacio. The old padre before him made Papa give us saints' names for our baptism. Then he died—our father I mean, not the old padre. Well, the padre died, too, though later. Gave us saints' names and died. I guess the saint part didn't stick." She laughed. "I'm actually Peaches Theresa and Cherry is Cherry Beatrice—and if you really want to make her mad, call her that."

Morgan studied her eyes and began to paint eyelashes on the senorita.

CHAPTER 47

The last Saturday in May, Jack took off work early and went to Abigail's. She opened the door and stepped out on the porch. "Jack, what a surprise." She touched her hair, moistened her lips with a flick of the tongue, and whispered, "It's not a school day—Cyrus is here."

Jack grinned. "That's not the only reason I come to see you, you know."

Cyrus appeared in the doorway.

"Hey, Cyrus, you want to play catch?" Jack said. "Get your ball and glove."

Cyrus spun around and bounded upstairs as fast as his little legs could carry him.

"No running in the house," Abigail said out of habit.

Jack stole a kiss before Cyrus came back. "What are you doing tomorrow?"

"It's Sunday. Going to church, I guess."

Cyrus returned and raced out the screen door. "Come on, Jack."

Not only had he fallen in love with Abigail, but he'd started to develop fatherly feelings for her son.

Abigail and Jack followed Cyrus into the yard.

Jack paced off a little distance and held up his hands. "Okay, Cyrus, toss me the ball." He'd never played catch with his father, but found he enjoyed doing it with Cyrus.

While Jack and Cyrus threw the ball back and forth, Jack said to Abigail, "What about after church?"

"No plans. What did you have in mind?"

"Rebecca wants Morgan to show her the mountain scenery—his thin places —but he thinks it's too far for her to walk. He sent me to ask if we'd take them in your carriage. It might be nice to spend an afternoon in the mountains."

Abigail eyed Cyrus. "Jack, can you throw very far?"

"Sure. I guess."

"Cyrus, show Jack how you can field a ball in the outfield. Go way, way back and he'll throw you a long one."

Cyrus ran to the other end of the yard.

Abigail arched her eyebrows. "Morgan and Rebecca?"

Jack's eyes crinkled. "Friends, not lovers, believe it or not. I'm pretty sure she's a twenty-three-year-old virgin."

"Not for long, around you New Yorkers."

"Why do you care? To you, virginity is worth less than a sunburn."

"It is, but a female Universalist minister already has two strikes against her. She becomes a free-lover, and she'll never get a job."

"She has a job."

"Not for long, I fear."

Cyrus had caught the ball and tried to throw it back, but his throws only went about a quarter of the way back. He'd run to where it landed, pick it up, and throw it again. He'd almost reached them, so Abigail said, hurriedly, "Tomorrow's Sunday, Penelope and Walter may have other plans. What do I do with Cyrus?"

"Bring him. We'll have a picnic. What do you say? It'll be good innocent fun."

Cyrus bounced up and down. "A picnic!"

Abigail smiled. "I suppose you want me to fry chicken, too."

"I don't know if Rebecca can cook," Jack said, "but I'm sure we don't want Morgan's cooking."

* * *

Sunday afternoon, Morgan closed the store and walked with Jack and Rebecca to Abigail's. Jack carried a pail of beer with a lid on it. Abigail was waiting on the porch with a basket. The horse, already hitched to the carriage, nibbled a carrot from Cyrus's hand.

"Cyrus, come and sit in the back seat between Rebecca and me," Abigail said.

"Aw, I want to ride in front."

Morgan tugged on Abigail's sleeve, and whispered, "You drive."

"Why? You know where you want to go."

"Er . . . Jack and I can't drive a carriage."

"You're joking."

"Never had a reason to learn. In the city, a train or hansom took us anywhere we needed to go."

"But you've lived out here for a year—"

"Never drove a rig."

"Well, it's time one of you learned. Jack, you and I'll drive. Morgan, you and Rebecca can ride in back."

"Oh, goody," Cyrus said. "Now, can I ride up front?"

"No, you better sit in back with Morgan and the Reverend—Jack is driving."

"I am?"

"Grab the reins. I'll show you how."

Jack followed Abigail's instructions and soon learned how to handle the reins without annoying the horse.

Tall conifers lined the twisting incline as Jack drove the carriage up the mountain road. The Taos Mountains were carpeted in verdant forest that reminded him of the Catskills back east. Puffy clouds in the cerulean sky cast shadows on distant mountains, creating patches of darker green. The trail snaked upward, with steep ravines appearing alternately on one side of them and then the other.

When they came to a grassy lea overlooking a canyon with a burbling creek hundreds of feet below, Morgan said, "Jack, pull over here."

Abigail and Rebecca spread out a blanket while Cyrus struggled, trying to carry the basket. "Jack, get that for him, will you?"

Jack bent over Cyrus, helped him lift it, and the two of them duck-walked it over to the blanket.

"Good job," Jack said. "Why don't you see what mommy put inside while I get the beer."

Cyrus lifted the covering and peeked in. "Wine."

"Go ahead, Cyrus," Abigail said. "You can unpack it."

Cyrus got out glasses, plates and silverware, a jar of pickled cabbage, a plate of cold chicken wrapped in waxed paper, and a gooseberry pie.

Jack pried the lid off the bucket. "Rebecca, beer or wine?"

"Beer please. I haven't had a pint since I left Boston."

"I'll have wine," Abigail said.

Jack grinned at her. "I know what you want . . . What's this? Oh, look Cyrus, a sarsaparilla."

* * *

After a jovial lunch, Jack took a nap while Abigail and Cyrus picked flowers. Rebecca and Morgan opted for a walk.

In the high altitude, distant mountain ranges west of them were colored in striated bands of smoky blue. "I see what you meant," Rebecca said. "The light seems softened, bent somehow."

"Yes, and for an artist, the colors are . . . just ethereal."

"Not just artists. Anyone can sense this place is magical. The separation between planes here feels as diaphanous as a bride's veil."

Morgan extended his arm toward the vista. "Perfect evidence that Ireland doesn't hold a monopoly on thin places."

"Oh, I never said it did. But if such places exist, shouldn't I visit the ones my ancestors held to be thin?"

Morgan shrugged. "Your Easter sermon postulated that it is people who are too thick, not the place we're in. You said the divine is everywhere."

"It is. Behind religious beliefs, beyond ecclesiastical creeds and pious rituals, a part of us touches infinity. Within our being there's a point of oneness with eternity that places in the external world can't surpass—even this one."

"Yet, you're still leaving Taos to search for them."

"I don't think I'll have a choice. The Protestants want a more orthodox minister, and the Catholics want me run out of town. Rather than fight it, I've decided to go willingly."

"Don't give up that easily. I mean, I preferred painting luminous landscapes to portraits of town folk, even though the landscapes didn't sell. But the portrait work was necessary to keep the emporium growing. So I set aside my personal desires to make a go of the greater cause."

"I noticed you'd gone back to portrait work. Surely Mrs. Romero doesn't pay you."

"No, that's something my agent pressured me into. But once I started painting Peaches, I realized I can combine both styles into pieces that satisfy my artistic sense and may earn me a place in a gallery."

"I hope it does." Rebecca walked to the edge of the gorge, swept her hand behind her skirt, sat down, and dangled her feet off the ledge. "Why don't we sit for a while and enjoy the peaceful place you've found?"

Morgan peeked over the rim at the depths below, swallowed a lump in his throat, and sat down beside her.

CHAPTER 48

Morgan was in the middle of adding minor refinements to a recent painting when he heard a familiar voice behind him.

"Is that a portrait of Peaches?"

Morgan turned. He could smell Bryce even over the turpentine. He suspected Bryce hadn't bathed since he left in April, and this was June. "Don't get me started about what you did on her birthday, Bryce."

Bryce grabbed his crotch. "Like President Roosevelt says, 'Walk softly, and carry a big stick.'"

Morgan shook his head. The Medicine Man obviously hadn't cured Bryce's crass humor. "Jack and I told you to leave the Romero girls alone."

Bryce pointed at the canvas. "Looks like you didn't follow your own rule."

"I never touched Peaches. You're lucky she didn't get pregnant. Those girls weren't using any protection."

"Funny you should know that." Bryce dropped the defensiveness and spread his hands. "Anyway, it wasn't my idea, and we were careful."

Morgan doubted if Bryce was ever careful. He studied his canvas a moment longer and decided it was finished. The scene portrayed Peaches standing at the kitchen stove, spoon in hand, strainer full of vegetables on the counter next to her, water flowing from a hand pump on the sink behind her. The store didn't have a kitchen pump, so he'd sketched the one at Abigail's house and filled in the details here. A loose strand of hair hung over Peaches' eye. Her lips, slightly pursed, like a bride married barely a week, anticipating her husband. He'd found Peaches could project any sensual expression he requested. But she didn't care for the painting, saying her mother's dress made her look like an old married woman. Morgan told her he'd name it *Frontier Newlywed*.

"Beautiful subject, you know," Bryce said.

"That one, too." Morgan pointed to the senorita overlooking a panorama.

Bryce went over for a closer inspection. "Amazing. If I didn't know, I'd think she was a classic Spanish princess."

Morgan cleaned his brush. "A real chameleon, that one."

"Doesn't diminish the talent of the artist."

Morgan capped the turpentine. "So, you're back. Have you changed your mind about selling out?"

"No, but I need money."

"None of your jewelry sold. You may have to melt it for the silver."

"No, I couldn't do that. You mentioned it might sell back east."

"There's definitely a market in New York for all things Western. That's the reason I'm adding images of southwestern women to my canvases."

"You mean Peaches in different costumes."

"Yes, unless your Indians would let me paint them—"

"They're not *my* Indians—"

"You know what I meant. Brag to a few of them about my work. See if anyone will pose for me."

"Sure. Now, about the jewelry, you had a place in mind?"

"I'll give you the address. You can ship it to them on consignment."

"I'll do it today. Can you loan me some money until they sell?"

"Bryce, we don't have any money left."

"Surely there's enough for a bath, a shave, supper, and a drink."

"You do reek, I'll give you that."

Bryce held up his palm as if taking an oath. "I'll go straight to the laundry and barber."

Morgan opened the cash box and retrieved a silver dollar.

Bryce eyed it. "How much will shipping to New York cost?"

"I have no idea. You'll have to box everything up and get it weighed."

"Okay, let's do that after I get cleaned up." Bryce snatched the dollar and was out the door.

When he returned, both he and his clothes were clean, and he smelled of bay rum. He brought with him a wooden crate and a couple of old newspapers.

"You can't wrap the jewelry in newspaper."

"Why not?"

"Appearance counts. When they open the box in New York, you want to convey that the contents are precious, not some aunt's second-hand pewter. There's tissue paper under the counter."

Morgan helped Bryce wrap and pack each piece. He located the address of his friend's store in New York and wrote a cover letter, which he placed in the box before Bryce nailed on the lid.

"You should send a wire telling him a shipment's coming."

Bryce pulled the coins out of his pocket and studied them.

"You've got enough for a telegram," Morgan said.

Bryce and Morgan each took a side of the crate and carried it outside. They set it down while Morgan locked the store.

Rebecca came out of the church and saw them. "Bryce? How are you?"

Bryce took off his hat and waved it. "Ecstatic! Especially now."

Rebecca took a step back. "Euphoria's good . . . I guess."

"It certainly is. You should try it."

Morgan tipped his hat. "Rebecca."

"Hello, Morgan." She pointed at the box. "Shipping more of your paintings?"

"No. I'm helping Bryce take his things to the freight office."

"Bryce, are you leaving again?" she said.

"I'll be here a few days. We're meeting Jack for supper—"

"We are?" Morgan said.

Bryce nodded. "Sure, why not? Would you care to join us?"

"Thank you, but no. I have a dinner invitation from Mrs. Hoffsteader."

Bryce touched the brim of his hat. "Perhaps another night while I'm still here."

After Rebecca departed, Bryce and Morgan picked up the crate and walked to the freight office.

"She's leaned out," Bryce said.

"What do you mean?"

"Slimmed down, lost her pudginess."

At the freight office, Bryce put the bite on him for money to pay the freight. Morgan knew that was coming and had a couple more dollars in his pocket.

Next, they went to collect Jack. They entered Manby's house and Bryce gave a long whistle, "This place is looking good."

Morgan looked around. It was. Half-paneling in the main room, beadboard wainscoting running down the hallway. Door and window surrounds with an interesting profile and roundels at the corners. All very sharp and professional. "Most of it is Jack's handiwork."

Bryce spied Jack sanding the chair rail that ran along the wall. "Hey, Jack!"

Morgan waved. "Bryce's come to visit—wants to have a little reunion. Can you get off work?"

"I'll be right out." Jack took off his tool belt.

They postponed supper and headed to a bar where Jack ran a tab. Morgan was grateful to be done spending money on Bryce. Things were still tight every day, especially with most of their spare cash going to record companies back east. Bryce knew that when he left, but then again, Bryce couldn't pour sand out of his boots if the instructions were printed on the heel.

Bryce ordered round after round as if the tab didn't matter. Of course, he did. Morgan didn't see where time with the shaman had changed him a bit.

"Bryce," Jack said. "I thought you didn't need money on your spirit quest."

"I don't. The tribe is willing to share everything they have. Problem is they don't have anything. Even though they never say a word about me mooching off of them, I don't feel right about it. I felt I should get a little money so I can contribute, too."

"Well, you've come to the wrong place for that. I'm working full-time to get us out of debt, and Morgan's agent's got him painting like John Henry laying steel."

Bryce slapped Morgan on the shoulder. "You got an agent? That's great news!"

"It's even better. He's got two gallery shows lined up for me later this summer. That's why I'm painting in the store. With you gone, I had to find a way to run the shop and paint at the same time."

"Sorry, about that," Bryce said. But he didn't act it. "Business ceased being meaningful for me. I've heard a higher calling."

If that was true, Morgan thought, Bryce might need to invest in an ear trumpet.

"How's that going for you?" Jack said.

"More to it than I thought. Years to go, yet . . . years to go. Can I get a refill?"

Jack grabbed their glasses and went to the bar.

When Jack returned with the beers, Bryce said. "We saw Rebecca today."

"Not surprising," Jack said. "She lives in your old room."

"What? With you and Morgan?"

"Don't be ridiculous. The town would never let that happen. No, I'm at Mrs. Romero's and Morgan sleeps on a cot in the back of the store."

Bryce winked. "Morgan, you ever slip over there in the middle of the night?"

"I would never—And Bryce, don't be putting ideas in people's minds. She's had to put up with enough animosity."

"I wouldn't judge you for it. Rebecca's skinnier now, makes her look younger, too."

"Bryce, get off it."

"I'm saying something made her lose weight. Maybe it was living at Abigail's."

"Now, hold on, Bryce," Jack said. "Abigail is a great cook."

"I wasn't maligning Abigail's cooking. Merely suggesting a plump woman might feel the need to slim down to compete with Abigail's looks."

Morgan would have laughed once, but now he just shook his head. "Bryce, you just say stuff to be saying it."

"No, seriously. Rebecca's tall as a telegraph pole. Now she's twice as thin. Problem is, when she shed pounds, they took her curves with them. Oh, on second thought, Morgan wouldn't sneak into Rebecca's room—he doesn't like them flat, even though a two-by-four is the easiest board to nail."

"Oh, shut up, Bryce."

"Come on, Morgan, she may be the last virgin left in Taos. What was it we used to say? If any woman sleeps alone tonight, we're all at fault."

"I hope that's not your plan," Morgan said. "You were reckless with Peaches."

"She was eighteen. And any recklessness ran both ways. I assure you that girl hasn't got a modest bone in her body."

"That's true," Morgan said.

Bryce wagged his finger at Morgan. "Hah! You claimed you never touched her—"

"I didn't, but Peaches offered to model au natural. She imagines herself one of Renoir's bathers."

Bryce grinned. "I'd buy that painting."

"You don't have any money—remember?"

"Right," Bryce said. "But you should let her pose if she's willing. I'll bet there's a big market for nudes."

"Hell, no! If Mrs. Romero saw it, she'd have us run out of Taos. Listen, if I ever need a nude model I'll use one of Sneed's women."

"Oh, no!" Jack said. "Don't go to Sneed. He'll make us pay for you even looking."

All three of them roared with laughter.

CHAPTER 49

Mrs. Romero handed Jack a platter of fried eggs. He served himself two, passed it on, and took a swallow of coffee. He had a slight hangover, but since he'd started working on Manby's house, he made it a point not to miss breakfast—too long until dinnertime. Jack uncovered the biscuits, took one, and offered the basket to Cherry.

Mrs. Romero handed him a bowl of fried potatoes. "I hear Mr. Holloway is back."

Jack buttered his biscuit and marveled at how much displeasure she could work into such simple words. "For a few days."

"He is?" Peaches' voice went up an octave.

Mrs. Romero scowled. "You're not to pose for Mr. Silver until Mr. Holloway leaves."

"Oh, Bryce isn't staying at the emporium," Jack said. "Reverend Sullivan took over our apartment there."

"You may believe that, but he and that woman heretic are together as we speak. Milkman told me he saw them hiring a rig over at the livery just after dawn. Said they had a jar of nasty looking greenish-brown liquor and a bedroll. No need to guess what those two are up to."

Jack choked on his biscuit and hurriedly gulped a swig of coffee. Damn Bryce. Damn, damn, damn . . .

"Goodness, are you all right, Mr. Diamond?"

Jack took another swallow of coffee. "Fine. I just remembered something urgent. Please, excuse me."

"But you didn't finish your breakfast."

Jack grabbed a biscuit and sliced it open. "I can't dally any longer." He laid his bacon and one of the eggs between the biscuit halves and stood up. "I'll take it with me, if you don't mind."

Mrs. Romero sniffed. "Highly irregular."

"I know, but . . ." By the time he realized he couldn't think of an excuse, he was out the door.

Jack raced to the emporium, got Morgan—who also cast imprecations on Bryce—as they walked to Abigail's. She was sitting on the porch sipping her morning coffee. "Kind of early for you fellows."

Jack brushed biscuit crumbs off his shirt and wiped his hands on his pants. "Needs must. We have to rescue Rebecca."

Abigail jumped up, splattering coffee on the porch deck. "What's happened?"

"Bryce happened," Morgan said. "He's back, and we think he's taken Rebecca up in the mountains to give her peyote and seduce her."

"She wouldn't do that," Abigail said. "Believe me. I lived with the woman for four months. Besides, she's not his type."

"Bryce's type is anyone without a penis," Morgan said.

"Morgan and I had drinks with him last night," Jack said. "He sounded mighty interested in Rebecca. Kept commenting on how she'd lost weight. This morning Mrs. Romero said the milkman told her he saw the two of them renting a buggy, carrying a bedroll, and, what we think must have been a jar of peyote tea. And, believe me, if he persuades her to drink it, she won't be responsible for her actions."

"That's likely a false rumor," Abigail said. "Bryce can't handle a horse. He told me so himself."

"Maybe she's driving. I don't know. Anyway, we need your rig. They have a head start."

"One lesson, Jack, and you assume you can drive?"

"No, we're hoping you'll come with us."

"Best to have another woman there," Morgan added, "in case things have already progressed too far by the time we find them."

"Rebecca won't—with Bryce—peyote or no. But yes, I'll go. Jack can help me hitch up the horse." Abigail tied her hair into a bun. "Cyrus is still eating breakfast. Morgan, tell him to finish because we're going on a picnic."

"A picnic?"

"We certainly don't want to embarrass the Reverend by charging up there like we suspect something's amiss. No, I'll throw together a basket, and we'll pretend to stumble across them on our outing."

* * *

Rebecca and Bryce had spread out a blanket in the grass not far off the trail. The liveryman's horse and carriage were tethered to a nearby pine. Bryce lay on his back looking up at the clouds. Rebecca lounged beside him, propped up on her elbows, gazing at the sun-kissed vista.

Bryce had been sipping from the jar of tea at regular intervals and was showing its effects whereas Rebecca had yet to sample it.

"You don't need to go anywhere to experience a thin place," Bryce said. "Peyote thins any place out. Try it. See for yourself."

"How many times have you taken peyote?"

"I can't say at the moment . . . quantitative measures tend to escape one in this state."

"So a lot?"

"A lot."

"It would seem, if partaking in it that frequently actually worked, then you'd remain in higher consciousness permanently. Right?"

Bryce put his hands over his eyes. "Too much if-then logic. The visionary abhors the syllogism. It's the antithesis of mystical."

Rebecca shook her head. "A vision or a thin place should change you, wouldn't you agree? If you need to keep revisiting the experience, then perhaps the gap hasn't become as narrow as you imagine."

"Come on, Rebecca. Don't think all the joy out of a thing."

Bryce rolled on his side and threw his arm across Rebecca's hips. She didn't take his arm away, but she didn't move closer to him either.

Bryce wiggled his ears.

Rebecca laughed. "You're like a rabbit."

"In more ways than one."

She shook her head and looked away.

"There is ecstasy in an orgasm, but you don't know that, do you?"

Rebecca met his eyes.

He held her gaze. "Virginity isn't worth anything. By definition, it merely means someone without sexual experience. Even greater is the ecstasy in this elixir because orgasms are momentary and this stuff lasts ten to twelve hours."

He slid his hand a little lower down her thigh. "You're a smart woman with a college degree. You know a lot. But one thing we never know is, what we don't know . . . until we find out. Then, people say, 'If only I'd known sooner.'"

Rebecca laughed at him.

"Here we are in this beautiful place, and I'm offering two wonderful experiences you've never had. I promise you once you've felt them you will never be the same. So, drink a little of this tea, raise your petticoats, and we will marry two extraordinary experiences together—higher awareness and physical bliss."

He leaned in and gave her a soft kiss on the lips, letting it linger. She let him.

A horse and carriage clattered up the nearby road. Rebecca sat up on her knees and arranged her skirt.

Abigail turned the horse into the clearing and stopped. Jack shouted, "Hey, Bryce!" He leaped from the rig and tied the horse to a juniper. "Fancy running into you two here."

Bryce sat up, looking bewildered.

Jack helped Abigail from the carriage, and lifted out Cyrus, who raced over to Bryce and hugged his neck. "You want to play? I didn't bring my trains, but we could pretend."

Morgan retrieved the picnic basket and carried it over for Abigail.

"This was all so impromptu," Abigail said, shaking a blanket open and spreading it next to Rebecca and Bryce. "Jack said to me, 'It's such a lovely day, let's have an outing.' Next thing you know, we're riding along and there you are. You don't mind if we join you, do you?"

"Not at all," Rebecca said. "Hello, Jack, Morgan, Cyrus. Your timing was rather fortunate. I was growing hungry and Bryce neglected to bring any food. I was about to start foraging for berries."

Abigail smiled. "Don't worry, we have plenty. There wasn't time to prepare anything epicurean, but what it lacks in quality we'll make up in quantity. Jack, be a dear, and open the wine."

Jack had a corkscrew on his pocketknife, and when he'd uncorked the bottle, Abigail poured.

"This early?" Rebecca said.

"Let's call it brunch."

"While you ladies lay out the comestibles," Morgan said, "us three men are going for a walk."

Cyrus jumped up. "Me, too."

Morgan gave Abigail a quick, small shake of his head.

"No, Cyrus, I need you to help the Reverend and me get brunch ready."

"Aw, I want to go with the men."

"After lunch, you can."

"Bryce, you're with us," Jack said with a smile.

The men walked to a distant ravine out of earshot. Jack kicked a stone over the edge. "Come on, Bryce, not Rebecca."

"This whole town's full of willing women," Morgan said. "Yet you pick the one you would literally ruin."

"Ruining a virgin? You've never called it that before. Besides, Rebecca's searching for something, and I can help her find it."

"With peyote?" Jack said.

"And more. You both experienced its effect on consciousness. What I've discovered since then is the effect it has on sex. When you combine the mystical and sexual experiences—well, there's no way to describe what happens in that union. You guys *have* to try it. I've got extra. We can all take it and make love together."

"Cyrus is with us," Jack said. "Besides, there aren't enough women."

"Oh, right. Well, I'll give you some to take home, and you and Abigail can try it later. Morgan, I'm sure you're acquainted with some woman worthy of the experience. Maybe Peaches?"

Morgan spat on the ground. "Stop being stupid. We're not letting you drug the minister and seduce her."

"It's not a drug, it's a sacrament, and she *is* seeking a sacred experience."

"Not like this, Bryce."

"Morgan, I know you think I'm being selfish. The opposite is true. She deserves to find what she's seeking. We all do. Why should she have to wait a moment longer? Her kingdom is at hand." Bryce swayed.

Morgan grabbed Bryce's arm to steady him. Jack took his other arm, and together they turned back the way they had come.

Bryce dug his heels in. "You're not going to throw me into the ravine, are you?"

Jack laughed. "Tempting, but no."

They walked arm-in-arm down the path, back toward the blankets. Morgan kept his voice low. "Rebecca's an educated woman who knows more about what she's searching for than any of us. She's perfectly capable of deciding what's right for her. It's not up to you to charm her into it. You're planning to leave anyway. Don't take a virgin to bed and then flee."

"I didn't mean her any harm," Bryce said.

"You never do," Jack said.

While the men were gone, the women attempted to have a circumspect conversation over Cyrus's head. Abigail had Cyrus practicing arithmetic by counting the spoons, forks, knives, and plates he'd unpacked and arranged on the blanket.

"Believe me, I understand," Abigail said. "Bryce awakens powerful emotions in women."

"Feelings are complicated," Rebecca said. "We don't have them one at a time, but rather they arise in a tumult, like a muddle of mewing kittens. Don't they? The thing I do is decide the course I choose to live during times of clarity and peace, and then stick with my decision when the heart is in an uproar."

"Twenty-four," Cyrus said. "Six of everything."

"Very good. Now imagine there were six more of everything. How many would that make?" Abigail touched Rebecca's hand. "You're aware, I'm sure, that I am a strong advocate of equality between sexes."

"Between socks?" Cyrus said.

"No son, it means men and women should be equal. Are you through unpacking the basket?"

"All done."

"That's nice. Look, Cyrus, Jack's coming back."

Cyrus jumped up and ran toward the men.

"To finish what I was saying, Rebecca, women's choices shouldn't be foisted on them by outdated societal mores, but neither should our decisions make us feel guilty. Guilt is a futile emotion. What's the point? Whatever we're feeling guilty about has already happened, and the past cannot be changed."

"Nothing happened, you understand."

"Oh, I believe you. But whenever your time comes, remember it's a woman's right to choose who we love and when—as men do—guiltless and free."

Cyrus and the men arrived. Jack and Morgan deposited Bryce on the blanket. Jack reached over and, in one smooth motion, scooped up the jar of peyote and lofted it out over the canyon. Seconds later, they heard it shatter.

Jack tousled Cyrus's hair. "Looks like you did a good job getting everything unpacked, son. Shall we eat?"

CHAPTER 50

Jack and Morgan had enough troubles without worrying about Bryce. After his failed attempt to seduce Rebecca, he claimed the peyote had given him a new direction, and disappeared again. Two weeks passed, and no one was sure where he'd gone this time. He wasn't with the local Indians, who, when asked about Bryce, simply pointed toward the mountains.

Jack took the morning off work to help Morgan determine if the declining store income could support both of them. To keep the store going he'd have to quit working on Manby's house and run the store while Morgan traveled east for his gallery openings. They did still get customers for books —various members of the Ladies Book Club looking for salacious books they could read on the sly. And they sold some of their remaining records to Gramophone owners desperate for novelty. So someone needed to run the emporium. But this gallery opening was an opportunity he couldn't let Morgan pass up.

The empty strong box sat on the table between them. Silver dollars were stacked next to an even shorter stack of Eagles, and only one, solitary Double Eagle. To Jack's eye their cash on hand came to about seventy dollars. That would just about pay Columbia and Victor, with nothing left over to buy new stock.

While Morgan was doing sums on a sheet of paper, scratching out numbers and retotaling expenses, Jack thumbed through the May issue of *Popular Science Monthly*. "Did you read this article on radioactivity?"

"No, I haven't had a chance. I've been trying to figure out if we can save the emporium."

"Professor Rutherford says this heavy metal called uranium gives off invisible rays of charged particles. He's identified three distinct types of rays."

"Uh-huh."

"It boggles the mind that a stream of electrons can penetrate solid matter."

"It's all I can do to imagine how we can go on."

Jack pointed at the bin of gramophone records. "Can't you refill that when you go back east?."

"Maybe, if Abigail lets us skip next month's rent. But I've been trying to figure out our profit-loss statement—it's something Hoffsteader put me on to. Record sales don't bring in enough to cover living expenses for two, and book sales aren't much better. The book club has pretty much dried up. The ladies still meet, but they're so preoccupied with arranging Rebecca's replacement they aren't buying anything new to read."

Jack put down his magazine. "Let me help work the figures."

After another hour, Jack had come to agree with Morgan. The Emporium just wasn't going to be a going concern any time soon. There just wasn't enough modernity or enough market for it to support their lifestyle.

Jack stared at the figures a moment. He thought he would feel sadder than he did, but he'd guessed this day was coming for a while. "We can sell the remaining records to Deitwiler."

"What are we going to do with all those stereoscopes?"

"Can't we return them?"

"If we could, we would have done that a year ago."

Jack nodded. "Same with the generators. So let's donate them to the school. The kids can use the stereoscopes to learn geography and the generators for science experiments."

"What about the books?"

"No. These aren't exactly school books. I guess we should have a going-out-of-business sale."

"Pretty humiliating," Morgan said.

"Yeah, but we need money to live on while we find something else. You've got your art shows, but you'll be coming back afterwards. And I've got to buy tools for my new profession."

"What are you thinking of?"

"Turns out, I'm pretty good at carpentry and enjoy it. Not outside framing, but inside, cabinetry and finish work. If we clear enough cash from the sale to afford some tools, I'll leave Manby's job and become my own boss."

"We're alike in that respect—never cared for jobs where someone told us what to do."

"Of course, once we close the store, Morgan, you'll need somewhere to live."

"I guess I'll move back to Mrs. Romero's, if she has room."

Oh, damn, he'd meant to tell Morgan when he got here, but they'd got caught up in the store ledgers. "No, you better try the hotel instead."

"That's too expensive."

"I know. I considered moving there, but it's beyond my means, too."

"You? Why would you leave Romero's?"

"She's real sick with La Grippe and it's extremely contagious."

"I heard that's been killing people, but I didn't realize it was striking so close to home. Careful you don't catch it."

"Aw, I'm tough. I might starve to death first, though. She hasn't the strength to leave her bed and if you thought you were a failure as a cook, you should try eating what Peaches and Cherry tried to put together. I had to bring soup from Abigail to feed them all. Makes you wonder that a woman running a boardinghouse never taught her girls to fix a meal."

"Told me she planned to marry them to men who could afford to hire maids."

"I expect she did, but now they're in a hell of a mess."

Morgan returned the money to the strong box. "So are we, Jack, so are we . . . I hope you won't think me a coward, but one of us has to inform Abigail she's about to lose her one and only paying tenant."

"I don't mind. I'll do it now. This is Cyrus's last week of school." Jack spruced up his hat, put it on, and walked to Abigail's. Along the way he picked flowers from neighborhood yards until he had a nice bouquet. Jack had come to realize—had for some time now—that he didn't need a dozen women. He loved Abigail. Cyrus, too. So what if he and Morgan's dream of the emporium bringing eastern culture to the west hadn't succeeded, at least Morgan would show New York the beauty of New Mexico. Even though they no longer owned a store, they still had Taos. He might start out penniless again, but he was going to make a home for Abigail and Cyrus. If she'd have him.

Abigail met him at the door and kissed him on the mouth. "How nice. You're not working on a school day for a change." She accepted the flowers and put them in a vase on the dining table. Then she locked the front door and dragged Jack into the bedroom.

Afterward, as they lay varnished with each other's sweat, Jack said, "Did you ever consider remarrying?"

"Haven't yet."

"Me, either. Married, I mean." Jack absent-mindedly caressed her abdomen. "I've got to get out of Romero's, she's still deathly ill."

"My soup didn't help?"

"It did, and they were grateful. But La Grippe isn't something you can cure with chicken soup."

"You're not sick are you?"

"No, but Peaches is starting to show signs. I need to stay somewhere else until the disease runs its course."

"Where?"

"I was thinking of here."

Abigail sat up with a jerk and covered her nakedness with the sheet. "Jack! Absolutely not. You know better."

Jack nuzzled her neck. She pushed him away.

"Sweetie," he said, "this isn't another of your casual flings. We're in love." He kissed her hard and long, sliding her back down in bed.

She arched her body against him. When their lips parted, she adjusted her pillow to prop up her head. "You have persuasive lips." She kissed him again, briefly. "But we just can't. There's Cyrus to consider—"

"You've seen us together. I treat him like my own son."

"You do, but a parent has to protect her child from ridicule—from what other kids would say. They'd call me a prostitute and worse. He's too young to even understand what those words mean."

"What if we made it legal and proper? Could I move in then?"

Abigail pushed him off her. "Very funny. Proposing as a cheap ploy to get you out of Mrs. Romero's."

"Why not? I already own a brand new suit, thank you."

"Don't tease a girl."

Jack's shadow fell across her as he leaned close. "Abigail Wythe, I love you madly. And I have never been more serious in my life than when I ask this. Will you be my wife?"

She said nothing for long moments. He swallowed.

He worked a pinky ring his dad had given him off his finger and slid it onto hers. "Abigail?"

Tears started down her cheeks. "Yes," she whispered.

They kissed and kissed. When they paused to breathe, Jack said, "Did you know I was going to ask?"

She nodded. "I was afraid you would."

"Afraid?"

"Afraid I'd say yes. I wasn't sure I wanted to take the chance again."

"I'm glad you did. When you didn't say anything, the suspense about killed me."

"I love you, too, Jack. It's all just happened so soon."

"When the time is right, it's right. When can I move in?"

"After the wedding."

"Get dressed. I'll go get my suit and the minister."

"Weddings take weeks of planning."

"If you say. But seriously, wouldn't it be nice to be married by Rebecca before she leaves town?"

"That may be soon. The Ladies' Book Club is at about the end of their tether."

"If you hurry the preparations, we can even have a June wedding," Jack said.

"I'll talk to Penelope—Oh! I've got to tell Penelope. She'll never believe it."

"Why not? Surely, she knows about us. You two never keep secrets."

Abigail laughed. "You're right. But when I first told her I was seeing you, she was flabbergasted. She said, 'I thought you couldn't stand that man.'"

"And what'd you say?"

"I said, 'I don't stand him, I lay him.'"

Jack roared with laughter. Her modern no nonsense manner made him love her even more. "You'd expect after I took care of Walter, she'd have a better opinion of me."

"Oh, she does. She was referring to a comment I made after we first met at Deitwiler's party. Remember, where you totally embarrassed yourself?"

"Well, occasionally liquor makes an ass of anyone."

"Jack, you're not an ass all the time. Somewhere inside you is a kind person who cares what happens to others. That's why I'm ready to take the risk."

Jack's face flushed, and he looked away. Abigail turned him back toward her and kissed him. "We better get dressed. I've got to tell Penelope, and you've probably got things to do."

"Yes, I need to figure out what to do about the Romeros."

"Jack, I'm sorry, but if you don't want to stay there, you'll just have to do like Morgan and put a cot in the store until after the wedding."

Jack slapped his face. "The store, I completely forgot. I came to tell you we have to close it."

"Oh, you poor guys."

"You're not upset you're losing a tenant?"

"No, but I feel bad for you. I know it was your dream."

"Not the reaction I expected."

Abigail gave him a playful smile. "Of course, you did just propose marriage without any means to support a family."

Jack's face fell.

"I'm joking. I'd marry you rich or poor."

"I can support you and Cyrus. I've discovered I'm a darn good carpenter, and there's plenty of work to be had."

"Cyrus! Oh, I have to tell Cyrus, too."

"I'd like to be here. I can come back when school's out, so we can do it together—if you don't mind."

"Mind? I'd love it. Why, Jack, you're already thinking like a father."

"Let's get dressed, then." Jack pulled on his pants and buttoned his shirt. "I'm going to stop by the apothecary and see if he has any kind of patent medicine that'll give Mrs. Romero some relief."

"See? That's what I mean about your kindness. You don't even try; it just leaks out on its own."

Jack waved his hand. "I guess I better tell Morgan the big news. You don't mind, do you?"

Abigail threw her arms around his neck. "I think he should be the first one we tell." She hugged him and then made a half-turn. "Button me up, will you?"

Jack reached around her and cupped her breasts in his hands.

She pushed his arms down. "The buttons are back there, Jack."

"Not all of them." And he reached lower.

So it was a little while before Morgan heard the good news.

CHAPTER 51

When Jack returned to the store, Morgan was blocking out a new painting. Jack could make out the outlines of the local mountains on a horizon that stretched on forever. "Nice picture," he said. "Do you know where the Sears & Roebuck catalog is?"

"In the privy?"

"I hope it's not missing too many pages."

"Why?"

"Morgan, old buddy, you better take a seat. I need you to do something for me."

Morgan laid down his brush and palette. "What's that?"

"I need you to be my best man—I'm getting hitched."

"What?"

"To Abigail. I asked, and she accepted."

Morgan grabbed Jack in a bear hug and pounded his back. "Couldn't have happened to two better friends."

"You're not mad?"

"Why would I be?"

"You and Abigail had something—"

"Oh, Jack, that was over by the time Bryce got here. Abigail and I have been best friends practically since we met at Deitwiler's party. I wish the two of you every happiness. I have no regrets."

"I wouldn't want to do it if you felt any other way. God, there's so much to do. I need to talk to Rebecca—we want her to perform the ceremony. Get tools ordered so I can start my business—I have a family to support now. Take medicine to Mrs. Romero . . . Oh, and Abigail says I've got to sleep here until the wedding. Do you mind?"

"Of course not, it's your store, too." Morgan laughed. "Find your own cot, though."

Jack ran for the door.

"Calm down," Morgan said. "It will all get done."

From the emporium, Jack went to the apothecary and then home to Mrs. Romero's. Cherry met him the door. "Peaches is weak as a moth, and Mama hasn't been able to sit up since yesterday. There isn't any way to even get soup in her, lying down."

"I know you're worried. I bought medicine. Try to stay calm, and get me a big spoon."

While Cherry was gone to the kitchen, Peaches came downstairs, holding desperately to the banister to steady her descent. As she reached the foyer, Cherry returned with a large serving spoon and handed it to Jack.

"Peaches," he said, "I brought medicine for your Mama, but you better take some, too." He poured a spoonful. Peaches put a hand on the wall to brace herself and opened her mouth. Jack put the spoon between her lips and tipped it up. She tried to swallow, but a little of it leaked from the corner of her mouth. He wiped her chin with his thumb and started upstairs when Cherry screamed. He turned just as Peaches collapsed with a *thunk*.

"Did the medicine do that?" Cherry said.

"No. It's La Grippe. It's weakened her, and I'm afraid it might get you, too." He scooped Peaches up in his arms and carried her to her room. "Cherry, bring that medicine and spoon." He laid Peaches on the bed, and when

Cherry entered, he said, "Your sister's got a fever. She needs to get out of those clothes, but your mother won't appreciate me undressing her, so I'll go check on Mama while you help Peaches into a nightgown."

Jack managed to get Mrs. Romero to sip from the medicine spoon, but the effort wore her out and she fell back asleep. When he came out of the room, Cherry was shifting from one foot to the other, eyes darting between Peaches' door and her mother's.

Jack laid his hand on her forehead and then lifted each eyelid to look. "How are you feeling, Cherry? Have you been vomiting? Have you had the trots?"

Cherry sniffled and shook her head.

"Hell, I don't even know what to look for. Come with me. We're going to the doctor."

Doc Martin examined Cherry—and Jack, for good measure. When he was satisfied, he said, "What you described sounds like gastroenteritis. Fortunately, neither of you have it, but it's been taking a lot of lives."

A stifled sob leaked out of Cherry.

"It'd be best for the two of you to stay elsewhere until it runs its course. I'll stop by Mrs. Romero's after office hours to check on her and the older girl."

"I gave them some medicine about a half-hour ago," Jack said.

"What'd you give them?"

Jack shrugged. "Something the apothecary sold me. I didn't bring it with me, but you'll find it on the nightstand when you visit them. It's in a blue bottle."

"I know what he's selling. It's mostly opium. Won't cure anything, but it will make them sleep. Sleep's probably as good as anything we can do. Any other boarders who might be in peril?"

"No one but Jack," Cherry said. "Mr. Smith and Mr. Jones haven't been home in weeks."

"Lucky for them," Doc said.

They walked back to the house, and Jack made Cherry wait on the porch while he went in to pack for her. He found Peaches snoring—probably a good sign.

He opened the wardrobe and paused, unsure which dresses belonged to whom. Well, the girls were about the same size, so he stuffed several dresses into a carpet bag. From the chest of drawers he randomly grabbed stockings and underthings. Tossing in a comb, brush, and a handful of hair ribbons, he fastened the bag closed and went to wake Mrs. Romero. Jack explained that she needed to send Cherry to stay with a neighbor until she and Peaches recovered, lest Cherry catch it too. Mrs. Romero was groggy, but she nodded her consent.

Jack and Cherry crossed the street to the Hoffsteaders where he explained the situation to Ida. Despite his assurance that the doctor said Cherry wasn't sick, Ida didn't want to risk her family's health. And he could understand that. They tried several more neighbors without luck. Finally, an exasperated Jack took Cherry to the church and asked Rebecca if she'd let the girl stay in her apartment for a few days. Rebecca said she could.

Jack was so relieved he completely forgot to ask Rebecca if she would perform the wedding.

CHAPTER 52

Mrs. Romero died that Wednesday. Doc Martin told Jack La Grippe seldom lasted longer than a week—patients either died quickly or got better. Peaches was going to recover, but she wouldn't be well enough to attend the funeral. Jack knew she'd never be able to wash and prepare the body and he didn't want Cherry to do it. Cherry said they hadn't any relatives nearby, and none of Mrs. Romero's fellow parishioners volunteered, so Jack hired the undertaker. The service would, of course, be at the Catholic Church, but the undertaker said if they delayed it more than a day, there'd be an extra charge for ice.

Jack and Abigail, though not Catholic, accompanied Cherry to the funeral so she wouldn't have to sit in the front row alone. Abigail feared the death of a mother would be too traumatizing for Cyrus, so she left him with Penelope and Walter.

In the days following the service, Father Ignacio expressed his displeasure that Cherry was staying with the Protestant minister, but members of his congregation were uniformly more afraid of La Grippe than they were of their padre's disapproval. So Cherry continued to stay with Rebecca.

No one seemed to recognize how much her mother's death and sister's grave illness affected Cherry.

Several days after her mother's funeral, in the middle of the night, Cherry slipped from her bed, crossed through the church, and entered the store. She headed straight for Morgan's cot, lifted the sheet, and wiggled in beside him.

Morgan was lying asleep on his side. Cherry slid her leg between his legs and pressed against him. His eyelids fluttered and then popped open. "Cherry?"

"Morgan."

"What are you doing?" he said in a hoarse whisper.

"I miss sharing my bed with Peaches. Can't I just snuggle with you?"

Morgan shot up. "No, you cannot. And whisper. Jack's sleeping on the other cot."

Cherry buried her face in his neck, the sadness and loneliness more than she could bear. "I don't want to sleep alone."

Morgan put his lips to her ear. "Well, you can't sleep here. Go back to Reverend Sullivan's apartment and be quiet about it. Make sure you don't wake her or Jack in the process."

Cherry whimpered like a puppy lost from her mama. Which was how she felt. She'd hated her mother's restrictions all these years. And now she'd give anything to get her back.

"Shhhh." Morgan scooted her off the cot, whispering, "It's a terrible thing you're going through, I know. But this isn't a solution. Doc says Peaches will get better; then you'll be back home."

Cherry, now forced from the bed, leaned over and tried to kiss him. Morgan turned her away and gave her a light smack on the butt. "Go back to your own bed."

* * *

Jack found cabinet work within a day and quit his job at Manby's. His order from Sears and Roebuck hadn't arrived, so he borrowed tools from Fred.

When he returned to the store, he said, "Morgan, we still have a little money, don't we?"

Morgan laughed. "You think so?"

"Give me enough to pay the doctor to keep checking on Peaches. I mean, I take her meals, but I don't know what medical things to do for her."

"I feel sorry for the girls, losing their mother and all, but isn't there some Catholic charity that can help?"

"I don't know if they will or not, but I'm not going over there to ask them. Are you?"

"We're broke, Jack."

"I've got a job. We'll be okay soon as I get paid, but Peaches needs medical care now."

"I agree. Cherry's already an orphan, we can't let her lose her sister, too. But extra money? We haven't any." Morgan scratched his head. "Tell you what, Doc likes to read, and he accepts barter. Tell him in exchange for taking care of Peaches he can come to our store and pick out as many books as he wants."

* * *

As soon as Doc said Peaches was no longer contagious, Morgan suggested they move Cherry back home to nurse her sister. For everybody's good. To preserve the girls' reputation, Jack continued to stay at the store. Tongues would wag if two teenage girls were living with Abigail's fiancée without supervision. It was a decision Jack regretted when Smith and Jones returned. He'd always resented the way Smith was forever poking his pudgy fingers into Cherry's dimples.

Jack came by every day to check on them. Once Peaches recovered, she discussed their financial situation with Jack.

"Smith and Jones offered to sell the house for us. They don't think we can run a rooming house on our own. And they're right. After all, Mama always planned to marry us off. She never gave us any business training or practical skills. We can't even cook very well."

"I agree, you two aren't capable of coping with a houseful of male boarders, and lord knows, neither of you can cook anything as complicated as chicken soup. But the house is paid for and could provide you with a steady income if you found someone to help you manage it."

"I don't want the house. I've always felt trapped there, and this just prolongs the prison sentence. I want to sell it and move to New York City."

"What will happen to Cherry if you do that?"

"Um . . . I'll figure something out. Mrs. Deitwiler is having her baby soon and won't be able to mind the store. Maybe Cherry can clerk for them."

"Well, if you're determined to sell, I don't believe you should trust land agents. There are too many shady real estate deals going on in New Mexico. I suggest you get advice from Mrs. Wythe before making any arrangement. She's been handling her own business affairs for years, and she won't misguide you."

Peaches agreed to talk to Abigail before doing any deal with Smith and Jones and went there that afternoon.

Abigail greeted her affectionately and invited her into the parlor. "You look like you're on the mend."

"Much better, thank you."

"Would you care for some lemonade?"

"That would be lovely, thank you."

Abigail excused herself and returned with two icy glasses. "I'm so sorry about your mother."

Peaches pressed her lips together, turned her head, and wiped her eyes with a hankie she pulled from her sleeve.

"Please, have a seat."

Peaches sat on the divan with her hands in her lap, twisting the hankie and wrapping it around her fingers.

Abigail sat down next to her. "Try the lemonade."

Peaches took a sip and returned her glass to the coaster. She smoothed out the wrinkled hankie, refolded it, and then squeezed it in her left hand.

"Jack tells me you're selling the house."

"Yes, I am."

"You need help to settle your mother's estate, but you mustn't trust land agents—or most lawyers. They'll have their fingers in your purse as soon as you shake hands."

Peaches stared, wide-eyed. "So what can I do? What do I do?"

"Calm down. There's a lawyer in Santa Fe I trust. I'll take you there to meet him. Let me wire ahead for an appointment. School's out now, so we may have to take Cyrus along, unless my sister can watch him."

"If not, my sister can," Peaches said. "Or does Cherry need to go with us?"

"You're eighteen, right? Is she?"

Peaches shook her head.

"We'll ask the lawyer to have the judge make Cherry your ward. That way no one outside the family can become her guardian and claim her share of your parent's estate. Also, Jack spoke to your teacher. She's going to let you take make-up tests so you can graduate."

"Oh, I don't care about that."

"You should. You may need that diploma once the money from your estate runs out."

"I won't. I'm going to meet a famous artist and become his lover."

Abigail couldn't help but smile. "That won't pay the bills, honey. Take your finals."

CHAPTER 53

Rebecca came into the store and slumped into a chair. "Well, it's official."

Morgan looked up from the wooden container he was building. He'd been scavenging crates from neighboring stores and reconfiguring them to hold his artworks for the journey to New York. There were too many paintings for him to carry aboard like he did last time, and they wouldn't fare well in the baggage car without sturdy protection.

"The church has found my replacement," she said. "I'll be leaving as soon as he arrives."

"Back to Boston, or have you found another church?" Morgan paused to test a canvas in one of the slots to see if it fit snugly.

"No offers yet."

"Well, we're young. You have a dream and it doesn't succeed, so you try something new. That's what Jack and I are doing."

"The church committee has offered a severance, so I have a little traveling money and that's exactly what I'd like to do—travel."

"To Ireland looking for thin places?"

"I do think there are places where it's easier to feel closer to heaven, much like the one you showed me a few weeks ago. Not that a person necessarily has to go to a certain place to touch something higher."

"I agree," Morgan said. "But it's nice to visit them. For me, it's not the place that's thin, it's the light. When I paint, it's as though a luminous energy is shining from a higher plane."

"Have you ever considered painting the Irish countryside or its rocky coasts? Many famous painters claim the greens are more vivid there, the seascape more dramatic."

Morgan gestured at the emporium's bare shelves and the 'Going Out of Business' sign in the window. "I think passage to Ireland is beyond my means. I'm still trying to make train fare to New York."

Morgan finished nailing strips of wood inside the crate to keep the canvases separate. He slid wrapped canvases into the slots while Rebecca watched in silence. Then he nailed the lid on and started building the next container. There were still several stacks of canvases to crate. This was going to take him a while.

"I'd always hoped to travel with Granddad when he retired, to visit the land where his parents came from. But he passed away last month."

Morgan stopped. He hadn't heard. "I'm sorry for your loss."

"It's . . . it's all right. At least he died thinking I was a success."

"You are a success," Morgan said, as he pried apart another salvaged crate. "It's the town that failed you." He laid out the rough boards, trying to imagine how to turn them into the shape he needed. "Jack can do this faster and better, but he's building new kitchen cabinets for Ida Hoffsteader. I don't begrudge him. He needs the money—wedding, new family, and all that goes with it."

"Yes, he asked me to perform the service, even if my replacement arrives before then."

"So you'll be here until the end of the month?"

"At least, but I may need to move to the hotel if the new minister gets here before the wedding."

"Can you afford that?"

"Granddad Fitzpatrick left me something in his will, plus there is my severance pay."

Morgan selected a board to saw into strips to make inside rails for the next crate.

"Do you want me to hold that board for you?"

"Thanks, but no, it's too narrow. Jack taught me to clamp it." Morgan attached the board to a sawhorse with three C-clamps and began cutting.

Rebecca stepped back from the spray of sawdust. "I have a brochure from the Cunard Line. The *R.M.S. Umbria* sails from New York to Queenstown, Ireland every other Saturday in the summer. It says, 'From Pier 40, at the foot of Clarkson Street.' Do you know where that is?"

"I do." Morgan gathered the strips he'd cut and carried them to where he was assembling the crate. "So, definitely Ireland, then?"

"I'd like to—not merely to find out if there are thin places, but also to see where my great-grandparents came from."

"An ancestral pilgrimage?"

"That's one way to put it." Rebecca placed her hand on Morgan's shoulder and he stopped hammering. "The problem is, Granddad is dead. It was a scary thing to come west on my own, but I felt safe in America where there are telegraphs, telephones, and a train back home. This would be different. I'd be cut off, alone, a single woman in a strange land an ocean away."

"There's always the transatlantic telegraph cable. You could send a message from Ireland to Boston if you had to."

"Morgan! Are you being deliberately obtuse? Are you going to force me to say it? All right, I'm afraid to voyage on a ship full of strangers without a companion."

"What about your family?"

"None of them have the time or desire. Will you go with me? I've checked the price. If we go second class, I've enough money to pay for two cabins."

Morgan laid down his hammer and turned toward her. "That's too generous. I can't. It'd be like living off a woman's fortune." *Except that isn't even a fortune.*

"You could paint in Ireland."

"If I were there, I'm sure I would. But I can't. I've got to be in New York this summer for two gallery shows. Then I'm coming straight back here. Taos is *my* thin place."

Rebecca wrung her hands. "I've got all this money. What good does it do?"

Morgan pried apart her hands and held one gently. "I'm leaving for New York the day after Jack's wedding. We can ride the train together, and after we arrive, I'll help you find the port and make sure you get safely onboard."

"Much obliged, but I'm really looking for someone to accompany me on the voyage and in Ireland."

"What about a lady's companion?"

Rebecca put her finger to her lips. "Two women traveling together? Maybe . . ."

"With a woman you could share one cabin. It'd reduce your expenses."

"I suspect you already have someone in mind."

"Cherry."

"Cherry?"

"She's at odds and ends, losing her mother, and soon, her home. It sold in one day. A trip abroad with you might be the very thing she needs. She could be your companion and maid."

"Oh, I couldn't treat her like a maid. She'd be more like my younger sister."

"A role Cherry knows well. Peaches is her legal guardian now. Shall we go ask her permission?"

Rebecca nodded and stood up.

Morgan locked up the store and walked with Rebecca to the Romero place. They knocked on the door and Peaches let them in. The house was in disarray, with open trunks and packing boxes everywhere. Mrs. Romero's good china and silverware were displayed on the dining table.

"We're having an estate sale," Peaches said. "Cherry won't help."

"Where is she?" Rebecca said.

"Sitting in the parlor, pouting. She's afraid of moving."

"Let me talk to her," Rebecca said. "Where's your parlor?"

Peaches pointed to a pair of closed doors off the foyer and Rebecca went in.

As soon as the door closed, Peaches frowned at Morgan. "You *with* her now?"

"No, we're just friends."

"Never been that with a boy."

"Sure you have. You and I are friends."

"Are we? I thought I was your model."

"You were. But don't you agree we're friends, too?"

"You mean because we didn't have sex?"

Morgan realized something in that moment. Free love was a lot more complicated than he thought. It wasn't about men and women both having the right to have sex with whomever they wished. It was about men and women respecting each other, whether sex was in the picture or no. Peaches had the first part, but the last part was a complete mystery to her. But then, she had been raised to be a wife and nothing else. She might not know there was something else out there.

"No," he said, "I mean because I like you, and you like me, without sex. Men and women can do that."

"Does that mean you think I'm a woman?"

"You definitely are. And responsible for Cherry, now, too."

"It seems like if we were really friends, you'd take me to New York with you."

"I'm not moving there. I plan to live and paint here. Once I get arrangements set up with my agent, I'll be able to ship galleries art without needing to travel there, except for the occasional opening."

Peaches collapsed in on herself again. "You really don't understand. Taos may seem special to you, but for us who grew up here, it's a place to get away from. I have the same urge to leave Taos as you and Jack had when you left New York to come west." The parlor door opened and Rebecca and Cherry came out. "But now I'm stuck here with *her*."

"That's actually what we came to talk to you about," Morgan said. "Reverend Sullivan has been replaced. She's going abroad and needs a traveling companion. I suggested Cherry."

Peaches surged to her feet, slapped Morgan's face, and stormed out, slamming the screen door.

Rebecca started after her, but Morgan held the minister back. "Let me. What did Cherry think?"

"She was delighted," Rebecca said. "We were coming to tell you the news."

"You two wait here. I'll speak to Peaches."

Morgan opened the door and saw her standing with her back to him, her head against one of the porch columns, sobbing. He put his hand on her back.

She jerked away. "Leave me alone. You're not my friend. You knew I was the one who wanted to leave Taos. Now, it's Cherry who you want to go."

"Not without your permission."

"Then I say no. She can just stay here and suffer with me."

Morgan put his arm around her and began to walk her toward the swing. "Peaches, why don't we sit for a minute and talk this out."

"No, I don't want to." She hooked her arm around his waist and leaned into him, even as she said it.

They sat together and Morgan pushed the swing in motion with his feet. He waited silently for the gentle swaying movement to calm her. He thought about her situation. What would become of her if she stayed? Pregnant and married to some man who wanted her money? Or carousing and drinking until she'd spent her inheritance and ended up on the slippery road to Sneed's brothel? He didn't like either of those choices.

And neither would she. What she wanted was to be a model. He was going back east. He knew artists there. She'd proved she could hold a pose and maintain a constant expression for long periods of time. She had enough inheritance to try for the life she wanted. Still, he'd make her buy a round-trip ticket, so she'd always be able to come home.

"Peaches, the week after next, Rebecca's going on the train to New York with me. If you'd like, you and Cherry can come with us. If you'll let Cherry sail to Ireland with Rebecca, I'll introduce you around the city."

Peaches threw her arms around his neck and squeezed until he could barely breathe.

He created a little separation between them. "We need to be perfectly clear about this. I'm only staying long enough to hang my two gallery shows and attend the openings. I'm not going to become your lover, or pretend we're married so we can share a hotel room. I'll find you a suitable women's hotel and acquaint you with my artist friends. We'll see if we can find you a steady modeling job before I leave, but if not, you agree to take the train back here with me."

Peaches kissed him on the mouth, hard.

Morgan pulled back. "What'd I just say?"

"Oh, Morgan, you're the nicest man I ever met."

CHAPTER 54

The day before their June thirtieth wedding, Abigail and Jack were cleaning the parlor. "Just think, tomorrow I'll be Mrs. Diamond."

"Ummm . . ." Jack said, "Actually, we should talk about that."

Abigail clenched her jaw and stopped waxing the credenza. "Are you getting cold feet? Now?"

Jack took her hand. "Oh, no, not at all. It's just that . . . don't think I'm a liar like Bryce, I'd just completely forgotten to tell you—"

"What, Jack?"

"My real name—it's Julius Hornsby. Morgan and I changed our names when we moved here."

Abigail looked relieved. "There's nothing illegal about that."

"Good, I always hated the name Hornsby. And Julius? Do we have to tell Rebecca anything . . . for her records?"

"Out here, a man's name is whatever he says it is. That's good enough for me."

Jack kissed her. "You're an amazing woman, *Mrs. Diamond.*"

"Not 'til tomorrow."

He hugged her. "But amazing every day."

* * *

On the wedding day, everybody was nervous. Abigail had decided an evening wedding would be cooler, in case the day turned out to be hot. But her decision just gave everyone extra hours to worry. Penelope, her matron of honor, kept re-ironing the wedding dress. "I swear, Penelope, you're going to wear the iron out. You're worse than you were for your own wedding."

Peaches and Cherry, excited to be bridesmaids, picked the flower bouquets too early. The petals wilted by mid afternoon, and new bouquets had to be made. It gave them something to do besides obsessively undoing and redoing their hair, which they'd done all afternoon. Peaches thanked Abigail for the third time for helping them sell their house. "But I felt kind of bad having to put Mr. Smith and Mr. Jones out."

Abigail waved this away. "Don't worry about Smith and Jones. They're, no doubt, off swindling someone else."

As the afternoon wore on, Penelope made limeade because she'd read it calmed the nerves. She made everyone drink copious amounts. The principal effect was they all had to frequent the outhouse.

Finally, Walter's wagon pulled in, carrying Jack, Morgan, and several barrels of beer. "I can't see how many kegs Jack brought for the reception," Abigail said, looking out the window. "But I'm sure it's more than we need."

Penelope pulled her away from the window. "Get out of sight. It's bad luck for Jack to see you."

"Superstitious nonsense."

"Well, it was poor luck with Claude Wythe."

"He wasn't husband material, that's all." Abigail looked down the driveway. "I think we should line the drive with luminaries."

"You're deciding this now, at the eleventh hour?"

"Cyrus and your three have been underfoot all day. It'll give them something to do." Abigail started for the door. "Let me ask Morgan if the emporium still has any paper bags."

Penelope slammed the door closed. "No. I'll do it. Peaches, Cherry, keep her here. Sit on her if you have to."

Penelope walked out onto the porch. "Walter, Abigail wants the kids to make luminaries Ask Morgan if there are any paper bags left at the emporium. If not, get some from the general store. We'll probably need more candles, too."

"Will do. We're going back for ice, anyway."

Jack jumped off the wagon and started toward the house.

Penelope held up her hand. "Jack, you stay back. It's bad luck."

"Luminaries?" Jack said.

"Just . . . do whatever she wants. Abigail's as nervous as a cat on a cook stove."

"Am not," Abigail shouted from the bedroom.

When Walter returned with paper sacks and candles, he started the children filling them with sand while he unloaded the ice and packed it around the beer kegs. Jack and Morgan hadn't come back with him, so Abigail escaped Penelope's clutches and went out on the porch for air. Cyrus wasn't in view, and Peaches and Cherry had disappeared. Perhaps the three of them went to pick more flowers. If this wedding took any longer to start, there wouldn't be a blossom left in her flower garden.

Ida Hoffsteader appeared at the end of the drive and walked toward her carrying the wedding cake—the Hoffsteaders had volunteered their cook's services. Abigail met Ida halfway and took it from her. It was a lovely three-layer cake with white icing, decorated with delicate flowers made of frosting.

"How beautiful," Abigail said.

"She did a good job," Ida said. "Forgive me for hurrying away, but I've got to change my dress and make sure Henrietta and Mr. Hoffsteader are getting ready. You can't trust a man to dress on time."

Abigail thanked her again and carried the cake into the dining room where she set it in the center of the table and began to arrange silverware around it. There was a knock on the door. "Penelope, can you get that?" Penelope didn't respond. Whoever it was knocked again.

Abigail opened the door and found Ida holding Cyrus by his shirt collar. "I discovered your young man exposing himself in the yard."

"I was peeing," Cyrus said.

"I'll take him, Ida. You go on home and get ready."

Ida let go of his collar and hurried away.

"Cyrus, why didn't you use the privy?"

"The girls were in it. They take forever, and I had to go real bad."

Abigail tried not to smile. "Well, sweetie, there will be a lot of people here tonight and long lines for the privy. Try to plan ahead a little bit, so you're in line before it gets so urgent."

Cyrus nodded solemnly. "Jack says kind of the same thing. Although he says, 'Never pass up a chance to pee.'"

Abigail tousled his hair. "I'll bet he does. Now, go help your cousins fill luminary bags. We have to get you washed and dressed before long."

"Will the wedding be soon, Mommy?"

She sighed. "Not soon enough."

* * *

The emporium looked more like a warehouse than an empty business. Abigail and Jack had offered to take everyone to the train tomorrow, but when Jack saw the pile of crates and luggage, he said to Morgan, "These won't all fit in the carriage. We have to leave room for passengers."

Morgan's paintings filled three crates, plus his suitcase, which lay open on one of them. Rebecca, Peaches, and Cherry each had large steamer trunks.

The women also had suitcases, but those were over at the hotel where Rebecca was staying—Abigail had decided it'd be best if the Romero girls went back to the hotel with Rebecca after the reception. "That way they won't get in trouble, and we'll know where to find them in the morning."

Morgan rapped his knuckles on one of the trunks. "You're right. No way we'd fit all this in the carriage, or even on a stagecoach. We're going to load everything on Walter's wagon tomorrow morning, and he'll follow us to the depot in Santa Fe."

"Not taking the train from Tres Piedras?"

"No. Dunn owns the only bridge across the Rio Gorge, and he charges a dollar a person and fifty cents a horse. It'd cost us a fortune. Besides, Walter wants to pick up a load of seed in Santa Fe."

Morgan, as best man, was ostensibly helping Jack get dressed. Although, after they'd delivered the beer, they'd merely been killing time until the wedding and trying not to drink too much. Morgan patted one of the crates. "Isn't it ironic? My agent had a hard time getting me a showing in New York until I started using Peaches for a model. Now, I'm about to lose her to New York."

"She had nothing to do with it. It's purely your talent, whether it's mountain scenery or a pretty woman. Hell, you can paint Abigail if you want. I won't mind."

"Thanks, but isn't that up to her?"

Rebecca crossed the street from the hotel and came in the store, looking nervous.

"Making sure the groom doesn't run out?" Jack said.

"No. Making sure I don't. I've never performed a wedding before. I didn't want to walk there alone."

"Well, it's my first time, too," Jack said.

"Don't worry," Morgan said, "I think it'll stick."

Rebecca inspected Jack's suit and straightened his tie. She smoothed Morgan's lapels, patted her hair, and linked arms with the men. "It's time. Don't let me faint, boys."

They walked arm-in-arm down the road, into Abigail's backyard. Colorful strings of Japanese lanterns strung between the house and conservatory swayed gently, making the candlelight within them flicker. Fuchsia-tinted clouds tinged the western sky as the guests took their seats. Cherry, then Peaches, then Penelope, and finally Abigail came out of the house and walked in a procession to where Jack, Cyrus, and Morgan waited in front of Rebecca.

When the wedding party had gathered near, Rebecca made her introductory remarks and began the vows, "Do you, Jack Diamond, take Abigail Wythe —"

"I do," Jack said.

"You don't want to wait until you hear what you're getting into?" Rebecca said.

Everyone laughed. Then, Rebecca resumed the ceremony. When she reached the end, while Jack and Abigail kissed, the sun fell behind the mountains, and fireflies began to appear.

"What are those, daddy?" Walter's daughter said.

"Fireflies. First time I've seen them west of Kansas."

"When I was a kid we'd see them in the Jemez Mountains, around McCauley Springs," Mr. Wentworth said. "Never here, though."

Children began chasing them around the yard.

Jack squeezed his new bride. "Kind of magical, don't you think?"

"A whole new beginning," she said.

The reception jumped into a full gallop. Men tapped the keg, and the three-piece band Jack hired struck up a tune.

"I'll be right back, honey," Jack said. "What can I bring you?"

"Penelope's bringing it," Abigail said.

Penelope handed her sister a glass of champagne and studied the assemblage. "Seems all your past lovers are at your wedding. Shouldn't you have invited Bryce?"

"Oh, we tried, but he's off somewhere making himself over into a shaman. An old Indian told Jack he saw Bryce up on Wheeler Peak shouting, 'We're all hawks now.'"

"Not trying to fly, I hope."

Abigail clinked her sister's glass. "Here's to hope."

Emma and Fred came over, greeted Morgan cordially, shook Jack's hand, and then left to congratulate Abigail.

"I'm surprised you invited the Deitwilers to your wedding after the Gramophone debacle," Morgan said.

"You and I never were the type to hold grudges," Jack said. "Fred's been real nice. When I needed tools for my cabinet business, he loaned me his until my own arrived. And Emma helped Abigail sew her wedding dress. Hell, we're neighbors now. We've got to get along."

Morgan smiled. "I got nothing but good wishes for Fred and Emma."

"And the coming baby? Theirs, yes?"

"Fred's, not mine, definitely," Morgan said.

A sudden explosion jolted them, and a red starburst lit up the night sky.

"Fireworks at your wedding? You really went all out."

"I don't know anything about it. Let's ask Abigail."

Squeals of delight came from the children as a green one exploded. Jack and Morgan found Abigail and Penelope in a cluster of adults craning their necks skyward.

Jack leaned over Abigail and kissed her forehead. "This is a surprise."

"I didn't do it," Abigail said.

"There's your benefactor." Morgan pointed toward Walter, standing in the lane, surrounded by a passel of youngsters. A fuse sputtered, they all backed up, and another plume raced skyward.

Jack waved. "Thanks, Walter, absolutely beautiful."

"Tuesday's Independence Day. I'd already bought them, and I thought, what the hey, why not tonight?"

"Keep the children back when you light those things," Penelope shouted.

"Stand back, kids," Walter said, as he lit another one.

"Abigail," Penelope said, "after the reception, Walter and I are going to take Cyrus home with us, so you and Jack can spend your wedding night alone."

"Thanks, Sis."

"Much appreciated, Penelope," Jack said.

"We might be late picking Cyrus up, tomorrow," Abigail said. "Jack and I are taking Morgan, Rebecca, and the Romero girls to the train station."

"I don't mind keeping him," Penelope said. "One more doesn't add to the chaos much. Stay in Santa Fe for the night. Make a honeymoon of it."

"Good idea," Jack said, "because we don't know how long this party will go on."

"Not too late, I hope," Abigail said.

Jack embraced her. "We'll sleep when we're dead. Tonight, let's dance." And he led her toward the band.

CHAPTER 55

A Navajo silversmith was hammering out jewelry, using Morgan's head for an anvil. How he'd ended up in an Indian camp after the wedding reception, he had no idea, but the pounding continued in his ears.

"Morgan, wake up! Open the door. We've got to get the wagon loaded."

The door. Someone was pounding on the door. Morgan stumbled from his cot and banged his knee on Rebecca's trunk as he staggered to get the door open and stop the noise. He turned the lock and Walter burst in.

Morgan slid to the floor and put his head between his hands. "Walter, are you—"

Walter reached down and pulled him upright. "Come on. You can sleep on the train. Jack and Abigail will be here with the carriage soon."

"Coffee, I need coffee . . . If they get here before then, they'll just have to wait." Morgan ladled water into the coffee pot, threw in a handful of grounds, turned the kerosene burner on high, and went to the outhouse. When he returned, the coffee was brewing furiously. He poured himself a cup of black sludge—just what the doctor ordered. "Walter, you want some?"

Walter shook his head. "Looks like tar. You drink it while I prop open the front door." When he returned, he squatted down at one end of a trunk. "Anytime, you want to start, Morgan."

Morgan still wasn't quite himself, but he gripped the handle and bent his knees. The men stood, and the veins in their necks bulged.

"Jehoshaphat, these trunks are heavy," Walter said. "What have those women got in them?"

"Everything they own, I imagine. I'm just glad your back's healed well enough to carry the other end."

"Oh, I'm one-hundred percent now."

When everything but Morgan's suitcase was loaded, he poured water in the washbasin. "Thanks for doing all this, Walter. I'm going to wash up and change clothes. Why don't you go over to the hotel and see if the ladies' traveling bags are ready to be put on the wagon." Morgan braced himself and splashed cold water on his face.

Clean, dressed, and a half-pot of coffee later, Morgan was beginning to feel human. He topped off his flask and slipped it into his coat pocket. There was a little whiskey left in the bottle. He'd give it to Jack.

Morgan strapped his suitcase closed and looked nostalgically around the empty emporium. It had seemed like such a beautiful dream, to carry the future to the far reaches of the country. And that future was still out there, still happening. New York had a subway and electric lights. Telephone lines were spreading their spider's web further and further. Automobiles might turn from rich men's toys into practical transportation. And the world was shaking free of the limits of ancient ideas everywhere.

Well, everywhere except Taos. One thing he'd learned was that the future may be coming, but it couldn't be rushed. It had to arrive like it always had, one day at a time.

Over in the corner he spied a dusty Mexican cowboy hat with little bells dangling from the brim. He picked it up and brushed the cobwebs off. It made him smile.

Morgan fitted his bowler inside the Mexican hat, so his was hidden. He put the double-layered hat on and carried his suitcase outside, where Rebecca and the girls were waiting with Walter. Rebecca gawked, and then grimaced. Peaches and Cherry started giggling.

Morgan set the whiskey bottle on the windowsill and added his suitcase to the wagon. "We're going to have a little fun with Jack. When he gets here,

I'll ask you to compliment my hat. No matter what's said, you ladies keep a straight face and agree with me. Okay?"

A cloud of dust down the road predicted the arrival of the carriage. Jack pulled on the reins and brought the horses to a stop. He handed the reins to Abigail and jumped down to help the ladies aboard. Then he spotted Morgan. "Jesus, you're not wearing that to New York, are you?" Jack glanced at Rebecca. "Excuse my language, Reverend."

"Jesus doesn't mind, so why should I?"

"I think it makes me look like an authentic New Mexican," Morgan said. "Don't you girls?"

"Like a real caballero," Peaches said.

Jack spit on the ground. "Like a complete rube."

Morgan flicked the brim with his finger. "The bells really complete it. Wouldn't you say?"

"Have you lost your mind?"

Cherry and Peaches burst out laughing. Walter and Rebecca joined in.

Morgan took it off and separated the two, revealing his own hat underneath. "I thought sure you'd recognize Bryce's old hat—the one he arrived with. I found it in the corner this morning." Morgan made a side-arm throw and sailed the hat toward Jack. Centrifugal force spun the bells outward as it flew. "Here, you can have it."

Jack's reflexes kicked in and he caught it with one hand.

"For Cyrus," Morgan said.

"I don't want him seen wearing the darn thing," Jack said.

"He'll love it," Abigail said.

"Leave it," Jack said. "There's no space for it in the carriage."

Abigail took the hat from Jack and, copying Morgan's throw, sailed it to Walter. "Hold on to this until we get home, Walter."

Morgan picked up the whiskey bottle and offered it to Jack. "A little hair of the dog?"

"I believe I will," Jack took a swig and started to hand it back.

"Keep it." Morgan tapped his jacket pocket. "I've got a full flask."

"You know I'm driving?" Jack said.

"I'm sure it will only improve you."

Jack shrugged. "It certainly can't hurt."

Walter went to his wagon while Morgan and Jack helped the ladies into the carriage. Peaches sat in front next to Abigail. Morgan and Rebecca took the back seat, with Cherry squeezed between them. Jack climbed in and snapped the reins. "Giddy up."

Jack drove south, toward Santa Fe. About six miles out of town they passed the old Franciscan mission at Ranchos de Taos. A half-dozen shirtless Indians were dancing in a circle around a barefoot white man who wore a beaded vest. Cherry whipped her head around and craned to see past Rebecca's hat. "That was Bryce dancing with those Indians."

Rebecca glanced back the way they had come. "I believe you're right."

"He looked to be in his element," Morgan said. "Happy as an Irishman in a pub on Saint Paddy's day."

Rebecca blushed.

"Sorry," Morgan said. "It just slipped out. No offense intended."

"None taken," she said.

At the train station, Jack and Morgan helped the ladies down. Jack went to locate a porter with a baggage cart while Rebecca and Morgan went inside to buy the tickets. Peaches and Cherry stayed by Walter and Abigail until Jack and the porter returned.

The sisters were bobbing up and down on their toes by then. "Our first train ride, ever," Cherry told the porter.

"We want to see inside the depot," Peaches said.

"It's just a room full of hard benches and dirty spittoons," Jack said. "You'll see your fill of train stations between here and New York."

Walter and the porter began offloading the trunks and crates of artwork onto the hand truck. "This'll take more than one trip," the porter said.

Jack nodded. "Girls, wait here with Abigail until Morgan comes out. We'll leave your suitcases with you so you'll have them in your Pullman car. I'll be out on the platform, keeping an eye on the baggage until the porter gets everything transferred."

Jack accompanied the porter as he pushed the first load of luggage down the platform toward the baggage car. The hand truck had a bad wheel and thump, thump, thumped as they went. "Reminds me of the porter's cart in Tres Piedras. Do they all do that?"

"I don't know, sir. I've never been to Tres Piedras."

Morgan and the others came with the second load of luggage. Rebecca and the Romeros took their suitcases and went to find their car. Jack and Morgan were left alone on the platform.

"Does it seem possible, it was only a year ago we arrived in New Mexico?" Morgan said.

"Our emporium never lived up to its promise," Jack said. "But we talked a good game."

"We did," Morgan said. "But don't worry, I'll be back. I'm only going to stay in the city for a few weeks."

Jack cracked a smile. "At least you no longer have to avoid certain Irishmen."

"No thanks to Bryce. Still, I'm happy they gave us a reason to change our names. I kind of like being Morgan."

Abigail came over and put her arms around Morgan's neck. "Get lost, Jack."

Jack laughed. "Married less than a day, and my wife's already making time with my best friend."

"Oh, go kiss those pretty Romero girls goodbye."

Jack left them and walked to where Peaches and Cherry were waiting with Rebecca.

Abigail looked into Morgan's eyes. "When we became lovers, it'd been my experience that men who talked big dreams didn't stick around long. For a woman who wanted to remain single, you New Yorkers seemed like a safe bet. That was wrong—you two proved to be the kind of men who stay. I want you to know, when you get back, you've got a place with Jack and me."

"What do you mean?"

"While you're gone, I'm going to have Jack convert our conservatory into an artist's studio. It's got plenty of light."

Morgan squeezed his eyes shut and gulped a breath of air. "You can't imagine how much that means."

The whistle blew, and the conductor called, "All aboard!"

Abigail walked Morgan to his coach. He stepped onto the train and extended his hand to Jack. "Hey, dude."

"Hey, dude, yourself," Jack said. "Send me a wire when you're ready to come home and I'll meet your train."

Morgan shook Jack's hand vigorously. "'Home.' I like the sound of that."

The End

Ragtime Dudes Meet a Paris Flapper
Another Award-Winning Novel

Seventeen years have passed. Ragtime is old hat, World War I is over, and the Roaring Twenties are underway. Cherry, who now calls herself Cherie, is a flapper living it up in Paris, and vowing to never go back to New Mexico. But while visiting her sister in New York, a telegram brings word that they are needed in Taos . . .

Cherie and Peaches reunite with Ragtime dudes Bryce, Morgan, Jack, wife Abigail, and a now grownup Cyrus, to face the group's most serious challenges with warmth and humor.

Royal Palm Literary Award Judges' Comments:

"This is a remarkable historical novel... The story is riveting. The language is absolutely delightfully reminiscent of the flapper era. Everything these people say and think is worth the reader's attention I did not want to stop reading."

Acknowledgments

Thank you to fellow members of Writers Alliance of Gainesville who critiqued the book as I was writing it: Skipper Hammond, Pat Caren, Catherine Pucket, Kimberley Mullins, Jessica Elliott, Joy Southwell, Ken Campbell, Bonnie Ogle, Jena Liggett; my editor: Dave King; my proofreaders: Pat Caren and Cindy Elder; and my beta readers: Ken and Cindy Elder, Steven Combes, and Dick Gartee.

Many thanks to the Taos Public Library for use of their historical archives. Let me also acknowledge the following print resources. Aspects of my characters' peyote trip were drawn from observations made by Aldous Huxley in his book *The Doors of Perception* (Harper and Row, 1954). Mrs. Holloway's opinion of Ragtime was paraphrased from a quote in an 1897 newspaper article in the *St. Louis Dispatch*. "My Girl's a Corker," lyrics by John "Honey" Stromberg, 1895. The stereoscope on the back cover was photographed by Davepape (Public Domain,) and the stereo card of the St. Louis World's Fair was by T. W. Ingersoll, © 1904.